W9-BLA-233

# FOUR DAYS

Also by Gloria Goldreich

LEAH'S JOURNEY

# FOUR DAYS

## Gloria Goldreich

HARCOURT BRACE JOVANOVICH
NEW YORK AND LONDON

*C. Ht*

Library of Congress Cataloging in Publication Data

Goldreich, Gloria.
Four days.

I. Title.
PZ4.G638Fo  [PS3557.O3845]    813'.54    79-3352
ISBN 0-15-132802-1

Set in Linotype Janson

Printed in the United States of America

B C D E

For My Mother
Gussie Goldreich
". . . a woman of valor"

*The author wishes to thank the Jerusalem Foundation and the staff of Mishkenot Sha'Ananim in Jerusalem, where much of* FOUR DAYS *was written.*

# FOUR DAYS

THE SOLDIERS MARCHED toward them three abreast. Their booted legs thrust forward in perfect uniform beat, as though propelled by a secret rhythm audible only to them. It was a winter's day, and the harsh northern sunlight, peculiar to that region of Poland, turned the pale crescents of hair that rimmed their metal helmets into silvery aureoles. The insignias and the buttons on their gray uniforms glinted, and the leather neck straps on the high-collared jackets were polished to a lustrous gleam. Their uniforms were pressed to perfection: the crease on each trouser leg was razor-sharp. Ina thought that if she were to touch the fabric it would slice her finger, but she would not care. Her body, she was certain, was emptied of blood. She clutched Batya's hand and watched the marching men draw so close that she and her cousin shivered in their moving shadow.

The soldiers wore rifles slung over their shoulders, but they did not touch their weapons. They did not bother to glance at the two barefoot children who cringed before them but made no move to dash out of their shadowed path. They did not break step as they removed their gloves and let them fall to the ground. Their fingers were long and very white. (Always, in dream and memory, she saw their hands with perfect clarity— the pink circlets of flesh beneath the nails, the delicate creases

of skin about the knuckles, the fatted cushions of palms that
clapped politely at concerts and lustily in beer halls.) Deftly
and swiftly now, they unbuttoned the narrow openings in the
front of their pants. Their penises shot out erect, as though on
command. The rigid lengths of muscle, purple with pulsating
blood, quivered, throbbed. Still the soldiers moved forward,
their even-featured, dead-eyed faces frozen, expressionless.
Inches from the trembling children they halted.

Ina's fingers dug into Batya's shoulder.

"Don't be afraid," she hissed, and it was her mother's voice,
harsh and premonitory, that swirled from her mouth.

The soldiers halted. The small girls clutched each other and
swayed dangerously in a vagrant arc of sunlight. Blue veins
threaded their way across the swollen violet expanse of the
penis of the soldier who stood in the middle. His lips were
thinned with pain and tension.

"Fire!" (The order always emanated from a distance, and
she could never tell who shouted it.)

The tiny slits of penis mouths parted, and tear-shaped silver
bullets shot forth. The soldiers stood in place, small smiles of
pleasure and relief rimming their mouths, as their ejaculations
of death found their targets. Batya tottered and fell. Ina
screamed and screamed again.

"Ina!"

Ray's hand was gentle on her shoulder, his night breath sour
against her face as he shook her awake. The window was open
and she heard the shriek of an ambulance, the distant hum
of a plane lowering itself for descent into Kennedy. The
bathroom pipes gurgled gently. Somewhere in the building
someone had used the toilet. She touched the smooth, sweet-
smelling linen sheet, studied the luminescent numbers on her
bedside clock. The terror broke. She was not in the courtyard
of a Polish prison camp. She was home in her apartment
overlooking Central Park.

She stretched her body out full length, pressed her hands
deeply into her husband's back. She was not a small girl. She
was a grown woman. It had been a dream. No. *The dream.*

Sweat streaked her body, and her lips were dry and cracked.

"I'm sorry," she whispered into the darkness. "It was a dream."

"I know." His hand found hers, held it, pressed it to his lips.

"You're trembling," he said, and kissed her palm and then each finger. In this way, too, he comforted Rachel, their daughter, when the child was seized by a sudden and inexplicable fear.

"Yes. I'm sorry." She apologized again for the legacy she had brought into their marriage.

Now, to reassure herself, she studied the room, checking off each familiar object. The mirror shimmered gently, a mercurial refraction in the night. If she rose now and looked into it, she would meet a woman's face, full-featured and serious-eyed, not an urchin child's terror-streaked visage, pale and skeletal.

Her bedside phone glowed like a shining coal in the darkness. She could reach out and dial a suburban number. Her cousin Batya, now Bette Goldman, mother of three, PTA vice-president, and ardent campaigner for consumer rights, would answer.

"That same nightmare?" Ray asked. His hands moved across her body with practiced skill. He cupped her breast in his palm, brushed his cheek against the nipple. It was tender to his touch, and she flinched, stiffened. She had never described the dream to him. She feared his terror and his pity. He would not offer an analysis—he was too careful and caring for that—but he would look at her with new sadness. It was from that sadness that she protected him. The exclusivity of her pain pierced and exalted her. She hoarded her dream, only sharing fragments of it with Dr. Eleanor Berenson during that quiet hour when afternoon melted into evening.

"Feeling better now?" Ray asked, and she knew from the glint of gold in his eyes and the huskiness of his voice that he wanted to make love, to banish her nocturnal fear with the force of his tenderness and his desire.

"I'm tired," she replied. "So tired." Her voice was a breathless whisper. Fatigue swept over her in a great wave. Her limbs felt strangely heavy.

"Go to sleep then."

He caressed her shoulder, kissed her cheek, smoothed the blanket over her. She relaxed dreamily, wonderfully, beneath the ministration of his hands. She loved this sense of being cared for. This was how small girls should be treated—they should be cosseted, not threatened. Her eyes filled with tears for the frightened children of her dream. Ray turned over on his side and was asleep again, breathing rhythmically, an absent smile on his lips. But she lay awake in the darkness, one hand resting on the strange new fullness of her breast. Her fingers moved tentatively across the oddly tender flower of her nipple.

A small laugh rippled through the silence. The intercom that linked their children's rooms with theirs wafted it toward them. Ray did not waken but smiled, as though the sound of his son's laughter had pierced his rest. Some mysterious nocturnal merriment had visited the small boy, and sleeping Jeddy laughed. Once, she remembered, her brother Yedidiah, for whom Jeddy was named, had wakened in the night and, in a strong clear voice, had recited the alphabet. "*A–B–C–*" he had intoned cheerfully into the darkness, and upon reaching Z he had fallen silent, a smile of satisfaction brightening his sleep-swept face. When had that been? she wondered. In the forest, in the farmer's cabin, in the transit camp? She could not remember, and she was newly irritated by the way her memories of that time came in swift flashes, often sparked by a trivial incident, an absurd thought.

She was fully awake now, and dates fluttered through her mind. It was April—late April. Warm breezes teased them with promises. The children plunged through drawers and closets in search of light shirts and blouses. She had menstruated last in early March. She remembered now waking in the early morning to the familiar slight cramp. Snow had fallen in great lacy drops outside her window, and tiny petals of blood flowered her sheet. Early March and now it was late April. She was three weeks late. She had never been late before, except for her pregnancies.

"No," she said very softly into the darkness, "it can't be."

She closed her eyes then and fell into a deep and dreamless sleep. But in the morning, while the children scurried about looking for their books, for vanished cardigans and missing compositions, and while Ray poured a second cup of coffee, she dialed Dr. Isaacs's office and made an appointment.

"Just a routine examination," she told the nurse, and went to help Rachel find her math book.

She thought about the dream again as she sat in the doctor's waiting room later that afternoon. She had brought her briefcase because she remembered the many hours she had spent in this room during her pregnancies with Jeddy and Rachel. A three o'clock appointment often meant a consultation at four-thirty or five with constant reassurances from the self-important receptionist that there had been an emergency, an unscheduled appointment, an important consultation. The waiting women had all smiled understandingly at each other. The doctor's lateness, his busy schedule, his inaccessibility, were all good signs. He was in demand because he was the best. They were in good hands.

Ina noticed that today the room was less crowded than it had been in previous years and that three of the four young women waiting were not noticeably pregnant. The abortion law had apparently altered the doctor's practice if not his habits. The one pregnant woman sat in a corner near the window, and splashes of sunlight dappled the mound of her abdomen, loosely covered by a black linen maternity dress. She looked at Ina with great seriousness but did not smile. Ina opened her briefcase and took out a brochure a new computer firm had sent her, but she did not study the itemized description of the new machine. Her thoughts trembled instead back to the previous night and to the dream that had recurred now for the sixth—no—the seventh time.

"Why now?" she had asked Eleanor Berenson once, after recounting the dream to her. "All these years and no dreams, no nightmares." (Only daytime terror, she had thought, but had not given voice to the words. Only sudden fears so intense as to be palpable. Only the sadness that drifted over her without warning, trapping her in a silvery spiderweb of her own misery. The strands of that flimsy snare were so finely woven that they could not be discerned. Friends and family, even Ray, were not aware that she felt herself imprisoned in gossamer melancholy. The misery was her secret, and sometimes she thought that if someone else penetrated it, a terrible fate would befall her.)

The analyst had shifted in her seat, lit another cigarette, and said very softly, "That is what we shall have to find out. Perhaps now at last you have the strength to dream."

But they had not found out, although weeks and months had passed. The dream vanished for long periods and then suddenly recurred. Tiny, isolated details became clear. In one dream Bette (Batya, she was called then) had been wearing half-leggings, bandages of fabric pieced together from discarded scraps. During that last fiercely cold winter in the camp, Shaindel, Ina's mother, had fashioned such leggings for both girls, sewing them at night, the flimsy rags held close to her eyes in the dim light. Her needle was a guarded treasure which she concealed beneath the board of her barracks bed. Ina remembered that the leggings had been stolen just before the liberation, and she had given her cousin one of her own so that each small girl had one leg protected against the biting cold. But in the dream Ina was bare-legged and Bette wore both the leggings. In another version of the dream one of the German soldiers had a button dangling loose from his impeccable jacket. It was that button that intrigued and amused the children. Ina had wakened from that dream smiling because she and Bette had to restrain themselves from giggling at the officer's disarray as the silvery bullets of death spewed forth.

Carefully, with infinite patience, Eleanor Berenson tried to piece together any stimulus that might trigger the dream. Had

Ina had a good day? Could she recall any incident, however small, that might have jarred her? Could she recall reading anything disturbing before going to bed? Diligently, Ina tried to remember. Her hands trembled and her body grew rigid. The fifty-minute hour stretched on interminably. Small orange lights flashed frantically on the doctor's phone. Somewhere across the city another patient tried urgently to call, but Eleanor Berenson took no calls during a session.

"Everything was fine," Ina always said at last, acknowledging defeat. "Just fine."

And it was true. The dreams had begun when things were good, when a soft glow seemed to have settled over their lives. They had just bought the Amagansett house. (She had had the first dream the very first day she had worked in the garden. How good the earth had felt beneath her hands, how silken the young bulbs she would root in the soil that was their own.) Her computer business was finally running in the black, and the children were at good and easy ages. Ray had recently been named a department head, and he moved with new certainty and confidence. He was a man who had finally arrived at his destination. He smiled more easily (although with an elusive wistfulness), walked with a new swiftness, held out his strong arms for their son and daughter, and reached for her in the soft darkness with wild urgency. Why, then, should heavy-lidded, thin-lipped soldiers, wearing the uniforms of death that she had not seen for decades, suddenly haunt her nights? The question nagged her as she sat in the doctor's waiting room where the sunlight fell in slats of gold across the worn green carpet.

"It's because I've been too lucky," she thought suddenly with frightening clarity. "They are catching up with me." "They." The denizens of death and despair, of mischance and misfortune, of faceless soldiers whose death's head insignias glowed in the darkness. Almost, it seemed, she could recall a face, but like an aborted bolt of lightning, the memory flashed and was gone.

The brightly colored computer brochure fell to the carpet,

and she thought for a moment that she might have screamed because the other women in the room turned and stared at her, but it was because the nurse stood in the doorway repeating for the second time, "Mrs. Feldman? Aren't you Mrs. Feldman? The doctor will see you now."

Minutes later she lay stretched out on the examining table, the pale green paper robe tickling her shoulders, the steel stirrups cold against her feet. The doctor's plastic-coated fingers moved skillfully within her body, and he talked softly, idly. He was indifferent to her outstretched body, submissive beneath his touch, and chatted as though he were at a cocktail party. They were having an early spring. His wife was so pleased. She would go up to their place in the Berkshires early. They were putting in a pool. Had Edie felt any discomfort when he did that? "Ina," she said wearily. "My name is Ina." He laughed. Her name was not important to him. Her annoyance amused him. His finger moved imperceptibly. Had her menstrual cycles until this month been regular? She was, after all, forty-one. At such an age changes sometimes occurred. Abruptly he slipped his hand out, plunged a long metal instrument in, clamped down, and removed it. She shivered against the metallic coldness. He peeled off the flesh-colored plastic gloves, luminous now with her body's mysterious moisture. His hands were very beautiful. He had long white fingers, beautifully manicured nails. She thought of the hands of the soldiers in her dream. Deftly he pulled down the paper gown and exposed her breasts. His fingers moved tenderly across them, climbing and resting. He palpated the flesh between thumb and forefinger, then squeezed hard, digging into the mammary gland, sliding his palm across the nipples still so tender that tears brimmed her eyes.

"Sorry," he said absently, and continued to touch her right breast and then stroked her left one.

"Okay," he said, and she thought she saw small satisfaction curl his mouth. "It's still there. Not getting any bigger, but it's still there."

"Oh." She had almost forgotten. Months ago, during her regular checkup, he had found a small lump in her left breast. His fingers had worried it briefly. He had sighed, and at the end of the examination he had returned to it and kneaded it gently between thumb and forefinger like a small child toying with a bit of clay.

"There is something there," he had said, but there was no concern in his voice. "Probably nothing, but still you never can tell with these things. We should check it periodically. Make an appointment sometime next month." But she had been busy. And he had after all said it was probably inconsequential. Sometimes she passed her finger across it, imitating his gesture, and thought to call him, but she had not. He himself had been so casual. Now he touched it yet again and frowned, as though annoyed. She felt oddly guilty. She had not meant to irritate him.

"It should come out," he said. "There's nothing to it. Let's get it out."

He bent over the sink, washing his hands. She would report those hands to Eleanor Berenson. Had she ever noticed them before? She could not remember. It was, she supposed, what the analyst would call an unconscious association.

"But what about—am I?" She could not phrase the question, and she felt herself badly disadvantaged to be talking to him from a prone position, naked while he stood garbed in the immaculate white jacket, the uniform of his profession.

A buzzer rang in his consulting room.

"We'll talk when you're dressed," he said, and hurried to answer the summons, leaving the examining room door slightly ajar so that she heard the sonorous bleat of his voice as he spoke into the phone. She closed the door and stood before the full-length mirror. Her fingers quickly found the small lump, but when she looked at her naked breast, she saw nothing, only the rose-white mound of flesh crested by the sleepy-eyed, earth-colored nipple. She felt oddly deceived but not surprised. The deepest malignancies were so carefully concealed. Desperate illness masqueraded as health. A lawyer friend of Ray's died suddenly of a heart attack. He had been a florid, robust man who had always tossed the children high above his head when he visited them.

"We were so shocked," Ina said to a mutual friend at the funeral.

"But Steve had congenital heart disease from childhood," the friend replied. "Didn't you know?"

A young programmer Ina had hired, a beautiful girl with hair the color of topaz and grass-green eyes, asked her for a six-month leave.

"It's all right if you can't give it to me," the girl said, "but I have diabetes, and they're afraid of my eye hemorrhaging. They're going to do a corneal fluid transplant." The girl's eyes had glinted, betraying no sign of exploding vacuoles of blood, no warning veins of redness.

Once, Ina had sat beside a neighbor of Bette's at a pool and watched her cousin cavort with her youngest child in the rippling blue water.

"It's wonderful to see how happy Bette is with the children," the friend (who quarreled endlessly with her own toddler) said. "I think only people who have had happy childhoods can be happy with their own children."

Ina did not reply. She and Bette had shared the same childhood; they had shared hunger and terror and loneliness; they had shared tiny tricks of survival and strange antics of endearment. Now they shared memories. What Ina remembered of that time, Bette had forgotten. They traded. They had taught themselves how to laugh when they discovered that their masters liked the laughter of children. But happiness was not even a known word in their vocabularies. Still, Ina understood Bette's neighbor. Her cousin was a tall, strong woman with an easy laugh and a surging, almost riotous joy in her children. The congenital, malignant misery of her childhood was masked by the hard-gained vigor of her maturity, just as their lawyer friend's brief displays of strength had masked the weak valve through which life leaked from his body.

Ina dressed quickly now, applied makeup, straightened her skirt. She smiled at herself in the mirror. She did not look like a woman who awakened trembling in the night, pursued by ghostly soldiers marching through silvery sunlight. Like the others, like Bette and the bright-eyed programmer, she too was a skilled masquerader.

Dr. Isaacs leaned back in his leather chair, his eyes wandering from the folder on his desk to the intricate Persian prints that lined his walls. Finally, as though with an effort of will, he looked at the slender dark-haired woman who sat before him.

"What we know for sure," he said, "is that the fibroma should come out. As far as the missed period—I can't tell yet whether there is a pregnancy. It's very possible, of course, but I don't want to make a prediction. We'll get the lab results on the urine sample soon enough. Now, when can I schedule you for a removal of the fibroma?" He moved his appointment book toward him, a leather volume, its lined pages thickly notated.

"I don't know," she said, and was surprised at the reedy quality of her own voice, the trembling uncertainty. "Can't we wait until we have the test results?"

"I suppose so." He closed his book. He was disappointed. He liked to have things set and settled.

"My nurse will call you when we get the lab report. You can decide then."

"Yes," she agreed, and felt a sense of relief as though she had been granted a reprieve. Gratefully, she stepped out onto a Fifth Avenue bright with sunlight, eager suddenly to reach her office where humming terminals offered her neatly spaced, correct answers.

The nurse called the next night. Ray spoke softly into the phone, and she half listened as she sat at the dining room table helping Jeddy with his math homework.

"You put the carrying number here," she told the child.

"I see," he shouted excitedly. "The answer is five, isn't it, Mommy? Five!"

"Yes," she replied.

"Thank you for calling," Ray said into the phone. "Mrs. Feldman will be in touch with you."

They talked about it when the children were asleep and they were alone in their bedroom.

"The test showed that you are pregnant," he said. His tone was flat, and he did not look at her. She felt cheated because she could not read his eyes.

"What do we do?" she asked. Misery weighted her words, and her fingers stroked his hair. She had been right after all. They had been too lucky for too long.

"I don't know," he said, and she was angered. Surely he knew. They both knew.

What choices, after all, were open to them? They had reached a time of life where decisions had been made and courses set. They had charted their route carefully, made orderly, organized decisions. When her business prospered, they had bought the Amagansett house. Much of her income went for the small luxuries. But even without economic considerations (and she felt briefly shamed that they had occurred to her so rapidly), their lives were set. She wanted no changes. On the street below, a rock was tossed at a street light. Slivers of glass slid by their windows and streaked down like rapidly propelled tears.

They were lying across the bed and he moved closer toward her, cupped her head in his hands, breathed softly against her neck—true and tried tricks of protection and affection that this time did not work. She stiffened beside him, moved her head away. Her long dark hair escaped the bun and streamed across the pillow.

"I'll have an abortion, of course," she said.

Her answer was as flat as his had been, and yet the words had a dark tumescence of their own and settled weightily upon her. He shifted his position, and she felt his hands and feet deathly cold against her, but he did not answer. They fell asleep not talking, fingertips touching, shrouded in a strange, ineffable misery. It occurred to her as she lay there that surely the dream would come that night, in punishment or in penance, but her sleep was wonderfully dreamless.

"How do you feel?" he asked her in the morning.

"Fine." Her voice was too light, her smile was too quick.

When she reached her office, she neither checked her mail nor glanced at her messages but reached at once for the phone and called Dr. Isaacs's office. The nurse was quick to understand, efficient at scheduling.

"Suppose I book you into Mount Lebanon. You can have the fibroma removed first, convalesce for a day or so, and then have the abortion. The whole thing shouldn't take more than four days."

Ina was grateful for her matter-of-factness, her cool cadence. "Yes. Fine."

She noted the date on her calendar, and a nodule of grief settled in her throat. Her chest was constricted. She hung up and reached for a folder. Her work went quickly that day. Columns of numbers absorbed her. Phones rang. The computer terminal in the large outside office tapped almost soundlessly. By mid-afternoon she was calm, almost anesthetized. That afternoon she stopped at a new dessert shop and bought strawberry tarts for dinner.

# FIRST DAY

ONE WEEK LATER (the efficient nurse had been swift in her scheduling), Ina and Ray drove across the park in the sleepy stillness of the spring afternoon and watched the newly green trees arch tremblingly upward to the gold-flecked, nacreous sky. They felt themselves tourists in their own city: the hour and their destination were both so foreign to their regular work-bound schedules that the park they knew so well seemed transformed into an unfamiliar terrain which they observed as visitors. At this hour of the day the shaded walkways and battered benches were occupied by nurses and young mothers who rocked shining carriages and were ruled over by fierce toddlers in brightly colored overalls who plucked at tufts of struggling rough city grass and hurtled their small bodies at slides and jungle gyms.

Ray slowed to a halt to allow a heavy black woman, her body bulging within a yellowing uniform, to maneuver herself and a gleaming red tricycle across the street while clutching the hand of a boy with milk-white hair who wept with weary dispassion. Why was he crying? Ina wondered, and she knew that if she had seen the child on the Hampstead Heath or in the Tuileries, she would think of him always when she remembered those parks. But he was a child of her own city, and so the mystery of his small grief lacked drama; it could be likened

too easily to the tears and tantrums of her children so newly
graduated from their tricycles to small English bicycles that
matched hers and Ray's.

"Poor kid," Ray said, but she did not answer because her
sympathy at that moment had leaped toward the black woman
who bent to wipe the child's eyes and, stooping, had revealed
a gaping tear beneath the arm of her uniform through which
a tangled mass of gray hair jutted.

They crossed onto Fifth Avenue. He would cruise for a
while, and if no space turned up, he would head for the municipal parking lot a few blocks north. They were, after all,
shrewd city dwellers, canny about one-way streets, defective
meters, two-hour parking zones. The city held few surprises
for them. Besides, they knew this area particularly well: both
their children had been born in this hospital, in the wing
carved out of earth-colored concrete blocks that glowed
pinkly in the sunlight, its long walk shadowed by the bright
blue canopy that proclaimed its name in white cursive script.
The Nerenstein Pavilion, named for a man who had contributed money rather than children to the world and plucked
his posterity from a building where other men's infants would
be born or lost.

Their own children, Jeddy and Rachel, had in fact been
delivered there by Dr. Isaacs, who, bored, detached, but
always superbly confident, would enter her room within a
short while and turn not to Ina but to her chart. Although he
had seen her only a week before, he would not remember her
name.

Sitting in the car while Ray struggled to fit into a too-small
space on Eighty-ninth, she anticipated the doctor's entry. His
coat would hang capelike from his shoulders in a theatrical
gesture, and his opening lines were always the same, whether
she waited for him in his examining room, her legs straddling
the table stirrups for a Pap smear, her breasts exposed for
exploration, manipulation; or whether she struggled in the
labor room, her body writhing, her cervix dilated, as her children edged their way from her womb into the world.

"Hello there, Anne" (or Edna or Elaine—always handing her a misnomer that began with a vowel but never her own name), "what have we here today?"

His eyes would rake the clipboard as though he were a diner examining an elaborate menu. Would the *plat du jour* be a hysterectomy with complications, a simple curettage, the birth of twins, or a normal delivery? Ah, yes, our Caesarean sections are excellent today, and the anesthesiologist is featuring a new local especially prepared in France—an excellent year.

Still, Isaacs was a good doctor and he had mellowed. During her examination last week he had even made small talk. And the hospital was the finest in the city. She had researched that in years past, in the days of her first pregnancy, when such subjects fascinated and obsessed her—when she kept anthropological studies of breast feeding and *The Magic Years* on her bedside table. At countless cocktail parties she had argued the virtues of Mount Lebanon and the Nerenstein Pavilion with other young women who wore softly flowing maternity dresses and pushed the advantage of Lenox Hill (a central location—a staff composed almost entirely of diplomates), New York Hospital (a fantastic rooming-in program), and small neighborhood clinics whose nurse-midwives attended consciousness-raising groups and greeted their patients at the supermarket (a personal birthing—free of antiseptic and institutionalization). Ina, however, had been unwavering. Mount Lebanon had the park, an entire neonatal floor, and the coolly superior Dr. Isaacs, whose green-plastic-coated hands had been the first to hold the tiny glistening bundles of screaming pink flesh that had been Rachel and then Jeddy, saying calmly, without surprise, at each delivery, "It's a girl—it's a boy," his tone exuding the confidence of prescience.

"We're not going to get a spot," Ray said. "Let me drop you at the entrance."

He shifted into reverse and she took up her case and got out of the car, waving jauntily, carelessly, aware suddenly that her hands were sweating and her heart was beating too fast. She stood hesitantly on the sidewalk for a moment, then marched up the high stone steps, looking back for a moment, noticing how the spring sunshine danced wildly about the street and came to rest, neatly slashing Fifth Avenue in half with a liquid bar of broad bright gold.

It was dark inside the high-vaulted reception area, and Ina squinted, adjusting her eyes to the sudden dimness. She sniffed in the hospital odor of a pine-scented air spray, which mingled sickeningly with an ammoniated disinfectant. A small dark man in a soiled green overall moved a mop slowly across the tiled floor. When he lifted it to wring it out, gripping it in his slender fingers with sudden energy, sudden strength, the water that he wrung from it was tinged with pink, and Ina knew that it was blood he was mopping up. Perhaps, in that pail of soapy water, a clump of pink detritus floated, a shapeless embryo like the one that had dropped from her own body into the toilet bowl so many years ago. That had been before Rachel. One minute she had been pregnant, moving slowly, cautiously, taking iron, and drinking milk. Then, a tiny, teasing cramp and she was no longer pregnant but bereft, weeping, staring at the ball of pink plasma and rushing to the phone to call Ray out of a conference.

How calm he had been—home within the hour, his arms around her, talking quietly to Dr. Isaacs on the phone while she sobbed softly into the pillow. He and the obstetrician were two men in control of the situation, in control of her, at ease with explanations, predictions.

"Not uncommon," the doctor had said of her spontaneous abortion, her miscarriage, and Ray had repeated it, as though the words were talismans—a secret mantra of reassurance.

"Not uncommon." The doctor's verbal placebo, well learned in Bedside Manner 1A and dredged out again and again. "Not uncommon" another doctor had assured her when Rachel ran a fever of 105 with the chicken pox. "Not uncommon" had been Jeddy's minor hernia and the sudden temperature that had sent them dashing to the hospital, careening wildly through the sleeping city. "Not uncommon" was the mess on the hospital floor, and "not uncommon" too was the "procedure" she would (perhaps) undergo in a few days' time.

A "procedure" Dr. Isaacs called it, but still Ina thought of twisted coat hangers and bare kitchen tables and the girl a year ahead of her in college who had died in the back room of a Framingham pharmacy. Eda had been the girl's name, so like Ina's own that they were often confused, and there were some who thought it was Ina who had died. It was perhaps a "procedure," but it was also an abortion, and if it was not "uncommon," perhaps it should be. The thought surprised her, and she shrugged free of it as the small man cut a final swath with his mop and the floor gleamed slickly in the dimness. Pleased with his work, he smiled, showing the shining gold fillings of his incisors, and he waved in passing to the woman in the small glass-enclosed office. She was on the telephone and did not look up.

Ina, clutching her suitcase and feeling its heavy pull (she should not, after all, have packed the programs but allowed Ray to bring them later as he suggested), moved toward the office that was marked "Admissions." The door was locked. She was reminded of the motel they and the children had stayed at in Alexandria, where the proprietor had sealed himself within a Plexiglas cage and spoke to them through a tube. He had slid their bill and brochures through a small slot that snapped swiftly shut. But there had, after all, been cash in the man's office and bottles of liquor and a small color television set perennially tuned to game shows in which all the contestants had purplish complexions and the quiz masters glowed in orange jack-o'-lantern skins. What was the admitting clerk of a hospital protecting? Records of early childhood diseases? Pathologists' reports? Blue Cross forms? Ina shifted her case to her other hand and tapped on the door.

The clerk swiveled about in her seat, stared into her telephone as though the knock had come from its depths, and then turned to the glass partition. She waved Ina to a row of leather chairs to the left of the office and continued talking. She was a small, sharp-faced woman whose black hair was trained to rise in lacquered peaks about her forehead, and when she switched the phone from one hand to another as she searched through the papers on her desk, the tiny charms on her heavy gold bracelet skittered angrily.

Ina obediently took the seat and placed the suitcase next to her, resting her leg against it—an old and early habit that would not be unlearned. Her children left their valises in the corridors of trains, in the middle of hotel rooms, in front of reception desks. Ray set his down casually, indifferently. None had ever been lost. But she placed hers always in sight at the bottom of luggage racks, in touching distance between pieces of furniture or hidden in small crevices. What could not be seen could not be examined, appropriated. She was the daughter of many journeys and understood too well examinations, appropriations.

Holding a valise and approaching an official (even a petty hospital clerk with sprayed hair and nylon smock) made her feel vulnerable, uncertain—rocketed her back to the wandering days of her childhood. It did not matter that her Vuitton case (bought jointly by Ray and the children as a fortieth-birthday present) was hardly the crushed cardboard suitcase she had last seen hurled into her aunt's garbage pail the day they arrived in America. Her aunt had been afraid of lice, and it had been a real fear. But still Ina wished that she had managed to salvage that case, to salvage something that would prove to her that those years, after all, had been real and not some surrealistic nightmare of terror and evil—that they had happened and happened to her.

"Do you believe it happened?" her cousin Bette had asked her last summer as they sat on the terrace of Bette's Stamford house watching their children cavort in the long rectangular pool.

Bette was two years older than Ina. They had been children together in the camp, and now, together again, they were prosperous, successful young mothers wearing bright bikinis and hooded caftans. Ina had not answered. Sometimes she believed it and sometimes not. But if she had kept that suitcase (it had been yellow with a dark stripe going up one side and encrusted with pocks of grime), she would have absolute proof that it had happened and happened to her. Those laughing, sunburned children—Jeddy and Rachel—her children—their golden arms outstretched, claiming the sunlight and the water, claiming the world, would not disprove it.

The seat next to Ina's was taken by a very beautiful young black woman who carried a patent-leather hatbox. She smiled brilliantly, apologetically, as her arm brushed Ina's and opened a fashion magazine. Her own photograph stared up at them. She was modeling a lemon-yellow evening gown, and her hair was twisted into a thick knot at the top of her head. She turned the page quickly, throwing Ina an embarrassed glance. She had not meant to show herself.

The front door opened, and a pale, heavily pregnant girl came in, her elbow held by an even paler young man who seemed to propel her as Rachel had propelled her battery-operated doll. He held a plaid suitcase and a pale tongue of blue nylon licked at the zipper's teeth. There was no wait for this couple. The locked office door flew open, a buzzer sounded, and two nurses—one pushing a wheelchair—flew down the hall. The girl slid into the chair, clutched her husband's arm briefly, and then looked away, her hand on her heaving abdomen, surrendering to her pain. He, in turn, disappeared into the office. The girl moaned as the nurses hurried her chair past Ina.

"You'll be fine. You'll be fine," the nurse assured her, and winked at Ina, inviting her into a bittersweet complicity, a woman's pact for and against pain. They disappeared into the waiting elevator just as the office door opened. The young man stood there, holding the valise and a Blue Cross card. He wore the dazed look of an abandoned child.

"Third-floor waiting room," the woman in the office called after him.

"Thanks. Thanks very much." His face brightened as

though he had been offered a rare secret, and he too hurried into an elevator.

"Next!" the woman called harshly, imperiously. The office door stood open, and Ina heard the impatient jingle of her charms.

She took up her suitcase and entered timorously, betrayed by it. The admissions clerk would know that it contained nightgown, bathrobe, slippers, toilet articles—the accessories of invalidism, of passive surrender to uncaring professionals. When the clerk left to go home, shedding her nylon smock, Ina would be extending her hand at a technician's demand, shuffling to the bathroom in paper slippers to produce a urine specimen, exposing her breast to a resident's incurious eyes and nervous, probing fingers.

"I'm Ina Feldman," Ina said. "Your office called and said they had my bed ready. My husband is parking," she added too swiftly. It was ridiculous but still important to her that this woman know that she had a husband, that she was protected, that her watch was of real gold and the Wedgwood pin on her scarf had been bought during a holiday in England. But the clerk did not care. She was interested only in the admission form which she extended to Ina.

"Fill it out in triplicate," she said. "Don't shift the carbons. And make sure your Blue Cross number is accurate."

She turned to answer the phone, which rang in three short rings followed by one long one, as though in tintinnabulary code. Ina turned to the forms, pleased to see the blank spaces waiting. Easily, contentedly, she lifted her pen and began:

*Last Name*: Feldman

*Maiden Name*: Cherne

*First Name*: Ina

*Middle Name*: None

*Parents' Names* (in full): Norman and Shirley Cherne

How much more economic were these American names, Ina thought, but still wrote them slowly, pressing hard on the ball-point pen as though to offer silent tribute to the pale, thin

ghosts who had been Nachum and Shaindel Czernowitz when
they arrived in New York Harbor over three decades earlier.
Nachum Czernowitz had weighed a bare one hundred pounds,
and his height was cut by the odd stoop he had assumed sometime in 1941. It was not an unfamiliar posture among concentration camp survivors. Those who stooped thought themselves
more inconspicuous and thus in less danger of attracting notice
in lineups or "actions." Their slouches were a disguise against
death. Nachum Czernowitz had spoken softly, hesitantly, and
his laugh was a rusty rasp that began in the back of his throat.
Norman Cherne was a hefty, red-faced man who played golf
twice a week, laughed heartily, and spoke so loudly and
swiftly that the English language, his adopted tongue badly
learned, tumbled out in clumsy clumps of words that made
him laugh yet again.

Shaindel Czernowitz had been a frail, sad-eyed woman
whose long fingers trembled with each small gesture and flew
upward, almost involuntarily, to touch her head. She had had
typhus in the camp, and her hair had fallen out. It would grow
again, she had been told by the young American doctor who
visited her in the camp hospital. He had been a nice man who
bewildered her with his concern, hovering over her bed like
the father of a cruelly injured child who can offer only pellets
of sweet reassurance. She had believed him and worried the
fine new tendrils and stroked the fuzz that had begun to grow
about her pale pink scalp. Her parents, her brother and sister,
her small son Yedidiah—all were dead.

Her father had died in a cattle car. Perhaps of exhaustion,
perhaps of starvation, perhaps of a heart attack. It was not
important. His body had been heaved out and piled on a heap
of corpses that a Polish peasant dutifully trundled off on a
wheelbarrow. Wild flowers grew with fierce and lustrous
beauty across the meadowlands of Poland, where the decaying
bones and flesh of so many Jews added richness to the soil.

Her mother, still clutching the small valise absurdly filled
with embroidered panties and camisoles, had not survived the

first selection. She had been a delicate woman, and the selecting officer had not even hesitated. "To the left," he had said. "To the showers." Peshi, her sister, had survived the selection but surrendered to despair.

And Yedidiah, the large-eyed, double-jointed boy, had caught a fever. Shaindel had nursed him with single-minded determination. They were in a transit camp then, and small boys were allowed to stay with their mothers if they did not make trouble. Yedidiah did not make trouble. He lay there silently, his large eyes glittering with a brilliance that frightened her. She begged an aspirin from one woman, and another gave her a vial of costly perfume to rub across his brow. "The alcohol will cool him," she said, and dabbed a single drop behind her own ear, although she stank of sweat and dirt streaked her body with ribbons of darkness. Once, she had worn organdy dresses and smelled of lilacs.

Shaindel saved her own drinking water to cool the boy, holding him beneath the arms that were light as chicken wings when she lifted them. She gave her tiny diamond earrings to a guard in exchange for three oranges. When Yedidiah had sucked the juice, she begged him to eat the pulp, and when the pulp was gone, she fed him slivers of rind sweetened with bits of sugar offered by a tall gaunt woman.

"He'll be all right," Ina whispered to her. The small girl comforted her, reassured her. The war had reversed everything. Little girls became mothers, and mothers, who should be powerful, omnipotent, were frightened and helpless.

The fever broke. The dangerous, jewellike brightness vanished from his eyes. He said that he was hungry. He said that Ina had taken his toy—an old sock that one of the women had stuffed with grass. Ina gave it to him. The women rejoiced and offered him bits of their own food, treasures carefully hoarded—a lump of sugar, a hard candy, a peppermint. They had saved him by joint effort, by sharing and caring. They felt triumphant, and they were briefly, secretly, contemptuous of their guards.

Shaindel had not slept during the three nights of his fever. That night he drank a cup of weak tea and smiled and demonstrated for all how he could bend his fingers backward so that his small hand looked like a whimsical insect. They laughed and Shaindel fell asleep.

She slept through the night, and when she awakened, she turned, smiling, to tell him that she had dreamed of the apple orchard near her parents' home. He had loved to climb those stunted trees, to pelt his amused parents with unripe fruit and brittle branches.

"Yedidiah," she said, but she had known at once that he did not, could not, hear her. His small body lay inert. The pale veil of death was stretched across his face. His large eyes were open. Gently, she pulled the lids down. His long lashes were like strands of silk between her fingers. One tiny hair clung to her finger, and she blew it away but made no wish. Her boy was dead. She had relaxed her vigilance. She had slept and he had died. She moaned softly. Terrible things had happened to her, things she could not speak of. She had been orphaned and children had been lost to her. Yet afterwards, after the war, at terror's end, she spoke of only one loss—her hair.

Would it really grow again in all its thickness and color? She had, after all, had the most beautiful hair in her village— thick chestnut curls—and she had never cut it. Would it grow again?

It had grown in, thick and bright. Shirley Cherne's chignon was streaked with silver now, and she combed it with great care each morning and crowned it with wonderful hats of shimmering feathers and softest suede. She bought her fine winter tweeds and her double-weave cotton knits in the designer shop at Saks, and the seamstresses in the fitting room spoke approvingly of her figure. Some women her age were too heavy, and some worked so hard at keeping their figures that they ended up dried and skinny in the wrong places. But Shirley Cherne was perfectly and comfortably rounded. And she was a lady. She was European, of course, and that made a difference.

Ina's ball-point pen moved on, ever vigilant of the carbons in triplicate.

*Place of Birth*: Poland

*Date of Birth*: November 20, 1938

Should she perhaps add to the date *Krystallnacht*—as those who were born on December 25 sometimes playfully added "Christmas—Joy to the World!"? *Krystallnacht*—"Sorrow to the Jews!" Idiot. Why was she doing this? A new excursion into masochism unique to this day, a punishment for an act still uncommitted. Did she then, on some mysterious level, see abortion as a crime? Her analyst, sweet-voiced Dr. Eleanor Berenson, would be annoyed, disappointed.

"When you understand why you have set a destructive mechanism into operation, doesn't it make sense to stop it?"

Dr. Berenson's voice echoed in memory; the lessons learned in that dimly lit office scarred the heart and triggered the mind to belt back retort and reaction. Ina sat up straighter. Certainly she would stop it. Swiftly she completed the rest of the form, offering to the hospital computer bank the information that she was the mother of two children, Rachel eleven and Jeddy eight, born by normal delivery in this very hospital, that she had had pneumonia at sixteen, that she was a computer scientist and her husband Raymond (age forty-two) a lawyer. Carefully she copied out her Blue Cross number and added the code of her major medical insurance.

*Reason for Admission*:

How clever they were to save this (the best?) for last, but she too was clever and skilled at words. The reason was "gynecological," she wrote, exerting so little pressure on the pen that the pale blue letters were skeletal.

She passed the form over to the clerk, who read it with the abstracted gaze of a harried schoolteacher, going over those words written too lightly. At the word *gynecological* she paused.

"We'll need more than that," she said, frowning.

"Check with Dr. Isaacs," Ina replied. She was beginning to

form an intense dislike for this officious bureaucrat with her jangling charm bracelet and her lacquered horns. (A waste of emotion, Dr. Eleanor Berenson would say wearily, wisely, and Ina agreed and struggled to assimilate dislike into contempt, indifference, but could not.)

"Surely you know what you're being admitted for?"

Ina shrugged.

"Minor breast surgery. The removal of a fibroma."

"And?"

"And an abortion. A therapeutic abortion." How harsh the word was. They should find another, not so rooted in ugly imagery, a word that did not conjure up rusted coat hangers and bare mattresses.

The clerk smiled, satisfied. She made a quick notation on the form.

"Okay. Just wait outside and someone from five will be down to take you to your room. Next!"

The beautiful black girl brushed past Ina in the narrow doorway, but now she did not smile. She had left her fashion magazine on the seat, and Ina took it up and studied a photo of three blond young men clustered about a tiny Chinese model in a burgundy evening gown.

"Mrs. Feldman?" The blonde woman in a striped smock with a large pin that said "Volunteer" (the "o" forming a happy face) smiled encouragingly at her. "Shall we go upstairs? Your room is ready."

Room 502 overlooked the park, and Ina smiled her approval at the diligent volunteer who whisked about importantly, showing her the bathroom and the small storage cabinet, the closet where Ina's roommate, unseen behind a white screen, had hung her clothes. The garments dangled there like neglected scarecrows in an untilled field. There was only a long-sleeved blue maternity dress and a conventional shirtwaist—one worn on her arrival and one ready for her departure. Ina herself, usually so well organized, had never shown such foresight, and before she left Mount Lebanon when Rachel and Jeddy were born, Dot, Ray's sister, had had to scurry around searching out undergarments and clothing. It occurred to her that she might have done that on purpose, courting Dot's concern, her mothering—perhaps seeking out the mothering that Shaindel Czernowitz in Poland had been too ill and desperate to offer and that Shirley Cherne in America had been too busy and exhausted to bother with.

Shirley had had her reasons, of course. There was, after all, a business to be built, money to be earned, a life to be pasted together again, a new language to master. Leave it alone; don't read too much into small things, Ina told herself, and evoked Eleanor Berenson's soft voice, imagined even the snap of a match as the analyst bent to light a cigarette. Such advice, so simple, so obvious, was always followed by a cigarette, as though the veil of smoke added somehow to the transparency of the insight.

Ina looked at the maternity dress again.

"I thought," she said to the volunteer, "that Dr. Isaacs requested that I not be placed on a maternity floor."

She spoke softly. From behind the screen had come a small sleep-strangled cry and then the rhythmic breathing of a drugged and heavy slumber.

"This is not a maternity floor," the volunteer replied. "The woman in that bed has a special situation."

She paused and stared at Ina, inviting her curiosity, her questions. Ina recognized the look. She had known a girl at college, a corridor gossip, who extended the first strand of a story—almost always a malicious tale—and waited for the pull of questions before unreeling her ugly skein of innuendoes, inch by inch. Now, as then, Ina refused to rise to the bait.

"They'll tell my husband at Reception where I am?"

"Yes, of course." The volunteer was disappointed. "Well, I hope I'll see you again before you leave. I come by with the hospitality cart. Don't worry. I'm sure everything will go well."

She hesitated, waiting for Ina's confidences, uncertainties. When none came, she added, "The nurse will be in in a few minutes."

"Yes," Ina said. "Thank you."

The door was left open, and a woman's sobs trailed down the hallway. A buzzer sounded and footsteps hurried toward its summons, women's voices murmured and a man's was raised in brief anger; a sudden quiet came, pierced only by the ringing of a phone quickly answered. Ina closed the door.

She slipped off her shoes and moved, in stockinged feet, to the mirror over the washstand. She studied herself carefully as she always did when she entered a new environment. In the mirrors of hotel rooms, in the bathrooms of strange homes and offices, she stared hard at herself, registering her own image. She gazed with great concentration into her own gray-blue eyes, passed uneasy fingers on her dark hair pulled smoothly back and twisted into a loose knot. She adjusted her blouse over the soft slope of her breasts and sniffed her fingers. She was, even in such strange new rooms, still Ina Cherne (Czerno-witz) Feldman and safe within that name, behind that face.

Satisfied, she unpacked her valise, placing the programs in their stiff file folders, the soft-backed Ngaio Marsh, the worn copy of *Great English Short Stories* on the bedside table. Her identity was established. The bed belonged to Ina Feldman, computer professional and thoughtful reader.

She slipped into her apricot nightgown and matching robe and hung her street clothes in the closet, careful to place them as far as possible from the forlorn garments that already hung there. Her toilet articles went into the drawer, and she put the valise into a corner of the closet, glad to be rid of it, acknowledging wryly, hopelessly, that it was time she overcame such an aversion. Soon, she assured herself, and thought that Eleanor Berenson would be proud of her.

She was in bed, turning the pages of the program, searching out the bug that prevented it from running accurately, when the Chinese nurse came in. Smiling and nodding, she affixed the plastic bracelet to Ina's wrist.

"They should have done this in Admitting. She is careless, that one."

Ina agreed, glad to have a grudge against the thin woman with the overladen charm bracelet. But she was glad, too, of her negligence. She would not have wanted to submit to that woman's officious, abrupt gesture, to extend her wrist to a hostile hand to be numbered and taped. She thought of the patch of skin grafted onto her mother's arm, covering the small blue numbers that had marched up the pink flesh, tattooed there on the day of their arrival in the camp when a Kapo had told Shaindel Czernowitz to thrust her arm out and hold it stiff. They had been short of ink that day and did not bother with the children.

Ina's own arm now was smooth and golden with an early spring suntan because they had already spent two weekends at their house in Amagansett, planting the seedlings of their annuals. They would have marigolds this year and pansies and small beds of varicolored impatiens. She forced herself to think of the flowers now, to forget the numbers—an emotional exercise practiced on Dr. Berenson's tweed couch. Would the analyst charge her for the hours she missed during her hospital stay? Probably. She should have, perhaps, discussed the abortion with Eleanor Berenson. She had not even discussed the breast surgery with her. There had been no occasion to discuss them, Ina decided, absolving herself, and she turned to smile at the little nurse.

"I am Susan Li," the nurse confided. "If you need me, the buzzer is right on the table." She spoke very softly and glanced over at the screened-off bed. "Mrs. Gottlieb still sleeps. That is good."

Ina nodded, glad to enter into a complicity of concern over a sleeping woman. Silently, balanced on her rubber-soled shoes, Susan Li slid out of the room and softly closed the door behind her. Ina turned back to the program, pulling the sleeve of her robe over the hospital bracelet.

Her next visitor was Dr. Isaacs's resident, a tall, fair-haired young man whose pale eyes were obscured by very thick

glasses. His white jacket, sizes too wide for him, hung loosely
about his shoulders, and his stethoscope was entangled in his
tie. He was, Ina thought, proof positive of time passing, of her
ascent (or decline) into middle age. At her first gynecological
examination during her freshman year, the resident at the student clinic had been some years older than she and had adopted
an avuncular manner and delivered a brief lecture on the
emotional and physical hazards of premarital intercourse. The
resident who had attended her during her labor with Rachel
had been about her age and had been an undergraduate with
Ray. There had been a generational conviviality to his examination. His wife too was having her first child, and they too
had bought their crib at a small Danish shop. This they discussed through her panting and his cries of "one finger
dilated—two fingers dilated!"—because he wanted to be absolutely certain she was ready before he called Dr. Isaacs. He was
a careful prince who would not disturb his king unnecessarily.
At Jeddy's birth the examining resident had been some years
her junior, and now the young doctor who stood before her
was yet another generation removed. The war that involved
him had been fought in Southeast Asia. The bastions of her
childhood were vague history to him.

She had been a bride when he was just entering high school.
He wore no wedding band, and the folder in his hand trembled
slightly when he approached her. She wondered if he were
still a virgin. Perhaps he had enough of women and their
lubricated interiors during the day and reserved his evenings
for solitary reading and the preparation of gourmet meals.

"I'm Dr. Akins, Mrs. Friedman," he said. "Dr. Isaacs had a
very busy schedule today—emergency surgery just now—and
he asked me to take care of the preliminary examination." He
glanced at the folder he held and then back at her.

"Feldman," she corrected him. "I'm Mrs. Feldman." It was
important in institutional settings to get names right. Enough
individuality was lost without a name disappearing as well. On
that she was something of an expert.

"Sorry. Mrs. Feldman."

He smiled apologetically, and she saw that he had the clumsy charm that would gain him a prosperous practice of middle-aged women. He would remain boyish into old age, and his surgical jackets would never fit him properly.

"Now, it's only the breast thing we're interested in today. The left breast, right?"

"Right."

"If I could just have a look. Can you slide the straps down, or do you have to remove the gown?"

Woman-wise, she had selected the nightgown because the straps moved easily, and she shifted them now, sitting straight up so that her left breast was exposed and shone with golden opacity in the harsh light of her bedside lamp. The rosy nipple was taut and tender and throbbed dully. Dr. Akins's fingers were strong and certain as he probed the breast, skillfully kneading the mammary gland which would (perhaps) not again produce milk for a suckling infant, and searching out the minuscule lump of fibers cohering beneath the nipple.

"I see," he said. "Very small but still, it's wise to have it removed. They'll do a frozen scan immediately."

"A frozen scan? Dr. Isaacs assured me that there was no chance of a malignancy." She tried to keep her voice even, but a thread of terror tickled her throat, tightened around her heart.

"Oh, I should think probably not," he agreed cheerfully, "but still we want to be sure, don't we?" He had, she thought, lingered over the word *probably*.

"I thought we were sure," she answered sourly, but he was not listening, absorbed in marking her chart.

"And in two days' time you'll have the abortion."

All her secrets were spread before him in that folder. Did he know that she and Ray had made love that morning in the silver light of beginning dawn? That knowledge too would be available to him if he asked or examined.

The blithe certainty in his tone irritated her. He was too young to speak so casually about her body's secrets, too young to check life and death off on his chart with a ball-point pen.

Not that it was really life, she reminded herself, remembering the lectures she had gone to, the discussion groups she had attended. A woman gynecologist, wearing a safari suit, had told the assembled women that a beginning fetus—a zygote (even the biological terms were devoid of human association)—was no more imbued with life than the unfertilized ovum. The lecturer had tossed her luxuriant golden hair as though to emphasize her point. "We now pinpoint death from the time we discern brain death—a brain-dead person is no longer alive. The beginning fetus has no brain capacity. Doesn't it follow then that it is not alive?"

Still, Ina remembered that she had always thought of her children, from the moment she knew she was pregnant, as seedlings of life. She ascribed an intelligence to them, personality, hope, and fear. Life was not so easily shunted aside. I choose this one to live and this one to die. I send this one to work and this one to the gas shower. I choose this one to be born and that one to be suctioned, cut, taken from the womb. She knew the parallel to be erroneous, but it persisted. Her palms grew damp, and she felt the beginning of a headache, a dull throbbing at the back of her head.

"We're not definite on the abortion," she said at last, and thought that it was only the second time that she had used the word that day.

Dr. Akins did not care. His pen flew over the chart. Why had she said that? she wondered, leaning back. She had no doubt, no uncertainty. It was the statement of a spiteful child protesting that he would not do something that he knew he would eventually have to do. Just as the child must know that the homework will have to be done and the dental appointment kept, she too knew that she would do what she had to do. *Had to?* The question teased her, and she turned from it back to the doctor, who was issuing directives, instructions.

"Dr. Isaacs will operate at eight sharp. Please don't eat or drink anything after eight tonight. Eight-thirty the latest. Do you have any questions?"

He smiled appealingly at her, and she observed that his

fingers, so firm and steady across gland and flesh, moved nervously otherwise.

"No questions," she said, and smiled. It was not his fault, after all, that he was a technician of the body, a skilled manipulator of muscle and flesh. They each had their work, and as he left the room, she turned gratefully back to hers.

She had finished the section and was beginning to understand the problem when Ray came into the room carrying a spray of yellow roses and a box of Barton's candy.

"Assorted nuts, I hope," she said, putting her work aside.

She was as pleased to see him, as excited by his sheer presence, as she was when she returned from a midweek business trip to another city. Perhaps entering the hospital even for minor surgery did mean the crossing of borders, entry into a new land, hazardous separation. She put her arms around his neck and kissed him, pressing herself against him, tenderly washing his tongue with her own.

"Hey, come on. I was just parking the car." He laughed nervously and glanced over at the screened-off bed.

"She's sleeping," Ina said softly, and pulled the wrapper off the box of candy.

Passion had deserted her. They had, after all, made love that morning, arching urgently toward each other in the pale, metallic predawn light and willing themselves to climax quickly, excitedly, nervous that the children would awaken, but their energies peaked by that nervousness. Like excited guilty lovers arranging clandestine meetings, they stole their morning moments from their sleeping son and daughter.

"Let me find a vase for these flowers," he said.

"They're beautiful. Thank you. Just ask the nurse at the station. They probably have some of those hideous styrofoam things."

"Okay."

She watched him leave, knowing that the nurse would not only find a vase but that she would fill it with water and arrange the flowers for him. His tangled mass of brown hair, his green eyes oddly helpless behind their thick glasses, the student slouch of his very wide shoulders, the shy turn of his smile—all combined to send women scurrying to help that "sweet Ray Feldman." Salesgirls left their counters to assist him in departments not their own. Waitresses remained long in the kitchen making certain his steak was well done, his french fries crisp. Pool typists finished his briefs first and returned them with reassuring smiles. "That reads well, Mr. Feldman, it really does"—as though he, a senior prosecutor with a *magna cum laude* degree from the Harvard Law School, required their approval. But always he looked up at them with a shy smile, questioning eyes. "Do you think so? Do you *really* think so?"

It was the same look he had given her the first time she saw him, the summer after she graduated, when she worked as a waitress in a Waltham spaghetti joint while taking the computer science course in Boston. Her parents had wanted her to go to the Harvard School of Education.

"A teacher has security always," Shirley Cherne had said. She believed (had been taught to believe) in the acquisition of licenses, credentials, pieces of official paper that could be cashed in for work permits or hoarded as a personal armory against disaster.

But Ina had set herself against them, registered for the computer course, and then, to "show them," had taken the greasy job she despised, punishing herself and them with a single move. Ray had come in alone the second week she worked there. He was teaching summer school at Cazenovia— an elementary government course. Should he have the spaghetti marinara or the fettucini? He was so thin he looked as though he ought to have both of them. She brought him the fettucini and a large plate of bread with extra butter. He came again the next night and had the spaghetti. She saw that his V-necked sweater was of fine cashmere but that there was a hole at the elbow.

The third night he was waiting at the kitchen door when she left, and three weeks later she was holding his hand in his sister Dot's apartment on Central Park South while Dot and her husband Larry smiled at them happily, worriedly, and asked again and again—"But are you sure? Really sure? Three weeks isn't a very long time, you know." She had presented their engagement as a fait accompli to her own parents. The Chernes were busy people. They had no time for agonizing introspection. If Ina and Ray were sure, then it was all right.

They had been sure. They were young people who, perhaps because they had not known parental guidance, trusted strongly in instinct. She had seen a heavy sadness in his eyes, and her heart had turned in pity and in recognition. He had admired the way she moved with strength and certainty that dissolved in the darkness of the night to surges of fierce passion, desperate clinging. She melted beneath his tenderness. His hands found hers as they sat side by side at a concert; his fingers gently threaded her hair as they watched the dying sunlight streak the Charles River with gold. He loved her voice—so crisp, so decisive. She made plans, decisions. Her family had never had the time for hesitancy, uncertainty. She recognized the force of his intellect, the power of his gentleness.

They were married in the large Queens synagogue to which her parents belonged. Tears flowed throughout the brief wedding ceremony. Audible sobs were heard when the cantor intoned the marriage blessings. His family wept because he was an orphan. Both his parents had been killed in an automobile accident when he was fifteen. Her family wept because she was a miracle—a child who had been marked for extermination yet who had grown to womanhood and stood before them now, gowned in the white of innocence, holding a bouquet of wild flowers in her hand. They wept because she was not dead and because this marriage was a wondrous affirmation. In the rear of the synagogue, her mother's friend Ida Davidowitz swayed dangerously and left before the breaking of the glass. Her daughter, just Ina's age, had died a week before liberation.

Ina and Ray were bright-eyed and calm. Bette stood beside her wearing a yellow dress, the color of buttercups, the hue of the small flowers that dotted the meadows of Poland during the first days of spring and that had grown stubbornly, in sunny clusters, around the steel poles strung with electrified barbed wire.

They had been sure, and in the end they had been proven right. Their lives had been good, moving steadily, at even keel. There had been the sadness of the first miscarriage and then the births of Rachel and Jeddy. Ray's work had gone well, and she had managed to free-lance during the children's early years. She loved her work. The exactness and detachment of her skill soothed and intrigued her. The terminals hummed reassuringly, reliably. No irrational passions altered their course. She was in control. They had the comfortable apartment in the city and now, at last, the small Amagansett house. The children had grown and become their friends. It was true that they had their differences, that they quarreled sometimes, briefly and bitterly, but they slid from their anger into an easy peace. A lingering sadness clung to Ina, but she kept it secret, a nurtured, hoarded treasure. She did not struggle within its tendrils, but more and more she felt it tighten about her. The dream, the trio of death-bent soldiers, spurred her to action against it, and she began to see Eleanor Berenson, who had long been her cousin Bette's analyst. Neither she nor Ray were uneasy about the analysis. Many of their friends were in therapy. They belonged to an intellectually oriented, liberal group who discussed encounter marathons, belonged to Amnesty International, and subscribed to the publications of the Sierra Club. They had both been early advocates of the abortion law. They had signed petitions and even contributed to newspaper advertisements. They had argued the issue fiercely at parties and with their families, once even slamming out of Dot's apartment because Dot, who mothered the elevator man and worried about the shopping bag ladies on Seventy-second Street, could not imagine anyone not wanting a child, a growing, developing infant. Dot's three children were adopted, and she had the barren woman's awe of pregnancy and the birth process. Yes, she agreed with abortion in the abstract—the woman's sovereignty over her own

body and all that—but when you came right down to it, wasn't
it rather like murder?

"No!" Ina had shouted, frightening Rachel, who began to
cry. "If you want to know about murder, ask me. I'm an
authority. An expert witness, but only for the victims. How
can you call abortion murder?"

Murder was when names were called in the pale light of
sunless dawns and women disappeared and were not seen again
although their children called for them in silent darkness.
Murder was a booted soldier thrusting a bayonet into the limp
breast of a startled dark-eyed girl. Murder was a child playing
with pebbles and clubbed suddenly from behind. Such memories flashed through her mind at odd, unpredictable moments.
She saw a dark-eyed teenaged girl in a bright yellow bathing
suit move slowly across a deserted beach. The girl's breasts
swayed in the loose suit, and suddenly Ina saw blood streaking
across the bright fabric and remembered the glint of steel
against flesh. A child bent over a pile of stones in her yard,
and she heard again, with memory's ear, the impact of a truncheon against a small skull. She understood murder. Murder
was a hillock of children's shoes, the worn leather smelling of
sweat, the frayed laces weeping. Murder was Yedidiah, her
graveless brother, and the smoke curling endlessly against the
rose-clouded skies. How could Dot, her Aubusson carpet un-
derfoot, Stuart Davis prints on the wall, her children laughing
above the sounds of "Sesame Street," compare abortion to
murder?

They had left angry but knew their anger would not last.
Dot would not allow it to, nor did Ray and Ina relish it. Larry
invited them to dinner at the Fleur de Lys the next week, and
Ina bought Dot a new best-seller, and they made it up. But
they had not talked about abortion with Dot since. They would
have to tell her now, Ina thought. They must call her when
Ray got back with the flowers. If she were to call the house
and learn from Carmen, their housekeeper, that Ina was in the
hospital, Dot would get upset, jump to wild conclusions. She

and Larry had been on a family vacation in the Bahamas and were due back only today. Ray must call her.

Ina turned back to the program. The girl who had written it had excellent perceptions. She would make a good analyst one day. But not yet and not that soon. Abruptly, Ina reached for the phone and dialed her own office, waited for the single ring and her assistant's voice.

"Ina Feldman's line."

"Ricky, it's Ina. How are things going?"

"Oh, fine. How are you?"

"I'm fine, Ricky. I told you this was just a routine procedure. Has the Steiner program come in?"

"Yes. I sent it out for debugging. And Mrs. Conrad returned the contract."

"Hold that for me then. Anything else?"

"No. Gee, I hope you'll be all right."

"Ricky." Just the right tone of amused annoyance. "I told you it was just a routine procedure. I'll be in on Monday. Call if anything comes up. You have the number."

"Okay. Take care."

"Right."

She hung up feeling better and looked up at Ray, who held the vase of flowers. The nurse had arranged the blossoms as Ina had known she would and even added some maiden-hair ferns against which the thickly petaled roses leaned. It occurred to Ina that this was the first time Ray had brought flowers for her hospital room. When Rachel was born, he had brought her a spider plant, which grew now in the sunlit corner of their window seat. At Jeddy's birth he had arrived with a cluster of pink dwarf cacti planted in a sky-blue ceramic bowl. Ina kept them on the study desk, telling Jeddy they were exactly his age and just as prickly as he was. But there would be no souvenirs of this hospital stay. Clearly Ray did not want any, nor, she supposed, did she. She stared at the yellow roses that would be dead in a few days' time and thought that it had been foolish and extravagant of Ray to buy them so far out of season.

"You ought to call Dot," she said as he set the flowers down on the bedside table.

"Yes. I suppose so. They'll be back at the apartment now. Their boat docked at noon."

"Yes."

But still he made no move toward the phone.

"What shall I tell her?"

"The truth."

His question surprised her, left her bewildered, off balance. They had never lied to Dot, his elder sister who had been his surrogate parent since the shared deaths of his mother and father. Dot was mother, sister, and friend to them. She hurried over when a child was ill, listened with pride to their professional achievements, wrote generous checks for birthdays and anniversaries. It was to Dot that Ina turned with questions about the children. Was it normal for Rachel to cling so long to the pacifier? Weren't Jeddy's temper fits too frequent and too violent? Her own mother, Shirley Cherne, could not be relied on for answers. Her children's childhoods had been lost to her, and she kept her grandchildren at a safe distance with expensive gifts and excessive involvement in their clothing. (Danskin, she advised, wore longer than Healthtex. Look at the cut on Billy the Kid.) Once Ina had asked her, knowing it to be a mistake but forging ahead anyhow, whether Jeddy resembled his namesake, her brother Yedidiah.

After a long pause Shirley had answered in a strangely dreamy voice, "Yedidiah had beautiful hands. Piano fingers."

She looked at Jeddy's pudgy, outstretched hand, and her eyes grew sharply bright. Ina would have welcomed tears, but none came. Her mother disappeared into the bedroom, hemmed two jumpers for Rachel, and left without kissing either child good-bye. And so it was to Dot that Ina offered her anxious queries, holding no secret too intimate for this sister-in-law who loved them as well as herself. Of course they would tell Dot the truth. She would be upset, but that was her problem, not theirs. They were responsible only for their own honesty.

"Suppose," Ray said, his hand lingering on the phone, "suppose I only tell her about the fibroma surgery."

"Why?"

"The abortion's not scheduled for two days. We—you—might change your mind."

He did not look at her when he said this but moved to the large window that overlooked the park. The first tender leaves of spring had begun their thrust through the branches of the great oaks, and in the bright sunlight they shimmered like graceful emerald fingerlings. Ray had a fondness for things small and delicate. He hovered over young plants, and in the den he sheltered a row of miniature crystal animals. On birthdays and anniversaries she and the children bought him Steuben diminutives. He had been fascinated by Rachel and Jeddy in their respective infancies, bewitched by the small garments of their layettes, bemused by the miracle of their toes, the tiny shells of their ears. Watching him now, Ina realized that Ray wanted this child: no, not a child—she would not call it that, the kernel of unformed life developing within her unwilling body. *He* definitely did not want the abortion. She turned from him, sorrow and anger clutching her throat. He had not been straight. He should have told her.

But this, after all, was the pattern of their life, of their marriage. Always they shielded each other. He had suffered so much. She thought of him as the orphaned adolescent, the lonely boy who called his sister's house his home, now grown to a man who gently cared for tiny objects and was tender and patient with young children. She protected him from further hurt, from added sadness.

Her own suffering was ineffable, he knew. He trembled to think of it, and she seldom spoke of it. She had been a child who had lived with cold and hunger and death. She had stood by the dead body of her silken-lashed little brother. He could not add to her grief, and so he shielded her with his silence, protected her with his muted anguish.

When did a shield become a barrier? he wondered, and he

noticed that on one park-side tree, small white blossoms nodded in the lazy wind.

"Why should I change my mind?" she asked, keeping her voice hard. "We decided."

"No. You decided," he said.

"That's not fair." Anger replaced fear, and the program slipped to the floor, a shower of long white printout sheets fluttering from the folder that had held it. The programmer had corrected and crossed out in red ink, and the markings looked like small bloodied scars.

He scrambled for the pages and handed them to her. She restored them slowly to order, glad of the task.

"Think back," she said, using the cool professional tone she reserved for staff meetings. "We talked about it that night Dr. Isaacs's nurse called. I said I would have an abortion. Did you say anything against it?"

She remembered now the strange darkness of that night. The street light on the park side of the street had been shattered by a rock tossed by passing boys. She had seen the rock make contact, watched the icy shards rocket groundward, noted the sudden darkness, but never heard the crashing glass fragment. Their apartment was on a higher floor, and they were shielded by its height and their sealed windows from the sounds and sirens of the city. Rachel had had a cough that night, and the sound of it had scraped the silence. Ina had worried that Rachel might have to stay home from school the next day and Carmen had asked for the morning off. Ina would then have to stay home, and there was an important marketing meeting scheduled at which she was to make a presentation. Automatically she had chided herself for worrying more about her meeting than about her child with the raw and hurting throat. She acknowledged, shamed but honest, that it was the meeting that concerned her more. Would Dr. Berenson congratulate her for such honesty or would she simply raise an eyebrow, shift a journal, and light another cigarette?

"I'll have an abortion," she had said tentatively into the

darkness. Ray had not answered her. His feet had been icy against her legs, his fingertips cold upon her neck.

"We didn't really talk about it," he said now. "You decided."

He stared out the window. It was almost three o'clock, and on the street below, women were hurrying, intent on reaching home before their children spilled out of the yellow school buses. Two tall women in suede coats, carrying brightly colored shopping bags, crossed against the light, and a taxi skittered to an angry halt. Women seemed to travel in pairs at this hour. Two young mothers passed directly beneath the window pushing small canvas umbrella strollers. They wore gaily knit ponchos, and as they stopped for a light, they laughed. He wondered if their children slept or if they had twisted their heads at the laughter and smiled too, the bemused, wise smiles of children who gently tolerate their parents' inexplicable gaiety.

"But you didn't say anything against it." Ina's voice was as plaintive as a child's. She had been misunderstood. It was not fair.

She was right, he knew. He had not objected, had not even thought about objecting until perhaps a day or so later when Jeddy had come to him as he worked at his desk. At eight, Jeddy was a tall boy with a startling litheness. When he leaped for a fly ball, Ray's heart stopped with pleasure, and when the children swam naked at the Amagansett shore, he marveled at Jeddy's taut little body, perfectly proportioned, perfectly coordinated limbs cutting against the soft air, the sun-splintered water. His son. His baby. Jeddy's large dark eyes were fringed with long pale lashes, and his gums, too large and lowly set—he would need braces one day soon—glowed pinkly above his teeth. But Jeddy's eyes were troubled that day, and his cheek was smudged with gray Magic Marker as though it had been ash-scarred by a distant sorrow. Ray had cleaned it with a corner of his handkerchief and listened to Jeddy's question.

"Do you believe in God?"

"I think so." A careful answer, honest, hesitant.

"I don't." The child was fierce in his certainty.

"Why not?" He struggled for calm. They were treading on thin ideological ice, he and his dark-eyed son. A false question, a careless word or laugh, and they would crash into the icy waters of silence and missed understanding.

"George Goldstein's sister died. She had leukemia, and she died. That's a blood disease. She was in the sixth grade. Our class collected money to send flowers. What did they need flowers for if she was dead already?"

This last question came in a different voice. Practical curiosity. Why is there lightning? What causes earthquakes? Why do the dead need flowers?

"For the funeral," Ray replied, and knew his answer to be foolish, inadequate. Other answers fluttered in his mind. To dignify death. To beautify pain. To symbolize life. Or, "We send flowers because we don't know what else to do." Had there been many flowers at his parents' funeral? He should remember. He had been fifteen at the time. But he remembered nothing except the sound of his jacket ripping against the rabbi's razor and the feel of the severed fabric (symbolizing grief, final separation) against his fingers. What of death without funerals? The deaths of Ina's brother, Yedidiah, of her aunts, uncles, and grandparents. What would Jeddy's questions (and Ray's answers) be when the boy's own history was revealed to him?

"Her name was Beth. She was very bossy. But sometimes she was nice. And she was only in the sixth grade. God shouldn't have let her die. He shouldn't let there be leukemia. There probably isn't any God." With each sentence Jeddy's voice rose, inviting argument, challenge. His fists were plunged into the pockets of his faded jeans, and his plaid shirt trailed over his cowboy belt, a button tangling with the buckle.

"Probably there is a God, and it's hard for us to understand him," Ray offered. He remembered Beth Goldstein. Straight dark hair and bangs that fell into her eyes. She and Rachel had been friends briefly and then had quarreled over a game or a school assignment. It had been Rachel who clung to the grudge, small heiress to Ina's tenacious righteousness and reasonableness. Poor Rachel. She would suffer because she had disliked the dead girl, but she would not worry about God.

"There are lots of things we don't understand," Ray had added, feeling the inadequacy of his answer. "We don't understand why grass grows and why it is that birds fly and why some flowers grow red and others yellow. And we don't understand a lot of things about God. But Jeddy, there are some things you just feel and don't understand."

His own words made him feel foolish and helpless, and a slow anger began.

"Think about it, Jed," he said in defeat.

"All right."

The child took his hands out of his pockets and stared at him, and Ray saw the terrible gravity in his son's gaze, the dark wells of struggle and loss. The boy's small shoulders slumped as though weighted down by a new and unfamiliar burden, by complex considerations. Ray watched Jeddy walk slowly from the room, and although minutes later he heard the boy's voice lifted in loud laughter as he joined Rachel in a game, Ray did not turn back to the brief he had been working on.

He stared at the door through which Jeddy had disappeared and thought that his children were growing up too quickly and soon they would leave him behind. He thought of the infant clutch of their tiny fingers and their small sleeping faces turned upward toward a wintry sun. Though they laughed and played in the next room, he missed them in their sweet helplessness and felt suddenly the shadow of loneliness, the shadow of age. It was a warm day, but he shivered and thought of how beautiful Ina had been in pregnancy, how wondrously warm had been the golden skin of her stretching abdomen, trembling with life beneath his touch. He did not want her to abort this child neither of them had wanted.

But Ina was right. He had voiced no objection and only nodded assent when she said that now would be the ideal time to remove the small fibroma on her breast. It was harmless, Isaacs had assured them, but still it should be looked at. She could enter the hospital for the minor breast surgery, rest for a day or so, and decide about the abortion. In all things Ina was grudging of time; she dispensed days, hoarded hours, grew miserly with minutes. It was the heritage of those crowded first years in America when she dashed home from school to make the beds and turned from homework to dinner preparations while Shirley Cherne labored with her husband in the small factory that would establish their future, ease the pain of the past, give them at last something that would be their own.

Ray had been glad of the extra time. It was a reprieve of sorts, a time for him to marshal his arguments, present his case.

"You should have said something," Ina insisted.

He turned from the window.

"You're right. I should have. But I wasn't sure. And I wanted to be fair."

"And now you're sure? And fair?" Her voice was harsh, distant, but it did not wound him.

"Yes. I'm sure. But the decision is yours."

"Thank you."

"Ina, we'd have three children. Not such an enormous family."

"No," she agreed. She would be fair.

"It wouldn't change our life-style. We can afford another child. We even have the room."

But it would change their life-style. She would not abandon all care of another child to hired help, and if she worked less, she would earn less. Their seaside house, the small luxuries in which they indulged, came from her income. She disliked herself for the thought. Could she say, "I will not have this child because I want to build a deck"? She shivered. Her mother spoke bitterly of a survivor she knew who had emerged from the camp with two large diamonds. "He could have used them to buy lives," Shaindel said. Life took precedence over money. This, she of all people must know. Ina felt a wave of heat wash over her. She lay back, overtaken by a sudden, unfamiliar weakness.

"I don't want another baby." Pleading, not certainty, cased her words. He did not recognize her tone but pressed his advantage.

"Why not?" He was a skilled prosecutor, and he tossed the question deftly out. She was girded for persuasion, not for defense.

"We always said two children."

"We never anticipated this."

"It wasn't my fault."

A silence grew between them. They had not before talked in terms of fault, culpability. They were not a couple geared to acrimony. When the car ran out of gas, they did not debate who had forgotten to fill the tank. Once there had been a small grease fire in the kitchen of their Amagansett house, but never had they discussed who had forgotten to clean the broiler. They had each survived childhoods that hissed in memory with grief and anger, and they strove mightily for a home in which soft voices and gentle laughter mingled, expending great effort on the seemingly effortless. But now, in this white hospital room, its walls thick with the odors of death and hope, its floor scarred by the wheels of mobile beds and breathing the sharp fumes of disinfectant, fault would have to be affixed and weighed in on the scales of decision.

"It had to be you," he said evenly.

She was the one responsible for birth control. She used a diaphragm. Of course, diaphragms were not infallible. She knew of half a dozen cases where they had not been effective, but still—she leaned back against the pillows and thought hard.

They had never made love without using the diaphragm. Of that she was absolutely certain. She remembered talking about it in her consciousness-raising group, discussing it easily with that cluster of women who had gathered together weekly to sit on the living room floors of each other's apartments, clutching mugs of lukewarm coffee, nibbling at sesame seeds while disgorging the most intimate worries, the fiercest angers. They traded feelings hesitantly and then more swiftly, tingling with the electric excitement of recognition.

"You've felt that way too! I thought I was the only one."

They had each believed themselves to be emotional monopolists: selective frigidity, tightly contained fury, petty resentment were their unique holdings. In those first months empathy masqueraded as friendship, affinity as affection. Curiosity and frankness chased each other in webs of words, recollections, revelations. Friendships flowered quickly, colorfully, and faded swiftly like the briefly lived wild flowers of spring. Two of the women got divorced and two others stopped speaking to each other. Other women joined them. One wept uncontrollably and another sat silent. Ina went less and less frequently and then stopped going at all. She retained only her friendship with Ruthie, who wrote children's books peopled with animals in unconventional sex roles and who had been amicably separated from her husband for five years. They were, she explained, too lazy to get a divorce.

But she did remember discussing the diaphragm with the group. Didn't it destroy spontaneity? asked a woman whose fingernails were bitten down to bloody stumps. Ina did not think so. She inserted it automatically, just as she brushed her teeth, put moisturizing cream on her face. It was part of her routine. It was not a routine she had ever broken. But still, always fair, conscientious, she thought back. She had conceived six, perhaps seven, weeks ago. About the time of the Texas assignment. She remembered that the night before she flew to Dallas there had been an electric storm and she had awakened to see laser beams of bright gold light flash across the black sky. The light splintered into fragments, as though shattered by the sudden rolls of thunder, now muted, now reverberant; blue sparks danced at their window. She sat up in bed, and Ray awakened too. She leaned against his chest, and they watched the storm together. When it was over, she was trembling, and his heart was beating rapidly, as though a momentous secret had been revealed to them. A large gray cloud veiled the heavens, trembled against the force of the wind, and wafted westward. They made love then, urgently, swiftly.

She had not bothered to take off her nightgown, and she remembered that it moved silkily at her neck as Ray moved wildly within her. He fell asleep at once, afterwards, murmuring something she did not understand, his hand heavy on her breast. She had glanced at the clock. Two A.M. Her plane left at ten. She was up at six, and then, yes, she had removed the diaphragm without thinking about it (just as she brushed her teeth, washed her face). It had been in then only four hours. Not long enough. All right. It had, after all, been her fault. But that did not alter anything. It was almost inconsequential. She said so as she told him about it.

"You think you took it out too soon by accident?"

"Yes. Of course."

"But doesn't Dr. Berenson say you don't do anything by accident?"

She was newly angered by his question. He did not like Eleanor Berenson, she knew. He had not objected to Ina's psychoanalysis but accepted it carelessly, mildly annoyed at the expense it involved. Yet now he was quoting the analyst whom he had always refused to take seriously. Damn him, Ina thought. Damn, damn, damn him.

"Call Dot," she said, and glanced at her watch. Almost four. Rachel and Jeddy would be just getting home from school. At her office the last of the day's cups of instant coffee were being stirred. In the Woodside factory her father, Norman Cherne, would be studying the day's receipts while Shirley's fingers flashed across the keys of the adding machine. She would have to call her parents soon and tell them. Soon but not yet.

"What shall I tell Dot?" Ray asked.

"That's up to you. But I don't want to talk."

She could not, just then, face Dot's warm concern, her anxious questions, her talk of her own children and Ina's. Children were the pivot point on which childless Dot's life turned —the children she had adopted and the children she could not herself bear—the child her brother Ray had been (and, for her, still was), and Rachel and Jeddy, his children. She haunted toy stores and cunning children's boutiques. The salespeople at Creative Playthings knew her by name and called to tell her of a new toy, a new craft kit. She spoke earnestly about "small motor skills" and "hand-eye coordination." The silver-haired saleswomen in silk shirtwaists hurried toward her in the Bloomingdale's children's wear department.

"We have just what you're looking for, Mrs. Weinglass. We were hoping you'd come in."

And Dot smiled gratefully, as immersed in the small garments, in the labels that read "flame-retardant," in the helpful "Guide to Parents" in cleverly packaged kits, as Ina was in her programs, Ray in his briefs, and Larry in the investment brochures that littered his walnut desk.

Ray dialed, and she listened to him absently, as though the phone conversation had nothing to do with her, was between strangers. The light above her neighbor's bed flashed impatiently, but there was no sound, only the rustle of linens.

"Sounds great," Ray said. "We'll have to try the Bahamas. Dot. The kids okay? Larry? Great. Fine. Everyone here is fine except that Ina's decided to have that little thing on her breast removed. Isaacs thought it was wise, and she had some time now so she decided to do it. We're at Mount Lebanon. She'll be in for just a couple of days. No big deal. Oh sure, she'd love to see you. Well, she's not in the room right now. Why don't you call later? It's extension 502B. Good. Send our love to Larry and the kids."

He hung up but did not look at her. He had not told Dot about the abortion. The ball was back in her corner.

"Please." The voice from the neighboring bed was timorous, fragile, as though worn thin by stress and tears.

Ina sprinted out of bed, but before she could cross the room the door opened, and a nurse and a young man hurried in. They disappeared behind the screen, but their soft voices filled the silent room.

"There's no change, Miriam, I swear to you." The young

man's voice was insistent, yet pleading. "He's sleeping quietly. The doctors say that it's good that he sleeps. Sleep brings strength."

"Strength." In the woman's small voice the word echoed dolorously, accusingly. There was a stirring of bedclothes, a rustling of papers.

"Don't upset yourself, Mrs. Gottlieb." The nurse's voice was cool, laced with professional kindness. It did not work. The weeping began. Slow, rhythmic sobs rose and fell. Ina felt her own heart constrict, her eyes burn.

"Now, Mrs. Gottlieb. That won't accomplish anything." The nurse was disappointed, disapproving, her tone that of a nursery school teacher whose charge will not listen, will not understand.

"Miriam." Grief and love burned helplessly in the young man's voice. "Miriam."

The nurse walked over to the sink. She was a tall woman and older than her voice had indicated. Her white cap was perched on silver hair, and a worn navy-blue cardigan covered her white nylon uniform. She held a hypodermic needle up to the light, studied its milky contents, and returned to the bed.

"Just turn on your side now, Mrs. Gottlieb."

"No needle. No needle!" The plea was earnest, exhausted. "Ben. Please."

"Miriam. They only do what's best. Everyone wants to help you."

His shadow slid across the screen as he moved forward to help the nurse. His hands pressed down, holding her still while the needle pierced her skin and the drug mingled with her blood, soothing, neutralizing the chemicals of fear and anguish. There was a low moan and then silence.

Ina and Ray looked at each other, and he moved closer, his hand covering hers.

"I'm sorry," she said softly, but did not know why she was apologizing.

"Me too. I'll get us some coffee."

They watched the young man named Ben walk out, his

shoulders bent, huddled within a green sweater that was too heavy for such a day. He wore a knitted skullcap which he touched suddenly in a swift and jerky movement. The nurse and Ray walked after him, smiling awkwardly at each other. They did not close the door after them, and the sounds of a woman softly crying drifted down the corridor. Ina looked down at the sunlight that formed an almost perfect golden square on the linoleum-covered floor, worn thin and colorless by endless scrubbings.

"Mrs. Feldman, Mrs. Feldman."

The soft voice in her ear mingled with the fragile sounds of her dream, and, still sleeping, she smiled lazily, unwilling to awaken and abandon the vivid mid-afternoon dream in which she danced effortlessly, dressed in a gossamer gown, at the center of a circle formed by softly clapping, faceless women.

The three soldiers watched them, grim and faceless, their arms folded at their chests.

"Mrs. Feldman."

The voice, still gentle, grew more insistent. Ina, reluctantly, forced her eyes open and saw Nurse Li standing beside her bed with a tall, olive-skinned technician who held a tray on which test tubes, slides, and needles glittered importantly. Blood samples glowed ruby red within plastic cylinders and were neatly labeled with name and date. A chain heavy with many keys dangled at his belt, and he fingered it impatiently— a harried sommelier of leukocytes whose professional smile did not desert him.

"Mr. Sanchez needs some blood," Susan Li said.

"Why? Doesn't he have enough of his own?"

Ina smoothed back her hair, straightened the sleeve of her apricot gown, and tossed the weak crumbs of humor at them. They smiled appreciatively although surely they had heard it so many times before, and she was grateful for their acceptance. She wanted them to recognize that she was not the usual demanding, self-pitying patient but one of their own kind— corridor-smart, casually courageous, independent. It was important at this moment that Susan Li and Raphael Sanchez, both of whom she would probably forget in a week's time, like and admire her. The "everybody love me" syndrome, born perhaps of the uneasy feeling that perhaps hardly anyone did. The booted custodians of her childhood, her uniformed masters and mistresses, had emanated hatred and anger, and she had the child's tentative, uncomprehending fear that somehow she had earned that anger and that hatred. She must have done something wrong. Always, therefore, she had worked harder to please, smiling up into set, indifferent faces, offering jokes when there was no need for laughter. Lucid memory eluded, came and went in swift flashes, but feelings were constant.

She held out her hand and grimaced only slightly as the finger skin was coldly cleansed and the needle plunged in to thirstily suck up the bright crimson beads of blood that were sandwiched beneath the slide.

"Once more and we're through," he said.

His fingers danced lightly across her skin. He was good at his job, and she was grateful to him for his swiftness and gentleness.

"I must have fallen asleep," she said as Susan Li placed a Band-Aid on her finger. "My husband went out for coffee, and I guess I just drifted off."

"Yes. He stopped at the desk and said to tell you he was going home for a while and would be back to have dinner with you."

"Oh, good," Ina said, but Susan Li was not listening. She had waved Raphael Sanchez out and now slid behind the white screen of the neighboring bed. Ina watched her silhouetted form bend to straighten a pillow, to pluck something up from the floor.

"Is Mrs. Gottlieb sleeping?" Ina asked softly when the nurse reappeared.

"Yes. Poor thing. It's very hard on her."

"Her baby was born sick?"

"Very sick. A preemie. Jaundiced and then with a respiratory defect—the same thing that killed the Kennedy baby. Still, it's four days now and he's alive. I went down to see him on my break. Not that you could see him really. He's just a little bit of a thing lost in that tent. But his hand moved. That's what always gets me with newborns—those little perfect hands." Susan Li stared at her own hand, the tapering fingers outstretched and unringed, the very clean nails neatly curved and clipped.

"These things happen," Ina said, summoning up the meaningless words she herself despised. "And she's very young." The voice behind the screen had quivered and trembled in the lightness of late girlhood.

"She's young, but she's not very healthy," the nurse said softly. "And she's miscarried twice. They're very religious Jews. I guess something like this means more to them." She fingered the gold cross that hung around her neck. Something like that would mean more to her also, and that was why she had used the precious free moments of her break to glance at the small life that struggled for breath within the life-sustaining tent. Only to Ina would it be sad but negligible.

"These things happen," Ina said. Ina heard her own words echo back, saw herself through Susan Li's dark eyes, a cool young woman in the apricot nightgown who had checked herself in for an abortion.

"I'm not like that," she wanted to explain, but Susan Li was checking her chart, tucking in the sheet, catapulted back into brisk professionalism.

"If you need anything else, Mrs. Feldman . . ."

"No. I'm fine. Really. Just fine."

To demonstrate that "fineness" she reached for the program and took up a page she had read before. See. She too had her work, her obligations. She did not look up until Susan Li had left the room, and then she replaced the program and dialed her apartment. It was just five o'clock. Jeddy would be back from his swim and gym session at the Y and Rachel from her flute lesson. The living room would be strewn with their bookbags and jackets, and the television set in the den would be

playing in the empty room. Jeddy had the unhappy habit of
turning it on and allowing it to play even though no one
watched.

"It makes me feel unlonely," he explained when they chal-
lenged him, armed with arguments about waste, their utility
bills, and the nonsense that one found on television in any case.
His reply had silenced them, drowned their arguments in
hidden but ever-present whirlpools of guilt. It had brought
Ina back to her own childhood afternoons, her after-school
arrival at the empty Queens apartment which smelled of
ammonia because Shirley Cherne had a passion for antiseptic
cleansers. She had, after all, lived with the stink of offal, with
encrustments of garbage. Filth and germs were her enemies,
and she fought them and urged Ina into the fray. Ina would
rush each day, coat and mittens still on, to turn on the radio
and fend off the silence with "Helen Trent," "Mary Noble,
Backstage Wife," "Portia Faces Life," just as Jeddy shored up
his own quiet "unloneliness" with the "Brady Bunch" and
reruns of "Marcus Welby."

It was, she and Ray acknowledged, their fault that their
small son had to struggle to be "unlonely." Their lives were
too active, too involved with their work, their causes, the
demands of their friends. To this Ina added the hours of her
analysis, Ray his New School courses in photography. And so,
in small penance they allowed the television set to play unheeded, to drown out the silence that was of their making.

The phone rang, and Ina was glad that Ray had decided to
go home, that the children would at least share part of their
day with him.

It was Rachel who answered, her small girl's voice imitating
Ina's own cool tone, even tinged with Ina's barely perceptible
accent.

"The Feldman residence. Rachel Feldman speaking."

"Rachel. It's Mommy."

"Mommy! How are you? How do you feel? Are they going
to let us come and visit?"

"I'm fine, darling. Exactly the same as I was this morning. I haven't even seen Dr. Isaacs yet. All I've done is have a marvelous nap and read a little. And of course you can't come and visit. I'll be home before you know it."

She kept her tone light, reassuring, using her own mother now, as always, for the role model of all the things she must not be.

"Where are you going, Mama?" she had asked Shirley Cherne, each time her mother left the house during those first years in America. "When will you come back?"

"God in heaven, she doesn't let me live!" Shirley Cherne's voice had whipped the air, her body rocked with anger. "I have to give her reports. I have no life. What? Am I going to disappear? You think I am going to disappear?"

"No, Mama."

But of course she had thought her mother was going to disappear. Hadn't Halina Lansdorf's mother disappeared and Anya Rutlinger's and her own Aunt Peshi—Bette's mother, her own mother's sister? They had all walked through the door of the barracks one morning, Halina's mother stopping to brush a white crust of sleep from her daughter's eye, her aunt turning to look at Bette with the preoccupied, worried gaze of a mother fearful that a fragile child is about to come down with yet another cold. They had not come back. *They* had disappeared. All that night and for nights afterward, Halina, Anya, and Bette had wept silently and without hope, their muted voices meeting each other in the silence of the sleepless night. "Mama." "Mama." "Mama."

"I have my ballet recital Saturday afternoon," Rachel said.

"I know. We'll be there."

"But I need money for a new tutu."

"I'll tell Daddy."

"Can we watch the TV special tonight?"

"Yes."

"Great. I'll get Daddy."

The phone clattered to the table, and Ray picked it up.

"Have a good nap?"

"Terrific. It was a good idea to go home to be with the children."

"Yes. I think I'll have dinner with them and then come back to the hospital. Is that all right?"

"Fine."

"Do you need anything?"

"No, I don't think so."

"Oh, yes. Your mother called. I had to tell her you were at Mount Lebanon."

"What did you tell her?"

"Only as much as I told Dot."

"I see."

He was leaving everything open-ended, tossing the decision neatly back at her.

"She said she'd visit tomorrow afternoon."

"God."

"I know, but what could I say?" He too stood helpless before Shirley Cherne, her fierce energy sapping his own, her strident voice muting his answers, silencing his explanations.

"Nothing, I guess. Let me speak to Jeddy."

There was a pause, and then Jeddy's voice, the cracked, tremulous, half-baby, half-small-boy voice that stirred her heart.

"Mommy, come home and give me a bath."

"Now you know I can't do that, Jeddy. I'll give you your bath next week. I'm fine, Jeddy, really." (I am not disappearing, Jeddy. There is no need to call me through the darkness of the night. These are new times, Jeddy. Mothers do not disappear.)

"Okay. I'm working on my plane model. Aunt Dot's going to paint it."

"Good, sweetheart. Listen to Carmen and don't fight with Rachel."

"We're having spaghetti. What are you having?"

"I don't know."

"Good night."

"Good night, baby." But he had dropped the phone, and Ray's voice came on again, oddly strained, tired.

"I'll see you in about two hours then, Ina."

"Yes. All right."

"Ina. You're not angry?"

"No," she said, and wondered if she was.

"All right then, babe. I'll see you soon."

She waited for him to hang up and then replaced the phone and reached up to touch the velvet petal of a full-blown rose and to smile at the aide who pushed the metal meal cart into the room.

She was surprised, halfway through the meal, to discover that she was enjoying it, although she had grimaced at the sight of the heavy dishes, the plastic silverware, the small paper packets of salt, pepper, and sugar. It was, after all, a luxury to eat alone and in bed while slowly turning the pages of her battered copy of *Great English Short Stories*. She was lost again in "The Rocking Horse Winner," the tale of the house whose walls whispered of money. She thought that if her own children were to write a similar story, they would have the walls of their home whisper of time. They never seemed to have enough of it, and she and Ray rationed precious hours, scheduled meetings weeks in advance, wearily marked their calendars in pencil, reserving distant days for conferences and cocktail parties, Rachel's dance recital, open school nights, meetings to protest the Westway, the influence of Arab oil, the racketing of garbage trucks on Central Park West. She often remembered, guiltily, that her first reaction to the ending of the war in Vietnam was relief that they would not have to make time for any more midnight vigils or predawn fasts, that they were done with hastily assembled caucuses in the basements of churches and community houses, that they would no longer spend precious minutes reading telegrams to Washington into the telephone. They could turn that time to other calls and other causes.

Almost idly, buttering a roll liberally, she thought of what another baby would mean in terms of time. The long sleepless nights (Rachel and Jeddy had not slept through the night for years—perhaps because she had always hovered over their cribs, listening for the soft sweet intakes of their sleep-thick breath, watching for the magic movements of their tiny limbs, fearful of nocturnal terror, for she had had a brother who died in the dark hours before morning), the frenetic days of feeding and changing and coddling and caring, the house-bound winter weekends. Always, she had snatched whatever free time remained for her work, for the soothing concentration on those columns of symbols, so systematic, so rational. But she never went far from her children when they were smaller, fearful always of unnamed dangers, shadowy threats, perhaps of lurking faceless soldiers.

In this she was different from her sister-in-law, Dot, who was absorbed in her children but free of haunting fear. It was live germs that Dot feared, and current trauma, not death-eyed children and lurking ghosts. Bette, she knew, shared her feelings. Her cousin might discuss the efficacy of vitamin C with Dot, but it was not the common cold that she feared—it was the hidden face of evil, the thunderous tread of booted feet marching backward through her memories. It was only recently that Ina felt at ease when Rachel and Jeddy were on their own. They had emerged from the thicket of childhood unscarred by concealed branches, strangling vines. They had eluded the invisible soldiers. Yes, she had been lucky with Rachel and Jeddy, but she could not trust that luck. She could not begin again.

It seemed to her that she had followed a professional pattern in her thinking. She had balanced the scales, executed intricate calculations, decoded, and decided. She poured herself more coffee. She was not powerless. She could make decisions and protect herself, protect all of them. She was, she thought with brief bitterness, her mother's daughter.

"Miss. Mrs. Excuse me."

The voice, so thin and frail she barely heard it, severed the silence, and she jerked herself away from Lawrence's polished syntax and remembered that she was not alone in this hospital room and that the small voice belonged to the woman in the next bed, little Mrs. Gottlieb, whom she had not yet seen but whose tears and fears she knew.

"Yes. Yes, of course. Can I help you?"

"If you could ring for the nurse, please. And pull back the curtain if you're able. I feel so closed in here. I can't see you. I can't see the window. Only these flowers. And now they left the buzzer too far away." Her voice was plaintive, like that of a child bewildered by illness, surprised at newness.

"Of course."

Ina rang for the nurse, pressing the buzzer more sharply and insistently than she would have if the summons had been for herself. She hopped out of bed and pulled the curtain back, whipping the length of sheer cloth so that the rings to which it was attached hummed metallically as they moved across the steel bar of the screen.

Miriam Gottlieb's face and form matched the fragility of her voice. She was a small woman, and the arm that lay above the crisp hospital counterpane was so thin that the vein at her wrist splayed an azure wave toward the pale outline of bone barely covered by the thin layer of translucent skin.

Her hair, however, which covered the pillow in a cloud of darkness, was soft and thick and matched the woman's large, dark brown eyes, riveted now on Ina.

"The nurse will be here soon. You'll be fine," Ina said, suddenly and irrationally ashamed because she wore her apricot silk nightgown while Miriam Gottlieb's arms fluttered in the butterfly sleeves of the coarse white hospital gown that covered her loosely, like an ill-fitting shroud. Ina's own strength and health, the rose gold of her skin, the swiftness of her step, embarrassed her in the face of the sick woman's pallor and the fretful weakness with which the long white fingers plucked at the linen sheet.

She thought suddenly of her children at this hour of the evening, newly bathed, fresh pajamas clinging to their damp sweet skin, sprawled across the carpeted floor, laughing and playing while this young mother's baby struggled stertorously

for breath. There was imbalance here and privilege—all hers,
unearned and undeserved. Her own luck in the face of
another's misfortune frightened her; she was the sort of
woman who often crossed the street to avoid passing a cripple.

She was teased too by the thought of the tiny embryo that
adhered now to her own umbilical cord, nurturing itself at that
moment toward a life it would not survive to live. Jeddy and
Rachel had been wonderfully healthy infants, large and well
shaped, their skin bright and firm; they had been vigorous
sucklings whose mouths tugged eagerly at Ina's breasts, claiming with feral thrust their nourishment. Would this embryo
(this "thing," as she preferred to think of the clump of protoplasm unwelcome and unwanted within that dark chasm of her
womanhood where womb and uterus, fallopian tubes, and
cervical passage nestled) develop into a sturdy, pummeling
fetus, an active, kicking baby? Dark doubts trembled in her
mind. The life she carried now was the nuisance detritus of
chance and carelessness. Would it be marked in some mysterious way by that same carelessness? Fantasies of all that could
go wrong in gestation danced before her. She remembered
tales recounted by other women in awed and fearful whispers.
Babies born without noses and fingers, monster infants whose
mouths grew out of their cheeks and whose skin was purpled
with massive hemangiomas. In the camp she had heard of twins
born without legs and arms to a gypsy woman, but no one had
ever seen them, and it was said that the monstrousness of their
defect was the result of medical experimentation. She herself
had studied her infant children carefully when they were first
brought to her. She had counted their fingers and toes, passed
her hand across the petallike skin of their faces and bodies.
She had been lucky. What happened to women who birthed
monsters? Did they go slowly and secretly mad? (The gypsy
woman, they said, had strangled herself with her own bed
sheets.) Surely, for them there was no solace in fifty-minute
hours spent in Eleanor Berenson's plant-filled office, where
small orange lights flickered on and off on the unanswered
telephone.

"Everything will be all right," Ina said in foolish answer to an unasked question, and even as she spoke, Susan Li hurried into the room.

"Feeling better, Mrs. Gottlieb?" she said. Her voice was gay and determined; the question was posed in the tone of a mother who must reassure a sick and fretful child. It was not a question at all, but a coaxing demand.

"I suppose."

Miriam Gottlieb smiled wanly. As a small girl she must have struggled mightily to please. She reminded Ina of the college girl she had hired one summer to organize her files. The job had been a boring one, and the air conditioning in the archives had broken down.

"It's boring work, isn't it?" she had said sympathetically to the girl, who doggedly arrived early and stayed late.

"I suppose," the girl had replied dutifully, wanting to please, choosing acquiescence over protest. Miriam Gottlieb and that almost-forgotten summer helper were spiritual twins, and Ina was impatient and intolerant of both of them. She herself would have done the work, endured the pain, but still, she would tell the truth. Yes. It is boring. And hot. And stupid. No. I am not feeling better. I'm tired. And sick. And worried to death. Never in her life had Ina said in answer to anything, "I suppose."

She returned to her own bed and watched as the nurse helped Miriam to the bathroom, her hand supporting the girl's back as the hospital gown flew open to reveal the knobbed length of spine, the thin shoulder blades that moved timorously like the wings of a wounded bird.

Ina was again immersed in D. H. Lawrence when the two women emerged from the bathroom. Miriam had changed into a high-necked, pale blue nightgown, and she moved more easily now, as though the soft fabric and the flattering color had imbued her with new strength, new confidence.

"You look so nice," Ina said. "By the way, my name is Ina Feldman."

"Thank you. I'm Miriam Gottlieb."

"Here's your hairbrush, Mrs. Gottlieb," the nurse said. "I'm going to get your supper tray. We kept one hot for you on the warming table."

"She's very nice," Miriam said as Susan Li hurried out.

"Yes," Ina agreed. "She seems to really care."

"She does care. She went to see my baby on her break. My baby, a little boy, was born sick, very sick." She said these words slowly, as though their utterance would negate them. They echoed sadly in the silent room.

"I'm sorry," Ina said at last. "But Mount Lebanon has the best neonatal facilities in the city. I'm sure they're doing everything they can."

"Oh, yes. Everything." Now it was Miriam's turn to reassure herself and to smile brightly as the aide carried the tray in and set it down on her bed tray.

She lifted the aluminum cover and smiled as the steam swirled mistily up about her face.

"It's funny," she said. "I don't think I care about anything at all, and then I realize that I'm hungry. How can I not care about anything at all and still be hungry?"

She lifted a forkful of fish, sipped her apple juice, and bent with great seriousness and interest to survey the rest of the tray.

"That's a good sign," Ina said.

The words might have fallen from her mother's mouth. Interest in food, Shirley Cherne had said again and again, was always "a good sign." In the camp, the time to worry was when someone lost interest in food. Not to be interested in food, even in the weak mixture of cabbage soup and the dried hard bits of black bread that were the standard camp diet, was to acknowledge a forfeiture of life, a total human bankruptcy. That was how her mother knew that her own sister Peshi, Bette's mother, would die. A woman who worked in the kitchen had managed to steal a hunk of salami and to smuggle it out by thrusting it up the front of her uniform.

"Our breasts had shrunk to nothing, so there was plenty of room there," Shirley Cherne had said, her smile twisted and

bitter. "The salami smelled of sweat, but we didn't care. Everything in the camp smelled. Of sweat and vomit. Of *pishachs*
and *dreck*. Don't you remember, Ina?"

Ina did not remember. She remembered nothing but a
cavernous room, soft weeping in the night, and a coldness so
pervasive it seemed possessed of a corporeality of its own. Not
even Eleanor Berenson, during the long persistent quiet remembering of the analytic hour, could make her remember,
nor did the analyst exert pressure. There were, doubtless,
warnings, instructions, on how to deal with survivors as patients. Perhaps it was just as well that they did not remember.
But Shirley Cherne remembered everything. Every incident
and every odor. *Pishachs* and *dreck*. Urine and shit. The stench
pursued her. Never, when Rachel and Jeddy were infants,
would their grandmother change them. She had had enough
excrement in her life—she had eaten and slept with it, had
sometimes thought she tasted it upon her tongue. In the Cherne
household the bathrooms sparkled, the water in the toilets
swirled bluely, the towels were changed each day, and plants
grew on Lucite shelves.

Shirley Cherne remembered the meal they had made of that
salami. Someone had contributed a heel of black bread, and
they crumbled the bread and the meat together to stretch it
out. Another woman had miraculously given them a sprig of
parsley, plucked from the field near the quarry.

"But Peshi wouldn't eat," Shirley had recalled. "Nothing.
Not a taste. I knew then she was finished. I was almost glad she
was taken in the morning 'selection' that day. Don't ever tell
Bette, but if she had not been taken, I am sure she would have
become a *mussillman*—one of those crazy walking skeletons
who cared about nothing but stared with the eyes of death.
You were so scared of them, Ina. I saw it happening to Peshi,
and then I knew it. No interest in food. Me—I still taste that
parsley. We thought it was a miracle that anything could grow
in that cursed soil. Even the birds stopped flying over the
camp. Wiser than the plants, those birds. They knew. You

could search the skies for weeks and months and never see a bird. Birds you can live without, but not food. Remember— not to eat is not to care."

And Shirley Cherne, to prove that she cared, peeled a peach and ate it with pleasure, allowing the juice to dribble down her chin.

Miriam Gottlieb ate enough to show that she too cared, and when she had finished, she poured herself a cup of coffee from the small carafe and turned to Ina.

"Would you like some coffee? Mine is still hot."

"Yes. Yes, thank you, I would," Ina said, and closed her book.

She had not read a sentence during the minutes past but had seen her Aunt Peshi's face float before her, frozen into the defeated, lifeless stare of the skeletal *mussillman*, the walking dead of the camps, who had populated the sleeping and waking nightmare hours of her childhood.

She settled herself into the orange plastic armchair beside Miriam's bed and noted the small objects assembled on the bedside table—a small silver music box, a tortoiseshell comb and brush set, a young philodendron, and a large floral display of irises and tulips. Wherever they went, Ina thought, women built themselves small nests, no matter how brief the visit, how temporary the habitat—still they carried with them photographs and flowers, books and plants, their small artifacts of individuality, of home building. On the one occasion Ray had been hospitalized during their marriage, he had taken with him only his toilet articles and the biography he was reading, both of which he had kept in his bedside drawer so that his hospital room looked as it had when he entered. In their shared motel rooms, her side of the bed was strewn with her personal debris while his remained chaste and untouched.

Even in the camp, she remembered, the interned women had made small pitiful efforts to establish a domicile of sorts—a clutch of wild flowers in a broken jam jar, a fragment of bright cloth spread across a bare, thin pillow. Ina's mother had a small china penguin which had stood on the mantelpiece of their Warsaw apartment and which she hid throughout the war beneath the coverlet of her barracks cot. It had slipped to the floor and shattered on the day of their liberation, and when Ina wept with a child's terror at seeing a fragmented treasure that cannot be made whole again, Shirley Cherne (Shaindel Czernowitz then) had shrugged indifferently and kicked at the shards with her foot. "We don't need it anymore," she had said.

But clearly, Miriam Gottlieb still needed her philodendron, which she touched now, gently, tenderly.

"It's a pretty one," Ina said. "Do you have a sunny spot at home to hang it?"

"Our living room gets hours and hours of sunlight, and I take advantage of it. Ben—my husband—says I've planted a jungle there. But I love my plants. I get so excited when they get new leaves. I guess I just like to watch things grow."

Ina nodded. She was familiar with such fenestral jungles where plants swayed in clever ceramic hanging pots and towered above low tables and soft armchairs, throwing their patterned shadows across parquet floors. Such indoor gardens grew mainly in the homes of childless couples where the foliage was not threatened by small grasping fingers and runaway Tonkas. Her friend Ruthie's plants dominated half her studio apartment, and when their consciousness-raising group met there, the women had sprawled like urban Amazons amid the greenery, their heads rising to touch fronds, their brows tickled by dangling, verdant tendrils. Ruthie explained that she spoke to her plants because she believed in it. Hadn't Ina ever read or listened to Thalassa Cruso? It had nothing to do with loneliness, with misplaced nurturing, with the silence of wide-windowed rooms where women lived alone.

"I like plants, too," Ina said now, and proffered her cup, which Miriam filled with steaming coffee, although her hand shook slightly.

"Cream?" Miriam asked. "Sugar?"

They acknowledged comfort in the small ritual, knowing that women take secret strength from the metallic click of utensils, the twin rattling of china cups and saucers, as coffee and confidences mingle easily, intimately. They settled back, each cradling the thick hospital cup, as oddly comfortable with each other as neighboring women, who, though not friends, will meet in each other's breakfast nooks when children and husbands are gone, to banish the night and seize rein over diurnal demands while sipping mugs of reheated coffee.

"Do you have children?" Miriam asked, and Ina showed her wallet shots of Jeddy and Rachel, Ray's serious dark eyes shining up from each child's face and her own thick dark hair crowning their heads—Rachel's caught up in a ponytail and Jeddy's a natural Afro.

"They're darling," Miriam said. "He's eight? That's a terrific age. I used to teach second grade. The best time. They've gotten over the basics and are all caught up in the excitement of learning. I could really do things with that age group. Gee, your children will probably miss you a lot. Will you be here long? I hope it's nothing serious."

"Where did you teach?" Ina asked, trading questions rather than offering answers.

"I taught in the South Bronx, believe it or not. And I loved it. Don't believe everything you read in the *Times*. We had some terrific kids. But I quit as soon as I became pregnant this time. I had miscarried twice before, and we weren't taking any chances this time. And it was a terrific pregnancy. I wasn't sick at all, and I treated the whole time as a holiday—a very long vacation. I slept late, went to museums and matinees, met my friends for lunch. I shopped for baby stuff with my mother and mother-in-law. They didn't want to—they said it was bad luck. And now, I suppose, they'll think they're right."

The coffee cup trembled, then clattered angrily against the saucer. Blindly, she reached for a tissue.

"I'm sorry." Her voice, so full and strong just a moment before, relapsed into a wispy tone, and although she did not cry, she held the tissue tightly, a paper shield against a sly and wily grief.

"That's nonsense," Ina said, assuming the firm maternal tone she used to handle the children's nocturnal fears, operating on the principle that certainty, however mistaken, effectively banished doubts, however valid. "Superstitious nonsense. I shopped for my babies' layettes before they were born. And I'm sure your baby is going to be fine, and you'll use every kimono you bought for him." The certainty of her tone surprised her. She was, after all, a woman who dreamed of booted soldiers and awakened haunted by the fear that she had been too lucky for too long.

"Do you really think so?"

"I hope so. When I gave birth to Jeddy, one of the babies born then was so sick that no one thought she would live. She fooled them all, and we still exchange birthday cards because she and Jeddy were born the exact same day, and we've kept in touch. Her name is Sharon, and she's the prettiest, healthiest girl. Last year her mother sent us a photograph. There are lots of happy endings and yours will be one, too."

"Yes. Maybe." Miriam pushed her spoon about in the dregs of her coffee cup. "This baby is very special. Ben's parents are all alone in the world. They lost everyone during the war. They got out of Germany in '37 but everyone else in the family died. This baby was going to be a whole new family for them. Ben's their only child. Our baby is supposed to build an entire new world for them, to make up for all those lost lives, all the loneliness. They were going to have a family again—an extension of themselves."

"You must think of yourself—not Ben's parents or your own," Ina said fiercely, the echo of sessions in Eleanor Berenson's office ringing in her mind. ("You are *Ina*. You are important. You must think about yourself now. About Ina. What is good and necessary for Ina?") The therapist's voice was steady and insistent, and now Ina's voice imitated that steadiness and insistence. "You're the mother." (Mother—what a soft, susurrant word it was—a gentle hum of a word—so simple for the smallest tongue. Mother. Mama.)

"I think of myself," Miriam said tiredly. "Of course I do. But I must think beyond myself. We're orthodox Jews, Ben and myself. We observe the sabbath, go to synagogue, study the Torah reading. Do you know what the words *shaarit yisrael* mean? The remnant of Israel—the remnant that survives and remains strongly Jewish, even after a terrible tragedy. Like the Inquisition or pogroms or the Holocaust. Ben is part of *shaarit yisrael*. And our baby—he too is—will be, if—" Again her voice trailed off, unable to verbalize the possibilities that lay beyond that "if."

Ina looked up and was relieved to see Ben Gottlieb come in, a smile on his face.

"You're feeling better, Miriam? You ate something?"

"Yes. Much better. And I ate. I had company. This is my neighbor for today—Ina Feldman."

"Hello." Ina smiled, and he held his hand out to her. His palm was very soft, and in his firm grasp her fingers fluttered.

"That's good," he said. "I've just come from the nursery. They think, the nurses, that his color's better. Much better. Isn't that good, Miriam? His color's better. I saw myself."

"That's wonderful," she said happily, and new color tinged her own cheeks, a rush of blood beneath the pallor so that her color, too, could be called better by those monitors of health who roamed the corridors of Mount Lebanon.

"Do you think, would it be all right, if my parents came tonight?" he asked.

"Not tonight," she said. "I'm so tired. Tomorrow. In the afternoon. My mother and father will drive them. But not tonight, Ben. Please."

"All right." He reached for her hand, and Ina rose quickly from the plastic armchair.

"It was a good talk, Miriam. Thanks for the coffee," she said.

Slipping between the sheets of her own bed and taking up the program again, she realized that she had not, after all, answered Miriam's question. As Ray had done during his conversation with his sister, she had avoided the simple direct answer that she was in the hospital for minor surgery and (perhaps) to abort a child she did not want.

———————

It was dark when Ray arrived, and she realized, with regret, that she had forgotten to watch the sun glide to its death above the trees in the park and neglected to search out the first golden glimmer of the Fifth Avenue street lights, small rituals that had marked her afterbirth days in this hospital. But she had managed to finish the Lawrence story and work out a problem in the program. And she had had a long telephone conversation with Dot and a brief one with her mother, both of which she would report to Ray and use to flesh out the armature of her argument—using each in turn to support her decision. Not that she had told either her mother or her sister-in-law about her pregnancy. Rather, she had listened to them and assigned their words to the correct column in her mental ledger, casting each of them in roles her consciousness-raising group (any consciousness-raising group) would have little difficulty recognizing.

Dot was the Great Earth Mother, the Eternal Nurturer, so mindful of her children that she neglected to remember herself. And Shirley Cherne, who had called her from the offices of Cherne Knitwear, so that calculators hummed and typewriters clattered during their conversation, was the Consummate Career Woman who happened, to her own and everyone else's surprise, to be a mother. There was now, and always had been, time for Cherne Knitwear, which had been more tenderly nursed than any child could have been at Shirley Cherne's hands. The infant enterprise, begun in a dimly lit loft with Shirley and Norman running the machines, making sales (speaking a broken English that sparkled with terms like *discount, special order, original*), buying, designing, and packing, had grown to its second stage of development with an employee in charge of each section, and finally blossomed into full maturity—housed in its own building, diversified in production, and boasting a proud and reliable listing in Dun and Bradstreet. Cherne Knitwear had been carefully nursed to adulthood, but Ina Cherne had grown up by herself in a home whose yawning silence had been broken only by the sound of the radio, so that the inflections of soap opera actresses were more familiar to her than her mother's own voice.

Typically, Ina's phone conversation with Dot had focused on Dot's children. The youngest, Simon, had been sick during their vacation. Rampant diarrhea. They thought it had been caused by the changes in diet and climate, but they were having him checked just to be sure. In detail, Dot described the nature of the child's excrement. Yellow. Runny. Hadn't Jeddy's been like that when he'd had the chicken pox? Ina could not remember. She never remembered things like that. But Dot, who scrutinized each child's soiled diaper, who still stared clinically at each child as he sat in the bath, searching the small naked bodies for rashes, drooping testicles, incipient scoliosis, welded such knowledge into tenebrous memory.

She was even more concerned with the children's emotional and intellectual development. As each child learned to speak, she recorded known words, plied them with puzzles and intricately shaped wooden toys crafted in Copenhagen and Oslo. Motherhood was her career, a vocation that, like the assumption of orders, negated selfhood, self-concern. Even now, she was less concerned about Ina's health than about the arrangements that had been made for Rachel and Jeddy during Ina's hospital stay. She hoped that Carmen would be careful about assembling their schoolbags and make certain that Rachel washed her face with allergenic soap. Eleven was a crucial age for skin, Dot reminded Ina, who wearily agreed.

With her mother Ina had spoken about the unreliability of suppliers and the threat of the new import markets in Hong Kong and Sri Lanka. "After all, who can manufacture as cheaply as they can?" Shirley Cherne asked accusingly. A machinist had quit, and the switchboard operator was careless, lazy. Only seconds before she hung up did she remember to ask how Ina was feeling and whether she needed anything. She was going to "make time" to visit the hospital tomorrow. Difficult as it was, she would snatch a precious hour, leave the adding machines to racket wildly without her, and visit her only daughter in the hospital. Always, when something important happened to Ina—graduations, roles in school plays, even her wedding—Shirley Cherne spoke of "making time."

Whenever Shirley spoke of "making time," Ina flinched. Never had she spoken of "making time" for her children. The children took priority whenever possible. Always, arrangements were made for them first. It was true that there was little surfeit of time as she and Ray manipulated their careers and communal and social obligations, juggling hours and days. But they had developed skill and balance. They improvised and invented. She could not cancel out the mother-empty silence of the after-school hour when Jeddy turned for comfort to the television set, and there was the occasional missed recital or class assembly when neither she nor Ray could leave work in the middle of the day. But they tried mightily, and they had been lucky. They lived, the four of them, she and Ray and Rachel and Jeddy, in a self-contained square of closeness.

"I wish," said one of Rachel's school friends whose parents were newly divorced, "that I had a family like yours."

Ina had glowed with pleasure at her words. No one had ever wished for a family like Ina's own. The few friends she had brought home from school stared curiously at the empty, overclean apartment. They looked at the gleaming oven which had never known the aroma of a rising cake or baking cookies. They watched Ina pull out the frozen chop and the single can for her evening meal. "Isn't your mother ever home?" they asked. "Don't you miss not having brothers and sisters?" Her children would never know such questions. She wanted with fierce desperation to protect her family and to contain it. The small Amagansett house was a fortress, each happy time together a new bastion. She trembled as Rachel arched toward adolescence, grew secretive, protective of her privacy. Change was dangerous, threatening. And a new baby would not mean change but revolution, almost chaos, it seemed to her. She struggled against a strange encroaching panic and with effort kept her tone light as she told Ray about her conversation with

her mother while he unpacked the Bloomingdale's shopping
bag.

He handed her a crayon drawing of a golden sun by Jeddy.
The sun wept tears of aquamarine although its rays shot forth
in agile bands of gold. Oversized flowers in fluorescent fuchias
and greens drooped sadly, and above the picture Jeddy had
scrawled, "Me and the flowers miss Mommy." Rachel had sent
her a letter written in the style of L. L. Montgomery. She was
reading *Anne of the Windy Poplars* and had adopted the
formal literary tones of the young Prince Edward Island
teacher. "Class today was interesting but tedious. I had a slight
contretemps with Lisa but managed to make my point known."
Rachel, Ina knew, would always manage to make her point
known. Ray had also brought her a new nightgown spun of
soft yellow batiste and a box of Bloomingdale's chocolate chip
cookies. He lifted the nightgown just as she reported her
mother's last words.

"Just before she hung up, she said, 'This is a very incon-
venient time for you to go to the hospital, Ina. We're organizing the fall line.' "

"And what did you say?" Ray asked. He leaned back, the
nightgown a sunny cloud in his hands.

He enjoyed hearing tales of confrontations between his wife
and her mother. He had grown fond of the Chernes during the
years of his marriage, but he admitted that his wife's parents
confused and bewildered him. Their voices were too loud,
their laughter too shrill, their home overfurnished and under-
lived in. The wartime filter of tragedy that clung to their lives
shielded them from both his anger and his understanding. They
were his children's grandparents, and their history of horror
was an inescapable legacy to his own heirs.

Those five years of their lives, between 1940 and 1945, the
years spent in hiding and fleeing and, finally, as prisoners, over-
shadowed all that had gone before and all that came after.
During those years their only son, Yedidiah, had died, and Ina
and her mother had been separated from Nachum Czernowitz

in the camp. Ray thought often of that unknown brother-in-law
for whom his own child was named. He bought new sneakers
for Jeddy, and as the boy touched them, Ray remembered the
photo of a hillock of children's shoes he had seen in a book of
concentration camp photos. In a Hebrew school play Jeddy's
costume for his role as a Maccabean warrior included an arm-
band with a yellow star, and Ray had written the bewildered
teacher an irate note, berating her for her choice. Jeddy
carried a shield instead. Within the expensive clutter of the
Chernes' Forest Hills home the ghost of Yedidiah drifted. The
single snapshot of him they had managed to save had been
enlarged and encased in a silver frame. It stood on the mantelpiece. The boy had large dark eyes and an easy, large-gummed
smile so like Jeddy's own. He, too, they said, had shown aston-
ishing athletic grace. He had been double-jointed. He had
played the piano. They lit a candle for him on Kol Nidre
night. It occurred to Ray once, seeing those sad small candles,
that the ancient Jews who had conceived of this Yom Kippur
custom had been prescient. They had anticipated an era when
deaths were unmarked by gravestones and death days were
unknown. They had known then that small flames would have
to be kindled in glowing witness that a life had been lived, a
death endured.

To understand the Chernes it was necessary to remember
the five years that had shaped their lives and the terrible loss
that weighed them down. Did Ina herself remember to do
that? he sometimes wondered, sensing the febrile heat of the
anger she aimed at her mother, the brittle impatience she
showed her father. But Ina's life too had been shaped by those
years. She had been a small girl when the ordeal began, a wise-
eyed woman-child when it was over at last. What if her childhood had been undisturbed, if she had grown up in a carefully
bordered normalcy, its perimeters of school and lessons, birthday parties and outings, seaside vacations and mountain camps,
clearly defined? Would there be that angry abrasiveness he so
often sensed? Would it be necessary for her to spend late

afternoon hours on the couch in Eleanor Berenson's office, hunting memories as gossamer and elusive as the golden dust of that beginning twilight that marked her analytic hour?

But such speculation was foolish, he knew, as foolish as his own sometime fantasies of a Ray who had grown up with living parents, whose boyhood had not been so suddenly and definitively shattered by the shriek of automobile brakes and seared-flesh odor of his parents' burning bodies, by his own private holocaust of loss and loneliness. When Ina wakened, terrified by the mysterious dream that would not cease, he clung to her fear-damp body, and in the darkness it seemed to him that she was dreaming his dreams.

How lucky Rachel and Jeddy were to grow up free of such shadows, of such night terror, in their casual comfortable home ringed with music and laughter, care and concern. He touched Jeddy's drawing, envying his children and loving them doubly for that acknowledged envy, wishing himself beside them always—a silent guide, an invisible protector. He remembered oddly, irrelevantly, that though they had often seen Yedidiah's picture, they had never asked about him.

"I said I was sorry," Ina said now. "I thought of saying that in the future you and I would be more scrupulous in our practice of birth control, but that if we were careless, we would certainly not indulge when they were organizing their fall line."

"Ina."

He glanced nervously across the room toward Miriam Gottlieb's bed. Ben Gottlieb sat reading in the plastic armchair while she idly turned the pages of a magazine. Now and again he reached out and touched her hand, and once she took his fingers and pressed them to her lips.

"I'm sorry. You haven't met the Gottliebs. Miriam, Ben, this is my husband, Ray," she called.

He walked over to them, shook hands with Ben, smiled at Miriam. They were an attractive couple, and tall, thin Ben reminded him of a young lawyer who had recently been assigned to his bureau. Ray brimmed with advice he wanted to offer the young man, gentle guidelines on life and law: he and his wife ought to take a year off and travel in Europe— something Ina and Ray had not done before the children were born and always regretted; the young man should get a master's in international law; he should cultivate a hobby that required him to work with his hands. Instead Ray corrected the young man's brief and advised him only to join the New York County Lawyers' Association for their insurance program. There were warnings that could not be offered, lessons that must be self-learned.

"Would you like some coffee?" Ben asked. "I have a thermos and some cups."

"And we have cookies." Ina hopped out of bed and scrambled into her apricot peignoir.

Swiftly, almost gaily, they organized their bedside picnic, carrying over the plastic armchair from Ina's bedside and appropriating a steel implement bench for Ray to sit on. Ina got her cookies, and Miriam produced a gift basket of fruit. They cut the shining apples with Ray's pocket knife and distributed the gleaming white pieces in their polished thin red skins, relishing the fruit for the sickroom, selected to tempt the invalid, to coax the weary back to a world where fruit blooms brightly and the fragrance of citrus sweetens the air.

They chatted with the easy intimacy of compatible strangers thrust suddenly into a contained, insular situation. Once, on a cruise ship, Ray, who never discussed his parents' deaths, had found himself telling their dinner partners, acquaintances of a brief hour, about the distant day when he had found himself orphaned. Ben Gottlieb was an engineer, and Ray knew someone in the legal department of his company. The Gottliebs lived in a small Westchester town, although they often regretted leaving the Upper West Side where they had lived during the first years of their marriage.

"But we found a house at a very good price. And it is not far from a good Jewish day school. That is very important for us," Ben said, and pressed Miriam's hand. To speak of the day school was to pronounce an utterance of hope. Perhaps their infant child, struggling now for breath on the floor above, would hurry to that school one day, his bookbag bursting with Hebrew grammars and commentaries on the Bible.

"Our children both go to Hebrew school. At B'nai Jeshurun," Ina assured them, not adding that too often they did not go. Hebrew school was the first activity to be sacrificed for a birthday party or a recital. Ina and Ray were, after all, twice-a-year Jews, appearing in synagogue on Rosh Hashanah and Yom Kippur. Sometimes now they missed even the New Year's service if the sun remained strong and they could squeeze in a long weekend at the beach house. Consistent parents, they did not demand of their children a commitment they did not themselves demonstrate.

And Ina could not bring herself to discuss God with the children. She had, after all, never confronted her own religious feelings. She was firm in her Jewishness but evaded the concept of belief. Dutifully she mouthed the prayers. "God full of mercy," she repeated but thought that it could not have been a merciful God who allowed her friends to weep in the darkness while their mothers' bodies floated in spiraling clouds of soot-stained smoke in the unseen sky. "Guardian of Israel," she intoned and thought, with a harshness that had no place in the dimly lit synagogue where men wept and women swayed, that with such a guardian Israel's enemies need have no worry. She had been in synagogue during the first day of the Yom Kippur War and thought of her cousins fighting on the Golan and in the Sinai. The prayers in her own prayer book seemed incomprehensible. *Avinu, malchenu.* Our Father, our King. What paternal monarch treated his children or his subjects in such a way? "We are as clay in the hands of the potter," the cantor sang, and Ina thought angrily, irreverently—clay that will be shattered into shards. But still, they belonged to the synagogue, went to service. They were Jews, and that they would cling to despite (or perhaps because of) the black smoke that had darkened her childhood.

"That's nice." Miriam and Ben Gottlieb were clearly not missionaries.

The two couples talked on. Ray told a joke, and they all laughed easily. Ina showed them Jeddy's drawing. Miriam played her silver music box for them. An intricate Bach fugue. The hospital loudspeaker called, in cultivated tones, that Dr. Elisofon was urgently wanted in Emergency; Dr. Giovetti was needed at the fourth floor nurses' station; would Dr. Richards pick up any hospital phone please, Dr. Richards, any phone at all! A note of irritation, or perhaps desperation, crept into that controlled, amplified voice. Dr. Richards, Dr. Richards.

In the corridor outside their door, nurses hurried by, moving silently on their crepe-soled shoes. They wore brightly colored cardigans over their white uniforms, perhaps to ward them from the chill of the ammoniated pine odors that rose from the worn floors and mingled with the medicinal odors that clung to the concrete block walls.

The doctors moved more slowly, their stethoscopes swinging like elegant, oversized necklaces which they wore with self-conscious carelessness, steel implements poking out of the wide pockets of their hospital coats. One young intern walked by in a green jacket, its lapel lightly smeared with blood. Had he had no time to change, or was this a badge of honor, a display of confidence, experience? Two aides pushed a stainless steel dolly loaded with juices and medications. The tiny capsules gleamed like precious jewels in their translucent plastic cups. And in room 502 the two couples continued their improvised party, sharing hospital delicacies, grateful for the small carrel of intimacy, of near-normalcy, they had created in this building where sickness and death hovered in brilliantly lit rooms and the sound of a woman's sighs soughed through winding corridors.

And it was simple, too, when the party was over and the cups emptied and discarded, for each couple to withdraw into separate privacy. Ina and Ray returned to their side of the room, pulling their chair after them. Ben Gottlieb drew the screen around Miriam's bed. There were things each husband and wife had to say to each other, and neither begrudged the other the awkward privacy granted by canvas and whisper. Glancing across the room, Ray suggested that they go out to the lounge, and Ina was surprised at the excitement with which she accepted his suggestion, as though she had forgotten that it was possible now for her simply to walk out of this room; she was neither invalid nor prisoner.

To prepare for this outing to the world beyond her room, she checked herself in the mirror, applied fresh makeup, and ran a brush through her hair. Ray brought her her slippers and eased her feet into them. Had they been at home now, he would have bent to kiss her ankle, she knew, and out of that knowledge she smiled at him. He smiled back, patient with the recognition that small acts of caring excited him, infused him with a sweet flow of sexual tenderness. He took her hand and they walked down the corridor, Ina leaning on him slightly as though simply by entering the hospital she had abandoned her own strength and now needed his support.

The lounge, situated opposite the elevator, had been furnished with a determined effort at casualness and gaiety. Bright red curtains hung at the windows, matching the Formica tops of the low tables placed in front of each Naugahyde couch and chair. The Lucite-framed graphics on the walls featured red circles tumbling through blue triangles, red, white, and blue dancing squares, and a confusion of ovoids in muted blues. It reminded Ina of the decor of the progressive nursery school that Rachel had briefly attended. It too had been determinedly gay and decorated in red, white, and blue, with the pretty young teachers wearing jumpsuits to match. But its furnishings, unlike the hospital's, had not been scarred by cigarette burns and the telltale rings of coffee cups, although the small curious scratch marks on the arms of the Naugahyde chairs were not unlike the nail scars left by small children in their fierce and desperate play.

The magazines scattered on the tables were many months old, and their once slick covers were frayed and flapped loosely from weakened staples. A coffee machine stood in the corner, and although a sign proclaimed it out of order, a tall, heavyset man in a dark windbreaker pummeled it with rhythmic, controlled anger. He would not believe anything that was told to him in this hospital; his actions proclaimed his stance. His wife, a small blonde woman whose pale eyes blinked apologetically, clutched at her tightly belted purple robe and asked him in tones of practiced stoic embarrassment to *please* leave the machine alone. He persisted, snowy spittle forming at his lips. The machine, in surrender, disgorged a cardboard container of coffee, and he smiled in satisfaction.

"See?" he said to his wife.

She smiled wanly, accustomed to being mistaken, to having him proved right even when he was wrong. They left the lounge, he carelessly dripping the beverage, leaving a trail of coffee-colored tears across the white-tiled floor.

The only other couple in the room were a young mustachioed black man and the beautiful model Ina had sat with outside the admitting office. The man wore a well-cut straw-colored suit and a brown shirt that exactly matched his skin. He sat close to his wife on a couch, talking in an urgent whisper, pausing to light a cigarette and perhaps to give her a chance to reply. But she, wearing now a blue velour robe, her luxuriant hair tied back, like a small girl's, with matching ribbon, did not answer but stared at the graphic of blue ovoids which were the same shade as her robe. Ina smiled at her and received in reply a shy nod, a finger languidly lifted in acknowledgment, recognition.

Ray led Ina to a corner couch and pulled a chair over so that he faced her with his back to the other couple, who sat silently now, their fingers interwoven, substituting touch for word.

"We must talk about this, Ina," he said.

"About the abortion?" She used the word bravely where he did not, but her tone was dull, disinterested, as though he were discussing again a subject that had been exhaustively argued.

"Yes. About the abortion." He matched her dryness of voice but did not meet her eyes, and she, in turn, studied his hands. His palms were extraordinarily large, yet his fingers were slender and he took immaculate care of his nails. She liked that, and reaching for his hand, she pressed it to her cheek, breathing in the scent of the lemon soap they used at home. She wished she had thought to bring a bar with her.

In that, she supposed, she was like her mother. She too sought after sweet smells, light drifting fragrance. She gagged at the hint of any putrescence. Once, in the barracks, a woman had died in the night. It had been summer. (Sometimes, thinking of those lost years, she forgot that the seasons had turned inexorably in their cycle, that even within the confines of barbed wire, soft spring winds had blown and hot summer sun had blazed—it was easier to think of that time as a block of endless winter.) The body had begun to stink. She had gagged.

"Don't." Her mother's voice was harsh, protective. "We are alive. Think of how lucky we are."

It was her mother's harsh reprimand that she wanted to offer her husband now.

"We are lucky. Just think of how lucky. We have our children, our lives. We don't want to jeopardize that luck."

Instead she said, her voice brittle, almost detached, "You said that it was my decision. I'm forty-one. There are risks at my age. Birth defects. Mongolism." She was encouraged and impressed by the seriousness and certainty in her own voice. She might have been selling a computer campaign to a client. Almost, she began to believe herself. It would be madness to have another child. Wooed by her own arguments, she grew astonished that he did not see that.

"I spoke to Isaacs about it," Ray said. "There isn't even a risk these days. First of all, the main danger would be if this was your first child. Secondly, they have a test now—amniocentesis. They can tell very early in the pregnancy whether or not it's a healthy baby. If it wasn't healthy, of course there would be no question. You'd have the abortion."

"And when did you talk to Isaacs?"

A slow anger stirred within her. He had no right to call her obstetrician. The two of them, tweed-suited professionals, had no right to discuss her, each sitting in a leather chair behind

paper-laden desks, while she sat in her hospital bed awaiting
their ministrations. The mysteries of her body were revealed
on the record cards that Daniel Isaacs, M.D., kept in the manila
folder marked with her name. Although he could not always
recall who she was, he knew the strength of her uterus, the size
of her cervical opening, and the bell jar shape of her breasts,
one of which he would slice into tomorrow with gleaming
scalpel. She resented him for his knowledge, so essential to her
life, for the power he held that rendered her powerless. It was
dangerous to be so vulnerable. That was the lesson of her
childhood, of the lost years when she had been a creature to
be hidden and protected, when she and her mother had lived
on the mercy of strangers, of briefly sympathetic neighbors,
of a benign Kapo who ignored the presence of small children
in her barracks, and the fierce alliance of women who had lost
their own children and worked to save the small survivors who
lived covertly in their midst—herself, her cousin Bette, and
other small girls who had somehow managed to live. But she
did not want, ever again, to be an object to be discussed and
protected, whose fate was determined by the decision of
others.

"I can't think of why you called Isaacs," she said, lying now.

"I called him this afternoon. I didn't think you would
mind."

"I do mind," she said coldly.

She dropped his hand, felt in the pocket of her robe for a
handkerchief, and found instead Rachel's letter. "Dear Mother
. . ." When had she stopped being "Mommy"?

"Look, Ina, things are much easier now than they were
when Rachel and Jeddy were born," he said. "We have Carmen. We could get whatever help you wanted in the house.
Dot's au pair girl has a sister, I know."

"Have you hired her yet?"

He winced at the bitterness of her tone. Was she being
unfair? she wondered, and the answer ricocheted against her
with sudden anger. Yes, she was being unfair. She had learned
grim lessons in that great bare room where she had spent her

childhood. All weapons were acceptable when you were fighting for your life.

"Ina, stop that. It's your decision. I haven't done anything."

"No," she said, "you haven't. But you've been working out
details. Have you thought of what happens to my business—to
the agency?" She threw the question out in a final salvo, but
he seized upon it with the barest note of triumph.

"That's what really concerns you, isn't it? That's the most
important thing." Accusation rimmed the question. The truth
was out, and it worked against her—gave lie to all her arguments.

"Yes. No. Maybe. And why not?" She was defensive now
and angry. "Yes, the agency is important to me. Why shouldn't
it be? I built it. It's mine." She did not add that there had been
a time when nothing had been hers, not even the faded rags
that covered her skeletal form. In Italy a bronzed nurse had
brought her her first new garment—a pair of underpants of
yellow cotton, precious because tags were still affixed to them.

She thought of her office and how the sun slanted silkily
across the walnut veneer of her desk, so that by mid-afternoon
a bar of gold settled on the lower leaves of the large plant she
had placed evenly between piles of programs, those she had
completed and those still awaiting her attention. She liked
watching the piles grow and diminish, tangible proof of hours
of work, of talent and skill utilized. Two Chagall prints hung
on her wall—one a scene of a star-encrusted night canopying
a tiny Polish village and the other of a bride and groom dancing among sun-licked clouds. She enjoyed looking up from the
folios of black-and-white print and losing herself for minutes
at a time in the artist's moods and colors.

She enjoyed ushering clients into her pleasant work-ruled
room, settling them into the brown leather chair that faced
her own while she apologetically lifted the ringing phone. "Ina
Feldman. May I help you?" Her phone voice was practiced to
a timbre of efficiency and sympathy. She even liked opening
and dealing with her mail—the touch of thick office stationery.
She enjoyed working with Ricky, her assistant, on an accumu-
lation of correspondence.

Her work freed her from people, from their demands and their secrets. The computer did not deceive, did not inveigle. When she wrote a program of directives, a reliable answer was produced, independent of whims and emotions. Too much of her life had been governed by the unpredictable. "We should have known, but how could we have known?" her father asked mournfully. But within her work she had absolute control, maximum predictability.

She became aware of the sound of soft sobbing within the waiting room and listened to it carefully, almost fearful that it came from her own constricted throat. But it was the lovely, tall, black young woman who was weeping with her husband's large white handkerchief pressed to her face. When she hurried from the room, her silk slippers flapping across the floor, he followed her, carrying a large navy portfolio of the sort that very thin and beautiful girls clutch to their sides as they hurry down Madison Avenue, their faces bent so that their skin will be shielded from rain and wind. "Marnie," he called, but she did not turn.

"It is eight-forty-five. Visiting hours are over at nine o'clock. It is eight-forty-five." The amplified voice on the public-address system enunciated each syllable carefully, and Ray automatically checked his watch.

"I don't expect you to give your work up," he said quietly. "With adequate help at home you could manage. You know you've always said it was the quality of time with the children, not the quantity."

That too was a quote from her consciousness-raising group, and, irrationally, she resented his using it.

"And certainly you could work during pregnancy. You're in a position now where you could create your own hours. And a lot of the work you can do at home."

"Perhaps I shouldn't go to the office at all. That apparently would suit you most," she said bitterly.

"That's not fair. You know I've always been proud of your work."

"None of this is fair," she shot back. That, at least, could not be denied. She had entered the hospital thinking he was as indecisive as she herself was. She had not come prepared to counter his carefully prepared and delivered arguments. He had given her no warning, no time. Still, she had ammunition of her own.

"What about the children? Have you thought about the effect of a new baby on Jeddy and Rachel?"

"I know for a fact that they'd be delighted," he replied.

"Goddamn it! You haven't talked to them about it, have you?" She strode across the room to the coffee machine and stared at herself in the metal mirror. Small furious dots of red shone at her cheeks, and her eyes glittered dangerously. Stray hairs had broken through her chignon, and she tucked them angrily into place. Then she pulled each knob on the machine and walked back to her chair.

"No, of course not. But Rachel mentioned at dinner that Laurie Corwin's mother is pregnant. She and all the girls in her class think that it's terrific. They're very excited about it. In fact Rachel and Laurie spent their free hour at the library looking at that book of photographs on natal development."

"Marvelous. I'll be their health education project," Ina muttered. "Nancy Corwin and I can share it. Perhaps they'll do papers on comparative pregnancies."

Ray ignored her and continued. "And Jeddy loves babies. Anything helpless and tiny. You remember the squirrel?"

She nodded. It was difficult to forget the tiny rodent shivering in his mangy ash-colored skin, yellow mucus sealing his eyes shut, that Jeddy had found in the park and brought home. The child had nursed the creature painstakingly back to health, hiding him in a large shoe box beneath his bed when Shirley Cherne, his grandmother, came. All animals filled Ina's mother with fear and loathing. They might carry lice. Fleas. Disease. Who knew when they could turn on you? Jeddy and Rachel, her American grandchildren, were lucky that they didn't know from such things. Why did they want to chase after *dreck*, filth? The squirrel had been released finally in the spring and had sprinted away through the tall grasses of the park, never looking back. Its coat had been sleek and its eyes bright. Jeddy, sadly and bravely, had not begrudged it its freedom and turned his attention instead to a crippled gerbil at the pet center in his school.

"All right. The children want a baby, would accept it. But you, Ray, why do you want a baby?" She asked this question softly, seriously, because that, of course, was where the muscle of his persuasion lay. Nothing—none of the carefully phrased and presented arguments—matched the heat of his own desire, of his sudden and mysterious longing for a child—a longing that she saw as a bewildering betrayal, a sudden denial of all she had assumed they understood about each other and the life that they had built together.

He hesitated for a long moment. His hand lifted to touch his hair where a flag of gray draped its darkness in an uncannily even patch. Two nights ago, he had awakened in the night to the sound of his own heart hammering loudly, arrhythmically, its wild uneven beat so loud that he was surprised that Ina did not awaken. Sweat dampened his pajamas. He shivered. Two men in his law school class had recently died of heart attacks. One of them he had known well. Lately, after court appearances, he felt a strange weakness and walked very slowly through narrow downtown streets. He played squash still but had shortened his game. He wanted another baby to fight the fear of age and death. He wanted another baby to renew his grasp of life, his belief in his own ability to nurture and create.

And he wanted another child simply for the excitement and the pleasure of it: he wanted to see again an infant's (no, *his* infant's) lip curled smilingly in sleep; he wanted to grin at a toddler's tenuous first steps and to be surprised at the sudden shadowing of eyes, sweet intonation of voice that reminded him of himself, of Ina, of her parents, of his own. A new child would reverse their steps, slow their lives down, provide a detour from the ineluctible route they were traveling now, and carry them back to the season of hope, of unpredictability.

Dennis Robbins, a colleague at the office, ten years Ray's senior, both his children in college, had become a father again

some months earlier. The gray-haired attorney had passed out
cigars, blushing proudly.

"How does it feel?" Ray had asked.

"Feel? Well, I feel great. Years younger. About to begin
again. It's crazy, hard to explain."

But Ray had understood, and he had placed the cigar in his
desk, keeping it there for weeks, his fingers fondling the blue
strip of celluloid, crumbling the tobacco trapped within.

But mostly he wanted the baby because it had become part
of his life—because it had been conceived in passion and carelessness on a night when the sky blazed with electric energy
and the moan of a wandering wind was drowned by the clatter of distant thunder. Life had happened that night, as he and
Ina had clung together against the storm's fury. It was true
that he would not have knowingly urged Ina into a new
pregnancy, had not even consciously formulated such an idea,
but it had, after all, happened. That surely must count for
something. And the life that had happened was growing,
minute by minute, hour by hour. An "embryonic mass," Ina
called it, but he saw it as a nascent infant, his infant, a gestating child of his blood.

He remembered an article he had read somewhere—in
*Esquire,* he thought—written by a surgeon. In it, the doctor
had described his observations of an abortion, of the very
moment of plunging a death needle into the womb. The "embryonic mass" sensed the danger, the doctor reported, and
struggled to flee the needle; it contorted itself wildly, hideously,
in its futile struggle to escape the gleaming steel instrument
of death. Were there womb sounds that early, he wondered—
did the embryo shriek or merely vibrate in terror?

In a dream only a few nights ago, he had seen Rachel and
Jeddy running across a deserted wheat field, a silver meteor
pursuing them across a storm-darkened sky. He had told Ina
about that dream, and she had tried to analyze it, using her
analyst, Eleanor Berenson's, technique. What had happened to
him that day, that evening? Rachel had been late coming home
from a flute lesson, and he had been upset, frightened. To pass

the time he and Jeddy had looked together through a new folio
edition of Wyeth paintings. She dismissed the dream at once,
wrapping it up in a neat interpretive package. The golden field
and the threatening sky came from Wyeth's brush. The silver
meteor was time—Rachel's delay, his own fear. Ina had been
satisfied with her interpretation, but he knew her now to be
wrong. The children, his living children, were symbolic of his
unborn (perhaps never-to-be-born) child, and they fled, in
desperation, the abortionist's tool, the persistent silver meteor
that would pursue and seek them out. It was clear to him. He,
Raymond Feldman, whose name had appeared on countless
petitions advocating the right of abortion, did not want his
own child aborted. The former co-chairman of "Attorneys for
Free Choice," a short-lived, little-met pro-abortion group,
shivered at the thought of that annihilating needle, of his wife
lying quiescent on an operating table while life, that small life
of his own creating, was destroyed within her womb.

"I want the baby," he said to her at last, "because it is ours,
part of us. Because we have no real practical reason not to
have it. Because I think it can make our lives—all our lives—
yours, mine, the children's—richer. I can't give you reasons by
chapter and verse, Ina. It's a feeling, a gut reaction. It started
slowly, and it grew. But I want you to know that . . ."

"The decision is mine," she said quickly, impatiently, before
he could mouth the words.

He felt exhausted suddenly. He had done what he could.
The options were hers now.

He plucked a damp Kleenex up from the floor and tossed it
into the gaping red ashtray, overflowing with vermilion-
smeared cigarette butts. The tall black man stood at the elevator holding the oversized portfolio and whistling softly.
Two nurses paused in the doorway and bent their white-
capped heads together over a stack of charts. Somewhere a
telephone rang.

A heavyset man in a rumpled seersucker suit, gray shadows
of grief circling his eyes, came into the lounge carrying a
pillow. He put it on the royal-blue couch and twisted himself

across the unyielding cushions, pressing his head against it. He would not sleep, they knew, although he would pretend to try. He kept vigil against death, waited for the sound of a nurse's voice, the tread of an intern's step, a glint of hope, a murmur of optimism.

Once, Ray and Ina had spent such a night in a hospital waiting room, curled against each other, their hearts tight, their mouths dry, their eyes burning. Jeddy had been seized by a sudden fever that had rocketed frighteningly upward; their child had been a trembling toddler racked by delirium with terrible sobs and fierce laughter—his small limbs burned to their touch, a mottled fever rash distorted his tender pink flesh, and sweat soaked his thick dark hair. They had rushed him to the hospital—not Mount Lebanon but St. Luke's, because they did not want to waste time crossing the park. The fever had dropped as mysteriously as it had begun, and they took Jeddy home a few days later. He himself remembered neither the fever nor the wild outbursts it had produced, but for months afterward Ina and Ray awakened in fear and hurried to the children's bedrooms to place their hands on cool sleeping brows and to listen anxiously for rhythmic, sleep-ruled breathing. They had glimpsed the terror of losing a child, and the shadow of that terror clung to them.

"Ray." Her voice was very soft, almost frightened, and he took her hand. The gauzy apricot stuff of her peignoir fluttered against her wrist, and he thought of how translucent her skin was just there, of how he knew each pale blue vein and could find them with his lips in the dark. Rachel too had such skin. It seemed to him a sad and delicate legacy.

"What?" he asked. The last visitors were grouping at the elevators. An aide came to the doorway and pointed at her watch. He nodded. He was anxious to leave, to hurry home to his sleeping children. The mingled hospital odors of medicine, pine, and ammonia had made him slightly nauseous, and he thought that he would walk home across the park where the newly blooming trees exuded spring's first delicate fragrance.

"Whatever I decide, you won't be angry?"

"Not angry." He put her hand on his cheek.

"Disappointed?"

"Maybe."

"I see."

"You asked."

"Yes. Kiss the children for me. You'll be here early?"

"Of course. It will be fine."

"All right then."

He bent and kissed her cheek, but she clutched his hand.

"I didn't tell you. I loved the new nightgown. Thank you."

"Wear it tomorrow then," he said. He held her for another moment and hurried into the elevator that gaped open before him.

She remained in the waiting room for a few moments after he left and thought of him walking out of the building, crossing the avenue to the tree-thick park, his long body silhouetted in the golden glow of the street lamp. The man on the couch snored lightly, and she tiptoed about the room dimming the lights, leaving only a golden circle of light to fall from a table lamp in the corner.

She walked slowly down the corridor to her room, passing open doorways where women either slept or prepared for sleep. In one room a tall woman wearing a hospital gown washed at the sink. Her long gray hair fell in a single braid down her back. Tell me, Ina silently asked the woman, whose silvered hair bespoke her age and perhaps her wisdom, what shall I do? The woman closed her door, and Ina walked on. In her own room, she saw with relief that Miriam Gottlieb was again asleep. There was a small black panda on her bedside table, a bright blue ribbon tied crisply, hopefully, about its soft chubby neck. Ina paused for a moment, then left the room again, walking swiftly to the elevator.

There was no one at the nurses' station, and the elevator, when it arrived, was empty. She remembered that the neonatology unit was on six and pressed the button for that floor.

There, she turned right and walked instinctively to a large windowed wall. Beyond its shield, blue-gowned nurses, their hair encased in large caps, masks concealing their mouths and noses, moved with ghostly competence. The infants lay in small steel-barred cribs. Over some respirator tents had been placed, creating a small encampment of pale green shelters in that desert of sterile white. One tiny infant slept beneath a plastic bubble, flailing its small wrinkled pink palms in the air as though to protest its weakness, its captivity. A nurse holding a baby bent to check a reading on a mysterious machine whose stainless steel tendrils curled about each other and were attached to an incubator.

"May I help you?" A nurse stood at Ina's elbow, carrying a tray of Styrofoam coffee cups.

"Yes. I want to see the Gottlieb baby."

"That one. In the bubble."

Ina strained, standing on her toes. The baby's hands were motionless now, and its tiny legs curled beneath the diaper that hung loosely on the minuscule body. It had a lot of hair; fine dark tendrils covered the delicate pink scalp. Rachel had had little hair at birth, but Jeddy's hair had been like that of the Gottlieb baby. Ina had bought a special brush to use on it— sterling silver backing with the softest of bristles. Ina wondered what she had done with that brush. Surely she had saved it.

"I think, miss, that you had better get back to your room."

The nurse was an older woman. Her voice was gentle. It was irregular that Ina, a patient from another floor, should stand before the window beyond which infants struggled for life, staring at another woman's baby. But she would not question her: a reminder that it was time to leave was enough. Ina smiled at her gratefully and took the elevator back to five.

In her own hospital bed at last, she thought of the Gottlieb baby, of those minute shriveled pink palms that beat against the misty man-made air within the respirator, of how the tiny fingers had clutched at nothingness and relaxed into quiet sleep. Across the room, Miriam, the child's mother, slept, her fingers tight about a corner of the pillow slip. Surely, the baby would live, Ina thought. She worried again about that silver-backed hairbrush and then willed herself to sleep. Isaacs had said he would remove the fibroma from her breast at 8:00 A.M., and he was never late.

Her fingers found the small nodule and pressed it as the doctor had done. What did that gentle pressure tell him, she wondered? Did its texture contain secrets of life and death? She thrust the thought from her mind, drew her hand down to her side in rigid reprimand. There was nothing to worry about. She would be fine. She would be fine.

# SECOND DAY

RAY WAKENED AS dawn broke. Streaks of pale rose light slowly etched their way through silver clouds. It had rained in the night, and slivers of moisture were cupped in the hearts of the young, tender leaves. Sitting up in bed, he saw the newly blossoming dogwood across the street. Its pink and white blossoms shimmered wetly and pulled the fragile branches earthward. Several branches had already snapped beneath the weight of the flowers, and the severed arms of the newly blooming bush lay on the pavement; the wet flowers, the color of an infant's unmarred flesh, formed small mounds of fragrant softness on the damp concrete. Ina loved dogwood. Often, passing that same bush, she scooped up the fallen blossoms and put them in the smoked glass vase on the dining room table. Perhaps, if the flowers were still there when he left for the hospital, he would gather them up and take them to her.

The thought pleased him, and he reached over to Ina's side of the bed, felt the smooth contour of her sheet, touched her pillow, still plump and firm. He pressed his face against it, smelling the pine forest scent of her shampoo, the barely perceptible lilac tinge of her dusting powder. She used no perfume—perhaps because her mother, Shirley Cherne, used so much—yet always, when she was away and he slept alone in their bed, the intimate odors of her body suffused him with pleasure and longing. Often he slept on her side, sometimes absently touching her things, moving his fingers across the personal clutter of her bedside table—the silver comb and brush, school pictures of Rachel and Jeddy in Lucite frames, the enormous purple-veined conch they had carried back from their St. Thomas honeymoon, and a programming manual she had compiled and edited. Once, angered at her because of an absence he resented, he had looked at her things and thought that the small table was a shrine and that the objects upon it were talismans of her success and achievements—the children, her work, their marriage. The thought was unfair, born of a momentary hurt (she had chosen to go to an out-of-town conference during a week when members of his law school class were honoring a retiring professor), and he, a fair and just man, had thrust it aside. But he had not forgotten it. He slid over now to her side, stretched out on the cool sheet, fragrant with the breath of her skin, glanced at his watch, and saw that it was not yet six. He touched the conch and fell back into the luxury of sleep stolen against the coming of the light.

The ringing of the phone jarred him awake, pulling him out of a long dark canyon of forgotten dreams, although he saw at once that only a quarter of an hour had passed since his first wakening. Groggily, he reached for the receiver and hoped that the children had not wakened. They had at least another hour to lie wrapped in dark rest, and it was oddly important to him and always had been that his children should sleep undisturbed. During their naps, when they were smaller, he had walked the apartment in stockinged feet, gently opened and closed drawers and cabinets, and often stood bemused in the doorways of their rooms and watched their faces, so soft and peaceful beneath the veil of sleep.

"Hello." His tongue felt coated and his morning voice rasped, unready, bewildered.

"Ray. I woke you."

Shirley Cherne, at three minutes past six, vibrated with energy, he knew. Her voice bounced, punched its way into the telephone against his ears.

"It is early," he said mildly, although he knew Shirley would not care if he acknowledged angrily that she had awakened him and Carmen and the children too. If she were up, they should all be up. She slept very little, and the few times he and Ina had stayed overnight at the Chernes', he had heard his mother-in-law's steps through the night, found her fully dressed and made up in the morning, no matter how early he himself awakened. Sleep she did not need, she announced often, and what she did not need, others too could do without.

Wakefulness had been her savior during the years of darkness, and she did not trust those nepenthean hours over which she had no control. Nighttime was death time, and it was while she dozed through a winter night that her son Yedidiah had slipped from sleep into death. Ina had told Ray once that through the years of terror, the long nights in forests and camps, she could not remember her mother sleeping. Awake in the noxious darkness, Shaindel Czernowitz had prowled the barracks. In the darkness of a night lit only by the roving golden beam of the camp searchlight, she had listened to the worries of a German woman guard. The guard's mother had died of cancer, and she lived in fear now because a lump grew within the thick mammary glands of her right breast. The woman, large-boned and soft-fleshed, wept. She could not bear pain. A gun and a leather switch hung from the belt around her waist. She had had only one child because she could not bear pain. In the fetid darkness, an inmate whose small daughter had died that day sobbed quietly.

Shaindel Czernowitz comforted the guard. She was a nurse-midwife, she said, with medical training. It was not true, but the guard allowed her to probe the tender breast flesh, to knead the lump between fingers calloused by quarry work. Was it that little pimple the woman was frightened of? Shaindel laughed, and the guard, a heavy woman with very thick lips, smiled too, in relief. Of course, Shaindel assured her, she would check it periodically just to be safe. Soon, very soon, it would disappear. For weeks afterward, the guard came to Shaindel in the darkness and exposed her breast, waited for the probing touch of Shaindel's fingers against the milk-white, blue-veined skin. And the lump did grow smaller and disappear. The guard brought Shaindel extra bread, the heel of a salami, a sweater for Ina. The stocky uniformed woman felt that a bond had been forged between them. They were two women, both far from home, who sat together in the quiet night and worried over death. Shaindel felt no bond—only the pleasure of bitter triumph, the sweated relief of the exhausted climber who has managed to grab hold of a rung on the ladder of survival. Like the guard, she too had stood watch in the night, and her vigil had been rewarded.

Now, too, as Shirley Cherne, she was companion to the darkness, watched television deep into the night, and jerked from fitful slumber when the first light of dawn sliced through the sky. Ray had been relieved to learn that in the back room of Cherne Knitwear there was a couch, and that often, in the slowing hours of the afternoon, his mother-in-law slept on it. It was, after all, safe to sleep in daylight.

"So it's early," she said without apology into the phone. "Soon you would be getting up anyhow. I wanted to catch you before you got busy with the children. How is Ina?"

"She's fine. It's nothing major, you know. Just a small fibroma. Isaacs will operate this morning, and I'm sure it will be fine. I thought she discussed all that with you yesterday."

"She talked. I listened. And what I know is this—for a fibroma you don't stay in the hospital four days," Shirley Cherne said curtly.

"Well, it's always good to get the extra rest. You know, with Ina's schedule at work and the children . . ." His voice trailed off.

"In a hospital you don't rest," she said. "Why is she staying so long? My cutter here, Rosie—she had the same thing. Tuesday morning it was out, Wednesday she rested, Thursday back at the cutting table. So why with Ina four days?"

"Just some tests," he said weakly.

"Tests." She echoed him harshly. Her voice rang with disbelief, mockery. "Listen, Raymond. I want you to meet me for lunch. You have time?"

He was startled. Through all the years of his marriage he had never had a meal alone with his mother-in-law. She never had the time, and he had never had the inclination. She was his wife's mother, his children's grandmother. He was fond of her, amused by her, and sometimes, looking at her, he felt a sudden, inexplicable shaft of pity for her. She was a woman who wore many rings of flashing jewels on fingers twisted by arthritis—blood-red garnets, harsh green emeralds, frozen sapphires trapped in gold, crouched awkwardly on her gnarled knuckles. A nerve pulsed wildly in her neck, and her flaking skin was covered with flesh-toned liquid makeup and powder, with high-gloss rouge and creamy eye shadows, the colors of life artfully brushed across a mask of death.

"I have time," he said. He was relieved. He would see Ina at the hospital and consult with her on what Shirley should be told. Meanwhile, he arranged to meet her at noon at a luncheonette on Eighty-sixth and Madison. Shirley Cherne hung up without saying good-bye. He realized then that she had not said hello. She was a woman who treated the darkness as daylight and had no time to spare for amenities. Minutes could not be wasted on greetings and farewells. Hello. Good-bye. Did you have a nice day at school?

"Daddy?" Jeddy stood in the doorway. His chubby features were thick with sleep, and he rubbed his eyes with rounded pink fists.

"Come on in, Jed."

Ray moved over and Jeddy crawled in beside him, resting his head on Ray's shoulder, his body relaxed against his father's warmth. The child fell asleep again, but for Ray the night was over and he lay rigid, watching the morning light grow brighter until the alarm in Carmen's room jangled and was followed by the delicate chime of Rachel's clock. The horn of a car barked upward from the street below. He heard the elevator door yawn open and snap shut, the clatter of milk bottles, a neighbor's bell.

"Come on, Jed," he said softly. "It's morning."

He rushed the children through their dressing and breakfast, a routine that Carmen usually managed. It seemed to him that with Ina away they needed his presence and involvement, the active care of a parent. He realized at once that he had been wrong. They responded to his presence with questions to which they knew the answers, minor frenzied searches for a missing notebook, an assignment pad, Rachel's headband, Jeddy's sneakers.

"Does this match?" Rachel asked.

She stood before him in her plaid cotton skirt and white blouse, against which the small buds of her nascent breasts pressed softly. She was worried about whether her green knee socks matched the stripe of the plaid, and he looked down and saw that her legs had grown shapely and she moved them with self-conscious grace—the lessons of the ballet class and the generations of womanhood well learned. It was a family trait, those beautiful curved legs, and the women knew it and were proud. Shirley Cherne's legs were still slender, and when she sat, she crossed them carefully and lifted her skirts slightly. Ina searched out the clothes of a particular designer because the subtle slits in his skirts revealed her calves.

"The socks match," he said, smiling, and she kissed him on the cheek, an acknowledgment, he thought, of his admiration and perhaps his wistfulness.

"Are you going to the hospital this morning?" Jeddy asked. A scab of egg yolk clung to his lip, and Ray wiped it off and wondered how much longer Jeddy would allow him to dab at the corners of his mouth, to tuck his shirt into his pants. Already he pulled away irritably, embarrassed.

"Of course I'm going to the hospital. As soon as you leave," he said, and added, although they had not asked, "Your mother will be fine. Just fine."

"I know. I need money for a tutu." Rachel looked at herself

in the hall mirror, bit her lips, ran her hand across her blouse.
    "All right."
    He reached for his wallet, but he was annoyed. They should
be more concerned about their mother. She was, after all, in
the hospital, separated from them by the sprawling park which
they seldom crossed alone. He did not want them to be upset,
distraught, but he did want concern, involvement. (If they
were not concerned for Ina, what care would they have for
him?) He remembered suddenly a story a colleague had told
him, of young children whose father had died of Hodgkin's
disease. An uncle had found a shaded glen, a quiet moment,
and armed with the advice of their teachers and a psychologist,
had broken the news to the children, who were just about
Rachel and Jeddy's age. There had been silence, and then the
girl had asked only one question. "Who will drive us to the Y
for gym and swim?" Not unnatural, the psychologist had
assured the appalled uncle. Concrete realities masking dangerous, amorphous grief and loss. Defense mechanism.
    Ray too had not been surprised by the story. He could not
forget the afternoon of his own parents' deaths—Dot, his
mother-sister telling him, Larry's arm about his shoulder, and
his own question, "Will I still go to camp?" He had been
scheduled to take his lifesaving test that summer, and throughout the funeral he had kept his mind focused on the clear blue
waters of the camp lake, on the willow tree whose branches
dipped and swayed above its shimmering surface. He had
kissed his first girl there the summer before. This summer he
would get laid. The rabbi had intoned the Kaddish, and Ray
felt his penis swell into firmness even as he dutifully repeated
the prayer. What had that erection been but sublimation,
sorrow substitution?
    He watched Rachel hunt for a comb and tease the small dark
hairs of her bangs into a fluffy cloud. Jeddy stuffed two comic
books into his briefcase.
    "For recess," he muttered.
    Ray marveled at the wondrous egotism and narcissism of
children. They had no world but their own. Small megalo-

maniacs, they moved through their golden days and dream-
dark nights, seeing only the single track of their own paths,
gazing into mirrors that recorded only their own reflections.
Silently he gave Rachel the money for the tutu, zipped Jeddy's
briefcase. At the elevator they turned back and saw him standing still in the apartment doorway.

"Hey, Dad, tell Mom we hope she feels better," Rachel
called out.

He nodded and waved, but they did not see him. The
elevator had arrived and they disappeared within it, their
laughter trailing through the long and empty hallway.

In the kitchen Carmen sang softly in Spanish, her voice
drifting above the rumble of the dishwasher, the low groan
of the electric broom. She was a tall woman with lustrous
black hair. Her mother lived in the South Bronx, and her two
small children were at a convent school in Mayaguez. She
spanned the generations, speaking rapid Spanish into the telephone, enclosing money orders in laboriously written letters.
She laughed with Rachel and Jeddy but answered Ina in
monosyllables and barely spoke to Ray at all. But the apartment was spotless and his shirts ironed to perfection. At dinner
parties, during the inevitable discussions of household help, Ina
would assert that she did not know how they would manage
without Carmen. It occurred to him as he left the house,
calling out a good-bye to Carmen, that she had not asked him a
single question about Ina. She did not answer him but continued singing her sad song of birds deserting a distant shore,
abandoned by lovers and children. Carmen, he knew, could
and would manage well enough without them.

He took a cab across the park, and although he reached the
hospital at eight, the nurse told him that Ina was already
prepped and in the operating room. Dr. Isaacs had been early.
There was no point in seeing her before the surgery. She had
been heavily sedated. The doctor would be out shortly. The
entire procedure should not take more than fifteen or twenty
minutes. The nurse spoke with the absolute certainty of the
very young, and he did not argue with her.

He sat down to wait and remembered then that in his rush to grab a cab he had not bothered to gather up the dogwood blossoms that littered the pavement with petaled clouds of blushing whiteness.

Ina lay stretched out on the operating table and listened to the voice of the anesthesiologist. He had a pleasant voice and an accent she could not at once identify. French perhaps. No. Italian. Yes. Definitely Italian. She had been to Italy twice. The displaced persons' camp to which she and her mother had been sent and where her father had found them some weeks after the war had been just outside Naples. The nurses there had fed her semolina, cooking the fine-grained pasta to a tender softness. They had spooned it slowly into her mouth, murmuring their unknown language as they fed her. Their words wept with sorrow, pity, and they stroked her thin hair as they worked. It was necessary to feed the survivors carefully. Their stomachs had shrunk, their gastric juices had dried, their teeth were too soft to masticate the food. Many who had survived starvation and death marches had died of the Hershey bars and salamis given to them by the American soldiers who had come from a land and life of such plenty that they could not bear to look upon hunger.

Her second trip to Italy had been different, of course. Three years ago she and Ray had taken a holiday there. They had stayed at the Eden Hotel in Rome and spent two or three hours each night over a late dinner. They had eaten every variety of pasta, but never semolina. They had traveled to Florence and Siena, Venice and Genoa, but not to Naples. Ina's cousin Bette had spent an academic year in Italy, but she too had avoided Naples, although a shopping center stood now on the site where their camp had been, and although all their memories of that camp were of smiling, gentle nurses who spooned snowy tender grain into their war-weary, unsmiling mouths.

"Italy is very beautiful," she said now, dreamily, to the

doctor who stood behind her. The sedative thickened her voice, cushioned her thoughts. Her body felt light, free—yet her limbs were heavy, weighted. How odd, she thought and felt laughter gather and drift away. She was relaxed, at ease.

"Have you been to Turin?" he asked softly. "That is my city."

"No. Never to Turin." He had lovely hands. They fluttered above her, the slender, tanned fingers balancing a silver needle that caught the harsh light of the fluorescent beam that focused on the table. Sometimes, in her dream, the steel bayonets of the soldiers glinted across the pale skin of their fingers. She frowned. She did not want to think of that dream now. She shrugged it away and listened to the gentle-voiced doctor who came from Turin.

"What I am going to do," he said slowly, "is to inject this needle into the area where the surgeon will work. You will feel a little cold and then numb, but there will be no pain. If you have any discomfort at all, just tell me. Are you ready?"

He did not wait for her answer but eased down the white hospital gown and bent over her. He had very dark hair, and she saw that his eyes were amber-colored and fringed with black lashes.

"What's in the needle?" she asked, although it did not really matter. She would let him do anything. He was very beautiful and wore a white coat with a badge on it. A uniform. The garb of authority. She melted into submission at the sight of a uniform. Policemen and even mailmen caused her to shiver, walk faster. The elevator operator in her office building filled her with a strange temerity. Once she had held the elevator for someone, and the starter had looked at her coldly and said, "Don't do that." She was a tenant and he was an elevator man, but her hands had shaken and she had said, "No. I won't again. I'm sorry." It was ridiculous, she had realized with anger, moments later. Why had she accepted, submitted to, his non-existent authority? But she knew the answer. It was because once she had been a slave, and slaves are conditioned to obedi-

ence. It was that conditioning she had to fight, and she spent
her life locked in battle. It was an act of will for her to seize
control of her own life, to make every minute, every action,
count. How wonderful it was now, at this moment, to soar
easily aloft on the soft wings of the sedative and surrender that
control to the soft-voiced man with graceful fingers and
amber eyes.

"Novocain," he said, and she laughed. How funny to use
the same drug for the filling of a cavity and for the excising of
a troublesome lump of the flesh.

"Where is the joke?" he asked. He did not and never would
understand American women.

She did not answer. The needle had pierced her skin, and a
pleasant numbness spread over the exposed breast. The Italian
doctor touched her, but she did not feel his hand. Dr. Isaacs
had moved into place, his face set in the professional smile of
interest, the plastic lines of simulated concern. When he had
delivered Rachel, his hair had been a pale brown. Now it was
dusted with gray. New creases were etched into his face. He
had much on his mind. Women traveled from many cities to
consult him. He was a fertility expert. When Ina first went to
see him, in the early years of her marriage, his waiting room
had been full of pregnant women who wore maternity clothes
the colors of wild flowers and knit fiercely, passionately, as
though fearful that their babies would be born before the
sleeve of a sweater was rounded. They read *The Magic Years*
and flipped anxiously through *Parents Magazine*. Now that
same waiting room accommodated flat-stomached young
women who read de Beauvoir, Friedan, Lois Gould, Anne
Roiphe. They came to have life scraped away, not nurtured or
coaxed into gestation. On the day Isaacs first found the lump,
Ina had listened to two Barnard girls in madras blouses and
denim skirts hold a long discussion about *The Women's Room*.

"She's right, absolutely right," one asserted, and the other
murmured softly, "Yes. But too polarized, don't you think?
Too polarized."

They had not glanced up respectfully, as the pregnant women always had, when Dr. Isaacs looked into the waiting room. This, at least, had pleased Ina. Probably, she thought, as she watched the lacy pattern of light the fluorescent fixture tossed across the ceiling, he had never even heard of *The Women's Room*. The thought made her laugh again.

"Feeling good, Edith?" he asked, leering over her.

"Ina. My name is Ina." The scalpel glinted in his hands, and she closed her eyes. What she did not feel, she did not have to see.

"Ina then. There. It's out."

She heard a soft splatter and his voice, cool, authoritative: "A frozen section on that." The technician's dutiful: "Right away, Doctor."

What did it look like? she wondered sleepily, and moved her hand tentatively, as though to touch that serrated section of her breast. But her hand felt so heavy; her fingers were burdensome encumbrances that she could lift only with difficulty. She was tired. So very tired. Fingers flashed by her eyes. Isaacs's fingers, wrapped in slimy yellow plastic. A large needle threaded with jet-black suture danced within them.

"Just a couple of stitches," he said cheerfully.

Her eyes followed a blood-soaked gauze pad that fluttered to the floor. Her blood, the color of Passover wine.

"It's a new suture," the doctor confided companionably to her. "Self-dissolving. No stitches to take out." His voice was very pleased. She thought of the production manager at a publishing house who had shown her a new glue-together binding.

"No stitching at all," he had said gladly.

Stitching was a long, expensive process. But the glue, after all, did not hold well, and often pages of the books separated in the readers' hands. She did not want pieces of her breast to flutter loose. She giggled, and Dr. Isaacs's face loomed above her, smiling.

"See there. We're through. And soon we'll have the frozen section reading." He pulled the hospital gown up, and a nurse covered her with a light flannel blanket. She felt cold suddenly.

"Thanks, Andreotti." Isaacs was talking to the anesthesiologist.

"Yes. Thank you," she added, although she was of course not expected or invited to say anything at all. Did the meat on the cutting block thank the butcher? She giggled again.

"When the injections wear off, you may feel some pain," the anesthesiologist said. "Just ask the nurse for something. You will be here overnight?"

"She'll be here for a few days," Dr. Isaacs said. "We've got some other minor business to take care of."

He peeled off his gloves and flashed her a grin of complicity, but she stared blankly back at him. A heavy sadness had replaced her giddiness, and strangely, inexplicably, she began to cry.

"It's not minor." Her voice sounded, to her own ears, like the whine of a small girl, and the flow of tears increased.

The tears were rapid and bitter, and she could not control them. The doctors murmured to each other above her supine body, and then a hand touched her torso and again a needle pierced her flesh.

"You're tired, just tired," Dr. Andreotti said.

How lovely his voice was, how wonderful his accent, reminiscent of that land of golden sunshine and bright smiling faces where snowy grains of nourishment were gently proffered on spoons that glinted in the sunlight of freedom and caring.

She was wheeled out of the room, down the corridor, and she felt herself disembodied, floating above the stretcher table. It paused in its progress down the corridor, and Ray stood beside her, his hand in hers, his eyes strangely clouded. What a good man he was, she thought. Ray. Her husband. Her children's father. Her heart turned in love for him and sorrow for them both.

"I'm fine," she assured him, but her tongue was thick in her mouth and tasted of the salt tears that fell and would not stop.

The nurse was talking softly, explaining. Ina was just tired. Everything had gone well. Just fine. But the doctor would like to see him.

"Come back and see your wife in the afternoon," the nurse suggested. "She'll want to sleep now."

"Oh, yes. Come back. In the afternoon. Please come back," Ina repeated.

Her voice sounded small and high to her own ears. Like Rachel's voice, rising from a dream, shredding the sleep-laden silence of the apartment. Rachel, she thought. Jeddy. Children. My children. She put her hands protectively across her stomach, and as the stretcher bed was wheeled down the corridor, she fell into a deep and dreamless sleep. Ray stood in the hallway feeling bewildered, abandoned. He felt in his pocket for a dime and went to call Dot.

"Fine, she's fine," he assured his sister. "The doctor wants to see me, but she's fine. Just fine."

He hung up and saw that the receiver was damp where he had clutched it. Gently, he wiped it. She had been crying. Ina, who never cried, had been crying. Her cheeks had been pale and streaked with ribbons of moisture, and her eyes had glinted with a febrile brightness.

Swiftly, he walked to the elevator and nodded to the young man who passed him and greeted him by name. Only when he had entered the car and was shooting downward, edging carefully away from an elderly couple who held hands and looked at each other sorrowfully, did he realize that the young man was Ben Gottlieb, the husband of Ina's roommate. He should have asked him how the baby was this morning, but then Ben had not asked him about Ina. It did not matter. They were men rushing down hospital corridors, so absorbed in their private worries and their secret griefs that they were exempted from the brief male niceties exchanged over water coolers and on commuter trains.

As he got off the elevator, he noticed that the elderly couple were huddled together now and that the old man, whose twisted fingers trembled, was wiping his wife's eyes with a handkerchief on which a flower of blood had been washed to a rusty shadow.

"Sha, sha," the old man murmured just as the elevator door snapped shut.

Ray imagined them holding vigil at the bedside of an only child, weeping over the death-still body of a beloved brother—perhaps the last of their surviving siblings. Always—at least since his parents' deaths (and perhaps before?)—he had dreaded hospital elevators, forever ascending and falling with their carloads of fearful and grieving passengers.

Dr. Isaacs's nurse motioned him at once into the office where the doctor sat behind a desk across which small pieces of paper had been spread in a neatly tessellated pattern. Square sheets of green onionskin were set at right angles to pale yellow rectangles and balanced by long sheets of intricately annotated computer printout forms. The doctor was on the phone, and he waved Ray to a seat. Professional boredom weighed his words. He twirled a pencil and closed his eyes.

"Yes," he said. "No. By all means seek a second opinion. I'll be glad to send the laboratory reports on."

He reached for a pile of green squares, removed the top one, and made a note on it. Like a weary player in a long board game, he tossed it onto his metal tray.

He hung up without saying good-bye, and Ray thought of his mother-in-law. There was clearly a special category for people who could be bothered with neither greetings nor farewells. He glanced at his watch. It was just past nine-thirty. The morning had barely begun, yet he felt weak with the weariness of a long day.

"Yes. Mr. Feldman. How are you? The children?" Now the doctor spoke with rehearsed heartiness, extended a dry plump hand for shaking.

"Fine."

Ray offered no details, knowing that Isaacs did not give a damn, did not even remember how many children there were. He did not mind. The man was competent, and they paid him for his skill, not for his emotional involvement in their lives. That area belonged to Dr. Eleanor Berenson, who specialized in insights and sensitivity. Perhaps it was Dr. Berenson with whom he should be consulting this morning. He had met her only once, several months after Ina began seeing her. The analyst had suggested the meeting, and Ina had nervously agreed that it would be helpful, and so he had gone.

He had wondered again, as he sat in her waiting room which was so crowded with plants that he felt himself a giant trapped amid diminutive interior foliage, why Ina had decided to enter the long and expensive analysis that stole precious, measured hours from her busy days. But he did not raise objections or question her. There were mysterious terrains in her past across which he did not dare to trespass. She shared dark memories with her parents; with her cousin Bette; with her friend Halina, who visited them once a year, laughed with a harshness that frightened the children, and drank too much. Sometimes when Ina and Bette and Halina spoke in soft, urgent tones, he stood uneasily with their husbands in the doorway. Their wives had secrets they would never share, memories they were fearful of knowing. In a way he was relieved when Ina began to see Eleanor Berenson. The burden of her drifting sadness had shifted.

Ray did not find it strange that Ina's cousin and closest friend, Bette, was also a patient of Dr. Berenson's. It was only natural to act on the recommendation of relatives and friends. Bette had also recommended Dr. Isaacs to them, and the hump-backed piano tuner who bent over their Bechstein twice a year also tuned Bette's Steinway.

Ray's meeting with Dr. Berenson had not been helpful. He had listened carefully to what the woman said but had difficulty understanding and assimilating her words. The doctor gave the impression of height and strength, but her voice was startlingly soft and cultivated. He remembered that she kept her hands perfectly still when she spoke, and although the light on her phone had blinked insistently during their meeting, she had ignored it. (Unlike Isaacs, whose fingers fluttered over his paper patterns and who excused himself now to take yet another call, leaning back in his large leather armchair while Ray sat too straight in his own seat, struggling to recall the analyst's words, wondering why, suddenly, on this spring morning, they seemed so important.)

"I can help your wife with current difficulties, but I think you should know that I am not sure we can really reach the root of what may cause the difficulties. Her early childhood years were extremely complex, overwhelmingly traumatic, and she's covered them with many layers. If we start stripping away, we may cause a landside. I think Ina understands this, and I wanted to be sure that you did."

He had nodded. The woman's tone was reminiscent of his own when he told a client that they could commence an action but anticipate only limited success—an out-of-court settlement perhaps rather than a definitive judgment. He himself was a courteous, responsible professional, cautious about raising false hopes, and clearly Eleanor Berenson shared his approach.

But he was mildly mystified, and he had told her so. He cultivated no illusions about Ina's analysis, harbored no hopes. The analysis was purely her own experience. Neither Ina nor Eleanor Berenson owed him any explanation or qualification. Eleanor Berenson did not quarrel with him.

It had occurred to him once that it had been after that meeting, after Ina had been seeing Eleanor Berenson for several months, that the dream began. Terror had ridden through her sleep, thrusting her into wakefulness. She wakened with a nascent scream frozen at her throat. Once she had whispered into the darkness. "Don't shoot," she had hissed. Once, loudly and clearly, she had shouted, "Bette, run! We must run!" On a rainy night her fingers had raced across his arm. "They're coming," she warned him, and clung to him, seeking to hide herself within the curve of his body.

When he asked her what the dream was about, she pleaded forgetfulness, confusion, fatigue. He was strangely relieved and did not press her. But he knew that the dream involved soldiers poised to shoot and that Ina and Bette were their defenseless targets. Why, he wondered, had the dream begun now, after all the years of calm? He had read somewhere that dreams were therapeutic, that they released and thus reduced fears. Perhaps the dream, then, was the beginning of progress in Ina's therapy—the first pebbles rolling slowly down the slope of memory. Like Eleanor Berenson, he too hoped that it would not cause a landslide, and to protect Ina from hidden danger, he held her tightly in the darkness, stroked her hair and shoulders, and whispered softly into her ear, banishing those advancing soldiers who would aim death at the sad-eyed child his lovely wife had been.

"It was good to meet you, Mr. Feldman," Eleanor Berenson said as she walked him to the door, and he had been oddly pleased that she did not call him by his first name. Again, unlike Dr. Isaacs, who completed his call, reshuffled his papers, and sighing wearily, said, "Well, now, Ray, what do we have?"

"I'm here to find that out."

"Well, we removed the fibroma and did a frozen scan. It was larger and deeper than I suspected."

"But still not dangerous?"

Ray's heart beat faster. By "dangerous" he meant, he knew, malignant—festering with evil, metastasizing until it grew large enough to smother life, to congeal into a ball of pain oppressive enough to kill. *It could not be cancerous.* The word shivered in his mind, and he thrust it away, scattered its letters: c-a-n-c-e-r—the sharded word fluttered into nothingness, mutilated, banished, but still he felt the arrhythmic beat of his heart, the tremor of terror in the fingers he forced into stillness on his lap.

"We can't tell yet," the doctor said carefully. "But I'll know definitely after I have the results of a permanent section."

"Ina seemed very upset," Ray said. Had Isaacs said anything during surgery about the size and depth of the fibroma? No. Of course not. The bastard was insensitive but not a fool.

"Yes. Well. The breast always stirs up an emotional reaction. The most minor treatment sometimes has that effect." The doctor was casual. He made a note on the chart spread in front of him, and Ray seethed with annoyance. It was not Ina's chart. He would not consult with one client and read the file of another. Damn Isaacs. Damn them all. He hated the building, the hospital with its odors of death and healing, its sterile whiteness, and its wheeler-dealer practitioners. But Isaacs continued, neatly placing the chart on a new pile. "And then she seems to have some ambivalent feelings about the abortion. At least that's what I gathered. Have you reached a final decision on that?" He looked at Ray questioningly, his pen poised as though prepared to take down the answer.

"We're not exactly sure," Ray said.

"Don't rush it. I would have had her stay an extra few days in any case, as it turns out. I didn't expect the incision to go that deep. I'll call you when I have the biopsy results. As for the other thing—just be very sure that you both know what you want to do."

He stood, and Ray saw that he still wore the blue surgical apron. A clot of damp blood clung to a pocket. Ina's blood. Wine-red and warm. Only last week she had cut her hand on the pruning shears as they cleared away the overgrowth in the Amagansett garden, and he had bent and sucked the blood that oozed from the small wound, desire stirring wildly within him as its taste filled his mouth. How beautiful she was with the sun golden across her face, her hand so firm and certain even as tears of blood flowed from it, revealing a brief and sudden vulnerability. He, the orphan boy, had married her for that strength, that definition of purpose that caused her to walk swiftly and in a straight line, her head erect. She was fine. Of course she was. The small lump would be proven benign. She was his wife, wonderfully healthy and strong, and life grew within her body—not death. He shook the doctor's hand and hurried out of the office, almost running to the elevator. He wanted to see her, to touch her, to make sure that she was not crying and that if she was, he was there to wipe away the saline streaks of her sorrow.

She was asleep when he reached the room. The Gottliebs sat

together at the window, using the covered radiator as a card table. They were playing honeymoon bridge, and their voices were as soft as the rustle of the cards in their hands. Miriam wore a belted pink robe, and a sprig of matching dogwood nestled in her hair. Because she wore lipstick and laughed softly at something Ben said, Ray knew without asking that their baby was making progress.

Miriam smiled at him and glanced protectively at Ina.

"She's been sleeping since they brought her up. It's good for her. I took two phone messages."

He thanked her and took the slips of paper she held out. Ruthie, Ina's close friend, had phoned and asked that Ina return the call. He was annoyed. They had told so few people that Ina was going into the hospital. How did Ruthie know? Had Ina called her? He crumpled the flimsy message form and quickly straightened it out. He did not want Ina to talk to Ruthie, but of course he would tell her that she had called. And it was not that he himself did not like Ruthie. He thought her interesting, clever, attractive.

She was a tall, lean woman who allowed her red-gold hair to sprout from her head in a wild Afro that she seldom combed, although she circled her eyes with purple shadow and painted her long golden lashes so that they danced stiffly upward when she opened her very large green eyes. Ray had seen her wedding picture and knew that she had once worn her hair tamed to silky lengths and no makeup at all. Older than Ina, she had been married in the late fifties, when all pretty girls wore their hair long and straight and got married two weeks after they collected their B.A. degree. She and her husband, an agreeable, bespectacled man whose name Ray could never remember, had settled into a ranch house in Dix Hills where Ruthie designed fliers for the League of Women Voters, the Committee for a Sane Nuclear Policy, and the Southern Christian Leadership Conference in turn. She learned to speak ardently and decisively in support of each current cause, and she prepared fewer and fewer clever casseroles. The summer *The Feminine Mystique* appeared in paperback, Ruthie enrolled in classes at

the Art Students League. Her husband nodded pleasantly, be-
nignly, and raised no objection to the cold salads he ate by
himself in the evening.

A fellow student brought Ruthie to the consciousness-raising
group where she met Ina and heard for the first time women
translating into words the vague thoughts and feelings that
had sent her restlessly from her quiet orderly house to frenetic
meetings in the basements of churches and synagogues. Late
one night, when the coffee had grown tepid and the talk harsh,
she had shouted wildly and loudly that she hated her life. She
was *bored.* The word made her weep because she belonged to
a generation that had been valiantly protected against boredom,
thrust from earliest childhood into a maze of clubs and camps,
lessons and excursions. Talent had been coaxed forth and nourished, personal vistas broadened. Ruthie had taken art lessons
and sculpture classes, modern dance and elocution. Her parents had gone to teacher conferences and discussed maximizing
her potential, realizing her creativity. And for what? So that
she could vacuum her living room in Dix Hills and make yet
another clever flier for a garage sale. She was *bored!*

"Do something about it," one woman said drily.

Ruthie did. She sold her first children's book, rented a studio
apartment on the West Side, and left her husband, who had
not been unduly upset. They were not yet divorced and occasionally met for dinner. Often he stayed the night, but Ruthie
had other lovers and spoke about them as casually and indifferently as she spoke passionately and convincingly about amorphous, insoluble problems. World peace, hunger, human rights
—Ruthie argued them all with heated conviction, and boredom
was vanquished in the hot fire of her involvement, her rhetoric.

She did not want to remarry, and she definitely did not want
to have children. She had strong feelings on overpopulation
and talked of adopting a slum child. Why, Ruthie had asked
Ray, would anyone bring more children into the world when
so many were given only marginal care? Her question had
come on a wintry Sunday when they sat together in the living
room. Jeddy and Rachel were in front of the fire, crouched

over the chess board, and when Rachel moved a pawn cun-
ningly, she smiled wisely and proudly—her mother's smile of
achievement, accomplishment. Her face shone golden in the
firelight. Jeddy ran his fingers through his hair, pondered each
move with his chin cupped between bent fingers. It was Ray's
father's posture during such a game on such a day.

Ray had thought his answer to Ruthie: "We have children
of our own, of course, because they are our own. They are
extensions of ourselves, and we need these small perpetuators
of our lives and loves, with their golden firelit smiles and the
gentle curve of their small hunched shoulders." But he had
not answered Ruthie, knowing that emotion was no adversary
to reason—that there are arguments that can never be argued.

He put her message now on Ina's table and knew that he
did not want Ina to speak to Ruthie today and receive rein-
forcement from Ruthie's arsenal of phrases, the fiery salvos of
reason with which Ruthie defended her tenuous liberation.
One lost battle, perhaps, and the fortress of hanging plants she
had erected on West Ninety-fourth Street would fall and she
would surrender again to the captivity of Dix Hills. Poor
Ruthie. He thought he knew the answer, simplistic though it
might seem. She had simply married the wrong man and turned
that single tactical error into a lifelong campaign of anger and
anguish. She should get a divorce and find someone else. One
day when they had all had enough to drink, he would tell her
so and watch her blink wildly so that her stiffened golden
lashes beat against her cheeks like trapped and frightened
butterflies.

Ina moaned softly and he bent over her.

"Ina?"

"A drink. Thirsty."

A glass with a curved plastic straw stood in readiness, and
he held it for her, lifting her head slightly. She took a few
sips, and her head slipped back on the pillow.

"Tired. I'm so tired."

"Sleep."

He drew the white cotton blanket gently over her and

kissed her forehead. Her long dark hair was spread across the pillow, and he hoped she would allow it to fall in loose soft folds through the day. But he knew that it was more likely that she would take control of it when she awakened and fashion it again into the tight chignon held in place by many unseen pins. Her eyes closed, and she slept again.

"How is she?" Miriam Gottlieb asked softly.

"Tired. How is your baby today?"

"Oh, he had a very good night. The doctors are more optimistic now." She smiled and took her husband's hand. "Ben spoke to a friend who's an actuary—for an insurance company, you know. He said there's definitely an upward curve on chances for a baby like ours:"

"No, Miriam." Ben Gottlieb's voice was gentle, cautious, wary of too much optimism. "He said that the curve had risen slightly over the past several years."

"Yes. Of course it's risen. Because of all the research and the new techniques. You know, the nurse, Miss Li, told me that if the Kennedy baby was born today, he'd surely survive." Her voice was breathless, sputtering like a small flame burning fiercely with hope. The cards trembled in her hands, and she set them down carefully. She did not look at the two men but inched herself back to bed. "I'm a little tired too," she said, and Ben eased her down against the pillow and adjusted the bed, turning the crank until she held a hand up. "Fine. Good. I think I'll sleep a little too."

"I'll go look at the baby," Ben Gottlieb said. His knitted skullcap was askew on his head, and he straightened it. Ray saw that although he was a very young man, his hair was thinning and his fingernails were bitten to bloodied edges.

"Yes. Yes. Go look at him. He's so sweet. So darling." She smiled, her eyes closed, and he walked quickly from the room.

The other message was from Bette, Ina's cousin, who asked that Ray call her, and Ray dialed her number in Connecticut and waited patiently while the phone rang. Bette had three children, and while the older boy and girl were almost the ages of his own children, the youngest was still in diapers. He

wondered now why there had been such a long interval between the births of the second and third child, but he supposed
that Ina knew. She and Bette knew everything about each
other.

They had even been born within weeks of each other to
mothers who were sisters and so alike that they were often
mistaken for each other, although Shaindel, Ina's mother, was
two years younger than Peshi, Bette's mother. The cousins had
been carried in their mothers' arms from the ghetto to a forest
hiding place. They had taken their first steps in a cave hol-
lowed out beneath a pigpen, where a Polish farmer had created
a refuge for them. At three they knew how to hold their breath
to block their cries of fear and rage. Tears, being soundless,
were not dangerous, but they seldom cried. They were pretty
children and were not sent to the death camp when their families were at last interned. Clinging to their mothers' skirts,
winsome, large-eyed little girls, adept at survival, they smiled
shyly up at a woman guard who kept them as barrack mascots,
tiny human pets trained to do tricks, to beg for scraps of bread,
jump up, roll over. When the women's band of inmates played,
the small girls, in striped jackets that swept about their bony
knees, danced with each other. A waltz. A minuet. A tango.
The German guards and officers clapped and smiled at each
other as they watched. They congratulated themselves on
their humanity. They were not such bad sorts. They allowed
the charming children to live. They tossed rusks of bread to
the emaciated musicians and chocolates, white with age, to the
children.

Ina and Bette saved the flaking squares of sweets for their
mothers until the day came when Peshi would not eat. At
war's end they went together to the camp in Italy and then
traveled with Bette's father and Ina's parents to the aunt in
Brooklyn who clutched them and wept and cursed and made
them take hot baths twice a day.

Once settled in New York, distance separated the cousins,
but they spoke on the phone several times a week and spent
long weekend afternoons behind the closed doors of their bed-

rooms, talking softly, laughing, playing records. They had become Americans and shed all but the faintest vestige of their accents with the same ease they had discarded the over-sized clothing given them at the camp near Naples. Sometimes they danced with each other, but never a waltz, a minuet, or a tango. Only lindies and fox-trots, and after a while, as though they had suddenly remembered something long forgotten, they did not dance with each other at all.

They went to neighboring New England colleges and married within months of each other. Bette's husband, Richard, owned a small engineering company, and they lived in a large, comfortable house in Stamford with a rectangular pool in the backyard. Bette did not work, although she was a talented designer and occasionally sold a pattern. She could not work, she would explain earnestly, because she had to be near her children, her home. When she was away, she called often. Was everything all right? Was everyone at home? And she asked to speak to each child, even the baby, who sputtered happily into the receiver.

Bette's hair, like Ina's, was thick and dark, and she allowed it to hang loosely about her face, crowned always by a tor-toiseshell headband. Some years ago Bette's father had died after a long illness. His death had been expected, and his funeral had been small and solemn, but for weeks afterward small things made Bette cry. She dropped a bag of groceries and wept for several hours. Someone criticized her bridge game and her tears showered the table, dampening the quilted cover, and continued to stream as she drove home; and she wept crazily, inexplicably, deep into the night. It was Richard who arranged for her to see Dr. Berenson. How long ago had that been? Ray wondered—perhaps three years ago. A year or so later she became pregnant with her third child. Was there a connection? Ray wondered. He did not think so.

"Hello." Her voice was breathless, as he had known it would be. The baby was active—into everything.

"It's Ray. I got your message. Ina's sleeping."

"Yes. Of course. How is she?"

"Fine. But tired."

"Do you think she'll want to see me today? I'm coming into the city for a session with Dr. Berenson, and I could manage it if she's up to it."

"I'm not sure. Her mother is coming, I know. I guess the best thing would be to give her a call from the city and check with her. I just don't know how she'll be feeling."

"All right. That's what I'll do. She's all set for the other thing?"

"The abortion?" He was not surprised that Bette knew about it. He would have been surprised if she had not known. In the camp the cousins had often slept together for warmth. Once, overcome with thirst during those last terrible days before the liberation, they had drunk each other's urine. Of course they told each other everything. "You'll have to talk to her about it."

"Yes. All right. I will."

"Say hello to Richard." He thought, with unexpected and rare malice, of asking her to say hello to Dr. Berenson as well and smiled thinly as he replaced the receiver.

Ina stirred, and in the bed across the room, Miriam Gottlieb murmured softly in her sleep. Ray opened his attaché case and studied the brief he had brought along, glancing now and again at his wife, whose features in sleep surrendered to an ease, a relaxation, they seldom knew during the urgent, busy hours of her waking.

It was almost eleven-thirty when she opened her eyes. She smiled up at him, and then her hand flew to her breast, found the bulky bandage, fingered it lightly, wonderingly.

"I didn't think it would be so big," she said.

"It's only a dressing." He took her hand gently in his, guided it downward, away from her breast.

"It's all right though." She allowed no question to linger in the sentence, and he was therefore excused from offering an answer.

"Isaacs will probably be up sometime this afternoon. How are you feeling?"

"Okay. It just throbs a little, and I'm fuzzy from the sedatives, I guess. But I'm okay—really I am. How are things at home?"

"Fine. Okay."

He had known she would not complain of pain. She never had—not even in labor with Jeddy, when the pains had rushed in with a fierce brutality that made her grasp the bed rail with whitened knuckles, bite her lip until blood trailed down her chin. She had moaned softly but had not cried out, the lesson learned long ago in a distant land, ineradicable, persistent.

"What did the doctor say?" she asked. "It was benign, right?"

"Oh, they are pretty sure that it was," he answered, struggling to keep his voice casual. Again, the mechanism of protection came automatically into play. He would protect her from his own uncertainty, spare her the doctor's evasiveness.

"Yes. I'm sure, too." Her voice was fuzzy, but she focused on shielding him from her own doubt. Their twin fears, unspoken, unacknowledged, were spread taut between them.

"How are the kids?" she asked, because that subject at least was safe.

"The kids are fine. I gave Rachel the money for the tutu. And your mother called. She wanted to have lunch with me. I'm meeting her in about an hour on Eighty-sixth Street. Ina, she knows something's up. What do I tell her?"

"The truth, I guess."

A nurse came in with a tray and smiled with trained brightness at them.

"How are you feeling?" she asked, setting the tray down as she lifted Ina's wrist with one hand and deftly inserted a thermometer in her mouth with the other. She required no answer. She would know how Ina was feeling when she had the pulse and temperature reading. She was very young, and her fair hair floated in straight sheaths about her shoulders. Her newly earned gold pin shone brightly on her uniform collar, and her cardigan was woven of the finest aqua cashmere. Ray envied her her youth and certainty, the poise and assurance her newly acquired knowledge gave her. It would be years before she learned that that knowledge was, after all, not enough—not nearly enough.

"Good, fine," she told them, answering her own question with a glance at her watch and at the darting streak of mercury. "Any pain?"

"A little," Ina admitted.

She eased herself up to a sitting position. The oversized hospital gown hung loose about her shoulders, and dark clouds of fatigue circled her eyes.

"I'm hungry though. Starved." She drained the apple juice and spooned Jell-O into her mouth. She hated to be hungry and always kept a small box of raisins in her purse.

"You'll be able to have a regular lunch," the nurse assured her. "And just ring if you need anything." She flashed them another brilliant smile, which they returned weakly, and went importantly from the room, making hasty notations on the chart.

"I should tell her that you're pregnant?" In the habit of the long married, he slipped easily back into their abandoned conversation as though the nurse had not interrupted them.

"Yes. I guess so."

"And?"

"And that's all. Anything else she wants to know, she'll have to come out and ask. My mother has never been known for her reticence." She stirred sugar into her tea, took a sip, and frowned but continued drinking.

"She wanted to know why you were staying so long in the hospital."

"She hates hospitals. I don't blame her." This Ina shared with her mother—their grim knowledge of hospitals in which no one recovered and doctors and nurses served as experimenters and morticians rather than healers. "I guess maybe you'll have to tell her we're considering abortion."

"Considering," she had said. He took guilty hope and did not dwell on it.

"All right. I'd better leave now. Oh, yes. Ruthie called and wants you to call back. And Bette called. She'll call again from the city. Something about visiting today."

He stood, attaché case in hand, and looked down at her. Pale without makeup, her body strangely frail within the coarse cambric folds of the gown, her hair curtaining her face in thick dark drapes, she looked very beautiful to him.

"Take care," he said, because he could think of nothing else to say, but when he bent toward her, she reached up and her arms went about his with strength and need, and her lips were moist and warm against his own.

"You'll come back right after dinner?" she whispered, and there was fear in the softness of her voice.

"Yes. Of course." He traced her eyes with his finger and left, walking too swiftly past a cluster of young interns, proud in their ill-fitting jackets, who trailed dutifully after a balding, rotund doctor.

The intercom blared. "Dr. Stevenson—any phone please. Please pick up the nearest phone, Dr. Stevenson."

At the elevator he stood beside the beautiful black model he had seen in the waiting room the previous evening. She wore a rainbow-striped robe, and her fingers nervously tied and untied its taffeta sash. When the elevator arrived, the girl's face froze into a smile, but no one exited. Ray entered, and as the door closed, he saw her turn and walk very slowly down the corridor. She wore the disappointed look of someone who has come to meet a train that arrived without discharging a single passenger.

Although it was not yet noon, a small line had already formed at the hostess's station in the small restaurant that only New Yorkers would call a luncheonette. Tiffany lamps dangled from the fake wood beams of the low ceilings, and the chairs around the mahogany-stained Formica tables were of a rich maroon leatherette, their color matching the coarse carpeting. It was called a luncheonette, he supposed, because paper doilies rather than tablecloths covered the tables and because counter service was available. Every stool there was

already occupied by men and women who ate quickly with
fierce concentration, glancing from their unread paperbacks to
their watches. Muzak teased the air with a medley of songs
resurrected from the fifties. "Dance, Ballerina, Dance," "Harbor Lights," "In the Sleepy Town of San Juanita . . ."
Vaughn Monroe's voice carried him back to distant days
when he and Ina danced to caressing tones in tiny Cambridge
bars, listened to the car radio in Ray's old Dodge, their bodies
pressed close in warmth and promise.

Ray took a place in line and watched the entry. Just as the
last chorus of "The Miracle of the Bells" came to its mournful
end, Shirley Cherne pushed through the revolving doors and
walked immediately to his side. She had not doubted that he
would be there before her. She did not expect to be kept waiting and seldom was. Even Jeddy, an inveterate dawdler, hurried when he had to meet his grandmother.

She wore a pale lilac linen suit with a matching blouse of
fine batiste, and when she stood on tiptoe to kiss him, he
smelled her perfume—the thickly sweet aroma of early spring
flowers seeped from her pores and mingled with the dusty rose
scent of her thick face powder. Silver waves crested across the
upswept torrent of her chestnut hair, teased and lacquered into
submission, each hair fearfully, obediently, in place. She
worked long and diligently at teasing her hair into a semblance
of thickness. It had grown back after the war but not as heavy
and luxuriant as the fabled tresses of her girlhood.

"Ray-Mond, how are you?" She always pronounced his
name as though it were two separate words, and he smiled
because he had, long ago, decided that that indicated affection
rather than affectation.

"Fine. Good. You look marvelous, Shirley."

"Saks." She patted her skirt, her fingers knowledgeably ap-
preciating the fabric. "The blouse from Bendel's." She touched
its tie. She was a manufacturer and had access to showrooms
and wholesale houses, but she would buy only in the best Fifth
Avenue stores.

"I like the salesgirl to wait on me," she said half defiantly, half apologetically, but Ray suspected that what she liked was the catering to her individuality, the calling of her name, the gentle obsequiousness and subtle pampering she received from the elegant saleswomen. She had, after all, spent long years of her young womanhood in ragged scraps of clothing, in thread-bare uniforms that did not fit, and then in hand-me-down dresses plucked from the overcrowded closets of the benevo-lent. She had earned the luxury of trying on carefully selected garments in private dressing rooms with thickly carpeted floors through which soft music floated gently, persuasively.

"Hostess! A table for two, please," she called out.

There were two couples ahead of them, but the hostess, a tall blonde woman who stared sadly out at her customers through eyes weighted down with thick blue mascaraed lids, motioned them forward with her great fan of oversized maroon menus.

"These people called for a reservation," she said defiantly to those who stood ahead of them, and she winked at Shirley Cherne, whose mascara matched her own. Survivor blue, Ina called it bitterly, Ray remembered. The hostess, he decided, was probably divorced and supported an autistic child and an invalid mother. Tragedies, like opposites, attract. As they sat down and she handed them their menus, Ray saw a dollar bill slip from his mother-in-law's hand into her fringed pocket. He was annoyed but said nothing. It would, after all, do no good. Shirley Cherne was an expert on the handling of queues—years of her life had been spent standing on them.

In return, the hostess herself took their orders—a tunafish salad for him and a cottage cheese salad plate for her. There was a choice between a large salad or a small one, and she ordered the large one although she would not finish it. She enjoyed seeing food on her plate when she was through eating. In this she was very unlike her brother-in-law, Bette's father. Ray thought of him now as Shirley spread a luncheon roll with a thick cloak of butter. She would take only a single bit of it, he knew, and then lavishly butter another before the end of the meal.

When Bette's father died, Ray and Ina had helped to close his tiny Bronx apartment because Bette was so distraught. He had lived alone and bought little because he ate little, yet his refrigerator had been packed with tiny packets of leftovers, encased in torturously constructed envelopes of plastic, silver foil, brown paper. Ancient crusts, dried scraps of meat, pale and brittle, withered rinds of cheese covered with verdant mold, had flaked and crumbled in their hands. Lemon peels, faded to the color and thinness of old gold, gravies congealed into graying masses of fat trapped in tiny jars, had crouched in corners of the greasy shelves. Peshi, his wife, Bette's mother, had starved to death. So had his parents, a brother and sister, a half-remembered infant son. He took no chances now and walked always in the shadow of fear, scooping packets of sugar and crackers into his pockets when he ate his solitary meals at restaurant counters. When Ray opened a cabinet in that fetid kitchen, dozens of cellophane-wrapped clusters of Ry-Krisp and Melba Toast tumbled out, and Ina filled three paper bags with hardened clumps of restaurant sugar.

Ray had vomited in the dead man's bathroom. It was not the decay that upset him but the sour miasma of terror that hung like a mist in those three sad rooms where a man (his children's great-uncle), who had escaped death, had lived in fear of life. That same nausea teased him when Shirley Cherne overordered and then looked with satisfaction at a plate still full, as though she had won a victory, had outwitted a malevolent schemer who would see her wanting. Waste triumphed over want. He thought too of a distant cousin of Ina's, a veteran of Terezin, who spent two hours over a simple dinner, masticating each bite soberly, reverently, and he wondered if anyone had done a study of the eating patterns of survivors. If they had not, surely they would. The Holocaust was academically fashionable just now.

"So how is Ina this morning?" she asked.

"Isaacs removed the fibroma. It was a very short procedure, and it was larger than he thought it would be, but everything went well. Ina was a little more upset than I expected." He added this cautiously, hesitantly, a verbal fisherman slowly extending a lure.

Shirley Cherne turned to her salad, carved a tomato rosette into small petals that bled across the lettuce.

"Always women are upset when something affects the breast," she said harshly. She bit into her carrot and thought of the German guard with whom she had sat in the fire-rimmed darkness. The woman had wept, and Shirley (Shaindel then) had comforted her in word and wished her dead in thought. Not one cancer but a thousand should grow within that body, within all their bodies. She speared an olive and spat the pit out, unashamed of her thought, her memory. Hatred was a weapon, and it had sustained her. It was impossible to fight without hating the enemy.

"Yes, that's what Isaacs said," Ray replied.

Shirley nodded. He was a nice boy, Ina's Raymond. She had always liked him, from the very first day that Ina brought him to the house. She had known it would be all right even if they had decided so quickly. He was so soft and gentle, with a winsome helplessness in his eyes, an awkwardness in the way he moved his long, too-thin body. It came, maybe, from being orphaned so suddenly, when he was too old to be called a boy and too young to be recognized as a man. His sister, that Dorothy with the empty womb and open arms, had given him support yes, love yes, but not strength. Well, you could not give a child everything. You could say, maybe, that she had given Ina strength but not love, and Ina, maybe, would say she had given her nothing. All right. Let her say what she will. After all, so smart, computer lady. She, Shirley Cherne, knew what she knew. And Raymond, as it turned out, was a good boy and not weak. She had sensed that. He was good, competent, and only a strong man could be that gentle with his children. And he had wonderful hands. Long fingers. Yedidiah had had such hands. Yedidiah. She filled her mouth too full of cottage cheese and spoke with the snowy granules trailing from the corners of her lips.

"Maybe it's something else Ina is upset about?"

"Yes. There is something else." He hesitated, always uneasy with his wife's mother, whom he thought he loved but knew he did not understand. "Ina's pregnant. She's about five or six weeks pregnant, and I guess you realize we never planned on having another baby."

"So you didn't plan. So, an accident." Words did not frighten her. She used them harshly, accurately. "Cancer," she said aloud while others whispered: "It's very serious, dangerous." "Cancer," she said. "He has cancer." Never would she say "in financial difficulties—troubled times." "Bankrupt," she mouthed loud and clear. Not for her the euphemistic "We didn't plan another baby"—no, "an accident." A careless collision of ovum and sperm resulting in the casualty of a zygote, an embryo, a wriggling worm of life generated by an accident.

"So what do you do about such an accident?" She took a bite of coleslaw, snipped the head off her pickle, and pushed the plate away. It was still covered with vegetables and half a scoop of cheese.

"We're not sure," he said. He wanted her carrot, but then she would have less food to discard and he would deprive her of the pleasure of waste, of the temptation she tossed at gods she did not believe in.

"Not sure. For not sure you don't stay in the hospital an extra few days."

"We're undecided," he amended, weakly.

The waitress brought their coffee and gave Shirley two creams. She would open them both but use only half of each, he knew, but wondered how the waitress had known. He was right. She laced the coffee with sugar and stirred it. Often she ordered a side dish of whipped cream which she spooned onto the top of the cup, but seldom did she empty it. Once, in a restaurant Ina had protested when Shirley ordered coffee, called for whipped cream and brandy, stirred them in, and discarded the concoction after a single sip.

"Let your mother eat the way she wants," Norman Cherne had said loudly. "What do you know? American princess!"

Ina had blushed, and her father had looked sorrowfully at

her. He spoke to his daughter rarely but looked at her a great
deal. She looked so like his mother, whom he had last seen
walking with his father down a wide Warsaw boulevard,
hugging a bundle to her as though she cuddled a very young
infant. Like Ina, his mother had been a tall woman who wore
her long black hair caught in a knot at the nape of her neck.

"Ina wants an abortion?" Shirley asked.

Ray was startled. She had not said "You and Ina . . . " but
only "Ina," as though she had some defined prescience of
their situation, of their conversations, of his urging and her
reticence, his growing certainty and her slowly evolving
ambivalence.

"I think," he replied, "she's not sure of what she wants."

"Sure. What's sure? No one is sure of anything. Only dying.
You do what you have to do."

To his surprise, she lifted her coffee cup and drained it, even
spooning up the sugar encrusted at the bottom, as though
suddenly hungry for sweetness, for energy, for life sustenance.

"You want the baby," she said, and it was not a question.

He nodded.

She picked up her white leather pocketbook, extracted her
makeup case, and painted her mouth a shade of lilac that
matched her suit, adding a layer of powder to the dusty veil
that shrouded her skin. Her fingers were twisted with arthritis
and weighted down with heavy rings, but they moved to these
small tasks of vanity with surprising deftness. She did not
wait for the waitress to bring the bill but stood. Again, he
smelled the springtime sweetness of her perfume as she bent
to kiss him on the cheek.

"I must hurry now. A big shipment of fabric comes this
afternoon, and I have to check the bills of lading. They would
steal from the blind, these suppliers. And I go first to see Ina.
Thank you for the lunch. It will be all right, Ray-Mond."

Her lips brushed his cheek, and then she was on her way,
walking briskly, rushing past two young girls who stood in
her way. At the exit she paused to study herself in the mirror
above the cigarette machine. She returned a stray tendril to

her upswept crown of hair and hurried out. The waitress arrived with the check, but Ray ordered another cup of coffee and drank it very slowly.

"You do what you have to do," his mother-in-law had said, but then how did anyone know what he had to do? The simple imperatives of his life trotted through his thoughts, clearly defined. He *had* to earn a living, pay his bills, stop for red lights, make sure his children were in good health, properly cared for, and educated. But in all other things he was trapped in the dangerous prison of freedom. He did not *have* to urge his wife to have a child she did not want. And yet, and yet. Who was it who said, "We may not know what is right or wrong, but we always know where our duty lies"? Goddamn it, it had been Churchill, and he had not been thinking about abortions but about the future of Europe. For the first time that day Ray smiled, and he took up the check, leaving the waitress a very large tip.

Shirley Cherne took a cab across town and stared at the newly blooming foliage with the avid interest of an infrequent theatergoer absorbed by a unique stage set. She did not often see trees in great number or a wild overgrowth of vines and bushes. A neat parade of skinny maples marched up her Forest Hills street, and even the grass that thrust its green teeth tenaciously through pavement cracks was clipped away by the fastidious custodians who pruned the puny hedges and mowed balding patches of green. In Long Island City, where Cherne Knitwear occupied a narrow gray stone building, scrawny ailanthus trees struggled in sandy yards, and dusty urban sparrows perched on leafless bushes. Yet once trees and greenery had been an intrinsic part of her life, part of her personal landscape.

She had grown up in the Polish countryside, and the woodlands had been the playgrounds of her childhood. With Polish playmates she had scaled the great oak trees, slid down vines, gathered berries from bushes hidden in deep tents of soaring evergreens. When she married Nachum Czernowitz and went

to live in Warsaw, they found a flat near the great municipal
park so that when she awakened each morning she could see
the branches of trees scraping the sky. When the war came
and rumors of a ghetto began, she turned for refuge to the
forest of her childhood, but her wilderness playmates were
pale-eyed strangers. They had forgotten her laughter and remembered only her Jewishness, now a crime for which they,
like their German masters, found her guilty. They stared
resentfully at her fine city boots, her lined cloak, and turned
away from her.

Still, she and Nachum wandered briefly with her sister,
Peshi, and Peshi's husband. It was summer, and they found a
hunter's shack with a pine-needle floor. On that harsh and
fragrant bed, she and Nachum had come together in urgent
passion, breathing in the odors of earth and growth, grasping
at life as death pursued them hard. But of course they had to
leave the forest and the tenuous shelter of that shack. Winter
was coming, and the infant children, Bette and Ina, shivered
constantly. Yedidiah, the toddler, blew on his fingers and
hugged his small body but rarely cried. Perhaps he had known
even then that tears were futile. Crying, their children had
discovered, was a luxury reserved for Aryan children.

She stared out now, as Central Park rolled past, and breathed
deeply, contentedly, at the sight of a small pine copse at the
bottom of a gentle hill. The cab slowed, and the driver reached
for a cigarette. He was a heavy, pleasant-faced man with sandy
hair and blue eyes. A picture of twin girls with hair that
matched his own, wearing matching white organdy com-
munion dresses, was taped to his windshield. Shirley Cherne
looked at his name on the medallion and saw with relief that
he was Michael Flanagan. How long would it be, she wondered, until men who looked like Michael Flanagan did not
fill her with uncertainty, fear? Even on her Forest Hills street
she pressed herself close against a building when a group of
boys wearing club jackets passed.

"You are a stupid woman," she told herself severely, and

turned her thoughts, forcefully, back to the fabric shipments she expected that afternoon, the load of zippers she had accepted on consignment, the defective trimmings she had received that morning. The rickrack had been faded. Such *chutzpah* to send her faded goods. By the time the cab stopped in front of Mount Lebanon, she had stirred herself into an anger that threatened neither mood nor memory.

"You have very pretty daughters," she told Michael Flanagan, and gave him an extra dollar.

"Thanks." But he did not turn or smile, and she did not care. She had given him the dollar because his name had not been Mueller or Krantz.

She bought a box of candy for Ina in the hospital gift shop and knew that Ina would accept it with a thin, accusing smile. She should have gone to a store, not stopped at a convenience shop. She should have taken the time to buy a present that mattered—to think, touch, consider. Once, when Ina was away at college, she had told her mother that she was the only girl in her dormitory who did not receive packages of home-baked cakes, carefully selected clothing. The Chernes sent her money, generous checks, but Ina wanted the talismans of caring—the hand-knit sweater, the freshly baked cookies. It was not the candy Ina would object to, but the implied thoughtlessness.

"That should be all you're missing," Shirley Cherne had countered then, but she had known she was wrong, just as she knew she was wrong today. You did not bring a daughter still recovering from surgery, however minor, a box of chocolates she would not want to eat. Still, what could she do? She was what she was, just as Ina was what she was. And today they had more important things to discuss than why Ina had no mother-knitted vests. The woman next to Shirley at the gift shop cash register held an oversized blue velour elephant.

"For my new grandson," she said, smiling. "I know it's silly, but I couldn't resist it."

"Very nice," Shirley assured her. She had bought her own

grandchildren's layettes in Altman's and warm comforters in Bloomingdale's, but never had she bought a newborn infant an overstuffed animal.

Ina was sitting up in bed when Shirley arrived. Her dark hair was caught back in a neat coil, and she wore a negligee of buttercup yellow. Shirley saw the bulk of the bandage through the thin fabric, and her heart turned. She did not like to think of a surgeon's scalpel cutting through Ina's pale flesh. How close to the nipple was the incision? she wondered, and remembered how Ina had hugged her small body as a child, always covering the rose-brown tips of flesh at her breasts, fearful always of nakedness. She and Bette had known, with the sly wisdom of children, that there was only nakedness in the death camp, that the deadly gas sprayed down on vulnerable unclothed bodies, and in their last moments men hugged their genitals and women concealed their milkless breasts. A small boy who worked as a *sonderkommando* had shared his knowledge with the little girls, and they had accepted it as they accepted the blue mist of smoke that hovered over the camp, the stinking of charred flesh, the incandescent fires that burned fiercely through the night amid the moans and muted crying. Children are like that, a Warsaw psychiatrist who worked in the quarry with her had told Shaindel. If they are born in a forest, they think the whole world is nothing but woods. If they grow up in a concentration camp, for them the world is nothing but flames and misery. The psychiatrist had choked to death on a rusk of bread three days before the liberation, but Shaindel had told the woman's son, who sought her out at war's end, that his mother had died of heart failure. She could not tell him how another inmate had thrust her hand into the dead woman's throat, removed the masticated hunk of food, and eaten it hungrily, huddled in a corner. Shaindel had not, could not, condemn her. She had been human enough to be shamed by her action and brave enough to struggle for survival.

"Mother, you look marvelous." Ina set aside the book she had been reading.

Shirley kissed her awkwardly on the cheek, her fingers passing expertly over the fabric of the nightgown. "Batiste. Very nice material," she said.

"Ray picked it up at Bloomingdale's."

"Very nice detail work. Good smocking." Shirley held out the box of candy and saw a large red Blum's box on Ina's table.

"Mmm. Chocolate mints. Thanks, but I don't feel like any just now. Dot sent that box from Blum's."

"She had a good time on St. Thomas, your sister-in-law?"

"She was in the Bahamas, not St. Thomas," Ina said, and wondered why it was her mother did not like Dot. Everyone liked Dot. Not that Shirley had ever said anything—nor would she admit to her dislike. "Why shouldn't I like her?" she protested when Ina discussed it. "She ever did anything to me?" And of course there was no answer. Ina shrugged and lifted the box of mints.

"Miriam, would you like a mint?" she called to the young woman in the next bed.

"No, thank you."

"Mother, this is Miriam Gottlieb. Miriam, this is my mother, Shirley Cherne. Miriam has a new baby. He's had some problems, but today he is doing better."

"Much better," Miriam said emphatically.

Shirley looked at her uneasily. She had heard that tone before, that urgent emphasis, that near-belligerence of voice in which dying women insisted they were fine, and mothers whose children writhed in the last stage of dysentery said over and over: "It's just diarrhea. She'll be fine. Just a little diarrhea." Later, standing over a small lifeless body, a weak voice protested: "She's just sleeping. She's not dead. She's just sleeping."

Ach, she was reading too much into things today. The girl had said her baby was much better, so let her baby be much better.

"Good," Shirley told Miriam Gottlieb. "A lot of babies are born a little weak. It's okay. It will be okay. You should have a mint."

"All right."

Ina smiled. Miriam clearly knew when someone was in command. If Shirley Cherne told her to have a mint, she had damn
well better have a mint.

"That's a sensible fabric," Shirley said approvingly, looking
at Miriam's striped nightgown. "That you don't have to send
to a hand laundry. Now, you don't mind if I close the curtain?
I have to talk to my daughter private. Business matters. You
understand?"

"No. Of course not," Miriam said, and Shirley drew the
curtain around Ina's bed and pulled the bedside chair close to
her daughter.

"That was very rude," Ina said, her lips set in a thin line.
Her breast was beginning to throb fiercely, and she felt the
flesh beneath the dressing to be searing with heat. When her
mother left, she would ask the nurse for something for the
pain. Soon her mother would leave. She never stayed very
long. Not at the apartment or the Amagansett house, not at
weddings or funerals. Shirley Cherne was a busy woman who
had to keep moving, who could not and would not remain
still. Oddly enough, Dr. Berenson had once said that about Ina
herself. Why, the analyst had asked in her noncommittal professional voice, did Ina Feldman have to keep moving?

"It wasn't rude," Shirley retorted. "It was necessary. I have
things to tell you. Important things." She looked at her daughter and saw the glint of febrile pain in her eyes. "You don't
feel good?"

"Not so good. But it will pass."

"Everything passes," Shirley said.

She poured a cup of water and held it to Ina's lips, supporting her head. Once, in the camp, Ina had become feverish,
and Shirley had managed to obtain a cup of water from that
guard who thought herself a friend. She had fed it to Ina,
holding her head just as she held it now. She wondered if Ina
remembered that time. No. Of course not. Ina, and Bette too,
remembered little, if anything of those years. Most of the
children—those who had been children then—did not. She
envied them. It was a blessing to be able to forget. She and

Nachum remembered everything, everything. She sighed and looked at the large garnet ring, twisted into a setting of antique gold, on her middle finger.

"I feel much better. Really. What did you want to talk about?" Ina asked.

"I had lunch with Ray-Mond." Her voice sank to a whisper. "He told me you're pregnant."

"Yes. But only a few weeks."

"And you think about an abortion."

"We've talked about it." Ina's tone was guarded. Care was necessary in any exchange with Shirley Cherne. Verbal shafts had to be swift and accurate. Her mother was a dangerous sparring partner.

They spoke very softly now. Beyond the screen Miriam Gottlieb chatted into the phone. "He's so much better. I even went to peek at him today. He has the sweetest hands."

Shirley Cherne sighed and licked her lips. Always they spoke of the hands and fingers, the new mothers. And who could blame them? There was such a miracle in the formation of those tiny hands, those soft, perfect fingers. A scrap of lipstick settled on her tongue. It tasted of lilacs, the wild purple sprays that had flourished across the verdant meadows that dotted the lost landscape of her childhood. She turned back to Ina.

"Don't talk about it. Forget from it. I know what you should do." Her voice was quiet, defiantly definite.

"What do you know? How can you know?" Ina's eyes flashed with anger, and she forgot that only a moment before her head had rested in her mother's hand. Her back was tensed, and a new pain shot through the breast. She struck her fingers together in a fist, useless and impotent.

"I know that you shouldn't have an abortion," Shirley persisted. "And how do I know? I know because I had one, and I know what it did to me."

"*You* had one? When? Where?"

Ina sank back against the pillow, weak, disbelieving. She knew about abortions. Her college classmates had had them in dimly lit offices on narrow streets, offering names that were not their own for records that would not be kept. Women in her consciousness-raising group had had abortions in clinics run as efficiently as supermarkets—paper gowns and paper slippers, ERA literature and copies of *Ms*. on bedside tables, gynecologists who talked as fast as they worked: "A second of pain—that's all. Here, we're through. Have you thought about an IUD—having your tubes tied—how about your old man getting a vasectomy? Off you go. There'll be some pain, but don't worry."

And occasionally young programmers or a secretary in her office had taken Monday off and returned to work pale and sad-eyed. By week's end both the pallor and sadness were gone, and a subtle hardness lurked in their eyes. But classmates, friends, and young employees were not Shirley Cherne/ Shaindel Czernowitz, her mother.

Always, Ina thought of her mother in two dimensions. Shaindel was the bald woman shrunk to skeletal thinness, whose bony arms hurt the child Ina when they reached around her for a desperate hug. Shaindel stood straight among the women, broken and crippled, and her voice rang with strength and certainty when others wept and moaned. It was she who managed always to find an extra crust of bread, a wizened graying morsel of meat; it was she who knew that the soup meted out for lunch should be saved until evening when it would have jelled and thus could line the stomach so that sleep was not made impossible by hunger. Shaindel, the mama, meant life and hope to the child who played on the splintered floor of a barrack room fetid with the stink of vomit and ordure, where tired women lived in a miasma of disbelief.

Ina, the woman, remembered so little. ("Anything that comes to mind," Eleanor Berenson always urged gently.) The recalled incidents were small flashes of remembrance, isolated splinters of terror from which she could not construct a single plank. Even the dream offered no clues, no scraps of insight. But she did remember her mother's face, so strong, so sharply beautiful in its determination, the features carved starkly out of the bone of the fleshless skull. "Mama!" the small Ina had called in the night, the terrible fire-spewing night, and Shaindel's arms, her milky bones luminous through the wasted skin, would come around her child's body and rock her gently into the safety of sleep.

Shirley Cherne was the woman her mother had become in America—a transmogrified figure with newly fleshy arms and a thickness of newly grown chestnut hair, who rocketed into the new American life, startling her husband with a talent for business he had not known she possessed, with ambition and determination. Shirley Cherne was the businesswoman who came home from the factory irritable and exhausted and seemed surprised to find Ina in the apartment. Sometimes Ina, growing up lonely and alone, only Mary Noble, Backstage Wife, and Stella Dallas peopling her wintry afternoons (she envied then, with all her heart, Stella's daughter, Laurel, whose mother talked to her), thought that she had dreamed up the person who had been Shaindel Czernowitz, because certainly Shirley Cherne had never come to comfort her as she lay crying softly in the darkness.

"When did you have an abortion?" Ina asked. (Who asked a mother such a question? And yet she had asked it and had to know.)

"In the camp. The second week we were there. You won't remember. I was like you—only a few weeks pregnant, and I knew that for pregnant women there was no chance. Once you showed, they killed you. The women, even the guards, told stories. Almost all pregnant women were sent to the gas chambers. On some few others, they said, they did medical experiments. Monster babies were born. Monsters. You remember maybe the Grunwalds—second cousins to your father. Chana Grunwald gave birth to such a child—a head as big as a watermelon because of some hormone injections they gave her. Chana went to London after the war, and she had two more children—normal babies—but she killed herself. They told stories. A Latvian woman they let go to her eighth month, and then they induced labor—when the baby was born, they killed it, and the mother saw. She saw and died on the table. Her heart stopped."

"But why? Why did they kill it?" Ina whispered. She felt that her heart, too, would stop. Her breast throbbed, and her mouth was dry.

"Why? They needed reason? Maybe they had a new drug to try, to see how fast it could kill a newborn. Such important experiments they had—sterilizing young women—making twins. That was an important one for them—to make twins and double the Aryan population. That's what the world needed—twice as many Nazi animals to turn all of Europe into a death camp. Ach, I can't even think about it. I can't." She reached into her bag and found a tissue to wipe her eyes. Drops of mascara dripped like blood and stained the tissue blue. Ina turned her head. Her mother almost never cried. The last time had been at Bette's father's funeral, and her weeping then had been swift and silent.

"What did you do—about the pregnancy?" Ina asked softly.

Ben Gottlieb came into the room and waved to her. She heard his voice, soft and controlled, and Miriam's brittle laugh traveled over the curtained screen. "Cute," Miriam said, and there was the rustle of paper as a gift was unwrapped, held up, admired. All visitors to hospitals should be like Ben, carrying clever talismans of the world outside, cheerful tales of health and normalcy. Ina did not want to hear what her mother had come to tell her. She wanted to see Miriam's present, listen to her gentle laughter, her new optimistic plans. Where would they hold the circumcision celebration? What food should be served?

"What could I do?" Shirley offered a question in reply— a Shirley technique. The buck does not stop here—it goes on and on. "Someone told me about a woman doctor—a prisoner. A brave woman. She changed names on medical charts—the living became the dead so that they could escape the *appel*, the roll call. She was everywhere, hiding the sick, stealing antibiotics. Somehow she got hold of a set of surgical instruments. How she kept them hidden in the barracks I don't know except that maybe she made a deal with the guards—helped them. They needed doctors also, believe me. From the highest social classes they didn't get concentration camp guards. Maybe she helped cure them from venereal disease, performed secret abortions. Do I know? But something she did because they let her keep those surgical tools. I went to her, and in a corner of the barracks, with the other women forming a screen in case a guard should come, she aborted that baby, scraped out my womb. She had no drugs, no chloroform. They stuffed a rag in my mouth so I couldn't scream, and two of the stronger women held me down while she worked. They put newspapers on the floor where I lay, and I watched my blood soak through the headlines, and then a small thing, a bloody bit of flesh, maybe the size of a small mouse, fell onto the paper. I thought it moved, but later they said I imagined that. I fainted then. See—who says God isn't full of mercy? And she was finished when I opened my eyes. She was a tall woman, that doctor, with green eyes the color of tears. 'I'm sorry,' she said. 'Thank you,' I told her. I never saw her again, although I heard that she survived the war and went to Israel. I hope it's true. And for what I did, God will forgive me." She did not cry now but stared toward the window where the spidery green leaves of a newly foliated tree pressed gently against the smoked glass pane.

"You did what you had to do," Ina said gently. She touched her mother's arms and moved her hand up to stroke the hair, rigid within its lacquer prison.

A small, bloodied thing, the size of a mouse, her mother had said. Was sex determined at six weeks' gestation? She could not remember. Had it been her brother or her sister, that embryo, the bloodied bit of human detritus scraped from her mother's womb that distant day? She would never know, nor would it, should it, make any difference. They called a parentless child an orphan. Was there a word, then, for a child bereft of siblings? Her mother had undergone the abortion their second week in the concentration camp—only two weeks then after Yedidiah's death in the transit camp. Twice then, in only a single month, Shaindel had been bereft. Pregnant with a child she could not bear, she had watched the silken lash of her dead son tremble on her finger. Poor Shaindel. Poor Shirley. Poor Mama. Ina's eyes burned.

She busied herself with words so that her heart would not break, because she remembered suddenly Yedidiah's laugh and how he could twist his fingers into strange contortions. He had been double-jointed, just as Jeddy was. She had forgotten that, or perhaps she had not wanted to remember it. Her mother had not wanted her to give Jeddy Yedidiah's name, but Ina had insisted on it. Her brother had been denied his life, but she would keep him alive within her own. Atonement perhaps, or guilt—what would Eleanor Berenson call it? Survivor guilt, perhaps. Certainly she would not call it love. Love was not a neurosis.

"Yes," Shirley said. "I did what I had to do. You're right. But for me it was the end. It dried me up. When they took that life from me, from my body, something ended. A snap. A dying. I was finished. Nothing. I thought of only one thing. To keep you alive. To see you strong. And I did keep you alive. I made you strong. You blame me for a lot—that I know. But this you have to give me—I made you strong."

She sat back in her chair, spent. The tie of her blouse had become undone, and the crisp linen of her suit was wilted. Her face, beneath its mask of rouge and powder, sagged. Ina saw her for the first time as an old woman, weak with age and memory.

"Mama." She had not used that word for a long time. "Mother," she said, cool and removed. She took Shirley's hand in her own and pressed it hard so that the rings cut into her skin. "Why did you tell me all this now?"

"Why? Because I don't want you to live like I do. With regret. With wondering. With sorrow. Because I don't want to happen to you what happened to me. I dried up, Ina. I was a young woman—much younger than you today. But from that day, when life was scraped from me, I became old, dry.

When they took that baby, they took from me my life. That shouldn't happen to you. It wasn't for that that I kept you alive, made you strong."

"Mama. You did what you had to do. You had no choice."

"I know. But you, Ina—you have a choice. And something else I want to tell you. You know we go to *shul*, your father and I—we support the temple. Good Jews, they think we are. Your father believes in God. Still, he believes. He's a sick man. Stomach trouble. High blood pressure. But on Yom Kippur he fasts. A whole day. And sometimes he goes to *minyan* three times a day. More often with each year. It's a miracle. A man who saw his mother go in an action, whose son died in the night—he goes and thanks a God full of mercy. *Nu*—so I go with him. I wear a hat, a nice suit. I kiss the Torah. But in God I don't believe. What I believe in is the Jewish people. Every Jewish baby born is a slap in Hitler's face. A new baby to take the place of my Yedidiah and of that bloody little mouse from my body that the women wrapped in newspaper and hid in the bottom of the garbage. They thought I didn't know, but I knew. From my body they took a life, wrapped it in a Polish newspaper, and hid it with the eggshells and potato peels. They had no choice. I had no choice. But you, Ina, you have a choice. So choose right. This I came to say to you today. Was I wrong to tell you? With you, sometimes I think that whatever I do is wrong."

But she had recovered her strength. She sat up straighter in the chair, retied the bow on her blouse, reached into her purse for her makeup bag, for the lipstick that tasted of wild lilacs, for the powder that would mask the tiny lines the trailing tears had left on her dry and withered cheeks.

Miriam Gottlieb's phone rang. A radio played too loudly in the room across the hall. Two interns and two nurses paused in their doorway. The young doctors were very tall and the women were very short. They laughed in unison, and sunlight from the wide hall window fell in dazzling golden petals across their white uniforms. Nurse Li slid into the room with a paper cup of pills for Ina. The red capsules gleamed like tiny rubies. She smiled at Shirley Cherne and crossed to Miriam's bed.

"I've just been to see your baby, Mrs. Gottlieb," she said, "and he's sleeping so sweetly."

"Doesn't he have wonderful fingers?" Miriam asked.

"Wonderful."

Ina's phone rang, and she spoke very briefly and hung up.

"That was Bette," she told her mother. "She said hello."

"She's coming to visit today?" Shirley stood up, brushing a speck of dust from her skirt. She was tired, very tired. Perhaps she would not go to the factory at all. Nachum could check on that fabric shipment. She would go home. No. She would go to Ina's apartment and see the children. She would take them for ice cream sodas to Baskin-Robbins.

"You think the children would like it if I took them for ice cream after school? And I could go with Rachel to buy the ballet dress she needs. She'll go alone, they'll sell her some junk. They take advantage of children."

"That would be wonderful," Ina said.

Shirley did not bend to kiss her. She touched instead the thin batiste sleeve of the yellow nightgown.

"This," she said, "you'll have to wash by hand. All right. Why not?"

She moved aside the screen. Ben Gottlieb slept in the chair next to Miriam's bed, and the three women smiled maternally at him.

"Good-bye and good luck to you," Shirley said to Miriam, and walked from the room, her heels clicking sharply as she walked too quickly to the elevator.

When she reached the street, she saw that it had begun to rain. A light spring drizzle spattered the pavement with tiny teardrops. Two mothers, wheeling children in bright canvas strollers, walked past her. Laughing, talking, they moved slowly through the gently falling rain, and the children held up their faces and laughed as the droplets fell upon their eyes.

Bette Abramson was startled by the rain. But then she was always startled by the world she reentered after a session with Dr. Berenson. She emerged from each analytic hour oddly disoriented, like a bewildered child awakening from a mid-day sleep.

Eleanor Berenson's office was in the East Seventies, so close to the river that the scent of salt air teased the street lined with tall apartment buildings and reminded those who paused long enough to notice it that their city was grounded on an island, their great buildings and bridges girdled by a sullen river and a raging ocean. On the hottest summer days a soft breeze drifted over the street, and in the winter the river breathed up a harsh and cold wind; those who walked the narrow street huddled close to the buildings for refuge.

The nearness of the water always surprised Bette, because within that dimly lit, book-lined consultation room, lying on the worn tweed couch, the unseen analyst behind her, she lived again in a wooded world, with moss soft beneath her feet and twigs snapping sharply as she walked. In her memories, the shadows of great trees blocked the pale light of the winter sun, and when the wind sighed, Peshi, her mother, wept, and she, Bette, did not walk but ran, outwitting the wind, hurrying to stanch the tears that fell unceasingly as though some great artery of grief had been severed and all the sorrow in the world gushed from her mother's eyes.

Sometimes, in that quiet room, with the analyst's breath soft and even in the silence, she was spirited back to the long, low barrack buildings of the camp, to the mud-clogged roads that connected the hovels of misery to each other, linking them into a world in miniature, an organized community of suffering. She saw again the sad blue smoke that floated endlessly between the buildings and the blazing orange torch of fire that soared upward from the crematorium.

"What are you thinking?" The analyst's voice would be gentle, yet insistent, like the soft but constant wind that tosses about the brittle detritus of autumn—the fallen leaves and ancient flakes of bark that carpet the forest floor. Eleanor Berenson's trained voice breathed hard against the fragile barricade of denial and defense that had shielded the woman Bette Abramson from the lost world of the barefoot child Batya, whose mother had died of grief and hunger, surrendering her life to endless night, and whose father had lived in terror long after the shadows had passed.

It was not of her father that Bette had spoken during that day's session but of a dream in which Ina appeared, not as her cousin but as her child, dressed in baby-doll pajamas of the sort Bette's daughter wore. The child, Ina, in the dream danced and sang, sat on her haunches and begged for bread, giggled wildly until the laughter became tears and the small girl curled up and wept, then crawled about the room searching for something. Bette, a grown-up Bette with an infant in her arms, followed after her, speaking in Polish, firmly but imploringly, as one speaks to a child who will be neither understood nor consoled.

"What were you saying?" the analyst asked.

"I don't know. I was speaking a language I no longer understand." She laughed uneasily and waited for the doctor to laugh too, or to offer a comment, to pierce the confusion with a sharp and knowing insight.

But Eleanor Berenson said nothing, only lit another cigarette. Seconds later the delicate chime of her small clock signaled the end of the hour, and Bette Abramson left the quiet, dimly lit room and stood in the street, allowing the soft rain to moisten her dark hair.

Bette decided to walk to Mount Lebanon. The rain was a light one, and the hospital was not far away. Bette liked to walk, and she wanted to stop at the small patisserie where she and Ina occasionally went for eclairs or charlotte russes. They would walk down Seventy-fourth Street, licking the swirling whipped-cream colonnade that topped the crown-shaped pastry, not talking, totally absorbed in enjoying the frothy sweetness that swirled about their tongues. Occasionally passersby would turn to look at the tall, elegantly dressed, dark-haired

women who ate their treat with the delighted concentration
of schoolgirls.

Their husbands indulged Bette and Ina in their passion for
sweets. At a meal's end, in the small restaurants where the two
couples often shared Saturday night dinners, Ray and Richard
would lean back in their chairs, content with their pipes and
coffees, while Ina and Bette attacked huge pastries, soft and
thick with delicate creams, painted lavishly with chocolate
brushes. The men watched their wives with understanding,
with stoic wisdom. They knew that it was not the attractive
women who bought their groceries at Gristede's and their
clothing at Saks who ate the quivering mounds of cake, but
rather the small starved girls their wives had been—the children with shrunken bellies who had slept on hardwood bunks
and wept with hunger through endless, fear-filled nights. The
men understood but said nothing. They were gentle and careful and would not trespass in a world that was not their own.

Ina would want a charlotte russe today, Bette guessed, and
she walked quickly to the small bakery. She bought the
pastry, and as she paid for it, she was gripped by a sudden
fear. Mattie, the baby, had a cold, and often his colds developed into croup. The older children should be home from
school soon. Had they arrived safely? There had been a series
of bus accidents recently. Her heart beat faster, and damp
beads of terror erupted beneath her arms. The sweat stained
her pale green dress the color of dark grass. She had to find a
phone. Eleanor Berenson's remembered voice, calm and dis-
passionate, echoed in her thoughts: "When you feel that way,
it makes no difference that you recognize the fear as irrational.
You must subdue it, and if the only way to do that is to call
home, do just that. Don't think about the housekeeper's annoyance or the children's irritation. Just do what makes you
feel comfortable."

Bette felt in her pocket for change, her breath coming
shorter. A month ago, a child around the corner had been
killed crossing the street. In a neighboring house a small boy

had gone to sleep on a summer evening and never awakened again. A teenaged girl had gone for a walk and disappeared. Terrible, the neighbors said. Extraordinary. Mysterious. Bette nodded in assent, but she did not agree with them. She found it extraordinary and mysterious that her son and daughter returned from school happy and healthy each day and that her youngest, her baby Mattie, slept peacefully in his crib, a smile curling his rosy lips. The good, the normal, was extraordinary to her. It was tragedy and terror that she anticipated, sensing them so sharply that her sweat glands excreted her certainty of disaster and her breath struggled through the asphyxiating pressure of heartache.

She called home from a phone booth in a drugstore. Her son answered the phone on the first ring. The baby was sleeping. His sister was practicing her piano lesson. He himself was going out to play kickball. Not in the street, he added, as though reading his mother's thoughts. Like his father, he understood her, and when he was not annoyed, he strove to reassure her. He had taken a class on the Holocaust in Hebrew school and came home, his eyes wide with questions. Had it really happened? Had it been that terrible? "Yes," she replied, and was relieved that he did not press her for specific incidents. Her memories were fragmented and wafted in and out of her mind.

When in the night he screamed in his sleep: "Mama—I want my Mama . . ." she rushed to him, remembering the night she too had called out but no mother had come. It had been her Aunt Shaindel whose arms encircled her and whose sharp, hissing voice had whipped her into silence. "Sha, girl, or you'll go the way she went."

Bette loved her Aunt Shaindel, that fierce and angry woman who had saved her life, and she hated her because she was alive and Bette's own mother was dead. She longed for Peshi, whose tears had flowed like the spring rain and cursed her because she had died and deserted the child who cried in the night: "Mama—I want my Mama . . ."

"Mom," her son said, "ask Aunt Ina if they can come up

this weekend. I want to show Rachel my backflips." He admired his cousin Rachel and relished her admiration in turn. Like their mothers, the American cousins shared their childhoods and whispered sometimes about the mysterious dark years when their mothers had been children together.

"I'll ask," she said, and listened for his breezy good-bye, the sharp click of the phone. Relief settled on her, leaving her so limp and fatigued that she took a cab the rest of the way although the rain had stopped.

Visiting hours were at their peak at Mount Lebanon, and Bette, clutching her white bakery box, stood in an elevator crowded with men and women who carried cornucopias of gay spring flowers, brightly wrapped gift boxes from which gently colored pajamas and negligees would tumble forth, gold-sheeted thick tomes from Brentano's, and strangely shaped parcels from Creative Playthings. A tall black man in a cocoa-colored leisure suit stood next to her, staring down at his brown plaid Saks Fifth Avenue box.

A tired-looking, small woman stood in a corner of the elevator holding a worn shopping bag. It was, Bette knew without looking, full of newly washed and ironed pajamas and underclothing. She would carry the same bag home, packed with similar garments flecked with small stains of mucus and blood, smelling fetidly of sweat and vomit. Small lines gathered at the corners of her watery eyes, and her shoulders drooped with the fatigue of those who rush between the worlds of the well and the sick, the dying and the living. Other passengers in the elevator edged away from her and held their own packages aloft, as though their gifts of whim and luxury might be sullied by her burden of the faded garments for the listless limbs of the very ill. They looked away when she exited from the elevator on the fifth floor, where the hallway sign read: "Visitors limited to the immediate family only."

Bette and the tall black man got off the elevator together and smiled companionably at each other as they walked down opposite ends of the corridor. He whistled softly, and Bette wondered if the sweet sound was a signal to his wife. Richard whistled the opening bars of the overture to *Oklahoma* as he came up the walk each evening. She hummed it now, as always intrigued by the innocence of American music. She wished Richard was beside her at that moment and thought that perhaps she would call him from Ina's room and they would meet for dinner in the city. The housekeeper would not mind staying an extra few hours, and her anxiety about the children was allayed. Perhaps, after all, she was getting better—an expression Eleanor Berenson found "inappropriate." "Not better—stronger," the analyst would say reprovingly. It occurred to Bette that although Eleanor Berenson surely knew that Ina was in the hospital, she had not asked about her. But then she was careful to avoid talking about the cousins to each other and had hesitated before agreeing to take Ina on as a patient sometime after Bette had begun her analysis.

"Bette!" Ina was sitting up in bed, a massive printout sheet covering her lap. Her hair was swept neatly back in a smooth coil and tied with a ribbon that matched her delicate yellow negligee. But her eyes burned too brightly, and her face was pale. When Bette bent to kiss her, she drew her hand protectively about her breast, and her fingers trembled.

"Are you all right?" Bette asked, but she knew the answer before Ina spoke and was certain that she was right.

There were siblings, Bette knew, possessed of instinctive and accurate knowledge of each other. Her Stamford neighbor had wakened one night, knowing with harsh certainty that her sister in California was deathly ill. She did not telephone but journeyed at once to San Diego, arriving only moments before her young sister underwent surgery for a ruptured appendix. Bette had always felt that she and Ina had such built-in perception of each other. Ina had known, without being told, when Bette's father died, and on a distant winter night when Jeddy was taken ill, suddenly and dangerously, Bette had wakened Richard, and they had traveled to New York because Bette knew that Ina needed her. Just as she knew now, sitting beside her cousin's hospital bed, that

Ina was not all right and that the "simple" procedures for which her cousin had entered the hospital had somehow become quite complicated.

"What's happened?" Bette asked.

"Let's eat first," Ina said, opening the pastry box. "This is the first solid food I've seen all day. No breakfast before the surgery. No lunch until after I'd recovered from the anesthesia. They make an awfully big deal out of Novocain."

Bette licked the cream topping of her charlotte russe. "Listen, there are three of these," she said. "What do we do with the extra?"

"Maybe my roommate wants it," Ina said. "Miriam," she called.

The screen was drawn around the bed, although Ina could not remember when that had been done. She herself had sat quietly after her mother left, thinking of what Shirley Cherne had told her. Where had she been, she wondered, while that struggling bit of life, that mouse of an embryo, had been aborted from her mother's womb? Probably with her Aunt Peshi and Bette. There was a game they played in the barracks. The small girls marched their fingers up Peshi's thin arm, reached her shoulder, giggled, and let their fingers tumble down. What had they called that game? Oh, yes, Moses goes up the mountain, Moses goes down the mountain. Such an odd mountain, her Aunt Peshi's shoulder had been, crowned with its knobs of bone shining bluely through the thinnest veil of skin. The game must have been Peshi's invention because she had never heard of it before or since the war. It had been a game invented to amuse children trapped in a land of death, in a world where play had ceased and both laughter and tears were forbidden.

"Moses goes up the mountain," she had perhaps called gleefully, while not far away her mother writhed, rags clogging her mouth as her womb was emptied of a life that would never be lived. "Moses goes down the mountain." Her fingers and Bette's had raced each other, and very often she had won.

Lost in that rare memory, Ina had fallen asleep, and when

she awakened, she reached at once for her work. She did not want to think of her mother on the barracks floor, of herself on the operating table, of the mute, moist appeal in Ray's eyes, and of the tiny baby that struggled for life in the ingenious plastic respirator. She did not want to think of that tiny clump of tissue, that odd, unwelcome growth that had insinuated itself upon her flesh and had now been excised. A pathologist was studying it now, peering at it through a high-powered microscope, searching diligently for deadly cells, for threatening hints. No, she would not think about it. She riveted her mind to the numbered columns before her, forcing her professional judgment to control her rambling thoughts. The program was good, innovative, and she worked on it with such concentrated urgency that she had not noticed the screen being replaced or Miriam slipping from the room.

"Maybe the nurse will want the other charlotte russe," Ina said.

Nurse Li was passing the door, and Ina called to her.

"Are you in pain, Mrs. Feldman?" The Chinese woman wore a bright green cardigan over her white uniform, and her long ringless fingers fleshed expertly across Ina's dressing, smoothing down a loose strip of tape.

"No, I'm fine, but my cousin brought me an extra pastry, and we thought perhaps you might like it."

The nurse laughed. "I'm sorry. I'm on a diet."

"Oh, dear. And Mrs. Gottlieb isn't here."

"She's in the nursery, checking on the baby."

"He's all right, isn't he?"

"Yes." But her voice was hesitant, troubled. "Pretty much the same. But the jaundice doesn't seem to be responding to lamp treatment. Still, that sometimes happens. It's always so unpredictable with these preemies."

"Yes. Of course." Ina thought of the baby's tiny fingers clutching so earnestly at the blanket. How perfectly the tiny nails were formed, the pink flesh glowing beneath the translucent ungulae. Surely such infinitesimal perfection must survive, endure.

"He'll be all right." Her voice was insistent, and her heart beat faster.

It had grown strangely important to her that Miriam's baby emerge from the isolette ruddy and kicking—as Jeddy had been in early infancy when Ina laughed into his own chortling, laughing small face. Why did she feel so involved in the progress of this baby born to a couple she had known for only a day? Every Jewish baby born is a slap in Hitler's face, her mother had said, and the Gottlieb baby was the last seed of life for a family lost in the cinders and ashes of the war some called Hitler's war. Perhaps her mother's words had affected her, but then Ina had sought the baby out long hours before her mother's visit. In the artificial brightness of a hospital night, she had stood in the corridor and watched through the nursery window as Miriam Gottlieb's baby stirred in uneasy sleep. It was not only her mother's words, Ina thought. It was something else—something she felt but did not understand. She felt a brief irrational anger against the Gottliebs for mingling their sorrow and uncertainty with her own.

"But if you want to give the cake away, there's a patient down the hall who just told me she's been craving something sweet like that," Nurse Li added.

"Yes. Of course." Bette handed the nurse the pastry box, smiled, and licked at the golden crumbs that clustered at the corner of her mouth. But when the nurse had passed off, moving silently down the corridor in her crepe-soled white oxfords, the white pastry box extended before her like an appendage to her white uniform, she turned to Ina and her tone was knowing. "Now, what's the matter?"

"Different things. It's crazy, but I'm edgy about the final pathology report, and then my mother was here today."

"Aunt Shirley was here? At the beginning of the season? She must be mellowing—taking time out to visit you when fabric shipments are coming in."

"She wasn't motivated purely by worry about my welfare. Oh, that's not fair, maybe she was. I don't know. I never know with her. I think she came because somehow she guessed

I was pregnant. She had lunch with Ray, and he told her that I was and that we were considering an abortion."

"I thought you were pretty well decided." Bette kept her voice neutral. She would wait until she knew what Ina wanted her to say. It was her job to support her cousin. Always, they had supported each other.

"I thought so, too. But Ray wants the baby. He says, of course, that it's my decision, but he wants to have it."

"Why?"

"I don't really know. He says that there isn't any real reason not to have it—we have the money, the personal resources. I keep getting the feeling that there's more to it than that— something he hasn't told me. I don't know. We'll talk some more tonight."

"And your mother? What did she say?"

"She told me something I'd never known—never guessed. It's funny. You think you know everything. Could anything worse have happened? And then suddenly, you're holding a new secret. Something you didn't know before and that you don't want to know, but it's yours, and you'll remember it always."

"That happens," Bette said. She looked out the window. There were many things, too many, newly revealed, that she would remember always.

"My mother had an abortion in the camp. Did you know?"

"No," Bette replied slowly. "But I knew, I sensed, that something terrible had happened to her—that is, something terrible beyond what we knew, what we could perceive." There were gradations of horror. There were secrets unshared, mysteries unsolved. Her voice was monotonous, dulled. It was in such tones, insulated by vacuity, that the cousins spoke of those years.

"Yes. We were lucky to be children, I suppose. Think of all we couldn't understand, didn't even have to try to understand." Ina laughed harshly.

Her mother, though, had not been hidden in the fortress of childhood, protected by the uncaring innocence of the very young. "Up the mountain, down the mountain," the children had called, as men and women writhed in pain and pale skeletons were pulled from windowless, noxious rooms. Had Peshi laughed as they played? Had her flesh trembled beneath the light touch of their tiny fingers through which fragile bone poked?

"I thought later," Bette said, still in that toneless voice, "when I could sort things out, that maybe something had happened with that guard. That tall woman who seemed to be always near us—the one who thought Shaindel was some kind of a nurse. I thought—years later, of course—that maybe she had forced her into some sort of lesbian relationship. I guess I thought that because once I saw a guard with Halina's mother, grabbing at her breasts, kissing her. It was the guard with the blonde hair that she wore in strips over her ears. Do you remember her?" Bette's voice trembled, and her hands flew to her eyes as though she would shield herself once again from the sight of her small friend's mother being forced to submit to the sexual advances of a woman who twisted her hair into whips and carried a truncheon.

"I remember very little," Ina said. "Sometimes I don't think I remember anything at all. And then suddenly something comes rushing back. Like today I remembered that game we played. Moses goes up the mountain—Moses goes down the mountain."

"And I don't remember that," Bette said. She frowned. Selective memory, Dr. Berenson called it. You remember what you can bear to bring to mind. Could she bear the memories of horror that engulfed her through sleepless nights more easily than the memory of a children's game? She set the thought aside like a tattered garment she would mend when she had the time. "So it was an abortion," she said thoughtfully. "I knew there was something because she changed so much, Aunt Shaindel. Suddenly it seemed as though all her warmth was gone, all the life drained out of her. Something had to have happened—something more than the ordinary horror of it all. I remember being suddenly afraid of her."

"I thought it was because of Yedidiah," Ina said softly. "Poor Mama. First Yedidiah. Then the baby."

"Not a baby, really," Bette said. "It was so early in the pregnancy. Only a few weeks." At the same stage of development, it occurred to her suddenly, as the life that clung now to Ina's womb. Only a few weeks into gestation. Would Shaindel's grandchild, then, be aborted as her child had been? Bette shivered, fumbled for a Kleenex.

"She called it her baby. She saw it. She said that it moved, but they told her—the doctor and the other women—that it was her imagination. She saw it move."

Bette said nothing. She stared out the window at the trees along the park, newly crowned with tender young leaves that glittered emerald-green where the raindrops had bathed them. When she spoke, her voice was so soft that Ina strained to hear her.

"Do you remember how after the war, when we were in Italy, the women in that DP camp seemed to become pregnant so quickly? I couldn't stand to look at them. Their eyes were still sunken into their faces. Their skin was like ours— the color of death. Their hands twitched. Some of them cried. All the time. But they didn't care. In those shrunken, skinny bodies they were carrying new life. I couldn't understand how they could bring babies into the world after all they had seen and suffered. I didn't even want to pick a flower then. If I touched it, I thought, it would die. How could I go near anything living? I used to dream about Death, a person. He was a man—so handsome—wearing an SS uniform, and he danced out at me from behind my mother's skirts. He was so handsome that I wanted him for my partner always. After all, whom did I know better than Death?" Bette's hands dropped to her lap, clasped in the manner of obedient small girls who speak only when they are spoken to.

"But you got over that years ago. We both did. We came to America. You met Richard. You had children." Ina's voice was harsh. It was dangerous to think back and remember; it was far safer to pretend that they were ordinary American women whose very faint accents lent their speech a certain charm.

"I didn't want the children," Bette said flatly. "When I was pregnant with Lonnie, I lay awake wishing that I would miscarry, wishing that they had sterilized me too. When I began bleeding when I carried Patty, I was glad. I didn't want to bring a child into such a world. I had the children for Richard. I didn't want them. I didn't think they could survive. I felt, I knew—something terrible would happen to them. It was different only with the baby, with Mattie. He was the only one I was ready for. I don't know if you understand that."

"Something to do with your analysis—with Dr. Berenson?"

"That, of course. But it was my father's death that triggered it. We went to clear out the apartment after he died. I know that you and Ray went to take care of the kitchen. I don't have to ask you what you found there. I don't want to know. But did you go into the bedroom?"

"No."

"My father lived those last years as though he were waiting for a knock at the door. His clothes weren't in the bureau but in suitcases—five of them, all packed, complete with Kleenex and packets of powdered milk and sugar. Clothing for all seasons with money sewn into the linings of jackets and the hems of his underwear. Dollars. Swiss francs. Pictures of me and the children hidden in shirt pockets. Iron pills. I guess he remembered how much you had to bribe a guard to get some iron pills. Shaindel used to get them for us. Horrible orange capsules."

"Oh, Bette, I didn't know." Ina reached out to touch her cousin's hand. She remembered the stink of decay that leaked from the dead man's refrigerator when they opened it.

"Who would eat such garbage?" Ray had asked, and she had not answered, although a reply trembled in her mind: "Anyone who was hungry enough would eat such garbage. I have eaten that and worse. In the end we filled our stomachs with dirt which was, they told us, safer than grass. Once, a dying woman vomited, and someone picked clots of undigested food from the puke that lay on the floor and swallowed them so quickly we saw her throat move. And when you are thirsty enough, you drink urine; and when you are hungry enough, you eat garbage. When you are frightened enough, you save every scrap." Her uncle's hoarding had shocked Ina, but it had not surprised her. She had not explained it to Ray. It was her secret, hers and Bette's, hidden always on the dark side of their souls.

"And one very strange thing," Bette continued. "He had no pajamas. When he went into the hospital, I went to the apartment to bring him pajamas, and there weren't any—I bought some new ones, and I asked him what he slept in. 'In my clothes,' he said. 'It is always better to be fully dressed and ready when they come.' You see, he had gone mad. He had only enough reason left, after the war, to raise me, to get me married off and settled into a normal life, and then he let himself go insane. It was easier than coping with what was supposed to be normal. And I didn't know it. He came to visit and played with the children and had dinner and told me that Richard was too thin and I should put in another bathroom, and he helped build the patio at the pool and wondered why your parents didn't invite him more often—all that time he was crazy. He went home and slept in his clothing surrounded by packed suitcases. And he grabbed food from a refrigerator stuffed with garbage and went to international currency exchanges and bought francs and rubles and kroner and sewed them into his underwear. This time he was going to be ready. How many times did I hear him say that my mother would have been alive if only he had currency or jewels to bribe the guards? He looked normal, he passed for normal, but Ina, he was crazy. Emotional cancer. Terminal. After that I would look in the mirror and think: I look normal, I pass for normal, but I am a little crazy too, and I will get crazier unless I do something. I cannot live in terror every time a child misses the school bus. I cannot go on wishing my children dead because I live in fear of their lives. That's when I began seeing Eleanor Berenson. I started analysis because I was scared that

I too would begin to sleep in my clothing and end up hoarding sugar cubes." She sat back, her face pale with exhaustion, her arms limp about the arms of the chair.

"But Mattie—the baby?" Ina asked.

Mattie was eighteen months old now—eight years younger than Patty, just as the baby that Ina would bear (*if, if* she allowed her pregnancy to come to term) would be eight years younger than Jeddy. Clusters of golden curls clung to Mattie's rosy pink scalp. His eyes were flashing sparks of blue in his bright chubby face, and he was fond of seizing the faces of visitors between his pudgy palms and kissing them wetly on the cheeks, gurgling softly with laughter. He was, Ray had said, and Ina agreed, the happiest baby ever born.

"Mattie I wanted. When I decided to become pregnant again, I was ready for life—ready to live it myself and to give it to a child. It took a long time—a lot of hours—years of them —and I can't explain how it happened—you know, but—but I was ready. Mattie is a gift, a bonus. Of course I still have worries about him, too—anxiety attacks I suppose is the technical term. But I don't live always at the edge of a cliff and pretend to others that I am at home in a peaceful valley."

Bette glanced at her watch and then at the phone, but she made no move toward it. She would go home after all—not because of fear but because she wanted to. Mattie was marvelous at bath time, funny and cuddly, and she wanted to hear Richard march up the walk singing from *Oklahoma*. She would go home. She was so tired. She had, perhaps, talked too much that day.

"My mother said something funny today," Ina said dreamily. "She said every newborn Jewish child was a slap in Hitler's face."

Bette thought for a moment, and when she spoke, her voice was quiet.

"I can understand that. I think now that was what all the pregnancies in the DP camps were about. They were saying something, those half-starved, half-alive couples who had buried children or seen them burned and buried. Maybe they

were saying: 'We survived. We're here. We're going to stay
and be fruitful and multiply, and we spit in the face of the
murderer and show him our children, newborn and laughing.'
I read somewhere that there were so many pregnancies at the
transit camps the British set up in Cyprus and at Athlit for
the illegal immigrants that Hadassah Hospital had to send over
teams of nurse-midwives. I suppose that when I had Mattie
it was a sort of declaration of life for me—and a slap in the
face for them. I don't think it's such an odd thing for your
mother to say or think."

"Maybe not," Ina said tiredly.

Her hands rested on her stomach, and the ache in her breast
had become a dull throb. She touched it and was again surprised at the size of the bandage. Just a small fibroma, they
had said. A small incision. Why, then, was the dressing so
large and bulky? She felt a shiver of fear and sought again to
calm herself. She was trained in reasonableness, in the construct of orderly thought. She would not panic. If they had
found anything, they would have told her. Isaacs was a bastard, but he was straight—he would not take the trouble to be
dishonest.

"Ina, did you ever have feelings like that?" Bette asked.
A note of fear sang through the question. She wanted reassurance. She wanted to know that others felt as she did, that Ina,
her cousin, trembled with the same cold fear.

"I didn't let myself," Ina said. "I don't let myself now. I'm
not afraid. I keep too busy."

She had, she knew, worked all that out very early. Activity
was the answer, achievement the panacea. She ran from meeting to meeting. She concentrated on new systems designs,
new contracts. She dashed from a recital at Rachel's school to
a meeting of the tenants' council. She left herself little time
to think and remember. The web of fear, of nameless terror,
encroached when she was not on the move. Dreams came only
in the emptiness and inactivity of the night. No. Not dreams.
*The dream.* Remembering it, she felt light-headed, nauseous,
and thought suddenly of confiding the dream to Bette. Per-

haps her cousin held a clue. Perhaps Bette could remember
what she had forced herself to forget; there must be an
explanation for those advancing soldiers who ejaculated pellets
of death from slit-mouthed penises.

Ina thought of the last time they had lunched with their
childhood friend Halina (Helene Kramer now) in a smart
Manhattan restaurant. Halina had had one drink too many.
Her eyes brimmed. Blotches of red bled beneath her cheeks.
She had told them how a guard had pulled her into the
shadows of a storeroom once and stuffed his penis into her
mouth. She had bitten down on it, gagged against the slimy
taste of his sperm. He had smacked her hard and hurried
away, and she had spat out the bloodied sliver of skin. She
had feared for her life then and skulked away when she saw
him, but he had ignored her, and it occurred to her, years
later, that he too had been frightened.

"I was eight years old," tweed-jacketed Helene had said.
Her red-tipped fingers clutched the martini glass. "God help
me, I was eight years old, and his scum was in my mouth."

She had spat into the ashtray on the table, and the slender
waiter who watched them had stared in amazement.

Perhaps Bette knew of some buried secret, Ina thought.

The phone rang then. It was her office, and she welcomed
the call, the questions that could be so easily and definitively
answered.

"Send that program on to the client for approval. I think
we'll have to buy some terminal time for that project. I'll take
care of that when I get back. I'm feeling fine. Really. It was
just a routine procedure. Thanks for keeping on top of
everything."

She hung up and glanced at her cousin. The question would
remain unasked. It was not Bette's problem. It was her own.

"See," she said wryly. "The busy life. No time to think, no
time to brood."

"Well, I'd better get going if I'm going to catch the train,"
Bette said. She looked hard at her cousin, but Ina turned away.
Bette combed her hair swiftly and applied fresh lipstick.

"Thanks for the charlotte russe," Ina said.

"Oh, I almost forgot. I have a new snapshot of Mattie."

Bette fumbled in her purse and came up with a color print that showed the golden-haired child laughing exuberantly and hugging an enormous stuffed elephant.

"That's great. Thanks."

Bette bent to kiss her.

"Not to worry," she said softly, "not to worry."

"No, I won't," Ina promised. She watched Bette walk from the room. Her cousin moved with a graceful, swaying gait, and although she was a tall woman, she held her head very straight—the remembered posture, perhaps, of distant days when a strong, determined stride might determine life or death.

The pain in Ina's breast grew sharper, and she clenched her fist against it and saw that she was still clutching Mattie's picture. What if I have cancer? she thought wildly, bringing the word to the fore from the darkness in which it had lurked. What if I die and leave behind me a beautiful little baby like this one? She forced herself to smile at the thought and set the snapshot down amid her bedside clutter.

The pain gripped her again, and she took the tiny gleaming red pill that Nurse Li had left her, gulped it down with water, and took up the printout sheet. If she kept her mind on it, she could finish that afternoon. She set her face in lines of stern concentration and reached for the notebook and pen that lay next to the picture of the joyous baby, grandson to her Aunt Peshi who had died because she was too exhausted to live, and to her uncle who had lived lost in the shadows of fear and the threat of dark and nameless danger.

Minutes after Bette left, Miriam Gottlieb returned to the room. She walked very slowly and was followed by an elderly couple who watched her carefully, as parents watch a small child who has only just begun to walk and may stumble and fall. The woman's hair was a yellowing gray of the same shade as her husband's, and they were both thin and slightly bent as though they had spent so many years crouching tensely over work tables that their posture had become a habit that could not be broken. Even their clothing was similar. He wore a tan summer suit worn lustrous by many washings, and her simple cotton dress was of a faded brown cotton, although its white collar and cuffs were the color of new snow and ironed to a starched crispness. They were, of course, the lonely survivors, Ben's parents, of whom Miriam had spoken. The sickly new-born was their grandson, the first root of a new family—it was he who would end their aloneness and make of them a family again, with a past and a future. The couple looked, Ina thought, like brother and sister, twin heirs to familial melancholy and tragedy. Their thin shoulders sloped beneath the burden of a long sorrow, and they moved slowly, reluctantly, as though no path, however promising, would lead them to anything but sadness and disappointment.

"Miriam, I'm glad to see you out of bed," Ina said, forcing a cheer she did not feel into her voice.

"Yes. We went to see the baby. Let me introduce you to Ben's parents—Mama, Papa, this is my roommate, Ina Feldman."

"You are also a new mother?" Mrs. Gottlieb asked.

"No," Ina said. "I had to have some minor breast surgery and perhaps another small procedure." *Procedure*, she decided, was a wonderful, all-encompassing word.

"How is the baby?" she asked.

"I think about the same. But we're a little concerned because the jaundice doesn't seem to be responding to the sunlamp."

"That often takes time," Ina said reassuringly, but her own words jarred her. She had no right to offer such a reassurance. She knew nothing about premature infants and jaundice. But she did know that such verbal placebos were necessary, even essential, in white-walled rooms furnished with high beds on wheels. "Don't worry." "Everything will be all right." "These things take time." What other comfort did people have to offer each other when children lay ill and dying and hospital windows were wet with the tears of a swift spring rain? She was relieved when her friend Ruthie burst into the room and the small, pale Gottliebs withdrew, smiling apologetically.

They sat at Miriam's bedside and looked sadly and appreciatively at the gifts and cards sent to mark the birth of the
struggling newborn.

Ruthie wore a gold jumpsuit that matched her wild golden
hair, which spiraled upward in ringlets dampened by the rain.
Long strings of coral beads dangled from her small, wonderfully shaped ears, and bracelets of turquoise and silver shimmered at her wrists. She carried a bright red ceramic pot in
which masses of African violets nestled, and an enormous
leather tote bag crammed with magazines and manuscripts,
drawing pens and pads, cellophane envelopes of dried fruits
and nuts. When Ruthie moved, the bag rustled intriguingly,
mysteriously.

"What a day." She sank into the visitor's chair, breathless
and bright-eyed. "I would have been here earlier, but Jerry
Wilder was in New York between planes, and he spent a
couple of hours at my place."

Ina smiled. Ruthie had brought the subtle scent of recent sex
into the hospital room. Her eyes still radiated the afternoon's
consuming intimacy; her rose-gold skin glowed with the
rough sheen of her lover's touch, the polish of his caress.
Ruthie would not see Jerry Wilder (of whom Ina had heard
much, as she had heard a great deal about Ruthie's other
lovers) again for weeks or perhaps for months. She might
never hear from him again in fact. But she did not care, or if
she cared, it would not obsess her, become the focus of her
feelings. Only her own life and her own work were important
enough to occupy Ruthie's thoughts and feelings. Lovers, her
husband, the house she had abandoned, the children she had
never had, were peripheral to her being. If Ruthie found herself pregnant, she would not even view it as a dilemma requir-
ing a decision. She would check into the abortion clinic at the
Women's Center, assure all the women in the waiting room
and her ward that they were doing absolutely the right thing.

While she waited, she would make pen-and-ink sketches of
a boy squirrel washing a floor while a girl squirrel built a
scarecrow. As she waited for the doctor, she would ask

disingenuous questions and offer the nurses advice on how the ward could be managed more efficiently. And she would be back at her easel the next day, at work in the whitewashed studio where plants flourished against every wall and filled every corner, as indifferent to the experience as she might be indifferent to the excision of an ingrown toenail, an impacted wisdom tooth.

"Biology is not destiny," she once told the members of their consciousness-raising group angrily, defiantly.

"But without biology there would be no human destiny," a young woman who taught philosophy at Hunter College argued logically.

"Why is all human destiny dependent on the sacrifice of women?" Ruthie had retorted, and the argument had circled back, inevitably, to changing sex roles, to more shared responsibilities in marriage, to the feasibility of contracts defining household roles. Ina grew bored and irritable during such discussions.

She wondered, then, what she was doing there. What common forum did she have with these women? She had drifted into the group, drawn there by other friends and acquaintances who were involved in the women's movement. She was naturally drawn to causes that spoke of "liberating," of "fighting oppression." She knew what it meant to be oppressed and then to be liberated, although her memory of the transition from one state to the other was vaguely confused with being spoon-fed snowy grains of semolina and dressed in a white hospital gown that smelled strongly of bleach. Clean clothes meant freedom, and enough food and soft voices and gentle hands signified liberation. The very words stirred her and reminded her.

She had carried a banner when Martin Luther King, Jr., marched on Washington, and later she had read somewhere that concentration camp survivors, in disproportionate numbers, had participated in that march. It did not surprise her.

Deep within her there lurked a kernel of suspicion (a kernel planted by the child she had been—the small bony girl covered

with rags) that they were slaves in the camp because they
were women. She had, she remembered, been startled to
learn that men too were enslaved and imprisoned (although
Yedidiah had died at her side and although her mother told
her that her father too lived behind barbed wire). She knew
now that her suspicion was foolish—ridiculous. They had been
imprisoned because they were Jews, but still the memory of
that enslaved community of women haunted her; it had perhaps impelled her to join this consciousness-raising group
which argued against any enslavement of women—economic
or emotional. She had listened attentively as other women discussed their relationships with their mothers, but she did not
participate. She, after all, had two mothers—Shaindel Czernowitz and Shirley Cherne, and neither of them did she understand. But after a few months the group bored her, and she
listened without involvement to the discussion of problems
that were irrelevant to her history and to her marriage. She
and Ray had, as a matter of course, without contract or discussion, divided the chores of parenting. She had said as much
to Ruthie, who laughed harshly.

"Your liberation rests on Carmen," she had said. "If you
couldn't pay someone to do it, you and Ray would be arguing
about who cleaned the toilets and washed the floors."

Ina had not answered. It was impossible to win an argument
with someone who belligerently proclaimed certainty, recti-
tude. Perhaps that was why she had asked Ruthie to visit the
hospital that afternoon. She had needed an injection of Ruthie's
unswerving conviction. She wanted Ruthie to tell her bluntly
and urgently that abortion was not even her choice—it was her
duty as a feminist and a humanitarian. Ruthie did not even
believe in zero population growth. Not even that, she argued,
until the orphanages of Asia were emptied and no child in the
world suffered malnutrition.

"Where is Jerry off to?" Ina asked.

Ruthie's friend, she knew, worked for an international
health organization. He traveled widely, and Ina, who loved
the excitement of airports, the sweet sounds of languages she

did not understand, the swirl of unfamiliar landscapes, envied him. They had taken a two-week trip to the Caribbean with the children last summer, and Ray had talked of a vacation in Greece and Israel. But a new baby would mean the long postponement of such vacations. A new baby. It was the first time she had formulated the phrase, and she felt a rush of sadness, a sinking premonition of defeat. If Bette were beside her, she surely would have cried, releasing bittersweet tears for which Bette would require no explanation. But Ruthie was impatient with tears. She saw them as women's ancient weapons, symbols of repressed anger, impotence. Several times she had slammed out of a room when another woman had wept, and only when the group met at her apartment were tissues unavailable. Everyone else kept them as readily at hand as the steaming coffee, the dry white wine, the loosely rolled joints that kept their talk surging and flowing.

"He's going to the Middle East," Ruthie replied. "A couple of weeks in Syria and Jordan, then Egypt and Israel."

"I wish I had known. I would have given him the addresses of my cousins in Israel," Ina said, but she was glad, after all, that she had not known. What right had she to foist off the unknown lover of a friend on cousins whom she barely remembered although they wrote to each other faithfully and in detail at each Jewish New Year?

Her cousins were the children of her father's brother, who had himself died at Belsen but who had made his children, only a few years older than Ina, promise that if they survived, they would go to Palestine. The brother, Avremel, had settled on a kibbutz high in the Galilee, and the sister, Chana, had graduated from the Hebrew University Medical School, married a fellow student, and lived in Jaffa. Avremel's eighteen-year-old son, named for his father, had died in the Yom Kippur War, and a year later Avremel's wife had given birth to twins. Chana's children had been too young for army service then. She had three daughters and sent Ray and Ina a new color photo of her family each year. In 1974 the picture showed her cradling an infant son. She had been past forty at the time of the birth but wrote with all the enthusiasm of a new mother of the baby's wondrous laugh, the pleasure of again having an infant in the house, of how easily she had been able to accommodate the child's needs to her thriving practice.

Ina thought often of her Israeli cousins' children, born in the aftermath of a war that had frightened them with its ancient threat, its dread, immediate danger. She knew that the twins, both boys, had been given life to sustain their parents against the loss of death. They were survival insurance, witnesses to endurance. An Israeli sociologist had told Ina that the birth rate in Israel had always risen dramatically after a war. Why not, Ina had thought, why not?

"Jerry wouldn't have had time to look them up," Ruthie said. "He's doing research on population growth—attitudes toward birth control, abortion."

"In Moslem countries?" Ina asked incredulously.

"Come on. He's not interested in official or religious policy but in individual attitudes and reactions. He's got a lot of different names."

Ruthie reached into her leather bag and plucked out a sketch pad and drawing pen. Deftly, with broad strokes, she sketched the stuffed panda that sat on Miriam Gottlieb's bedside table.

"How'd it go this morning?" she asked.

"All right, I suppose. Apparently the fibroma was a little bigger than they thought it would be. Not that anyone told me anything. Isaacs hasn't been down, and I haven't seen his resident either."

"I told you to go to a woman gynecologist." Ruthie put a baseball cap on the panda's head and drew in a pitcher's mound covered with flowers. She was having a good time with the flowers, some of which had faces, and she smiled as she worked.

"That's a lot of crap, Ruthie. You pick the best doctor available. It's sexist to choose a doctor because of sex." Ina was glad to argue something about which she held an opinion as definite and firm as Ruthie's own. Certainty was a delicious luxury.

"Oh, I don't know. I still think women doctors are more sensitive to other women. Especially for abortions."

"Ruthie!" Ina's eyes flashed angrily, and she nodded in the direction of Miriam's bed and was relieved that Miriam was on the phone and her in-laws were conferring sadly in a corner of the room. Clearly no one had heard Ruthie. Old Mrs. Gottlieb's eyes were red-rimmed as though she had begun her mourning, resigned to its inevitability.

"Sorry." Ruthie lowered her voice. "Actually, I thought of calling you. Jerry wanted to know whether Judaism had an official position on abortion. But I guess he'll get all the material he needs in Israel."

"I don't know that much about it," Ina replied. "I'm sure the official religious doctrine is definitely anti. But I think that it's history more than religion that forms the attitudes of most Jews."

"What do you mean?" Ruthie allowed a rose to grow out of her panda's mitt.

"I think in view of their history, a lot of Jews see abortion as genocide—whether consciously or unconsciously," Ina said slowly.

"You're joking." Ruthie's voice shivered with disbelief, and she looked at Ina as though she were seeing her for the first time. "Abortion is purely an individual decision—a woman's decision about her own body, her own life. It has nothing to do with history or nationalism."

"It does if you belong to an endangered species," Ina said. She thought of her mother's emaciated form spread across newspapers, watching in agony as a bloody cluster of cells was scraped from her body. That tiny embryo was not included among the six million and yet belonged in that dread count. That aborted bit of life had been a casualty of war and belonged within her own personal circle of loss. Death-eyed, they danced around her on sleepless nights—Yedidiah, her brother; Peshi, her aunt; her uncle; women who had hugged and fed her; faceless playmates who had scrambled about with her on the splintered barracks floor.

"Surely you don't believe that," Ruthie protested. Ruthie's world was divided neatly, dialectically, between the oppressors and the oppressed, the exploiters and the exploited, men and women. Religion was irrelevant to her. She scarcely remembered her own. She worshipped faithfully at the altar of individual freedom, free choice, maximized human potential. She did not recognize any "species" as being endangered because she saw only one "species," one large human family in which all children laughed with shared merriment at wide-eyed pandas who carried roses in outstretched baseball mitts.

"I don't know," Ina admitted. She looked at the flowers Ray had brought her and saw that a tiny bud, lost and unnoticed amid her yellow roses, had yawned gently open.

"You can't believe it. If you did, you wouldn't be having the abortion," Ruthie said. She kept her voice very low this time, but her eyes did not leave Ina's face.

"I'm not absolutely certain that I'm going to," Ina said, and she touched the new young flower. The petal was velvet-smooth against her skin.

"But Ina. That's wild. You were all set, all decided. You had it all thought out."

"I'm just not sure now," Ina said defensively. She had been wrong to tell Ruthie about the pregnancy, to ask her to visit. But then that had been before Ray had told her of the strength of his feelings; before her mother had come to visit wearing a lilac suit, her twisted fingers wreathed in rings glistening with the earth's dead and secret brilliance, and carrying with her her sad secret of lost and terrible years.

"But you know, Ruthie," Ina continued, "even leaving out the Jewish thing—there are other arguments to be made. We talked before in the group—you remember that night at Helen's place before Cynthia had the abortion—about genetic responsibility."

"We were all stoned that night."

"We still said it, and it was valid. If the only group practicing zero population growth—or no growth or even rigid birth control—is composed of people like us, we're going to end up with a large population of know-nothings and a very small group of competent, intellectually responsible people."

"That's racist!" Ruthie's voice was harsh, angry.

"Bullshit. That's reality. If the only people who fuck and reproduce are blonde and blue-eyed, you're going to end with a lot of blue-eyed blondes. If the only people who limit their reproduction are those who are enlightened and educated, the balance is obviously going to shift. It's not racist. It's common sense."

"The idea is to educate everyone," Ruthie said.

"Wonderful. But that's not something that's going to happen overnight. It's not going to happen in our generation or in Rachel's. So what do we do until then? Hedge our bets?"

Ina was tired. She was impatient with the argument. Ruthie peppered the air with feminist verities, universalist clichés. But it was Ina who would have to make a decision. It was within her womb that cell metastasized upon cell and a life slowly developed. It was she, not Ruthie, who would wake in the night either to an infant's desperate cry or to the wispy presence of sad, unborn small spirit—a lost child who might have been.

An orderly rolled a stainless steel cart into the room, looked at them, then at the number on the cart. He cursed briefly and bitterly in Spanish, shoved the cart ahead of him, and walked out. Miriam's phone rang, but it was a wrong number. The tall black model and her husband walked slowly down the hall, arm in arm, glancing idly through the open door of each room as though they were window shopping on Fifth Avenue. Nurse Li and her evening replacement paused at their beds, read the charts together, murmuring softly to each other.

Ruthie opened her pad to a fresh page, held her pen poised, but drew nothing. Ina felt subdued by the vagrant loneliness of the late afternoon. The lost hours of the vanishing day were scattered behind her like drifts of floating, irretrievable leaves. She waited in the bright but waning light for the first soft shadows of evening darkness. There was a cruelty to the late afternoon hours in early spring—a harshness to that first lengthening of daylight when the sun stayed stubbornly skyborne and it seemed that the sweet release of evening would never come.

"I should be going," Ruthie said. She closed her pad, replaced it in her bag, took out her makeup case, but did not open it.

"I'm sorry, Ruthie," Ina said. "I didn't mean to get into a hassle."

"That's all right." Ruthie's voice was tired. Her fingers toyed with an earth-colored lipstick. She plucked a dead petal from the clump of violets, and it dropped on the leg of her gold pantsuit in a clinging gentian tear. "You've got to watch the flowers carefully. Clip the dead ones. Jerry brought me a new curly spider plant. I'll be able to give you a cutting in a few weeks."

"Great."

"Ina—just think of yourself, of whatever you want." She stood, holding her leather bag, a new moist smile painted on her face, her eyes turned toward the window, toward the city that stretched out below them. She was in a rush now to be lost in its streets, to hurry toward rooms where talk soared in rainbow-colored clouds of affirmation, reassurance, and strong hands reached out to touch and sustain while soft voices breathed recognition, agreement. "I know." "I think so too." "Have you felt that? I've felt that." It was dangerous to be alone in the hours before evening, and her friends were waiting.

"I don't know," Ina said in answer, not looking at her friend, "there are times when everything you decide is both right and wrong—in different ways for different reasons."

"Maybe." Doubt was a defeat for Ruthie, but she acknowledged it.

The sketch of the panda lay on Ina's bed, and Ruthie carried it over to Miriam Gottlieb.

"I thought you might like this," Ruthie said, and Miriam

smiled when she saw it. Her finger traced the rose in the panda's mitt, and a new brightness gleamed in her eyes.

"Thank you. It's marvelous. I'm going to frame it and hang it in my baby's room." She held the drawing at arm's length as though seeing it already in a bright plaid frame beneath a glass across which strips of sunlight glided.

"My baby's a boy," she told Ruthie.

"Great," Ruthie said. She bent to add her initials to the drawing and smiled. "I'll be in touch, Ina. Take care of the violets."

She waved and hurried from the room.

"Will do. And thanks."

Ina moved the small pot of violets toward her and adjusted the flowers so that she could watch the petals of the newly opened bud. The phone rang, but she did not answer it, and it did not ring again. Her breast throbbed, and she found the pain strangely welcome. The painkiller had made her drowsy, and as she drifted toward sleep, she wondered if the dogwood tree across from their apartment house was in full bloom yet; she remembered how its blossoms grew in delicate sprays of blushing whiteness, the color of a newborn infant's untouched flesh.

It had been a mistake, Ray realized, as he stood on the corner of Central Park West and Seventy-fourth Street, waving to taxicabs that slowed imperceptibly then sped wildly to pass him by, to take the children to Dot's for dinner. His sister had promised him a quick meal, but inevitably there were interruptions. The children quarreled. Simon, the baby, choked on a piece of meat. Larry was called to the phone.

Ray had called Ina to tell her he would be late getting to the hospital, and she assured him that he had done the right thing. Rachel and Jeddy enjoyed their cousins, and being with the family would relieve the strain of her absence, the anxiety the children felt about her hospitalization. Ray did not tell her that the children had scarcely mentioned her. Rachel had been absorbed in trying on her tutu and whirling through

Dot's living room in the short, skirted bit of pink froth. Her legs were slender and marvelously curved, and she swayed and dipped in the new costume with casual, sensual pride.

Jeddy had learned that afternoon how to roll a baseball down his arm and grasp it in his hand. He practiced the trick endlessly, showing it to his cousins, his uncle, to Dot's au pair girl, Ingrid, who had been taught to marvel effusively at anything a child said or did.

Again, Ray thought of the narcissism of children, of their wondrous self-centeredness, and of how they stood, for the brief years of their childhood, at center stage while their parents danced attendance on them in the wings, readying the lights, applauding, hiring coaches and teachers. It was only in the darkness of the night or in the shadows of moments of hurt and sadness that they reached toward the adults who waited for them with outstretched arms. Rachel wakened from demon-peopled sleep to call for her mother, her father, but in the deceptive brightness of the late afternoon sunlight, she hugged her tiny breasts and moved gracefully, languidly, to her own secret music.

The children loved Ina, he knew. They were concerned for her. But it was their own lives, their own small tricks and accomplishments, that absorbed them, and that was as it should be. It was only the infant, the toddler, who clung to a mother's skirt and would not let a father vanish from view without melting into misery. Ray held Dot's youngest on his lap, let the tiny fingers trace their way around his lips, through the soft furry line of his eyebrow. The child clutched a leaf, plucked from the small saplings that bordered the park. Delicate golden veins threaded their way through the sheer green stipule, and the child showed it to Ray.

"Pretty," he said in the high, sweet voice that was only just learning to form words. He was a large-eyed child named Simon for Ray's father, although he had been born in a Saigon hospital. His black hair fell in layers about his round tan face, and the children laughed fondly at him and called him Simple Simon.

"Very pretty," Ray agreed, and kissed his nephew's head.

He held the leaf the child passed to him. He had often picked similar leaves for Rachel and Jeddy on their walks through the park. On beach walks he would stoop to pick up a fragile shell from the sea-swept stretch of shore.

"Pretty," he would tell his children, and watch their small fingers fly across the intricate lines that patterned nature's sweet debris. He remembered sharing the mystery of twilight with a child, holding an infant in his arms while the sky shivered and shimmered its way through layers of fading gold to the death of darkness. Perhaps he would never know such a moment again. Jeddy and Rachel rushed ahead of him now and had no time to stand by his side and watch the struggle of lingering daylight.

"I'm glad Ina is feeling so well," Dot said over coffee. She had not wanted to visit that day, she explained. She had known that Ina would be tired after the surgery, and after all, both her mother and Bette had visited. It really was a bit too much for Ina only hours after the operation, didn't Ray think? Beneath Dot's question lay her uneasiness with both Bette and her brother's mother-in-law. They made her uncomfortable, moving as they did so easily through illness and death. Sometimes, it seemed to her, they studied her curiously, as though an aberration marked her life of ease and comfort, her childhood of laughter and gaiety, and it was their European experience of death and terror that was, after all, normal and ordinary.

"Yes, Ina's fine," Ray said firmly. He had decided that afternoon that no matter what Ina thought, he would tell Dot a lie of omission. There was no need for Dot to know about Ina's pregnancy.

Dot had shielded him from so much that he could shield her from this—from Ina's hesitancy about bringing forth the life she carried, when Dot, who hungered for such life within her own womb, was barren and bereft. His sister mothered children other women had borne and hurried from pediatrician to play group as she had once hurried from fertility clinics to

wonder-working gynecologists in distant cities. Why she did
not conceive remained a mystery, and she submitted at last to
its insolubility. She was content with her adopted children,
she assured him, but once, walking with her through the park,
he noticed her looking at two pregnant women who sat chatting on a bench. Her gaze had lingered on them, and when he
asked her a question, she looked at him in bewilderment, and
he knew that she had not heard him, and he repeated his query
softly, gently.

Jeddy, Rachel, and Dot's oldest son, Ethan, played a game
of Sorry as Dot and Ray talked. Jeddy and Rachel played as a
team, their heads bent close together. She wore a short plaid
skirt over her tutu, and Jeddy brushed his dark hair from his
eyes as he read a card. Fleeting slices of sunlight moved through
their thick night-colored hair.

"They're such beautiful children," Dot said. Silence swallowed the words she had not spoken, perhaps had not even
thought, although he ascribed them to her. Why were there
only two? She gladly would have birthed many such perfect
children who would play calmly through the soft hours of
encroaching evening. "Is Ina very upset about being away
from the office?" she asked, almost idly.

"She misses the children," he replied, a shade too emphatically. He felt restless, annoyed with the implied criticism in
Dot's question.

Claire, Dot's eight-year-old daughter, came in to seek help
on a current-events article. Patiently, Dot searched through
the newspaper with her daughter. If necessary she would, Ray
was certain, dash off to the library with her. His sister's
absorption in her children annoyed him, suddenly and irrationally. He thought of Ina bent over her work, absorbed in
the series of programs she would design into an intricate
system. He remembered an evening when she came home
from work glowing with pride. She had formulated an idea
for a new data bank. A major company was interested in it.
He surged with desire for her, proud of what she was, of what

she had accomplished. He would not want Rachel to have less of a life.

He would make sure that another child would not endanger Ina's career, the business she had built. There were ways to manage. A woman attorney in his office had four children and worked full-time. Arrangements could be made.

He rose to leave. It was already late, and he did not want Ina to be alone. Was Dot sure it would not be too much trouble for Larry to take the children home?

"Of course not." Where children were concerned, nothing was too much trouble. She smiled at him and took Simon on her lap. Claire stood at her side, disinterestedly reading about endangered species.

"Be good, kids," he said, tousling Jeddy's hair, kissing Rachel, who smelled of her grandmother Shirley's perfume. His mother-in-law had spent an hour or so with the children after visiting Ina. She had shopped with Rachel for the tutu and given Jeddy a crisp ten-dollar bill but had not kissed them when she left. What had Shirley said to Ina? Ray wondered, and he was suddenly eager to be at the hospital.

"Kiss Mommy for me. Tell her I hope she feels better," Rachel said, and turned swiftly to her Aunt Dot for the glance of approval her words would surely bring.

"Me too." Jeddy had had a man returned to "Start," and he grimaced. His mother was in the hospital across the park, but the game he was losing stretched before him.

Dot walked to the door with him, Simon nestled against her shoulder, almost asleep. (That, too, Ray yearned for, the moistness of a child's mouth, the flutter of small lashes against his neck as a baby drifted to sleep in his arms.)

"Yes."

"You'll call me as soon as you get the report on the permanent section?"

"Yes, of course." He bent to kiss his sister, to stroke Simon's silken mop of black hair. It was death Dot feared—not life. He shivered now as he stood on the street corner, although the

spring night was warm, and once in the cab he did not roll
down the window until the driver turned and asked him to.

Ina was in the waiting room when he arrived. She called
to him as he stepped out of the elevator, and he was relieved to
see that she looked much better than she had that morning.
Her color was high, and her hair hung in a single braid down
her back. She was talking to the tall black model he had
noticed the previous evening, and he was newly startled by
the younger woman's beauty.

"Ray, this is Marnie Coleman."

"Hello, Ray."

He had expected her voice to be deep and throaty, but it
was high and light and reminded him of Simon's child tone.
He shook Marnie's hand and kissed Ina on the forehead.

"No flowers. I'm sorry. I got held up at Dot's and didn't
have time to stop at the florist's."

"She can share mine," Marnie said. "I think every photog-
rapher in town sent me yellow roses and charged it off as an
expense."

"Marnie's a model," Ina told him, and he was amused at the
tinge of envy and awe in her tone. "In fact, I've been telling
her she should write a book on her background and what it
takes to be a top New York model," Ina continued.

"Especially if you're black," Marnie added, and both
women laughed, the laughter of clever, world-wise career
women who understood the stakes and did not resent them.

They sat in relaxed ease on the white plastic couch, their
filmy peignoirs falling in graceful folds to the scoured linoleum floor. Marnie wore deep purple, and Ina had changed
into her apricot-colored robe. A small woman in a faded
duster shuffled in and listlessly picked up a frayed magazine.
She looked at them, and a reluctant smile curved her lips as
though she had been reminded suddenly of a world where
women dressed in delicate fabrics, the colors of wild flowers,
and laughed gently into the sweetness of a spring night.

"Dr. Simonson—pick up any phone. Please pick up the
nearest phone, Dr. Simonson." A man's voice, bored and dis-

interested, blared into the public-address system. "Dr. Riss, please go to Emergency. Urgent. Dr. Riss, please report to Emergency."

"Look, Ray," Ina said playfully, girlishly, "Marnie did my hair. Do you like it?" She turned her head almost shyly, and he smiled. Ina loved to have people play with her hair, to fuss over her, just as her mother, Shirley Cherne, craved the attentions and ministrations of salesladies, an excess of food and jewelry. What they had been denied during the lost terrible war years, what they had yearned for, they garnered and hoarded now.

"I love it," he said.

The small heavyset man who had slept in the waiting room the night before glanced at them tiredly. He was eating a tunafish sandwich, and small golden tears of oil dripped on the red table. He finished the sandwich and wiped the table carefully with a napkin. His pale eyes were watery and red-rimmed, and a fleck of dried blood clung to his chin.

"See you." Marnie glided out of the room, and they watched her move down the hall as though she were a dancer on a receding stage.

"She's lovely," Ray said.

"Yes. How are the kids?" Ina asked. "And Dot?"

"Everyone's fine. Terrific. A bit worried about you. They all sent their love."

"I'll call later." She played with the belt of her robe, and he saw that smoky shadows had formed about her eyes.

"Shouldn't you be resting?" he asked.

"Well, I was in bed all day. My mother was here and Bette and Ruthie, but I slept in between. Besides, both Miriam's and Ben's parents are visiting, and I thought I'd give them some privacy."

"How's their baby?" he asked.

"The official report is that his condition is stable, but they don't sound as optimistic as they did this morning. I don't know." Her voice slid down, and he took her hand and felt its answering pressure.

What must it feel like to lose a child? he wondered. It occurred to him that he soon might know, and his fingers went limp at the shock of the thought. Some years ago he had visited his in-laws on a fall day and found Shirley Cherne pale and withdrawn. She, who loved bright clothing and jangling jewelry, wore a faded shabby robe, and her fingers were ringless. Ina and her father had spoken to her softly, gently, as one speaks to a mourner. Later Ina had told him that the day of their visit was Yedidiah's birthday. Shirley and Norman's son, Ina's brother, the namesake of his own Jeddy, would have reached his fortieth year that day.

Would he, too, think of their unborn child in years to come and mentally mark the year of school entry, bar mitzvah, graduation? He, too, would pause sadly at phantom dates and silently observe anniversaries that would never occur, mourning the loss of the unknown small shadow who had hovered across these bright springtime days of his middle years. *If.* The unspoken *if* weighed him down, rested in deadly heaviness upon his heart.

"Did you tell Dot?" she asked. "About the pregnancy?" She surprised herself. Until now she had thought only in terms of abortion.

"No. I decided not to," he said, and she did not argue with him.

It occurred to her that too many people had been told, too many opinions offered. She suffered from a surfeit of honesty and openness. Dimly, she wished she lived in more closed and secret times, in a Jamesian era when men and women talked softly of trivia over fragile teacups while grand passions caused their hands to tremble (but imperceptibly), their hearts to beat too rapidly beneath their ruffled blouses, their impeccably starched shirt fronts. Would Isabel Archer have attended a consciousness-raising group and discussed her feelings about contraception? Would the haughty countess have sought a friend's opinion on whether or not she should bear her love child? She would, Ina decided, reread *Portrait of a Lady* that summer.

The red, white, and blue waiting room was rapidly filling up with patients and their visitors. The men wore lightweight suits newly pressed for the new season and could find no peace for their hands. They cracked their knuckles, folded and unfolded their fingers, flipped through frayed magazines. They were uneasy tourists in this healing territory reserved for the treatment of women and the multiple and mysterious ailments that seized breast and womb, blocked the gleaming twin ovaries, the slender fallopian tubes, the hollow uterus.

The women wore new robes, bought especially for their hospital stays and generally worn only during visiting hours. Their fingers played with lengths of braiding, long satin ribbons, tiny pearl buttons. They wore too much rouge, and their eyes were bright with worry and fear. They spoke softly, but fragments of phrases slithered electrically through the room, gliding from one group to another: "A cyst, the size of a lemon." "A small fibroma—definitely benign." "We'll see what he says." "He will come in the morning." "He'll have the pathologist's report by the afternoon." Their doctors were magical messiahs, breathlessly awaited, wistfully worshipped for their knowledge and their skill.

At one of the small tables, a woman and her husband bent over checkbook and bank statement. She was very frail, and her scalp shone palely through her thin brown hair. Radiation, Ray guessed at once, and saw the blue shadows of pain etched beneath her eyes, the terrible fragile thinness of her wrist. Her small, depleted body swayed in the folds of a red robe, chosen perhaps for its brightness, its defiance. She was dying, Ray was certain, but she pursed her lips, held the pen tightly, and reconciled the statement while her husband followed her figures and nodded. Even the dying and those who attend them must balance their checkbooks. He was a short, serious man whose hair had grayed too young, and he watched his wife through very thick glasses. When she raised a question, he shuffled through a pile of canceled checks and offered her one, touching her wrist on which a blue vein pulsated warningly.

Coins jangled in the coffee machine, which was in working order tonight. A teenaged girl, whose long dark hair hung in glossy folds about her shoulders, opened a large white gift box and shook out a nightgown and a robe of bridal white.

"It's beautiful," she told her parents, who wore matching blue cord pantsuits and twin smiles of encouragement.

Why was such a child in the hospital and on this floor? Ray wondered. And why had her parents brought her such a gift? He thought of Beth Goldstein, the small girl in Rachel's grade, sister to Jeddy's friend, who had died of leukemia. She, too, had had long dark hair, and the last time Ray had seen her, at Rachel's birthday party, she had worn a dress of white linen—an off-white, the color of a shroud or, perhaps, a wedding dress. "God shouldn't have let her die," Jeddy had said of her, and Ray looked at the girl who sat now between her parents, twirling the hospital bracelet that dangled from her wrist and dutifully smiling. "God shouldn't let her die," he thought, and saw that Ina too was watching her.

"Let's get out of here," he said.

"Yes."

She rose quickly, and he put his arm around her shoulders. Slowly, silently, they walked the long corridor. Bed lamps were lit in the rooms they passed, and women sat up and pulled silver needles threaded with rainbow stretches of yarn through delicate frames of needlepoint and watched black-and-white shadows move aimlessly across the tiny screens of rented television sets.

They were relieved that only Miriam and Ben Gottlieb were in the room. Their parents had left, and Miriam's bedside table was crowded with the loving clutter of their visit: a bunch of daffodils, a bowl of fruit, a hunk of sponge cake shining golden through crinkling folds of Saran Wrap. Someone had brought a radio, and Ben fiddled with it earnestly, trying to coax its quivering wispy tones into full voice. Ray, who was oddly skillful with mechanical objects, offered to help. With great concentration the two men studied the antenna, and then Ray turned it slightly and shifted it halfway upward, and the rich tones of the *Eroica* filled the white-walled room. They looked at each other with the shared pride of achievement, the anticipation of enjoyment, and smiled.

The two couples felt, at that moment, like a family locked together in an overwhelming intimacy in which everything was known and nothing was concealed. In this white-walled room, high above the urban park that breathed the delicate fragrance of a new spring, of a season of growth and beginning, their dreams and fears hovered and met. They were isolated in the room where the odors of ammonia and cut flowers wafted together, the silence broken by the urgent ringing of bells and the toneless announcements calling for doctors who would surely not arrive in time at unknown bedsides.

In the brief hours that Ina and Miriam would spend together, new leaves would unfold on the great oak beneath their window, decisions for life or death would be made, an infant, an embryo, would survive or die, and all their lives would be forever altered. During this period a phone would ring and a voice would tell them whether the fibrous tissue plucked that day from Ina's breast was benign or malignant— good or evil. They were together now in a building where life was touched by death and hope and fear struggled together on scales that would not balance. All this the Gottliebs and the Feldmans, they who had been strangers only a day ago and soon would be strangers again, would share.

"Do you play Scrabble?" Ben asked.

Ina and Ray nodded in eager assent. It was a game they loved and played often and intensely on summer nights at the Amagansett house. Once, in an analytic session, Ina had spoken long and eloquently on a point that interested her— some cultural nuance she no longer remembered. She had admittedly been showing off for Eleanor Berenson. A part of transference, she supposed. Her mother had never been impressed by her facility with words and had looked with scarce interest at the essays published in high school and college magazines and later at the odd piece published in professional journals. But Eleanor Berenson had been interested. She had lit an English cigarette and leaned forward in her seat. But when Ina was through talking, she had sighed.

"Sometimes," she had said wearily, "words obscure feelings. You in particular must be wary of that."

Her warning had angered Ina, and she had missed the next session, inventing a conference out of town. But the truth of the analyst's observation had penetrated, and she remembered it now as Ben Gottlieb set up the Scrabble board and they gathered in a circle around Miriam's bed.

The familiarity of the board reassured them. It belonged to their life outside this hospital, to comfortable carpeted rooms furnished with deep chairs and many pictures. A grease stain had faded the pink star that indicated "Start" and Ina smiled. On their own board it was a coffee stain. The tiles were kept in a worn Hallmark paper bag on which Joan Walsh Anglund cherubs cavorted. They plucked letters from the paper bag and chose for first. Ina drew an *A*, selected her tiles, and the bag was passed around. They were all serious and secretive and covered their tile racks with their arms. A nurse stood briefly in the doorway and watched them with the benign smile of a mother whose children have at last settled into a satisfactory board game and are playing without a quarrel.

Ina set out the first word. BREATH. Eighteen points with the double word score she got for going first. Not up to her usual but she settled back, satisfied. Ben added an *E*. BREATHE. He built downward. ENDURE. Ray used his *R*. RAPID. Miriam moved her tiles about, fluttered over the board, and withdrew them to juggle them around on her rack yet again. An aide wheeled a cart of juices in, and they all took paper cups of apple juice.

"That's a nice game," the aide said companionably. She was a heavy black woman who wore gold-rimmed glasses that exactly matched the golden molars that gleamed when she smiled.

"Yes, it is," Ben agreed, and offered her a fruit from the

bowl. She took a peach and wheeled her tray down the hall, humming softly.

Miriam moved at last. DEATH.

"My letters are terrible. I couldn't do anything else."

Her voice was troubled, apologetic. Ina saw at least three other possibilities but said nothing. For the next several moves their words seemed to relate to geography. Ray contributed TERRAINS and gained fifty points. Ben managed a triple letter with VOLCANO, and they all clapped for him. Sixty-four points. They looked at each other admiringly and plucked tiles from the bag speedily, excitedly. The game was moving fast and well.

HEART, Miriam built down. RESCUE. That was Ray's. REGRET. Ben's word, crafted too quickly, earning too few points. TUBE, Miriam added, but it was Ray who put his letters down to utilize her *B* and produced BABY. They stopped playing then and studied the board, avoiding each other's eyes.

"I'm tired," Miriam said, and her voice was soft—a brittle barrier against the tears that trembled just beyond it.

"I'll add up the score," Ray offered, and while he calculated, Ina swept the tiles into the worn paper bag. It would not do to admire the board at game's end as they sometimes did, occasionally constructing a whimsical story from the words they had built. BABY, they had written, and DEATH and ENDURE, BREATH and BREATHE, REGRET and RESCUE. Their fears had trailed them into the game and in the end had defeated them. Ray had the most points, but no one cared. They put the game away, chatted for a few minutes, and then Ray and Ina, like polite guests who had sensed the right moment to leave, returned to her side of the room and Ben moved the screen around Miriam's bed.

Sitting on her own bed, Ina undid the braid Marnie had fashioned and let her dark hair float loosely about her shoulders. She wanted to brush it, but the incision on her breast ached when she moved her arm upward, and Ray took the brush from her and slowly moved it through the thickness of her hair, his arm encircling her waist, feeling her flesh smooth and hot beneath the filmy fabric of her nightgown. He wanted to make love to her and wondered why it was he always wanted her the most when she was inaccessible. On business trips he dreamed of her, reached across an empty bed to touch her absent form, called her as morning broke. Now he moved his hand down, rested it on her thigh, and stroked her hair rhythmically.

"What did your mother have to say?" he asked.

"She told me that she had an abortion. In the camp. When we first arrived. She told me by way of a warning. It dried her up, she said."

"Could it?" he wondered aloud, and she did not answer but leaned closer to him, pressing her body against his.

"Would you love me if I had one breast?" she asked.

"Yes." His voice was firm. He moved his hand up and cupped her other breast, bent to kiss the pale flesh of her neck that shone beneath the thick layers of dark hair.

"Don't," she said softly, and he recognized the desire in her voice.

"Whatever happens," he said, "I'll love you."

His own words surprised him. They were not a couple given to mouthing endearments, asking the teasing questions of playful lovers: "I love you. Do you love me?"

"All right."

She accepted his statement as knowledge that had been essential to her and lifted his hand to her lips, kissing it where the small scar of a childhood burn trailed whitely across his thumb.

Behind the screen the Gottliebs talked softly. A woman's voice sounded through the public-address system. "All visitors are requested to leave. Visiting hours are over. All visitors are requested to leave."

He settled Ina back against the pillow. Her hair spilled in dark waves across it. She looked very pale, and her fingers fluttered up to the thick dressing at her breast.

"Does it hurt?" he asked.

"A little. The nurse will give me something."

"All right then. Good night." He kissed her forehead, dimmed her bedside light.

"Kiss the children for me. Maybe they could phone in the morning—"

"Good idea."

He drew the blanket up and tucked it about her as he did with Rachel—briefly now father to his wife, just as he was often lover to his daughter.

"Sleep now," he said, and was glad to see that her eyes were closed and her body relaxed beneath the light covering.

He walked to the door and thought of saying good night to Miriam, but Ben joined him just then and held his finger to his lips.

"She's sleeping," he said, and they left quietly, not talking but sharing each other's company as comfort. Marnie's husband stood at the elevator clutching the oversized portfolio. His eyes were fixed on the dancing numbers that indicated the elevator's progress, and his lips were thinned into a compressed line of anger. He was the sort of man, Ray guessed, who called his answering service every hour, consulted his watch and his calendar often.

"I think I'm going to take the stairs," Ben said suddenly. "I want to stop and see the baby."

"Okay."

Ray watched him disappear up the stairwell. Should he have offered to go with him? he wondered, and was glad that he had not. He did not, on this night, want to see a newborn infant, stirring sadly within the transparent cocoon of a respirator. He took the elevator down and was pleased, when he left the hospital, to feel a sharp, almost wintry, wind breathe across his face.

In her hospital room, Ina stirred in half sleep and thought to call her mother, but she did not. Instead she mentally reviewed the neatly spaced and shaded Scrabble board and the words they had formed. BREATH and DEATH, BABY and BREATHE, RESCUE and ENDURE. These she remembered. A secret lay concealed among them, but it was not revealed to her, and she slept at last as the drug took effect.

She dreamed without waking that night. She wandered with her cousin Bette through the stillness of a leaf-carpeted woodland. They held hands and wore summer dresses that fell softly about their bare legs. As they came upon a clearing, Ray and Bette's husband, Richard, approached them. The men carried flowers, and their faces were bright with sunlight, although the forest was dark with shadows. The women danced lightly into their arms and felt the wondrous hardness of desire against the yielding softness of their flesh. In her sleep Ina smiled and whispered mysterious endearments in the lost, secret language of her childhood.

Ray walked home that night and paused opposite his apartment building to breathe deeply of the newly blooming dogwood. The fallen blossoms had, during the long day, been trampled into mounds of damp petals that exuded a faint odor; the scent of decay wafted above the fragrance of the burgeoning heart-shaped flowers that glowed whitely in the darkness.

# THIRD DAY

INA STIRRED INTO wakefulness reluctantly that morning. She moved through the eddying waves of sleep like a weary swimmer parting the waters for the last, exhausting final laps to shore. She rose and fell, now rocked in a lazy slumber, then soaring into fitful, unwilling awareness. Light and dark melded, and when she turned, her body moved heavily, slowly; her breast ached beneath the pressure of her weight. The pain, unfamiliar, intruding, angered her. She opened her eyes and looked in bewilderment about the white-walled room with its stainless steel appointments, its glacial sink. She could not, for a brief, heart-sinking moment, remember where she was. She felt befuddled and deceived by the lost hours of sleep, as she sometimes did when waking from an afternoon nap, and she wondered anxiously whether it was the gray light of morning or early evening that shone bleakly in through the high windows. And then her probing fingers found the bandage at her breast, and she sniffed the odor of the pine-tinged disinfectant, saw a red light flash brilliantly on and off over the doorway of the room across the hall. She knew then that she was in Mount Lebanon Hospital and it was early morning.

She watched as nurses walked down the corridor in pairs. Shifts were changing, and instructions were being relayed. The women in their white nylon uniforms paused at each door and bent their capped heads over the clipboards. Small notations were made, nods and sighs exchanged. Those who were going off duty wore fresh lipstick, and their bright cardigans were buttoned against the chill of early morning. They walked more slowly than the new arrivals, their bodies weighed down by the fatigue of long hours of work. They looked warily through the corridor windows, as though fearful that the world beyond their hospital fortress had undergone mysterious and threatening changes while they hurried down night-silent hallways with their silvery needles, their pills and paper cups, their gleaming stethoscopes and electronically controlled thermometers. Here, in their sterile professional domain, they were in control. They knew what to do when the mercury on the thermometer shot past the quivering danger point. Buzzers and phones were at hand. Linens were arranged in orderly, familiar stacks. But outside, on the street below, automobile horns shrieked; strangers in ill-fitting clothing darted past on peculiar early morning errands; lone women carrying laden shopping bags wept quietly as they walked the empty streets. Not long ago, a Mount Lebanon nurse had been raped and murdered on her way home; her body had been discovered in an alley only three blocks from the hospital. The night-shift nurses were tired and wanted to go home, but they were safe and wanted to stay.

The newly arrived nurses moved with rapid step, checked their watches, made notes with freshly sharpened pencils. Ina envied them their hours of beginning, their carefully organized workday. She wished herself back in her apartment overlooking the park, dressed for the office in tweed suit and turtleneck sweater, her attaché case neatly packed and ready. The elevator door slammed against the chatter of Rachel and Jeddy, whose damp kisses were planted on her cheeks. Before leaving the house, she would give her morning instructions to Carmen, who listened with bored indifference. The roast beef for dinner, Ray's shirts to the laundry, the shag rug in the study to be sent to the cleaners.

Ina's office, in the early hours of the morning, was a quiet expanse where terminals hummed with the rhythmic messages of data being transmitted, while keypunch machines bit their way through sheaves of cards. The machinery of her profession controlled her work space. It was mechanical, efficient, and often when a clerk or a programmer spoke to her, Ina was startled, almost annoyed by the human contact that interfered with the safe, undemanding whir of the mechanical apparatus that surrounded her.

She wanted now to be in her office, among her computers and keyboards, away from Mount Lebanon with its ambience of health and illness, life and death, fruition and abortion. The hospital handled problems that the most carefully coded program could not solve, the most intricately designed system could not predict. She turned on her side. A searing pain suddenly and unexpectedly shot through her breast, and she cried out softly and pressed the nurse's call button.

A nurse she had not seen before, middle-aged and plump, entered the room and padded silently over to the bed. Micaceous gray eyes looked down at Ina through rimless glasses. The white nylon slacks clung too closely to thighs that had spread too widely.

"Yes, Mrs. Feldman?"

"I have a bad pain in my breast." Her voice was weak. The complaint, the call for help, shamed her.

The nurse looked at the chart, glanced at the dressing. She pressed a thermometer into Ina's mouth, held her wrist, and checked her pulse. She read the thermometer, made entries on the chart, and smiled reassuringly.

"You're just having normal discomfort. The incision is fresh. But there's no fever, no sign of unusual drainage. I'll get you something for the pain."

She disappeared and Ina got out of bed, the ache oddly mitigated by the nurse's explanation. She glanced out the window and was perversely pleased to see that the day was overcast and that the few pedestrians hurrying through the street down below carried umbrellas and glanced apprehen-

sively up at the sky. She wondered if Carmen had reminded
the children to take their boots and decided that she would
call home after she had washed. She closed the bathroom door
gently. Miriam was still asleep, a bemused smile on her face as
though a dream had posed her a charming riddle.

She emerged from the bathroom pleasantly hungry and
wondered when breakfast would be served. Perhaps she would
take a fruit from Miriam's laden basket. She contemplated
oranges, apples, pears, and heard the voices of the nurses in
the hallway just outside her room.

"I'm just bringing her some Darvon for the pain. It's the
left breast. A fibroma they said, but it's a pretty big incision,
and there's a note that they're waiting for a biopsy report.
You never can tell with these things. Remember that nice little
Mrs. Lorimer—she was in the last room on the east corridor?
When they prepped her, I examined the breast myself, and
there was hardly anything there. 'A pimple,' I said to her. 'Are
they really going to cut you just to get that little pimple?'
And then they had to do a double mastectomy. Poor little
thing. Afraid that her husband would divorce her. Silly girl.
There's 505 ringing. I'd better get 502 her Darvon."

Like an eavesdropping child, Ina scrambled back into bed.
Her hunger had turned into nausea, and the pain shot sharply,
wildly. One hand flew to her breast, and with the other she
stroked her abdomen, a remembered gesture from the early
days of her pregnancies with Rachel and Jeddy. Sometimes
then it had seemed to her that the small gestating creature
nestled within her womb might take comfort from this small,
rhythmic pressure, the gentle stroking across the protective
mother-flesh. Had Shaindel then, in those distant days, passed
her own hand over the newly stretching skin and flesh that
sheltered the tiny embryo that would be pried out and tossed
across the yellowing Polish newspaper that covered the barrack floor? Had she too sought to bring brief, almost invol-
untary, comfort to the child she would not birth?

"Here's your pill, Mrs. Feldman." The nurse's voice was

falsely buoyant. Ina had preferred her competent indifference.

She tossed the pill down, and when the nurse hurried from the room, she clasped her hands above the counterpane, forbidding her body their touch. Patiently, sadly, she waited for the narcotic to spirit her lightly above the pain and allow her to drift off into a sweet half sleep.

When she awakened again, the stainless steel breakfast carts were being trundled down the hall. Trays were briskly set down on bedside tables. Phones rang insistently. The nurses and doctors walked swiftly down the corridor and no longer spoke in the muted, gentle tones of early dawn. An orderly dropped a tray and cursed harshly. Miriam Gottlieb sat up in bed, her hair neatly brushed. She held her orange juice in one hand and the phone in the other.

"He had a good night, the neonatologist said," she reported. "Perhaps there will be a turning point. It may come today. The first week is crucial."

Now, for the Gottlieb baby, Ina thought, the first week of life was fraught with uncertainty, an arbitrary measure of hours and days. But all of life was divided into time spans, zones of danger and decision. Her sister-in-law, Dot, bubbled with information gleaned from psychiatrists and social workers, child-rearing manuals and weekend seminars. The first six months of a child's life set personality patterns. The years from two to six were a vital period of growth and development. Adolescence was a time of crisis. Ina and Ray had hovered over Jeddy's hospital bed during his mysterious fever, and the attending physician had said to them, "The next twenty-four hours will tell the story."

Always, it seemed, all parents, like the Gottliebs, were destined to wait for hours and days, for months and years to pass, for one crisis to supersede another. The birth trauma would be followed by the hazards of infancy, give way to the mysteries of childhood and the terrible uncertain teenage years, as children trembled in the shadow of the adults they would become. Rachel hesitated on the threshold of that world now. New breasts jutted gently beneath her sweaters, and the baby fat that had padded the bones of her face had melted away.

"Am I pretty?" she asked, standing before the mirror, her hands delicately balanced on newly curving hips. "Will I be pretty?"

"You'll have to wait and see," Ina answered casually, and felt her daughter willing the months and weeks to rush swiftly by so that the secret of her beauty would be revealed. Ina felt her pain and apprehension. Just as Miriam Gottlieb longed to clutch her tiny sick infant and vault with him across the frontiers of danger, so Ina wanted to take Rachel's hand and lead her daughter to the corridors of maturity, assurance. But Rachel would have to wait, as Ina had waited, as Miriam Gottlieb waited now, for life to unfold itself, for the crucial hours to pass. Another child, Ina knew, would mean a replay of all vigils already endured with Rachel and Jeddy, a marshaling of energy for new and unknown times of crisis. She was on her way "Home." It was unfair to ask her to start again at "Go." She herself now felt a child's whining fretfulness. She reached for her coffee, and at the clatter of the utensils Miriam turned to her and smiled.

"Good morning. How did you sleep?"

"Fine. I got up earlier, but they gave me something and I fell asleep again. How's the baby?"

"He had a good night."

"Wonderful."

Ina turned to her breakfast tray, but the hunger of early dawn had deserted her and the sight of the food nauseated her slightly. Her fingers lightly touched the bandage at her breast. Did a cancer lurk within the softness of those tender glands? A lump, they always called it, and she thought that it must look like a dark resistant clot, spreading duskily across the milky network of ducts and tissue. She had no control over its growth, its unlimited and unlimiting mitosis. How much control did anyone have over his physical destiny? Involuntarily her hand moved to her abdomen. Yes, here she could exercise control, decision. Sadness settled on her, and when she lifted her cup, she found it so heavy that she was surprised that it did not fall from her hand.

The phone rang and she lifted it wearily, almost disinterestedly.

"Ina." Ray's voice was tender, concerned, and she felt irritated and angered. His love was unfair and overwhelming. It denied her recourse to anger and resentment. She did not deserve his gentle devotion, his careful fairness, but he insisted, persisted. What was not her fault became her guilt.

"What kind of a night did you have?" he asked.

"All right, I suppose. But I got up very early. At dawn."

"Why?"

"I don't know. A pain where he cut yesterday." She waited for his reaction but he was silent, and through his silence she sensed his worry. Swiftly she reassured him, tried to undo the damage. "The nurse said the incision was fresh. That caused the discomfort. She gave me something, and I went back to sleep."

"Good. Did you have breakfast?"

"Just coffee. I wasn't hungry." Again the phone grew electric with his worry. Was loss of appetite symptomatic? She sensed his lawyer's mind weighing this new evidence. "I'm hungry now though," she added, and was startled to discover that it was true. She bit into a piece of cold toast and toyed with the cardboard of the cereal box.

"How are the kids?" she asked.

"Fine. They left early. The bus made an early pickup so they didn't have time to call you. They'll talk to you this afternoon. Ina—Dr. Berenson called this morning."

"Oh."

"She wanted to speak to you. She said you had canceled your appointments this week, and she wanted to schedule alternate hours. She had no idea you were in the hospital."

"You told her?"

"Yes, I couldn't see any reason not to. In fact I was sort of surprised that you hadn't." He had, in fact, not been surprised.

He had been shocked. Hadn't Ina felt that the hospital experience was important enough to discuss with her analyst?

"It—it didn't come up." Her excuse sounded weak, trivial. It had not come up because she had not wanted it to come up. It had not come up because she had avoided conflict by avoiding discussion. She supposed that Eleanor Berenson would call that "resistance." She did not care. She was tired of explaining herself, justifying herself, shifting uneasily on the seesaw of decision and explanation where no weight was steady and no weight predictable.

"I don't think I understand, but we'll talk about it later," Ray said drily. "I'm leaving now. Is there anything you need? I'll be there right after work."

"I can't think of anything. If there is, I'll call Dot. She's planning to come today, I think."

"Yes. She's got you sandwiched in somewhere between the pediatrician and the orthodontist."

Ina laughed.

"Ina—Dr. Berenson asked for your hospital phone number, and I gave it to her. I expect she'll call you sometime today."

"Ray, did you talk to her about anything—about the abortion?"

"Of course not." Her question startled him, offended his professional propriety. Eleanor Berenson was not his analyst.

"Have a nice day, darling." Love for him overwhelmed her, made her tremble. He was so good, so fine.

She wanted to be next to him, to touch his large-boned hand and place her lips gently against the smoothness of his freshly shaven cheek. She remembered a distant spring morning when, at such an hour, they had prepared to leave for work. They were both in the study, each searching for a vagrant document on the desk they sometimes shared, dressed in their office uniforms of wool and linen. Suddenly their eyes had met, their hands had touched, and they were both laughing, amused at their own absorption, their earnest busyness. Minutes later, they were naked on the floor beside their desk, the sunlight that poured in through the venetian blinds striping their bodies, his attaché case a hard pillow beneath her head. They had arrived at their desks an hour late, and their co-workers had remarked on the splendid rush of color in their cheeks, the brightness in their eyes. Damn it—she wanted to be naked on the floor beside him now. But she said only, "Call me during the day if you get a chance."

"I'll try," he said. "Get some rest."

The phone clicked into silence. She replaced the receiver and very slowly poured the cereal from the box into a bowl. Across the room, Miriam shrugged into her pale blue robe and watered the African violets, plucking a dead petal from the blossoming plant.

"I feel so much better, so much stronger today," she said, and there was mild amazement in her voice, as though her own recovery mystified her. "I think I'll go to see the baby."

"Good morning, Ina."

Marnie Coleman stood in the doorway, her black hair twisted into an intricate coil, her rose-colored robe shimmering against her dark satiny skin.

"Marnie. Good morning. This is Miriam Gottlieb."

Miriam smiled pleasantly.

"Hi, Marnie."

They might have been three girls relaxing on a lazy morning in their dormitory, wandering from room to room in robes and slippers. How simple it was for women to slip into sororal patterns, to play with each other's hair, offer advice on dress and love, exchange sweet and mysterious secrets, desperate confidences.

"I wondered if you felt like a game of cards," Marnie said. "How about you, Miriam?"

"I'm sorry, Marnie. I have some office work to finish up and phone in. I rented time on a computer, and I've got to get this work done." Always, at college, there had been one girl eager for a card or Scrabble game at any given hour, and always Ina had had homework, a paper due, a test to study for. Her life, like the work she had chosen, was tightly programmed. There was little time for games, few stolen moments on a sun-streaked study floor. Constant activity shielded her from drifting inexplicable sadness, from vagrant moods and shadowed memories.

"Do you feel like playing, Miriam?" There was a pleading quality to Marnie's voice. She wanted more than a game. Her black eyes smoldered, and her long coated lashes moved against her cheeks like small frantic wings beating back grief.

"I was just going to see my baby. He's on another floor. Do you want to come with me?"

"To see the baby? Yes, I'd like that, I think," Marnie said. She smiled, a brilliant professional curving of glossy lips, revealing startling white teeth.

It occurred to Ina that she did not know why Marnie Coleman was in the hospital and on this floor. Some female thing, she had casually supposed, but the supposition no longer seemed simple or adequate. Women's bodies were so vulnerable, such fragile fortresses wherein systems of nurturing and procreation were linked together by organ and gland, by rushing blood and slowly streaming hidden hormones. Such secrets and such danger lurked within that gametic network which was shielded only by flesh and muscle.

Marnie's rose-colored robe swirled about her narrow hips, partly open. The nightgown beneath the robe was sheer, and Ina saw her new friend's dusky skin, the curly mound of thick, dark pubic hair jutting above vaginal bone and muscle. Through that narrow-lipped vagina, a dark-skinned infant might thrust itself into life, and the woman's body, Marnie's, would writhe and bleed and then wondrously heal itself and wait in readiness for new love to throb within it, for new life to grow into fullness. Marnie pulled her robe closer, knotted its silken sash.

"Come on," she said, and her voice was low and husky. "Let's go and see your baby."

Ina watched the two women walk from the room. The phone rang, and she listened to Eleanor Berenson's cool professional tone. The analyst thought it might be helpful if she spoke with Ina that day. She had some free time that morning. Would Ina like to see her?

"Yes," Ina said gratefully. "I think I'd like that very much."

Norman and Shirley Cherne were having breakfast, but they were not seated opposite each other in the cheerful alcove that their ambitious and optimistic decorator had designated the "breakfast nook." They stood and moved restlessly about the kitchen as they always did at that hour of the day, as though fearful of the matutinal intimacy of the day's first meal. There were, as yet, no pressing business demands to fill their conversation; talk at this hour would focus on themselves, and this was a danger they had recognized long ago. Shirley Cherne prowled the kitchen, her coffee cup in hand. She brushed away the stray crumbs her husband dropped as he wandered from the table to the counter top where the morning *Times* lay spread out. He read it, bending over the closely printed columns and raining the crumbs of his English muffin down upon them. The news was his daily obsession. He read the *Times* each day before leaving for Cherne Knitwear, and by noon he had sent Angel, the stock boy, down to Gordon's Luncheonette to see if the *Post* had come in. On his way home he picked up the Yiddish paper Gordon ordered especially for him, and he always fell asleep watching the news on television, a *Time* or *Newsweek* dropping from his hand.

"Look," he said now, thrusting a fleshy finger against an offending paragraph, "this English actress—she's making a film about the Palestinian refugees. One of the worst injustices in history, she says. She should know from injustices."

"She should know from being a refugee." Shirley Cherne laughed harshly and turned the hot water on full force. She herself read only the business section and the fashion columns. Current events she ignored completely. When bombs erupted on the television screen, she left the room and ran the vacuum cleaner above the din of crashing metal and screaming children, videotaped in from distant lands. The news made no sense to her, had made little enough sense when she herself might have been a photograph in the newspaper, a statistic in a long column of statistics. After the war, at the camp in Italy, a woman reporter had tried to interview her. Could she tell about her personal history? Did one particular wartime experience stand out in her mind? Why did she want to know? Shaindel had asked. "So that my readers will know your story." The journalist was plump and wore a GI field jacket. She gave Ina a packet of lollipops. "And so what if they know?" Shaindel had asked her. "Will it make any difference?" And she had walked away, leaving the woman with her pad still open to a blank page.

The war had taught her. She knew herself to be powerless against the waves of history, the bellowing of foreign dictators, the cool foreign policy statements about containing communism that ended with newsphotos of a jungle littered with the bodies of young men. She would stick only to what she knew and could cope with—the changing lengths of women's skirts, the new flowing sleeves on blouses, high-interest saving certificates. Weekly, she rushed from bank to bank, insuring her grandchildren's future, looking with satisfaction at passbooks made out to Rachel and Jeddy. What she could not give to Yedidiah she would give to Ina's children.

But her husband plowed daily through miles of newsprint, searching out symptoms, warnings, like a physician charting an obscure disease. Students rioted in Iran, and he studied their slogans and banners and muttered uneasily: "The Jews better get out of Iran. We saw the Hitler *Jugend* riots and we didn't move." A ranking American military official referred to the "Jewish influence on the media." He clipped the item and pondered it. "That's exactly what they said then. See, we have to watch it."

"What are you talking about?" Anger seared Shirley's tone, a rush of blood scored her cheeks. "That was there and this is here. The United States. America. You read anti-Semitism into everything."

"That's not true." He was calm in the face of her fury. He

understood it. She was safe at last, and she struggled to cling to that safety. Walking in this new American sunlight of freedom and prosperity, watching her business grow and her grandchildren flourish, she would not be drawn back into the shadows of fear and danger. But he stood guardian, retained his vigilance, remembering always, in a clinging penance, how dearly he had paid for his laxness.

"Before the invasion, we didn't read anything into the most obvious things. The handwriting was on the wall, but we covered it and read what we wanted to read. Hitler, we said, was a raving maniac—a mad dog. We forgot that mad dogs have rabies and that maniacs are dangerous. If I had read then and understood then what I read and understand now, everything would be different—everything."

She did not answer him. By everything, she knew, he meant Yedidiah, their small lost son; his parents, who in his dream-swept sleep endlessly wandered the Warsaw street where he had last seen them, on their way to death; his brother killed at Belsen, whose children lived in Israel now and sent them letters with brightly colored stamps printed in Hebrew. He saw them as a miracle—those stamps on which biblical birds soared and a bearded Herzl glowered, printed in the language of the Torah, legitimizing his people. A nation with its own stamps was a power to be reckoned with.

He turned the page and set down his empty coffee cup, which she immediately plucked up. He stood guardian over events she could not control, but she did daily battle with dirt and germs, with small grease spots and floating dust motes. She had lived in filth once and never would again. Dirty cups and plates were plunged into water so hot she wore two pairs of rubber gloves against the searing heat; she ran the vacuum cleaner morning and evening.

"I went yesterday to see Ina," she said, talking to him above the running water, as though her words needed the filter of its interference. She had worked late on the inventory after leaving Ina's children, and he had been asleep when she came home.

"So?" His tone was guarded. He had wanted to visit his daughter in the hospital, but in the end he had not gone. Hospitals frightened him. He had worked as an orderly in the camp hospital, and sometimes still he awakened sweating at night, his lungs burning with the nightmare odor of ethyl alcohol and accumulated vomit, the stink of putrefying flesh.

He had only once entered Mount Lebanon. During Jeddy's ritual circumcision in the special room at Mount Lebanon, Norman Cherne had stood beside his son-in-law, Ray, whose arm he had clutched when the scalpel was raised above the infant's quivering penis. He had closed his eyes, reminding himself that this was his grandson, born in the haven of the United States, named for his son who had died in a land without havens. He was not soothed and saw still, in his mind's eye, the white-coated camp surgeon swinging a bloodied steel instrument above the barely anesthesized young boy who was one of a hundred Jewish boys forced to submit to experimental sterilization. It had been Nachum Czernowitz's job, as inmate 8703, to wheel out the enormous green garbage can into which the tender pink flesh, still dripping scarlet flecks of blood, was discarded, like the detritus on a butcher's floor. He had turned away from the weeping boys stretched out on the operating table, kept his face expressionless, but once outside the room, out of sight of the Germans, he vomited, retching up bilious phlegm because his shrunken stomach would not yield enough to quell the nausea. Norman Cherne avoided hospitals and had bolted his grandson's circumcision party, seized by a mysterious virus that his wife neither questioned nor explained.

"How is Ina?" he asked now, folding the newspaper neatly and discarding it, glad to be done with it. He would try to get the *Post* earlier today. This new splinter party in Syria did not sound good, and the riots in Argentina were ominous. There the danger was clear and imminent. His cousin, Mendel, was in Argentina. Norman would write to him, but Mendel had already in his lifetime fled one country—would he leave another? And his children were settled there—mar-

ried, the grandchildren endowed with proud Spanish names.
The daughter's husband was a non-Jew, an assistant minister.
Mendel would not leave. Still, Norman would study the after-
noon paper carefully and write his cousin that night.

"Ina is all right. The breast surgery was minor. A little
growth—a nothing. Still, I wish they had the results of the test
already. With Rosa they told her right away it was nothing.
But there's something else."

"Yes?" He asked but did not want the answer. An arrow
of pain pierced his heart. His fingertips grew cold. Ina would
be all right. She was strong. She was all they had.

"She's pregnant."

"Ina? But she said—I thought they wanted only the two
children."

"They wanted." She laughed scornfully. "Sometimes you
get what you don't want. True. They didn't want another.
It happened. And now they are deciding what to do about it.
Ina is deciding."

"Deciding?" He was puzzled. "What's to decide?"

"Whether she should have it or not." Her tone was impatient. She wiped the counter top with the damp towel. She
was ready to leave for the office. It was their season, and there
was a lot to do.

He smoothed out his news clippings and did not meet her
eyes. He understood her but avoided his own understanding.
Nor did he want her explanation. He did not want to know.
He wanted only to be left alone with his mountains of newspapers, his maps and editorials. It was simpler to ponder the
situation in Argentina, to worry about whether the Vatican
would recognize Israel and Russia would ease emigration, than
to think about an unborn—perhaps never-to-be-born—grandchild floating in the milky waters of his only daughter's womb.
Always, he had kept a careful distance from Ina, fearful perhaps that to reveal his love would be to betray his fear. Ina
had his own mother's great dark eyes and her thick dark hair,
and when she laughed he heard his mother's laughter. Watching his daughter walk through a room, he saw again his

mother's strong and graceful pace. Often in his thoughts Ina and his mother melded and became one. In dreams they moved toward him together and vanished always before they reached him. He remained standing with his hands out-stretched and a mute cry frozen on his lips. Ina! Mama! His mother had vanished, and he trembled with terror for his daughter—the strong young woman who moved so purpose-fully through the days of her life.

Her purposefulness and her strength saddened and worried him. He knew that too much show of strength betrayed secret weakness. In the camp men who had wept (as he himself had wept—in fear and uncertainty, in weakness and in terror) had survived those who stood frozen in what they conceived to be stoic strength. The slender tree sways in the wind. The heavy, rigid tree shudders and snaps. His daughter did not, would not, sway in the wind. Yet in recent months he had discerned a new softness, a tentative uncertainty. Twice, when they found themselves alone together, she had turned to him, and he had felt a question tremble mutely between them, but both times the moment had passed and the elusive query had gone unasked.

"Why shouldn't she have the baby?" he asked.

Shirley Cherne shrugged. Her rings were ranged before her on the kitchen table. Tiny lights glinted in the hearts of the cruelly bright gems. One by one she slipped them on.

"Once, I also decided not to have a baby," she said.

"You decided." He mimicked her harshly. "It was decided for you. There is no comparison."

He looked at her, but she turned her head, staring instead at the sapphire twisted between talons of gold that sat above her wide gold wedding band. It was not the ring he had given her on their marriage day. That one had been tossed onto a mountain of gold taken from the other Jewesses who shivered fearfully with her in the bare cabin called, with German in-genuity, "Reception." The new ring he had bought for her with the first profits earned by Cherne Knitwear.

Only once, ever, had they spoken of the lost child conceived on the fragrant needle-strewn floor of a pine forest
and abandoned on the bloodied, splintered boards of the concentration camp barrack. She had told him about it at the
displaced persons camp in Italy where they had come together
after the war, a husband and wife strangers to each other,
tentative and shy after the years apart. She had covered her
head with a ragged checked cloth, ashamed because the typhus
had left her bald and he had so loved her thick chestnut-
colored hair. He had worn a bulky field jacket, given to him
by a Jewish GI, that hid his skeletal frame, ashamed because
on their wedding night he had carried her exuberantly around
their bridal chamber while she praised him and wondered at
his strength. Now his hand trembled beneath the weight of a
laden spoon.

It was then, during the first days of that Italian reunion,
while they spoke to each other in the measured cadences of
polite strangers and as the child, Ina, stared intently at him
and relearned the word "Papa," repeating it softly again and
again, that Shaindel had told him about her abortion. Grief
had filled him with silence then, and he refused to speak of the
unspeakable. He was a fragile wisp of a man, a bereaved
father, a mysterious orphan; he might be blown away in the
wind of yet another loss. It was only the urgency of the present that gave him ballast. There were letters to be written to
the family in America, visas and affidavits to secure. He could
not afford to think of that child—conceived and aborted, the
unborn victim.

"I had to do it," Shaindel, the bald woman whose eyes were
cavernous in her fleshless face, told him (not sharing with him
the details—the rags that had gagged her screams, the blood
that had surged from her body), and he had mourned for his
chestnut-haired bride whose skin had always been cool to his
touch and whose eyes had glinted golden in the darkness.

"Of course you had to," he had said then, and turned back
to the visa applications, the letters.

They had, until this morning, never spoken of it again.

She removed the sapphire ring, touched the smooth gold of the wedding band.

"You always blamed me for that decision, for having the abortion," she said. Her voice was very low, and she rubbed the ring between her fingers, scratching her flesh with the prongs of its setting.

"Never." There was honest astonishment in his voice. He blamed no one for anything they had done or refrained from doing during those years. He had read a book written by a survivor who described snatching a crust of bread from his own starving father. Norman had not blamed him.

He had seen men in the barracks strip socks and shoes from a dead man's feet, unroll bandages from the limbs of new corpses. He had not blamed them. The man who slept on the bunk beside him, a gentle dentist from Lublin, had awakened weeping one night and told Nachum that when he and his family had been in hiding from the Germans, his infant son had suddenly begun wailing. The sound of his cry might have betrayed them all. The dentist had placed his hand tightly over the infant's mouth until the German patrol passed. When he removed it, the baby lay lifeless in his arms. His wife had clutched the tiny rigid corpse for a full day, refusing to believe her child dead, her husband a murderer.

"You are not a murderer," Nachum Czernowitz had assured him. "You tried only to save your family's lives."

But the dentist, who knew whole sections of *Eugene Onegin* by heart (and recited them softly into the darkness) and who had translated Walt Whitman into Polish, could not be comforted. He had died of pneumonia three days before the liberation, and Nachum had taken his worn boots, his thick blanket, and a tattered jacket. In the jacket pocket there was a small book of poetry. The Hebrew verses of Bialik. Nachum had the book still, concealed beneath his handkerchiefs, its flaking pages emitting an odor of loss and death. On Yom Kippur he placed it next to the memorial candles.

He did not blame the poetry-loving dentist who had killed his own newborn child.

How then could he blame Shaindel, who had sacrificed an unborn child so that she could protect her daughter and her sister's daughter? Without Shaindel, Ina and Bette would not, could not, have survived. He had never blamed her. He had respected her courage. But they had never talked about it, and he had never told her so. He had assumed, always, that it was the war and the years apart that had destroyed the warm and easy passion between them and had turned them from young married lovers into the skeletal man and the death-eyed bald woman who had come together in Italy to rebuild their lives. It was their own silence that had defeated them. She had withdrawn in a shell of wordless guilt, and he had been fearful of trespassing into the echoing canyon of her sorrow.

He moved toward her now quickly, decisively, and placed his hand against her moving wrist, forcing it into quiet submission. Her pulse throbbed wildly against his restraining finger. Once, in the camp, he had caught a bird in his fist, a weary sparrow with a battered wing. He had held it and felt its pulsating heart and felt the bird's desperate fear and the strength born of that fear. He had released the bird gently, carefully. But he did not release his wife's wrist.

"Listen," he said, and his voice was very gentle. "Listen well. I never blamed you for it. I loved you for it. You were very brave. You stayed alive, and you saved Ina for me. And now you must stop blaming yourself."

There was a heaviness to his tone. He was weighted by the years of silence when they had been caught up with building their lives anew and had talked, in the new language of their new land, only of loans and interest, new machinery, stock and design and overhead, exhausting themselves with success and coming together as husband and wife in perfunctory, passionless coupling.

Her head came down on his shoulder. She leaned limply against him, and he thought for a moment that she might fall.

He bent to kiss her eyes, as he had done on their wedding night (holding her still in his arms—the proud, strong bridegroom), and his lips found her hair and moved downward to her mouth. Gently he lifted her fingers, gnarled with arthritis and beringed. He slipped the rings off and kissed her hands, kissed the soft palm flesh that smelled of lemon-scented soap.

Tears glittered in her eyes but did not slide down her cheeks. Just so he had kissed her on their wedding night and through the early years of their marriage—the years during which they had slept on their sheeted featherbed in the Warsaw apartment they had chosen because it overlooked the park and reminded her of the woodlands of her girlhood; just so he had kissed her during the long nights of the years of terror when they fled through a forest that was no longer a sheltering place of play. She wept unshed tears for the years they had lost and for the days that were left to them.

"Nachum," she whispered. "Nachumel." The half-remembered endearment was spoken in a bride's voice, shy and loving.

They left the apartment together, and for the first time in many years they did not triple-lock their door.

"I will talk to Ina," he said as they stood in the hallway, waiting for the elevator.

"Yes."

She did not ask him what he would say.

In the elevator, on their way to the subway, they discussed the new line. Wide sleeves were coming in. Tunics would be popular. The buyer from the J. M. Horne Company in Pittsburgh would call on them that afternoon. Should they call in a model? Did it pay? They moved quickly now, anxious to get to Cherne Knitwear, to get on with the life they had built. Before they descended into the subway entrance, Shirley Cherne looked up at the sky. A pale white sun fought weakly to be seen through a veil of misty grayness. It would rain before the morning was over.

Dr. Eleanor Berenson, a cautious woman, carried both a

raincoat and an umbrella. It was too early for visiting hours
at Mount Lebanon, but she asserted her right as a physician
and received a pass for the fifth floor, which, she was reason-
ably certain, no one would ask to see. At the bank of elevators,
she met a doctor whom she had known during her residency
at Mount Lebanon. They studied each other carefully, each
taking comfort from the damage that passing years had
wrought on the other. Dr. Howard Ross, who as a resident
had been toothpick-thin, was a portly, balding middle-aged
man now. Plastic surgery was his specialty, he told her, with
emphasis on reconstruction. He rebuilt damaged hands and
fingers. Only last year he had won an award for so skillfully
operating on a badly burned cellist that the musician swore his
new hand was defter than the one that had been so nearly
incinerated.

"What's your specialty, Ellie?" he asked her.

She answered politely, although no one ever called her
Ellie. Still, she was grateful that he had not kissed her.

"Psychiatry," she said, and thought grimly that she could
add that her specialty was wounded psyches with emphasis on
frayed and tattered egos. She had no awards to report, only
the odd article in *The American Journal of Psychiatry*.

"I didn't know psychiatrists made hospital calls," he said.

"We don't usually. This is a special case."

"Aren't they all?" He looked at her with commiserative
understanding, waved, and hurried to his own office. A
woman from Larchmont was bringing her daughter to see him.
The girl's nose was perfectly attractive, the mother had assured him, but she did get so many colds, had a deviated
septum, and was sensitive about a small bump. If he could
just talk to her gently. She was, after all, a special case.

Eleanor Berenson waited patiently for the elevator, wondering vaguely what she would say to Ina Feldman, who was,
after all, truly a special case. Ina and Bette and other survivors
who came to see her, carrying their memories of misery and
terror, of irrevocable loss and unarticulated anguish; the past,
like a treacherous ganglion, blocked their clear access to the

present—they were her special cases, and she made concessions and allowances for them that she would not grant her other patients. For Ina she left her consulting room on a grim, rain-threatening morning to follow an undefined instinct.

Eleanor Berenson's father had left Germany in 1935, and the analyst had thought always about what might have happened had he never left. She teased herself with small masochistic fantasies of horror and felt grief for the grandparents and uncles she had never known who had died in Terezin. She experienced a special empathy for survivors who came to her as patients—she might have been a party to their agony—certainly she was involved in their destiny. And perhaps that was why so many survivors came to her. She knew analysts whose patients were writers and artists. The newly separated and divorced filled the consulting room of another colleague. There was a subtle tropism between analysts and the patients they attracted. Survivors came to Eleanor Berenson.

She remembered, as she rode the empty elevator up, the emotional weariness in Ina's voice. It was that weariness that had resulted in her taking the unorthodox step of visiting the hospital. Her colleagues, she knew, would not approve. She was not sure that she approved her own decision, but it was taken, and there was no turning back. On the fifth floor she turned to the right. She had known this corridor well, as both doctor and patient.

Eleanor Berenson was a short woman who sat so well, so erectly in her chair, that she gave the impression of height. Patients, seeing her out of the context of the consulting room, were always amazed to realize how small she was. Ina, sitting up in bed, absorbed in the sprawling printout sheets spread before her, was, as always, newly startled by the analyst's size and even more surprised by the beribboned box that was held out to her.

"Chocolate truffles," Eleanor Berenson said. "I always like sweets when I'm in the hospital. And I know you like these."

"Thank you," Ina said. She could not remember ever having

mentioned her fondness for the sweet to Eleanor Berenson. Perhaps the analyst was thinking of Bette. She felt a flare of jealousy akin to the jealousy she had felt as a child when her mother seemed too involved with Bette. She loved her cousin, but she did not want to share her mother. (There was, after all, little enough to share.) She loved her cousin, but she did not want to share Eleanor Berenson. Did Eleanor Berenson, she wondered, ever confuse her with her cousin? Perhaps analysts, like parents, mixed their patients up and, thinking of one, called the name of another. No. Analysts could not afford the luxury of such confusion.

Eleanor Berenson settled herself in the Formica visitor's chair and glanced around the room.

"I see you have a roommate," she said, looking at Miriam Gottlieb's empty bed. "That's good. I always found being here in a private room very depressing."

An aide came in, smiled, and stripped Miriam's bed. The drawing of the baseball-playing panda fluttered to the floor, and Eleanor Berenson got up to retrieve it. She glanced at the drawing approvingly.

"My friend Ruthie drew it," Ina said.

"It's nice for a children's room." The aide stood back to study it, balancing the fresh linens in snowy hills on her arms.

"In the right frame," Eleanor Berenson agreed.

The casual exchange vaguely surprised Ina. This floor of women broke down so many barriers to create the atmosphere of a select sorority, a strong sisterhood concerned only with feminalities. Intimacy and involvement came swiftly on this corridor where women walked slowly in flowing dressing gowns or moved crisply in white uniforms. The male doctors and technicians were tolerated for their professional skills, but they were excluded from the earnestly exchanged confidences, the spontaneous rush of caring and compassion that the women extended to each other. Ina had been seeing Eleanor Berenson as a patient for two years, but only on this hospital floor had they come toward each other as people, drawn together by the common denominator of their woman-hood. Eleanor Berenson, who admired a whimsical drawing of a panda, had spent her own long nights in a hospital room, listening to the breathing of another woman in the bed beside her. She had experienced childbirth. Ina had seen her son, a tall boy whom she sometimes met at the elevator. He moved with the awkward gait of adolescence, and his skin was very bad. Ina took pleasure in the boy's acne. It humanized his mother.

"Miriam, the woman in the next bed, has a very sick baby," Ina said.

"I'm sorry. I guess that's why she's on this floor. I know they don't usually put obstetric cases on five."

"How do you know that?"

"I was a resident at Mount Lebanon," the analyst replied. "I'm a medical doctor, remember? And I've been a patient here, too."

"Yes." Ina touched the bandage at her breast. Perhaps she would ask Eleanor Berenson, M.D., who must know something about fibromas and cysts, melanomas and spreading malignancies, whether there was any significance to a deep incision.

"I was surprised that you never mentioned going into the hospital," the doctor said, her voice coolly professional now.

"Well, I did cancel the appointments."

"That's not the same as telling me why you were canceling. I assumed it was because of a business obligation—a business trip perhaps."

"I never said that."

"It's what you didn't say that counts." The analyst was quiet now, waiting. She wore a gray suit that exactly matched her short steel-gray hair. A black thread clung to her skirt, and she plucked it off.

"It didn't seem important enough to mention."

"Not important enough? Breast surgery? Most women feel very emotional about such an experience. Many women who are not even in treatment arrange to speak to a therapist about their feelings at such a time."

"I didn't have such feelings. It was only minor surgery. Now, though, I'm not so sure. They haven't given us a final report. And the other thing—I thought then—when I made the arrangement—that everything was resolved, our decision made."

"The other thing?" Eleanor Berenson's voice was gentle, prodding. She lit a cigarette. There was no ashtray in this room where a neatly lettered red-and-white sign requested patients and their visitors to refrain from smoking. She flicked her match into Ina's coffee cup.

"I should have told you," Ina said. "I'm pregnant. We didn't plan it—it happened. You know we'd never thought of having another child. It seemed clear to me that I'd have an abortion."

"And now—it no longer seems clear?" The analyst's tone was casual.

"Ray wants the baby. He told me so yesterday. And my mother visited. She told me she had an abortion in the camp. She's afraid it will do to me what it did to her. She wants me to have the baby." A fatigued listlessness weighted her tone, and she played fretfully with the hospital bracelet on her wrist.

"And what do you want?" Again that skillful, gentle voice, that incisive, probing inflection. Ina thought of the way Dr. Isaacs's scalpel had moved so expertly, so carefully and cleverly, through the soft glandular tissue of her breast. How skilled these doctors were, how insidiously they pried loose diseased tissue, deadly secrets.

"Me? I don't want the baby. I'm afraid not to have it—if Ray really wants it. I'm afraid to have it. Maybe, I don't know, maybe I want it after all. Miriam's baby—the woman in the next bed, her name is Miriam—her baby may die, and I— I may decide to kill mine. What kind of a person am I? I don't know what I want." She was crying now, odd, griefless tears that squeezed their way out of her eyes and trailed hotly down her cheeks. Her breast throbbed angrily. It was the damn painkiller that was making her so emotional. What was happening to her? Damn it—two jags in two days. She who so seldom cried, who remained dry-eyed through dreams in which a trio of death-driven Nazis pursued her—death spewing out of their swollen organs of life. Yet the barefoot child of the dream, small Ina, did not cry, while here, in the safety of this room, tears burned her cheeks.

The analyst held out a tissue.

"I think, Ina," she said quietly, "that it's going to be a very hard decision for you to make. I suspect that what you want most of all is to be free of any decision. You want things to simply happen because they must. But it won't work that way."

"Yes. That's true," Ina said. Her mother had done what she had to do. Her decision, her action, came of necessity. She had had no alternative. She had aborted her baby so that she might live and give Ina and Bette her protection. Ina, however, was the prisoner of her own freedom. She had too many choices, too many options. Like Ruthie, she danced to too many tunes and could not single out the melody that was clearly her own.

"There is something else," Eleanor Berenson said hesitantly. "It may affect your decision so I'll bring it up now. Otherwise I would have waited for it to emerge in our sessions. It is something I have often experienced in my own practice and that appears again and again in the monographs written by analysts who work with survivors. It is—let's call it a syndrome. I am speaking about survivor guilt. Do you think it may, perhaps, be relevant to you?"

"Guilt? You mean because I survived and Yedidiah didn't?" Ina's voice was very low. Poor Yedidiah, the little double-jointed boy with lashes so long they had brushed his jutting cheekbones. Jeddy had inherited the double-jointedness and Rachel the long, thick lashes. Perhaps a new baby would be born with jutting cheekbones and Yedidiah's high musical laugh.

"Yes." The analyst's voice was firm. She had crossed the danger mark. She could not turn back now.

"Maybe. I always thought that if it had been Yedidiah who had lived, my parents would have been different. He was so bright, so clever. They had such great hopes for him. He could have been anything."

"Even the president of his own business—perhaps a computer consultation firm?" Eleanor Berenson asked drily.

"Yes, of course," Ina agreed, and then her voice drifted into softness. "I see what you're saying. You think I've been trying, all these years, to be my brother."

"Exactly. And now, perhaps, you may even give birth to him."

Pain twisted Ina's face. Her heart pounded noisily. Sweat turned the yellow of her negligee to dark gold beneath her arms.

"What do you want?" she cried. "What do you want from me?"

"Nothing." There was a new soothing quality to the therapist's voice, not unlike the expression in Dr. Isaacs's voice as he had completed surgery. There now, I'm almost through. Soon—soon—you'll feel better. "I want you to know what you want from yourself. I don't want you to regret a decision taken too hastily or a decision not taken at all."

"Thank you," Ina said bitterly. "Thank you very much."

Eleanor Berenson glanced at her watch and rose to leave.

"Please, Ina," she said, "think about what I brought up. Flow with your feelings. Do what you want to do. Do what is best for you. There is no right. There is no wrong. And no matter what you decide, you will not be punished."

"I don't think that's true," Ina said softly, and wondered if Eleanor Berenson was thinking of the dream—her dream. What, after all, had those small girls, she and Bette, done that they should be so cruelly punished? The mystery worried her. It was a familiar fatigue. Sometimes she moved through that dream with a tiredness so heavy that submission to the advancing martinets of death seemed a relief, a release.

The analyst hesitated, but she did not reply. She moved toward the bed, kissed Ina gently on the forehead, and left swiftly, brushing past Miriam and Marnie in the doorway.

Miriam, when she entered the room, was deathly pale. Marnie's hand rested lightly, protectively, on her shoulder.

"Oh, Ina," Miriam said, "the baby's worse. I saw it right away. His color. And he hardly moves."

She did not weep but sat at the edge of the bed, her arms crossed at her breasts, swollen with the milk her child could not drink. Marnie eased her down, covered her with the hospital blanket.

"The baby will be all right," Ina said. Perhaps a bargain could be struck. If Miriam's baby died, she would bear her own. A life for a death. A slap in Hitler's face. A remnant of Israel. An irrepressible, hysterical laugh grew within her throat, but when she opened her mouth, a sob escaped—a brief, fluttery gasp of misery. The rain had begun, and tiny droplets wept softly against the wide-paned windows.

Ray had called Dr. Isaacs's office when he arrived at his own desk. The doctor was unavailable, and the pleasant-voiced receptionist who answered the phone knew nothing about Ina's tests. He called again an hour later. Her voice, still pleasant, was tinged with annoyance.

"I have no information for you, Mr. Feldman. Suppose you leave your number. We'll call you."

"No," Ray said. "I won't be at my desk. I'll try again."

He hung up, feeling a clutch of fear. Always, when a judgment was handed down, if it had gone against the interests he represented, he hesitated to make the call, often procrastinating transmittal of the bad news until late afternoon. Perhaps Isaacs followed a similar pattern. What if the news were bad? All right. He would consider that. If the permanent section showed a malignancy, the breast would have to be removed. Didn't they sometimes remove both breasts? He recalled a photo of Betty Ford and Happy Rockefeller and remembered that Happy Rockefeller had undergone a double mastectomy. Was that the worst?

He sorted out the facts available to him as he might prepare for an examination before trial. But in this case there could be no negotiations, no plea bargaining. He could not say: "All right, Dr. Isaacs, take the left breast and leave the right one. All right, Doctor, take both breasts, but leave me my wife." Or perhaps—and his heart sank at the thought that came without warning—"Take my wife, but leave me the baby she is carrying."

His hands trembled. He reached again for the phone, looked at his watch, and pushed it away. His eyes burned. That morning at breakfast Jeddy had looked up at him with strangely glittering eyes and asked, "Mom's not going to die, is she?"

She was not going to die. It could not happen to them, to her. He had been too often deserted. Too swiftly his parents had left him, had catapulted him into aloneness. It could not happen again. He had been too long alone, he loved her too much. She was fine. The lump on her breast was simply a benign growth. She would continue her pregnancy, and their home would ring again with the full-lunged bellow of an infant's cry, the prattle of a baby's voice. He would feel again the bony prehensile grasp of a child's—*his child's*—fingers around his own. Ina would want the child. Finally, she must want it. He willed her to his own desire, his own rationale. New life negated death, banished nightmares of fear and loss. He did not want his wife to awaken weeping in the night, haunted by nameless terror, elusive memories. During her pregnancies she had slept always with a small smile lightly upon her lips. He wanted to see that smile again, to place his hand upon her swelling abdomen and feel the small unborn child of his love and of his making skitter beneath his touch.

A sudden wind drove the rain in a fierce crescendo against his window, and through the streaks of falling drops a tiny rainbow webbed its way onto the plate glass and formed a delicate prism in the corner of the pane. He saw it as a lucky talisman and reached for the folder on his desk and buzzed for a secretary to come in. Ina would be fine. He knew that she would be fine.

By mid-morning the light drizzle had turned into a heavy rainfall. Fat, clumsy drops raced down the windows, and Ina drew the drapes. The thick white fiberglass muffled the sound of the wind but did not block the wail of a siren that drifted up from the street below. Miriam Gottlieb stirred uneasily in a sleep induced by grief and drugs rather than fatigue. Angry blotches of red dotted her cheeks and brow, and her lips moved as though to make mute protest. Earlier the heavyset nurse had brought her a white pill which she had swallowed with the disinterested obedience of a child too ill to protest.

"This will make you feel better," the nurse had assured her. "Everything will be all right."

She had glanced at Marnie and Ina, intercepting their glance, and nodded in complicity. Of course everything would not be all right, but was there anything else to say? She did not look at them as she left the room, and Marnie stayed only a few minutes longer.

"Did the baby seem that much worse?" Ina asked.

"I don't know. It was the first time I ever saw him. But the nurse said they were worried because a digestive problem had developed. I never saw anything so tiny, so helpless." The model clenched her fists, lowered her head.

"I know. I went to see him the other night," Ina said. "It's heartbreaking. Still, they have hope. They've done so much research, have so much new equipment."

"Yes. I suppose." But Marnie's voice was dull, unconvinced. She wandered the room, her fingers absently twirling the rose satin length of her sash, and left, waving absently to Ina, who watched Miriam as she sometimes watched Rachel. Miriam reminded her of Rachel, who collapsed into rigid despair in moments of hurt and disappointment. Often Ina coaxed her daughter out of the blackness with treats and promises, offering the child a movie, a bicycle basket, an afternoon at the ballet. What could she promise this young woman who wanted only her baby, newborn and half-alive? If your child dies, then I will have mine? Could she, would she, say that—mean that? Her yellow nightgown grew damp with sweat. She touched her pulse and felt it race as crazily and wildly as her thoughts. It was the damn painkiller that was making her think that way. She would not ask for it again. Exhausted, she leaned back against the pillow, and when she felt calmer, she picked up her work folder and concentrated again on the neat rows of figures.

She worked steadily for an hour. She was designing a system for a movie company that would help determine when films at local theaters across the country should be changed. She glanced at an input chart, checking the accumulated revenues for a science-fiction film playing in the movie house of a Kansas prairie town. According to her system, ticket purchases there would peak at thirty-five hundred and decline steadily for the next three days, when a comedy would be shown. To carry the system one step further she needed data on the success of that particular comedy in other theaters. Someone in her office had better check it. She reached for the phone and glanced at Miriam, who slept peacefully now, her cheek cushioned on her arm. Slowly, she replaced the receiver. She did not, at that moment, give a damn what film played in Goshen, Kansas. Impatiently, she gathered her data sheets together and replaced them in their folders. It occurred to her that it was the first time her work had seemed foolish to her.

She went to the window, pulled the drapes aside, and looked down into the street where a woman and a child wearing matching yellow slickers ran through the street. The child's hat blew off, and the woman dashed to get it. She threw it to the small boy, who caught it, and holding hands they rushed down the street together, butting forward against the sheets of rain.

Ina took out her makeup case and carried it over to the sink. She studied herself carefully in the harsh fluorescent light. She coated the shadows that ringed her dark eyes with compressed powder, brushed her lashes with mascara, applied circlets of blush to her cheeks. She would ask Marnie to do her hair again in that single braid. Ray had liked it, and it made her look younger. Young enough to be the mother of a new baby? The question teased and amused her. At the playground sandbox she would be the elder stateswoman, dispensing expert advice on toilet training and tantrums. There was one such experienced mother of older children at each playground. Ina had known such a woman when Rachel was a toddler. Her name was Karen, and her older children were in high school. She wore loose tent dresses and read Camus while her small son grabbed other children's pails and shovels. Like all knowledgeable veterans, she carried minimal equipment yet was always prepared for emergencies and dispensed Bactine and Band-Aids, zwieback and extra shirts. She had left a job lecturing on literature at a university to raise her new and (she admitted ruefully) unexpected baby.

"Was it worth it?" a mother of twin toddlers, her own eyes red-rimmed with lack of sleep, her loose shirt streaked with child stains, had asked.

The older woman had seemed startled by the question.

"Worth it? There was no alternative." She had turned back to her book. The week before she had finished *The Stranger*, and she was halfway through *The Plague*. She did not return to the park, but they learned that she was away at a sanitarium. She had swallowed an entire bottle of aspirin while her small son napped in his crib. Ina had not thought of Karen for years, but she remembered now, suddenly and irrelevantly, that the paper jacket of her copy of *The Plague* had a ragged rip. It had been a blue jacket with a drawing in brown of the port at Oran running across it.

Ina went over to her bedside table and leafed through her own books. One by one she picked them up and set them down. The closely printed words overpowered and exhausted her. She had no patience for them. What she wanted was a magazine showing brightly colored pictures printed on slick paper. She wanted photographs that would carry her out of the room into worlds where flowers were arranged in graceful bowls and women in tailored tweeds climbed out of sleek sports cars or dashed across broad lawns with russet-colored afghan hounds. She would ask Ray to get her a subscription to *Harper's Bazaar, Vogue,* perhaps *Town and Country.* But for now she would borrow a magazine from Marnie. She hurried out of the room, glad to have a destination.

Marnie was not in her room, where the bedside table was covered with flowers and rainbow-colored robes were tossed over the chairs and drifted down from hooks and hangers. Small silver-capped bottles of makeup were lined precariously along the sink, and the light fragrance of a very expensive perfume made Ina think of English country gardens at summer's peak. A large black portfolio was propped against the wall. It had fallen open, and photographs were scattered across the floor. On their glossy surfaces Marnie smiled from a mountaintop and Marnie stared seriously through an open window. She danced alone in a white gown against which her skin shone duskily. She skied, laughing, down a gentle slope. She held her head up to the summer sun, her naked breasts arched to meet the shooting rays of light. Marnie mused pensively over a letter. That photo, Ina remembered, had illustrated an advertisement for a better-grade notepaper. Marnie touched a strip of silk to her cheek. That had been an advertisement for an English fabric designer. Carefully, Ina replaced the photos in the portfolio and went to the waiting room, where Marnie sat on the red couch, combing the hair of the teenaged girl whose parents had brought her a negligee of bridal white.

"All you need, Tina, are three bobby pins and a ribbon or a rubber band," Marnie told her. "You do a quick twist and there it is."

The girl touched her long dark hair.

"I'm going to have radiation," she said. "They say your hair falls out from radiation." Tears, like raindrops brimming with light, stood in her eyes. She was full-breasted and had graceful womanly hips, but death lurked within her body and she was a child. She might live, but she would lose her hair and be ugly. She did not want to live if she were ugly. No one invited ugly girls to parties, and they were the last to be picked for clubs or teams.

"Hair grows back after it falls out," Ina said. "My mother had beautiful chestnut-colored hair. She got sick and lost it, but it grew back—even thicker than before. Don't worry about your hair. Just think about getting well."

Tina looked at her, dry-eyed now.

"I try," she said, "but it's hard. My mother cries. Oh, not in front of me, but her eyes are always red. The doctor says they've had very good luck with the radiation—and the chemotherapy. And if hair really does grow back . . . The doctor says so but I don't believe him . . ." Her voice drifted off as she balanced her accounts. She was a child trying to please. She was a child who knew that her mother cried when she was alone. Mothers, strong, impervious to all, wept and took whole bottles of aspirin only when the clouds of death and desperation hovered over them.

"When my mother comes to visit, I'll introduce her to you. She'll tell you herself, show you," Ina promised.

The girl nodded. Again she touched her fingers to the ponytail Marnie had fashioned. She walked from the room but turned shyly at the door to wave to them. She had been taught politeness.

"Cancer, I suppose," Ina said, looking after her.

"Yes. Ovarian cancer. She's only fourteen. She got her period a couple of months ago, and the bleeding just didn't stop. Clots. Small hemorrhages. They took X rays, did exploratory surgery, and found it. They removed the ovaries, and if it didn't spread, I guess the radiation will get the rest. At least I hope so." Marnie sighed and shivered.

"My daughter keeps worrying about when she'll get her period," Ina said.

"Oh, this sort of thing is very rare."

"Yes. Everything is rare."

Small Beth Goldstein, dead of leukemia at eleven—Rachel's classmate, Jeddy's friend's sister. Ina had gone to pay a con-

dolence call. So rare, a weeping aunt had said. The young son
of a systems analyst with whom Ina occasionally worked had
slipped from his seat at school one day. He had lain in a coma
for three weeks and drifted into death as silently and mysteriously as he had slid into sleep. So rare, they had said as they
collected money for a scholarship in the child's name. An
aneurysm. She had heard of three such rarities in the months
that followed. An aneurysm, a weakened vein in the brain, a
chimeric virus. She trembled for her children, longed to call
them, wished them at each side of her as they sometimes lay,
stretched out, watching television, their bodies warm and relaxed against her own.

"You had breast surgery, Ina?" Marnie asked.

Ina nodded. The dressing was a mound of sterile whiteness
beneath her buttercup-yellow peignoir.

"It was minor. A small cyst. We're just waiting for a
pathology report now, but they're almost positive there is no
malignancy." Her voice was steady as she used the word, but
she felt the dart of fear, the shadow of doubt. "What about
you, Marnie?"

"I'm fine now—at least the doctor seems to think so. I'll
probably go home tomorrow. I'm pregnant, and there was
some bleeding, and I got pretty frightened. I guess I'm awfully
nervous about this baby, and my obstetrician is pretty con-
servative, so he checked me in here. But I'm okay now.
Really. Just fine." She repeated the word as though emphasis
would evolve into truth.

"That's good," Ina said. "You seemed a little down this
morning."

"Yes. I guess I am. Bob, my husband, is sort of ambivalent
about the pregnancy. He just started his own agency, and we
need a couple of months to really get it going—to make sure it
will work without me. We could use another year for a
cushion. It would be a shame if he didn't make it. We were
a long time getting to where we're at. We didn't fall into a
gravy pot. We were kids together on 127th Street. Does that
give you some sort of a picture?"

"Yes," Ina said. "I know about Harlem."

"Oh, yes. Everyone knows about Harlem, but believe me,
it's the kind of thing you'd have to live through to know about.
There were five kids in my family. Five kids from three
different fathers, but not one father in sight, not one paycheck
coming home. Two of my sisters are on the street. You've
probably passed them on 45th, on the way to the theater.
They work together and dress like twins—high boots, short
leather skirts, cowboy shirts. Their pimps are good friends.
My kid brother is in Wiltwyck, but my other brother's on his
way to becoming a doctor. He lucked out. He got into a good
City University program and made it. We helped some, Bob
and I, but mostly it was him." She smiled, proud of the
brother whom she had been able to help and who had
triumphed even as she had.

Ina envied her that pride and felt again the clinging loneliness of the only child whose home is a cocoon of quiet and
whose games are limited to intricate spreads of solitaire and
fantasies whispered into the darkness. But even that loneliness
had come to her by default. She was not an only child. She
had had a brother with huge eyes and wondrous fingers. His
laughter echoed sometimes in empty rooms, and often, during
those first days in America, she had spoken softly to him in the
night. "It's nice here, Yedidiah," she had said. "It's warm, and
there's enough to eat. Why didn't you wait? Why did you go
away? Why did you have to die, Yedidiah? Now they want
me to do everything you should have done."

She had long since recognized her anger at her brother for
dying, for deserting her and Bette. This she had once told
Eleanor Berenson, on a wintry day when snowdrops pelted
the analyst's river-view window.

But only today had she acknowledged the full breadth of
her anger at her brother for leaving her alone with her parents,
for allowing her to assume the responsibility that should have
been his. She had to be the good child, the exemplary student,
striving and achieving. She had to make all their hard work
worthwhile and provide them with the dimension of life

Cherne Knitwear could not give them. She too mourned her
brother, but their grief would not be contained. Her children
were their grandchildren, her son named for theirs, but she
could not entice them out of their sorrow, woo them from the
loss of their boy, their son, their Yedidiah. Always and forever
his picture smiled down at them from their mantelpiece, and
his unlit birthday candles smoldered blackly in their hearts.
Instead, they kindled memorial flames for the child who had
not lived to become a man.

"I had a brother," she told Marnie. "He died very young."

"I'm sorry," the model said, and Ina was glad that she asked
no questions. Could Ina have said, as Marnie had, "That's the
sort of thing you'd have to live through to know about"?
There was, even to suffering, an arrogance, an exclusivity, a
subtle competitiveness. How did My Lai compare to Babi
Yar? What was Harlem compared to Belsen? What was a
brother at Wiltwyck compared with a brother dead in a concentration camp—two sisters lost to the streets compared to a
fetus killed so that a woman would not be murdered? Who
kept score, and was there a score to be kept?

"It was a long time ago," Ina said, and steered the conversation back to Marnie. "Your husband came from a large family
also?"

"Yes. But different from mine. His parents were together.
There were three other kids. His father had a good job with a
loading company, and his mother was a practical nurse. They
kept the kids in school, dressed pretty good, and they saved
enough to buy a house in St. Albans—that's a section of
Queens. They rented it out till they had enough money to
furnish it. Bob's mother wanted a couch from Macy's. But
they were on their way. Bob and I were in our sophomore
year in high school. We went to a New Year's Eve party, and
we were on our way home when we heard the sirens. There
was a fire in their lousy stinking building, and the damn rat-
trap exploded—just went up like a tinderbox. From a couple of
blocks off, people thought they were watching New Year's
fireworks. All of them went up. His mother, his father, the

twin boys, the little sister who sang like an angel. You could smell their flesh burning, cooking. We buried little pieces of burned bones. Sometimes I smell it still. You never smelled anything like that."

"Yes," Ina said very softly. "I have." But Marnie was not listening. Her hands were clasped in her lap, the dark tapering fingers woven together in a basket of desperation.

"Bob and I got married two years later. He finished school at night because he started working. We needed the money. For me. For lessons. Elocution and music and modeling. We needed cash for clothing and for everything that goes with selling yourself. Photographers. You can't get to be a model before you've got a classy leather portfolio filled with glossy, expensive pictures. Bob worked. I worked. We weren't going to burn up in any fire on 127th Street, and our kids weren't going to walk the streets." Her voice, trained into softness by expensive teachers, took on a new edge, reminiscent, Ina thought, of her mother's, of Shirley Cherne, who had looked up from the first account books of Cherne Knitwear and said, "All right. Now we begin again. No more dirt. No more rags. No more being hungry."

"Well, you've done it," Ina said. A magazine on the waiting room table was open to a picture of Marnie. She had posed wearing a long mink coat, her hair threaded with strands of pearls. Marnie looked at it and smiled bitterly.

"My looks won't last forever. The agency's the answer. Bob's right. We need time. A year, two years. That's why he doesn't want this baby. No. That's not fair. He does and he doesn't. But goddamn it—I know for sure. I do, and I'm going to have it. When I saw Miriam's baby today, my heart turned. I waited a long time, and I worked hard. What's the good of what we've done if it's just for ourselves?" She reached for the magazine and slammed it shut, tossed it to the floor.

"You don't know," she said quietly to Ina, "how it feels to be unsure about something as important as this. I'm sorry. I'm very lousy company." Abruptly she rose and hurried from the

room. Ina remained, staring down at the magazine she no
longer wanted to read.

"But I do know," she said in a loud, clear voice. A passing
aide paused, stared at her curiously, and moved wearily on,
pushing a steel cart laden with linens ahead of her. A single
washcloth slipped from its pile and fluttered, like a small white
flag of submission, to the waxed linoleum floor. Ina stepped on
it heavily as she walked back to her room, where Miriam still
slept, while swirling tongues of rain licked the windows behind the thick white drapes.

Mornings were a whirlpool of lost hours for Dot Weinglass.
She had meant to be at the hospital before noon, but one small
crisis after another delayed her. Ethan and Claire overslept
and had to be driven to school. Larry called and asked her to
trace a discrepancy in the checkbook, and she spent half an
hour with a sheath of rainbow-colored canceled checks,
searching out the error. Her youngest son, Simon, ran a low-
grade fever, and although the pediatrician assured her that the
temperature meant nothing, Dot had insisted on bringing the
child to his office. Before she left, she spent long minutes comforting Ingrid, the au pair girl, who had a brief and inexplicable crying jag in the kitchen.

The doctor had been irritated and perfunctory. When he
muttered something about the dangers of overprotection, Dot
made a mental note to switch to a younger man who had
opened a family practice in her building. The words *family
practice* intrigued and comforted her. The family was the
cornerstone of Dot's life, and determinedly she explored any
service or product designed to sustain and reinforce it. She
joined a health club because its prospectus emphasized op-
portunities for the family to play together. She belonged to a
reading group whose selections emphasized literature oriented
to the family. She enrolled religiously in courses at the New
School taught by psychologists and sociologists who distributed
impressive reading lists and discoursed on subtle dimensions in

family life. The only vacations she and Larry took without the children consisted of weekend retreats to a Westchester mansion where, between lavish meals and nature walks, experts (often the same experts who taught her courses) discussed child rearing. The couples in attendance listened earnestly and took notes in the leather-bound notebooks that the organizers of the weekend distributed to demonstrate their seriousness. One does not write drivel on thirteen-pound notepaper bound in Italian leather. Once, after subtle urging from Dot, Ray had suggested that they join the Weinglasses on such a weekend.

Firmly, politely, Ina had declined. But she knew that Dot was deadly serious in her dedication to Larry and the children, a devotion that included Rachel and Jeddy because they were Ray's family. Once, in her consciousness-raising group, Ina had talked about her sister-in-law and described Dot's long years of trying to conceive and her total involvement in the children she had finally adopted. Reactions were swift and bitter, and the pot-scented air trembled with harsh, predictable recrimination. Dot was archaic, totally unliberated, a stereotypic throwback, a modern caricature of the vanished Jewish mother. "Only instead of chicken soup she offers fulfillment of potential," someone said.

"She's nuts. A self-denying neurotic," Ruthie contributed. "And probably not very bright."

Ina, who loved Dot and relied and depended upon her, had, treacherously, not replied. She had tossed Dot out to them, knowing precisely what they would say, wanting them to prove Dot wrong and thereby prove Ina right. But she knew the truth. Dot was good and strong and very bright. She had graduated from Barnard *magna cum laude*, effortlessly earned an advanced degree in art education, and after several years of teaching had been offered an administrative position designing an art curriculum for inner-city schools. She had rejected the offer and concentrated instead on the family she was determined to have. She tried desperately to become pregnant, visiting fertility clinics in distant cities, undergoing exhaustive tests that revealed nothing. Eventually she and Larry decided to adopt, and her children's needs became her life. Often, when a child was ill, or when Dot suspected an illness, she did not leave the apartment at all but spent whole days at a time adjusting the vaporizer, fetching drinks and medication, and reading endless stories while the au pair girl watched her with tolerant amusement. If Ina were not in the hospital, Dot would not have left Simon, although the child was content enough propped up in front of the television set, watching Ernie and Bert cavort down Sesame Street.

"Bad," Simon said gleefully, shaking a fist at Bert, who had upset an apple cart.

Dot smiled. The sound of Simon's voice filled her with joy. When Simon had been brought to them, he had been shrouded in a silence so profound they feared him mute. Dot had taken the baby from the social worker's arms and felt him rigid and unresponding within her embrace. For long weeks he did not cry but only whimpered softly, like a hurt and frightened animal. When the other children laughed and played, he stared at them through his great dark eyes as though mystified by their joy. Dot had, during the first long months, despaired of making the child her own. He seemed, in his pain and angry sorrow, to belong still to the ravaged land he had left behind. She had thought seriously and fearfully of confessing failure and giving him up. Once, before the final adoption papers were signed, she had spoken of that fear at a family party, a birthday dinner for Jeddy at Ina's home. Shirley Cherne had looked at her sharply and reached for a huge ruby-colored apple from which she took only a single bite before discarding it.

"So don't sign the papers. It's an easy thing to walk away from what isn't yours. But what is your own, you fight for and you keep."

Dot had not replied. A subtle enmity existed between her and Ina's mother. Tenaciously, they competed for Ina's love that was already their own. The older woman had looked across the room where Ina and Bette sat together laughing over a private joke. They had by chance dressed very much alike that day, in dresses of soft blue wool, and both of them wore their long dark hair loose about their faces. They looked more like twin sisters than cousins. These lovely young women belonged to Shirley Cherne. They were her own, and she had fought for them and kept them safe and alive when others were lost to danger and death.

Dot had not answered Shirley, but a new and fierce determination had seized her. At that moment Simon had become her child, and she had, through the weeks and months that followed, battered her way through the fortress of misery that surrounded him. She had held him close for hours, and he had learned to laugh, to relax in her arms, to shake his fist at a cartoon character and call out, "Bad. Bad Ernie. Bad Bert."

"I'm going to the hospital to visit Aunt Ina," Dot said to the child, hugging him although he strained against her, more interested in his television show than in her embrace. "Be a good boy. Listen to Ingrid."

"Yes. Okay. Bye." Simon, like a small Oriental prince, waved her away. His arm flapped imperiously in the sleeve of his plaid flannel bathrobe. She bent and dropped a kiss on his silken dark head.

Before she left, she called Ina's house and asked Carmen to check Ina's shoe size. Dot wondered, not for the first time, why Ina continued to employ Carmen. The housekeeper was so distant, so cold. But then Dot knew that Ina instinctively kept her distance in most relationships. Closeness frightened her. Where other women proffered a cheek for a perfunctory social kiss, Ina extended her hand. It had taken Dot long years to develop an ease and warmth with her brother's wife, and even now, although there was genuine affection between the two women, she knew that an emotional no-man's-land stretched barrenly between them—a subtly mined area that she must tread with care.

Lurking in that bleak terrain was the mystery of Ina's war-seared childhood, the death of her young brother, her own internment—unthinkable and thus unspeakable. Dot Weinglass could not share the terror memories so tenaciously guarded by Ina and Bette and by Norman and Shirley Cherne.

Dot stopped at a small boutique and bought a pair of hand-knit slippers.

"Size six—in yellow," she told the salesgirl, who knew her well because the boutique stocked wooden puzzles from Sweden and she called Dot whenever a new shipment came in. "They're for my sister-in-law. She's in the hospital."

"I'm sorry. Nothing serious, I hope," said the salesgirl.

"No, I don't think so," Dot said, and was surprised by the uncertainty in her own voice.

It was raining hard when she left the shop, and she hailed a cab. Relaxing against the deep leather seat, she took out her compact and looked at herself with satisfaction in the small mirror. Her skin was bronzed by the week in the Caribbean sunshine, and there was a golden sheen to the light brown hair that exactly matched her brother Ray's. The children too had marvelous color, and Dot had been bothered because Rachel seemed pale and tired now. Ray and Ina should take the children away for a spring vacation. The weekends at the Amagansett house were not enough. But then Ina would not leave her agency. Perhaps after the hospital experience she herself would feel the need for a vacation. Dot toyed nervously with the ribbon on the gift box. Why was Ina staying in the hospital so long if the procedure was really so minor?

The cab stopped for a light, and Dot recognized a heavyset woman who hurried across the street, her head bent against the driving rain. She had been a member of a therapy group Dot had attended very briefly—a group composed entirely of women who did not conceive, although clinical tests had failed to reveal any physical causes. "It's experimental. The therapist is looking for underlying emotional reasons," the gynecologist who suggested it had explained to Dot.

She had attended five sessions. The heavyset woman had said nothing for the first three, and during the fourth she had spoken haltingly of loneliness and failure and cried uncontrol-

lably, bent almost double and clutching her heavy breasts. She
did not return for the next session, and Dot herself had
dropped out of the group, which disbanded a few months
later. She watched the woman hurry down Madison Avenue
now and wondered if, after all, she had ever had a child. A
young couple rushed past the cab, laughing at each other as
the rain coursed down their faces. Dot smiled at them, although they could not see her, and thought about Simon and
the way he had shaken his fist at the television screen. Determinedly she turned her thoughts away from overweight
women who wept openly about their barrenness in the company of strangers.

"Sweet baby," she whispered to the absent Simon as the
light changed and the cab careened forward and lurched to
a stop in front of Mount Lebanon.

She had not been to the hospital since Jeddy's circumcision,
when she had ridden up in the elevator with Shirley and Norman Cherne. For once she and Shirley had been relaxed with
each other, both overjoyed at the swiftness of Ina's labor, the
health and beauty of the newborn child. Norman Cherne had
been very quiet, starting nervously each time the elevator
stopped. He had left, pleading illness, even before the ceremony was completed. Well, at least today the Chernes would
not be there. Ray had told her that they would visit Ina only
in the evening.

"It's their season," Ray had said. It seemed to him he was
always apologizing to his sister for his wife's family, even
when no apology was necessary.

"Oh, I understand," Dot had assured him, but she knew that
she would never understand her sister-in-law's parents—the
flashy, abrasive woman who wore too many rings and the
florid-faced, heavy man who hid behind his silence and his
laughter. It was only Bette, of all that family, with whom Dot
could establish any rapport—gentle, quiet Bette, as concerned
about her own children as Dot herself was about Ethan, Claire,
and Simon. She would call the apartment from Ina's room,

Dot thought as the elevator stopped at five. Simon was fine, she knew, but Ingrid's tears had left her uneasy.

It was lunchtime, and the long stainless steel meal carts stood in the corridors as nurses and aides hurried from room to room carrying the plastic trays. The odors of overcooked vegetables and singed meat mingled with the antiseptic hospital smell.

"Dot!" Ina, who was settled in a chair beside her own table, reached out to her sister-in-law, taking her tanned hand in her own.

"Ina. You look fine. How are you feeling?"

"Okay. But not as good as you look. What a great tan! Sit down. Care for some watery cauliflower or burned pot roast?"

"No, thanks. But you go ahead."

"I'm just about finished." Ina pushed the wheeled table away and looked across the room.

"Miriam—meet my sister-in-law, Dot." There was no need for last names. The hospital room created an immediate intimacy. "Miriam, you'd better eat. The food's bad enough when it's hot, but cold—ugh."

"Hello, Dot. I'm just not hungry." The young woman's voice was weak, disinterested.

"Eat anyway," Ina replied brusquely, and dutifully Miriam slipped the aluminum foil from her lunch plate.

Dot recognized Ina's tone. It was the firm imperative she used with Rachel and Jeddy when she wanted them to help with chores, to practice, to do their homework. It was the voice she used when talking to junior programmers. Once Dot had stopped by Ina's office and heard her say to a flushed young girl, "I don't care how you do it, but that has to be coded by the end of the day." Dot had had no doubt that the coding would be completed, just as she did not doubt that little Miriam Gottlieb would eat her lunch. Ina's voice of authority, a mnemonic echo of Shirley Cherne's own, would not be denied.

"This is for you," Dot said, and held out the beribboned

package to Ina, who opened it swiftly, her face bright with pleasure. Dot chose her gifts carefully, unlike Shirley Cherne, who wrote careless checks or offered stale boxes of chocolates that would never be opened. Anger at her mother stirred and bubbled within her. It had been unfair, she thought with sudden fury, for Shirley Cherne suddenly to reveal to her the secret she had kept close all those years. Ina wanted no part of that which had for so long been withheld from her. The long-ago abortion was irrelevant. Her fingers found the soft wool, delicate as an infant's garment.

"Oh, Dot, they're lovely," she said.

"Ray told me he had bought you a yellow negligee," Dot said, pleased that her gift was a success.

"Marvelous. Just what I need. For this place anyway."

"But you'll be going home soon. I thought perhaps tomorrow." A note of anxiety crept into Dot's voice. Ina's color was too high, her gestures too quick and impatient. The thick white bandage gleamed whitely beneath the yellow nightgown. A small drop of green-gold pus had seeped through it and settled like a bilious stagnant tear on the snowy gauze.

"Maybe tomorrow. Maybe not. I have to decide," Ina said. Her voice was weak and strangely weary. She glanced across at her neighbor. "Miriam, Dot and I are going to walk down to the waiting room."

"I'll be all right," Miriam said. She looked wonderingly at the fork in her hand. "You know, I was actually hungry."

Ina smiled. She was not surprised. She was her mother's daughter and had learned her lessons well.

The waiting room was empty except for a sad-eyed, balding man in a rumpled shirt who sat hunched over one of the tiny red Formica tables, spooning rice pudding out of a Styrofoam container. He looked up as they entered and smiled the apologetic smile of a guest who knows he has overstayed his welcome but has no place else to go. Ina recognized him as the man who had slept on the narrow couch the night before. She fumbled for words of comfort to offer him, but what after all could she say? Perhaps your wife will be better today? Perhaps your wife will die today? In the end she said nothing, and the man shuffled from the room. A yellow clot of pudding clung to the surface of the table. Dot wiped it off with a tissue which she put into the wastepaper basket.

"I guess it's a relief to have the surgery over with," she said as they sat facing each other in matching red chairs.

"Yes. But it was really quite minor. It didn't even require a general anesthesia. Isaacs was practically sure from the frozen section that it was benign, but just to be on the safe side he sent it out for a permanent section. He'll call us today. I guess we'll really relax when we have the final word." Idly she played with the narrow ribbon, forming a simple cat's cradle, disentangling it, and creating a more intricate one. If Bette were seated opposite her, she would carry it deftly from Ina's fingers to her own, and Ina in turn would transfer it back. It was a small cousinly skill developed during childhood afternoons in the barrack when Shaindel had admonished them constantly to play quietly. Their string had been knotted shoelaces plucked from the rotting thin shoes of the dead or strips of thread unraveled from uniforms become shrouds.

"Isn't it unusual then to stay in the hospital? Mrs. Philips, who lives across the hall, came home the same day." Dot's voice was hesitant. She did not want Ina to think she was prying, but still there was something odd about this hospital business, about Ray's evasive answers, his heavy mood. "It's none of your business," Larry had told her that morning when she mentioned it, but Dot did not agree. The family was her business. Ina would not answer any questions she felt intrusive, she knew, and so she was within her rights to ask.

"Ray didn't tell you then?" Ina asked. The casual innocence of her question was deceptive, and she disliked herself for it. She knew that Ray could not and would not tell Dot about her pregnancy. She looked at her sister-in-law, who smoothed her blue linen skirt and unbuttoned the top button of her white blouse. Dot's light hair was damp with rain and curled about her face in natural ringlets. Worry glinted in her green eyes, the color of Jeddy's own.

"Tell me what?" Dot asked.

"That was stupid of me," Ina said. She did not meet Dot's eyes but bent to arrange the scattered magazines in a neat pile. "I know he didn't tell you. The fact is, Dot, I'm pregnant. We didn't plan it, and I'm not really sure what to do about it. So many things complicate it."

Now, again, pain pierced her breast, and her hand flew up and rested on the bandage in a soothing, protective gesture. It seemed to her that the pain was harsher now, and she wondered worriedly what that meant. Could that "minor" surgery they had dismissed so casually mean major illness? Cancer? Death? And if death cells moved stealthily through her body, what would she do about the small life that was also nurtured there? To have the child would be to strike a balance, to even the scales. There would be a death, and there would be a life. But I am not going to die, she thought, and the pain, as though on command, subsided, vanished, leaving her wearied but calm.

"What should I do, Dot?" she asked softly.

"Well, you can do one of two things. Either have the baby or have an abortion."

"What would you do?" Ina asked, and her hand flew to her mouth at the thoughtlessness and cruelty of her own question. "I'm sorry," she muttered, and wadded the corner of a magazine into a tiny pellet. Pain glinted in her sister-in-law's eyes.

"I've never had the luxury of such a decision," Dot said, "but of course we both know the answer. We talked about that once."

The memory of that argument drifted back to them. They had, during that brief and fierce exchange, exposed themselves, revealing their anguish and their yearning. Ina lived with memories of murder—the quotidian homicides of her childhood. Dot's barrenness clung to her like a cloak of sadness; she shivered within it and listened daily to arguments advocating the right of other women to destroy that which she herself could not create.

Ina got up, wandered over to the coffee machine, pressed the buttons, and went back to her chair. She picked up the satin ribbon and held it slackly between her fingers.

"What about Ray?" Dot asked.

"He wants the baby. Now. He didn't tell me before. I thought we were both decided on an abortion, but now his position is clear. The decision is mine, but he wants the baby. He's a lot like you—as far as children go."

"Maybe, but I'm not sure. I think for most men—at least for Ray and Larry—their children are self symbols. They send out a message—they advertise to the world what their fathers are like. I watch men at school plays and dance recitals. They applaud like crazy, but it's not their kids they're clapping for —it's themselves. Look what they've done. Look at their beautiful, bright children. Their kids bear witness to their lives. A man who is the father of a small child is a young man no matter how old he is. When Simon came, Larry got a new lease on life. He went out and bought a set of barbells. If he was young enough to be the father of a new baby, he was young enough to begin lifting weights. But the children aren't just a symbol for me. They're my life. Oh, I know what you think, Ina—you and your friend Ruthie. I'm obsessive about the kids, kinky, unliberated. Okay. Maybe you're right. But the children are me. They're everything I want." She looked at Ina defiantly. She would explain, but she would not apologize. There was no need to.

"You know," Ina said, "I've envied you sometimes. To be so clear about it. To be so absorbed in it. Never to resent it."

"How can I resent it?" Dot asked. "For me the children are the best thing that ever happened to me. The most creative thing in my life. I'm helping other people grow up—making sure they're getting the support they need to become the kind of people they can be. It's magic for me to hear Simon laugh."

"It's different for Ray. I don't know, but I think it has something to do with the way your parents died. We've never talked about it. I don't know why. Why haven't we talked about it?" There was a dreamy sadness in her voice, a regret for all the questions left unasked, for dreams unshared. They were too busy. There was no time. That would have to change. They would have to make time.

"Maybe," Dot said thoughtfully. "I remember their funeral. We sat alone in the family pew—just Ray and Larry and I. I felt such a terrible loneliness. We were such a small family. Ray and I were cut loose, set adrift, alone. I at least had Larry, but he wasn't enough. I had no parents, and I wanted children, but I was childless. It was much worse for Ray. He was too old to be a little boy and too young to be a man. He wanted to cry, and he was ashamed to cry. He moved into our guest room, caught between being our son, our brother, our guest. Poor Ray. I was so glad, so relieved, when he married you."

"And I was never sure you approved," Ina said. It occurred to her that this was the first conversation of any depth and intimacy she and Dot had ever had. They spoke, in this hospital waiting room with its clutter of impatience and sorrow, with the intense urgency of strangers who meet for the first time and sense an emotional affinity that affords them honesty, revelation. And yet they had been bound by ties of family for a decade and a half.

An aide came into the room and swabbed the floor with a damp mop, avoiding their feet so that they sat isolated on an island of dryness. The sad-eyed man, wearing his jacket now, came in, plunged a quarter in the coffee machine, and looked at it in unsurprised defeat when no coffee came forth. Nothing would work for him.

"Why do I bother?" he asked plaintively. Quietly, unobtrusively, he left the room.

"I thought you would be too strong for him," Dot said. "But then I saw that you were just strong enough for him. It was even. You balanced each other and wanted the same things."

"Until now," Ina said sadly.

"I don't know. Maybe you do want the same thing after all. You're not sure what you want. If you were, you never would have talked to me about it. You thought you knew what I would say, what I would advise." Dot took up the ribbon and stretched it taut. She too could conjure up a cat's cradle.

"But you didn't say—you didn't advise," Ina protested. She bent forward and transferred the web of ribbon to her own fingers.

"No. But you didn't know that." Dot smiled. "I've got to run. I have to pick Ethan up at school. The orthodontist."

"Yes, I know."

Ina put her arm around her sister-in-law's waist, and they walked slowly through the wide corridor back to her room.

"Your roommate's baby—will it be all right?" Dot asked suddenly.

"It's hard to tell. Pretty much touch and go. I had a crazy thought this morning. I thought that if Miriam's baby died, my decision would be made. I would go ahead and have my baby."

She looked at Dot, hesitant, apprehensive, frightened at her own words, at the wild thought that had come to her in a narcotized moment. But Dot did not lose step.

"There are," she said very softly, "stranger bargains."

Miriam was on the phone when they entered the room. Dot waved to her and put on her pale blue belted raincoat. Ina walked back with her to the bank of elevators, and the two women stood together silently, shy suddenly within their new intimacy. When the elevator came, Dot leaned forward and hugged Ina.

"Do what's right for you," she said, and vanished into the car, empty except for a tall, thin man in a well-tailored pin-striped suit, whose face glistened wetly with tears that continued to fall as he stood there. The door slid shut as Dot waved sympathy, encouragement, good-bye.

"Nothing is right for me," Ina thought.

A new, unfamiliar weariness weighed her down, and she walked too slowly back to her room. She stretched out on the bed without taking off her robe or pulling down the blanket and slept. The pain throbbed dully at her breast, a ghostly, slumberous companion.

At three-thirty that afternoon, Angel Martinez, who worked
as stock boy and messenger for Cherne Knitwear, followed his
daily routine. He went to Gordon's Luncheonette, where
Joseph Gordon automatically put down his copy of the
*Racing Form* and filled a deep cardboard box with a dark
tea, a coffee thickly laced with heavy cream, a slice of dry
toast, and a fresh bialystoker roll stuffed with cream cheese
and raspberry jelly. He jammed a new issue of *U.S. News
and World Report* between the Styrofoam cups, knowing that
Norman Cherne would want it.

"How are they?" he asked Angel.

He repeated the question each day in the tone of a concerned adult asking after small children whose set routine
must not be disturbed. He had, after all, been making coffee
for the Chernes since their arrival from Europe, since the days
they had operated out of a one-room loft on the other side of
Holroyd Street. He had watched their English improve, their
business expand, and their small frightened daughter grow into
the beautiful, self-assured woman who had a business and
children of her own. Once a year she came into Gordon's
Luncheonette with her father and smiled pleasantly at the
man who had given her boxes of Colored Dots in the days
before she knew a word of English, and provided her with
school supplies, ferreting out pencils, crayons, and black-and-
white speckled notebooks from the dusty supply in his storeroom. The Chernes had never forgotten that Joseph Gordon
would not let them pay for Ina's school supplies. New fast-
food takeout places with gleaming plate-glass fronts and
delivery service had opened, but they continued to patronize
the shabby luncheonette. Each year at Passover they sent him
a bottle of slivovitz and at Chanukah a bottle of Sabra liqueur
from Israel. Occasionally Angel would arrive with a package
containing a new garment produced by Cherne Knitwear.

"For Mrs. Gordon," Angel would say, although both he
and Joseph Gordon and the Chernes themselves knew there

was no Mrs. Gordon, only aging prostitutes who occasionally
visited the tiny room in the rear of the store which was Joseph
Gordon's home. The clothing was passed on to a niece who,
unlike Ina Cherne Feldman, had neither a business nor children of her own.

Angel hurried back across the street with his cardboard
tray. He bent his own frail body over the cardboard box to
protect it from the downpour. Like Joseph Gordon, he worried about the Chernes and wanted their food to be hot. Back
in the office he gave the coffee and bialy to Shirley Cherne
and the tea and toast to her husband. They faced each other
across their battered wooden desks, bought years before at a
city auction. Their carpeted showroom was furnished with
slick Naugahyde couches and chairs, and their receptionist
sat in sleek elegance on a bright orange swivel chair perched
behind a rosewood table, but the Chernes' own seats were old
kitchen chairs, and they piled catalogues and bills of lading
on the small secondhand dresser that they had bought for Ina
the year of their arrival. They did not easily discard pieces of
their past—so much of it had been lost to them without choice.
(Where was the featherbed of their Warsaw apartment, the
woven rug that had belonged to Ina's grandmother? Furnishings were landmarks, evidence of the way lives had once
been lived.)

"How is Gordon?" Shirley Cherne asked, and Angel
shrugged.

Norman Cherne took the magazine but pushed the tea and
toast aside.

"You drink it, Angel," he said. "I have to visit my
daughter."

Angel took up the box, remembering that Rosa, the cutter,
had told him that their daughter was in the hospital. Nothing
serious. Something like Rosa herself had had—a growth on
the breast. As he left, he noticed that Norman Cherne, who
had already put on his vest and raincoat, bent over his wife,
who was absorbed in a pile of invoices, and touched her hair.

Angel had worked for the Chernes for four years, and this was the first time he had seen them touch each other. He smiled and went back to the stockroom.

Shirley Cherne lifted a red pencil and studded a flimsy sheet of paper with question marks.

"A hundred yards," she muttered. "They never sent a hundred yards. If there were eighty-five in that shipment, I'd be surprised, but a hundred—never."

"Shirley. Shaindel." His hand was gentle on her shoulder. "I'm going to Ina. I want you to lie down."

"Later. When I straighten out the invoices, I'll lie down. If you're going, go." But she did not shrug his hand away, and when she looked up at him, there was a new softness in her eyes. "Be careful what you say to her. Our lives were ours. She has her own."

"There is nothing wrong," Norman Cherne said, "with wanting that your children shouldn't make the same mistakes you did."

His own errors had been myriad. He had not heeded the warnings. He had seen the clues but had not taken the time to solve the mystery. With the invasion of Czechoslovakia his cousin Mendel had taken his family to Argentina, another friend had taken his family to Palestine, a neighbor who could find no other route had turned eastward and gone with his wife and infant son to China. But he, Nachum Czernowitz, had stayed in Warsaw and watched his parents walk to the cattle cars. He had not left Poland, so his son, Yedidiah, had died and his wife, Shaindel, had emerged from the war frayed by a grief and guilt that had hardened into a bitterness he had never tried to dissolve. Her thick chestnut hair had grown back, but he had not forgotten how they had come together in Italy as emaciated strangers who hid shyly from each other. She had not looked at him when she told him about the abortion, and he had never told her what his work in the camp hospital had entailed. They shared the victim's shame at being victimized and buried their past in a frenetic absorption in the present. The business, the synagogue, the grandchildren.

He did not want Ina to repeat his mistake, to create a barrier in her marriage that might not be breached. There was a warning he could offer her, and she was smarter, wiser, than he had been. Perhaps she would listen to him, his capable, assured daughter who moved with the proud grace of his own lost mother.

But his mother had been a woman possessed of rare warmth, of sudden spontaneous bursts of affection. She had held him close when he was a small boy, but even when he was a grown man, a young husband, she had enfolded him in her arms and embraced Shaindel too when they arrived for their sabbath afternoon visit. They had eaten long lunches, listened to the afternoon symphony, and turned the radio off when the news spoke of Hitler, of the fall of Czechoslovakia, of the invasion of Austria. Silence meant safety. They had continued to fool themselves even when they recognized the charade and saw the desperate and dangerous reality.

Someone, an old neighbor, had told him that his father had died of a heart attack in a transit car, but no witness had come forth to speak of his mother. He liked to think, then, that she had died in her sleep, and he focused on his memory of her at a family wedding, surrounded by small children to whom she offered laughter and an abundance of silver-wrapped candies.

His daughter did not share that openness, that sweet optimism. But then his mother had grown up surrounded by love, promised every joy and every hope. By the end of the war, when he saw his child after the years of separation, she was no longer a child but a woman who had seen and survived death, imprisoned in a child's body. She had been pinched daily by spectral playmates—by hunger and cold, fear and evil. He could not expect of her, his war-crippled child, the plenitude of warmth his mother had exuded, but he knew she was capable of such warmth. It was there within her, trapped behind the defenses she had built. One day, he thought, his daughter would laugh with the fullness and gaiety of her murdered grandmother. Poor Ina, he thought, and cursed himself because he had misread the clues of history and so had lost his son and wounded his daughter.

He took the subway into Manhattan and wondered if the time would ever come when he could board a train without shivering or enter a hospital without choking back a swift, irrational nausea. He had gone once to a lecture at the Herzl Institute and heard a psychiatrist from California discuss what he called "the survivor syndrome." The man, who must have been an American toddler when Nachum Czernowitz listened to his radio in his Warsaw apartment, talked of clinical studies. Survivors had strange eating patterns. (Nachum thought of his brother-in-law, Bette's father, stuffing his pockets with lumps of sugar, bits of Melba Toast.) Some had strange sleeping habits. (Nachum thought of his wife, who slept hardly at all during the hours of darkness.) Certain phobias were consistent. Trains were feared and with good reason. The psychiatrist had abandoned his sheaf of notes and leaned forward to speak earnestly, conspiratorially, to his audience. They listened attentively, the young college students who sat with ball-point pens poised over spiral notebooks, the middle-aged women bored on the winter evenings, the weary men like Nachum, who avoided each other's eyes because they had come to nurture their own secrets and not to trespass on the emotional privacy of others.

"But understand this," the doctor had said to them, "since the Holocaust, no Jew anywhere will ever again board a train casually, innocently. I myself"—and here he blushed, and his eyes grew bright—"feel a strange anxiety even when I take the daily seven-thirty-seven from Oakland to L.A."

All Jews then were survivors, sharing survivor fears. Would Norman Cherne's own grandchildren, Rachel and Jeddy, intrepid young urbanites that they were, tremble in the canyons of Grand Central (which so resembled the great terminal in Prague from which Jews left for the camp at Terezin)? Would their great-grandparents' long-ago journey to death in a cattle car that had no windows and only cracks in the floorboard through which urine and liquid feces (for no hard excrement could be formed when no hard food was eaten) flowed diminish their pleasure in the exciting whistle of an engine, the fierce churning of iron wheels across tracks of steel? Was the grim heritage inviolate?

From the subway he walked the few blocks to the hospital, stopping on a corner to buy a bunch of daffodils from a young girl who stood in the rain enveloped in a huge green poncho. She held a flowered umbrella over herself and her wares. Raindrops glittered on the golden flowers, and when she had given him his change, she pulled out a book and read, standing patiently in the downpour. He admired her. She had fair hair and blue eyes and was surely unfrightened by trains and by the storms of early spring. He felt vaguely regretful that Ina had never sold flowers on a city street. She had always been so directed, programming her life, controlling her future.

At the hospital entrance he took a deep breath and passed beneath the sheltering canopy into the lobby.

"This is a hospital," he told himself. "Here people come to be taken care of, to be helped, to be cured. Here, if they die, it is in spite of all that is being done for them, not because of it." He repeated the words again and again, turning them into a mantra of reassurance. He was skilled at dealing with his own terror. The nausea abated, and he skillfully shunted away memories of strong young men who had become mutilated corpses, of frightened young women turned into barren skeletons whose mutilated breasts hung limply against ribs that gleamed through the sheerness of fleshless skin, of terrified children whose first cry of pain would be their last shrillness at life.

In the elevator he closed his eyes, and the other passengers glanced at him curiously, fearfully, and clutched their own flowers and brightly wrapped packages. They had troubles enough and turned from a stranger's terror. But the old man did not faint. At the fifth floor he opened his eyes and exited without looking back.

It was quiet in the corridor. The long, rain-swept afternoon was drawing to a close. Shifts of visitors and nurses were changing. Preparations were being made for the evening. An orderly worked in the waiting room opposite the elevator. He polished the metal mirror on the coffee machine, moving the cloth in slow, rhythmic circles, grinning widely at his dark-skinned, gold-teethed reflection. At the nurses' station, the white-uniformed women hurried through their paperwork. Long printed forms flew through their fingers and were deposited in metal filing boxes. They answered the phones on the first ring. There was no time to be wasted. Doctors in street clothes hovered over the desk. They initialed small green medication forms, wrote their full names on longer sheets of paper, checked their watches against the clock. A tall young man in a raincoat carried a medical bag in one hand, a tennis racquet in the other.

"Indoor game," he said to the cluster of white-coated men and women who stood in a group studying the same chart. No one looked up, and he headed for the elevator.

Norman moved down the long hall, walking slowly as the newly aged do in the dying hours of the afternoon when they realize at last that it is late in the day and they are no longer young. The doors to many of the rooms were closed, and behind them he could hear women moving slowly, water running, the whirl of a hair dryer. He passed a room in which a beautiful black woman who looked startlingly familiar, dressed in a peacock-blue robe of shining satin, bent over a young girl, fashioning her hair into a soft, loose bun. The girl was very pale. Her skin almost matched her robe and negligee of bridal white, and her eyes were very large in a face grown thin. She laughed as she was fussed over, and the lilt of her laughter told him that she was only brief years away from childhood. She might have been dressing for her first dance. He hoped, with sinking heart, that she was not dressing for death.

From somewhere came the sound of soft weeping. Here, along this long passageway where women readied themselves for the evening hours, where the stink of alcohol and drugs mingled with the fragrance of perfumes named for wild flowers and distant places, joy teased and shadows threatened.

Norman Cherne moved more quickly. He wanted to sit down beside his daughter's bed. He wanted to hold her hand. She had his own short fingers, his fleshy palm. Yedidiah had inherited Shaindel's graceful hand; he remembered her fingers so long and tapering before they had been twisted by arthritis, weighted down by the heavy rings set with smoldering dead-eyed gems.

Often, when Ina was a child, he had tiptoed into her room as she slept and sat quietly at her bedside and sometimes lightly touched her pudgy hand. He loved her best, felt most protective of her, during those silent hours of darkness when she slept, moist-lipped and flushed, and neither knew nor cared that he stood watch beside her. Once, when Bette had spent the night, he had tiptoed in and watched both girls as they lay together in the narrow bed, their dark curls damp from the bathtub, their bare arms flung above the covers because the night was warm.

He had said a prayer as he stood over their sleeping forms. "Blessed art Thou, O Lord our God, who has preserved a remnant of Israel." He was a religious man. In the days before the war he had belonged to a study and discussion group of earnest young men who read Graetz and Dubnov. He believed in the hand of God moving through history. His daughter and his niece had been saved. They were the remnant. They would be mothers in Israel. Softly, rhythmically, they breathed into the darkness, and softly and rhythmically he prayed. They had been saved. There was reason in the universe. They were beautiful, lying there in the shadowed room. The scent of their shampoo had tickled his nose. He smiled and wept and repeated the prayer. He remembered too how Shirley had sat in the living room that night, bent over the ledger. She had found a small profit that could be turned to a larger one, a use for a yardage of corduroy they had thought useless. Her chestnut hair was loose about her shoulders, and the lamplight was golden on her skin, but because she did not look up, he had feared to move toward her. Much later, hurriedly, mechanically, their bodies had met in the warm darkness, need subduing passion.

The door to 502 was open, and Ina was on the phone. She waved, blew him a kiss, and continued talking.

"Grandpa just came in," she said. "Now, Rachel, even if the assignment isn't fair, you must do it. We do all sorts of things in life that may not be pleasant or fair. No, I won't ask Daddy to write a note to the teacher."

Impatience crept into her tone. She grimaced and glanced at her watch. He heard the child's shrill, angry voice protesting, repeating her argument. Once, walking in Central Park, he and Rachel had passed a shabbily dressed child who had worn one blue sneaker and one red one. The canvas of both had been worn and ripped.

"Why is that kid wearing shoes that don't match?" Rachel had asked.

"Maybe her family is too poor to buy new sneakers," he suggested.

"But that's not fair." The child's eyes were bright with righteous fury.

"So everything is not fair." He had shrugged but held her hand tighter, frightened for her, fearful that the day would come when the full measure of life's unfairness would be revealed to her.

Ina hung up.

"That child. She'll fight windmills one day." She leaned forward and her father kissed her forehead.

"That's how it is with children." He touched his daughter's hand, held the flowers out to her.

"They're beautiful," she said, and put them in the vase, arranging them between the soft-petaled yellow roses.

"From Raymond?" he asked.

"Yes. They're lovely, aren't they?"

He nodded. He liked his gentle son-in-law, who was strong enough to reveal his tenderness.

"So. How are you feeling?"

"Fine. Really. I had a little pain earlier, but Dr. Isaacs's resident was just here to check the incision and change the dressing." She pointed to the snowy white cushion of bandages beneath the pale yellow of her nightgown. "He says it's healing already. Of course they don't have a final report yet." She waited for reassurance, but his thoughts were elsewhere.

He turned his eyes away from the bandage that covered the incision that was healing so cooperatively. He knew about incisions that did not heal but festered and stank and were covered not by bandages but by wads of newsprint, rotting rags. Expertly, with the skill of decades, he blocked memories of the way green globules of pus had leaked through the open wound of a man whom he had recognized as a friend of his uncle's; of how milk-white snakes of intestines gaped through an inexpertly sewn stomach wound; of wine-red hemorrhages that formed scarlet pods on the splintered plank floors. He had mopped those floors with his eyes closed, and because there were holes in his shoes, his bare feet were often stained and streaked with other men's blood. He had forgotten a great deal, willed himself to forgetfulness, but fragmented memories haunted him at night, thrust themselves forward and caught him unawares during the day. He protected himself vigilantly, yet was always vulnerable.

He looked across the brightly lit hospital room to Ina's roommate's unmade bed, the cheerful clutter of her bedside table.

"You have a nice woman sharing the room?" he asked.

"Very nice. A young woman. Interesting. An orthodox Jew but very modern. Her baby was born sick. He's in an incubator."

"Yes. Yes. Your mama told me about her. Well, maybe the baby will improve."

It was fortunate, he thought, that the young parents of the sick baby were orthodox. He envied those who lived so completely by their faith. He remembered them so well from the camp. They knew how to accept. They pulled their beards and rent their clothes, but in the end they turned from their grief to their God and praised Him as they stood at the foot-

hills of hell. Dutifully, they said the Kaddish over the dead—
the Kaddish, which did not speak of unutterable loss but
reaffirmed their commitment to God. Prayer quorums had
formed in the camp on the day of liberation. The chimneys
smoked and darkened the skies above them, and the air trembled with the keening of women, the bewildered weeping of
small children. Wandering urchins whimpered, the sick and
the dying moaned, and the orthodox swayed and lifted
their voices, "Blessed and magnified be His name. *Yitgadal
v'yitkadash.* . . ."

He shrugged the memory away, turned his eyes from the
empty bed. He was impatient with other people's misfortunes.
It was his daughter he must talk to.

"Your mama told me also that you're pregnant."

Her hand trembled, and her cheeks grew hot. She was
startled, strangely betrayed. She had not expected her mother
to tell her father anything beyond the barest details of the
minor breast surgery.

"Ina had a cyst removed," she imagined her mother saying.
"She's fine. They're almost sure it's nothing serious."

"Good." Her father's reply would come from behind a
screen of newspapers, while the radio and television set played
simultaneously, infusing him with the news he needed to
survive.

Her parents did not discuss, did not waste words. They
talked. They decided.

"Ina wants to go to New England to college."

"All right."

"We'll do a full line of jackets and skirts."

"Vests also. A big year for vests."

"One thousand to the U.J.A. Five hundred to Bonds."

"All right."

Ina had lived her girlhood in the impeccable cage of their
brief exchanges, their long silences. Like cautious scavengers
they hoarded their words, fearful of waste, terrified of revelation. Working together all day in the business, mind matching
mind across the battered desks, words had become unnecessary

to them, and the war years of separation had schooled them to silence. Yet this they had talked about—this third grandchild who might not be born to them. Her pregnancy. This unwanted, accidental conception, this small mass of protoplasm growing within her that had strangely shattered so many silences. Like a small stone tossed into a pool of still waters, it had set off reflex reactions—swirling concentric waves triggered new and deeper ripples. Old secrets and new fears, hesitant confidences, abrasive revelations—all had been held out to her so that she might pick and choose like an uneasy diner who feels no hunger but must study the long and extensive menu of a restaurant chosen by strangers.

"I didn't think she would tell you," Ina said at last.

"You think, maybe, it's not my business?"

"It appears to be everyone's business. Yours, Mama's, Dot's . . ."

"People love you. They want you to do what's right, what will make you happy."

"All of a sudden," she said harshly, and turned her eyes from him.

A lingering raindrop trembled on the edge of the daffodil. Shame filled her. Her father had brought her flowers. Yellow flowers to match the bed slippers that had been her sister-in-law's gift, the roses and negligee Ray had given her. How odd that all of them should have chosen gifts the color of sunlight. Yellow was the "safe" shade pregnant women chose when, uncertain about the sex of their babies, they hesitated to buy pink or blue.

"I'm sorry, Papa," she said. Her voice was very low, and he remembered how she had looked up at him in Italy and mouthed the unfamiliar word: "Papa? Papa?" It had been weeks before the query fluttered away and she could say the word free and clear.

"It's all right," he said. "I know how you feel. You didn't have it easy with us. It wasn't our fault. We tried. But I know. It wasn't easy for you. I'm sorry."

"I don't blame you. I never blamed you."

Who, then, did she blame? A question to be raised with
Eleanor Berenson when the drapes of the consulting room
were drawn against the waning light of day, the brief brilliance
of sunset. Who can I blame, Doctor, because surely someone
must be at fault? At whose feet do I lay down the burden of
my survivor guilt? Where do I rid myself of the compulsion
to be all things to all people—son and daughter to my parents,
wife and mother to my husband, the young orphan? The responsibility must belong somewhere. I cannot assign it to the
indifference and cruelty of history, to the whim of careless
destiny. I am not a historian. I am not a philosopher. Who will
make Yedidiah stop dancing through my dreams? Who will
halt the march of the faceless, death-burdened soldiers who
stalk me in the night, who would kill me—us—with their
organs of life? Tears burned at her eyes, and sorrow crouched
in her throat. A raindrop fell from the daffodil's golden petal
and settled on the bedside table, a shimmering drop of grief.

"You don't have to blame me. I blame myself. All of it I
could have prevented. We could have left. Others did. Didn't
my cousin Mendel take his family to Argentina? Others went
to Palestine, to Russia—even to China and Japan. I saw, I
heard, but I didn't believe. Will Mendel believe me now? Will
he leave his life, his children and grandchildren in Buenos
Aires? But he is an old man now, and I was young and I did
nothing." Pain weakened his voice, etched lines of anguish
about his eyes. Beneath his golfer's tan the pallor of sorrow
blanched his skin. He had been gray before his fortieth birthday, and his deep laughter had never rung true. Pity for him
stirred her. All things to all people, she would mother her
father, who had suffered and would not allow himself to stop
suffering.

"Papa. You couldn't do anything. How many people left?
Very few. And where could they go? Mendel had an aunt in
Argentina who got him the visa. You had no aunt in Argen-
tina. Could one go easily to Palestine? The White Paper, the
British quota. The refugee ships sank. You can't blame your-
self. There was no place to go, nothing to do." In a litany of

excuses she fought his misery, but he sat with his head in his hands. At last, he looked up at her. His eyes were dry, his hands steady.

"Your mother told you about the abortion she had in the camp?"

Ina nodded.

"Me, she told about it in Italy. In the displaced persons camp. We didn't talk about it again until this morning. More than thirty years. It lay like a cancer between us. No. Not a cancer. A cancer is alive, growing. This abortion, this baby she didn't—couldn't—let grow—this small death—it lay between us. It blocked our lives. To love you need life, and we had only death between us. My dead parents. Her family—dead. Peshi. Yedidiah. The baby who wasn't even a baby. Dead."

"I was alive," Ina cried. "Why couldn't you love me?"

"We didn't love you? Stupid girl!"

He smiled sadly, touched her hand. The hairs on his fingers were of fine silver. She had not noticed them before. She could not remember her father touching her like this before (as Ray touched Rachel and Jeddy, a fatherly flutter of skin upon skin, protective, reassuring). But she did remember waking at night in her Forest Hills bedroom and seeing him in her room, looking down at her. He had loved her. She knew it, and he would not argue it with her, thus proving it. She lifted his hand to her lips and kissed it.

"Today, this morning," he continued, "we talked about it. Through all these years your mother thought I blamed her. How could I blame her for doing what she had to do, for having the courage to do it, for saving you and Bette? But that is what she thought. And I—I thought she suffered from such grief and sorrow at the loss that there was no room for me. And so like that we lived. Good morning. Good morning. Pass the sugar. Make the deposit. Guard the secret." His shoulders quivered. The waste was awesome, the silence was resonant.

"You must not do what we did, you and Ray," he said. His voice was husky with warning. "You must not live between shadows of secret. You must not grieve for that which is lost and blame each other for what you both caused not to happen." He had noticed and been grateful for the way his daughter and son-in-law shielded each other. But there was danger in caution. To soothe was not to solve.

"It's different for us," she said. "We're not like you and Mama. We talk. We discuss."

"To talk is not always to say," he said. "And some things you can't discuss. There is no right. There is no wrong. What you do, you can't undo. Think on it, Ina. My Ina."

He stood, still touching her hand, and bent to kiss her brow. His lips were cool against her skin. The pain in her breast throbbed dully and perversely, she longed for a searing, punishing shaft of anguish, but there was only the steady, numbing hurt.

"Papa."

She wanted to thank him, to soothe him, to offer him the assurance he wanted. I will do what you want to spare you pain. I will have this child so that you will not worry over my worry, regret the possibility of my regret. We will all live happily ever after. The laughter of our newborn babe will echo through our dreams, and the lessons of the past will become the primer of the future. We will hold no secrets and assign no guilt.

But instead she pressed his hand, gently pulled at the silvery tendril that curled about the knuckle of his middle finger, and repeated softly, "Papa." The word was a caress that comforted them both.

He shook out his raincoat, patted his tie.

"You know what I will do?" he said. "I will go to your apartment and see the children. Mama will meet me there later, and after dinner we'll come back here and visit with you."

"Good. The children will like that. Pick up some chocolate for them."

"All right. You remember when you were a little girl,

Gordon used to give you those Colored Dots? You think they still make them?"

"I don't know." She smiled. There had been good days, the smoothness of a sweet on her tongue, the rattle of others in a bright cardboard box. There had been things that offset the loneliness of the Queens apartment and the silence of rooms where an only child wandered through waning daylight hours. There had been her parents' pride in her academic success. Her Arista installation certificate, framed in gold, hung still in their hallway.

"My Ina's," her father had said proudly, showing it to a friend.

They had loved her, but they too had been lost and alone.

At the doorway he waved.

"Papa!" she called after him.

He had walked a few steps down the hall but came back.

"Thank you," she said, and he nodded gravely and continued on his way, an aging man who walked slowly through the shadows of late afternoon.

Ray called the doctor's office for the fourth and last time that day when his own secretary had left. Before leaving, she had straightened his desk, poured him a fresh cup of coffee, and placed his umbrella in a conspicuous position next to his attaché case. She did not want him to walk bareheaded in the rain. She worried over him as his sister had, as Ina did, as his daughter Rachel was beginning to.

The phone in Isaacs's office rang several times. On the seventh ring the doctor himself answered it. His voice was bitter. He was a busy man, an important man. He banished death with his skilled fingers. He should not have to lift his own phone.

"Dr. Isaacs—this is Ray Feldman."

"Yes, Mr. Feldman—Ray?" The doctor was so busy he could not remember whom he knew and whom he did not know. Many women stretched prone before him on the exam-

ining room table. Expertly his fingers explored their bodies,
probed and manipulated their breasts. He laughed away their
fears and listened gravely to their sad secrets. He gave them
wise advice. Often barren women became pregnant and
pregnant young women were restored to freedom. He played
no favorites. He dreamed sometimes of white mountains of
thighs, hillocks of breasts, valleys of grassy vulvas. He could
not remember names. Often he forgot faces.

"About the lab report on Ina? You were supposed to get
back to me today. I called several times." Immediately Ray
regretted his tone. He had not meant to be accusative. He
could not afford to alienate this man who knew so many
answers, who sat in his hospital fortress protected by garrisons
of nurses and receptionists, impermeable in the bulwark of his
knowledge. "I'm sort of nervous," he added, keeping his voice
low and respectful.

"Of course you are." Isaacs was suddenly jovial; he recog-
nized deference and apology. There was a rustling of papers.
"I'm just finding the lab report now. Ah, here it is. Just what
I thought. After all, it did run pretty deep."

"Then the report shows a malignancy?" Ray asked the
question through painful gasps of breath. His fingers held the
phone in a death grip. The calm of his voice surprised him.

"No. Just the opposite. All benign tissue. We're free and
clear. Absolutely. I told you we'd call if there was a problem.
There was no reason to worry." The doctor sighed. He could
afford a restrained reprimand now. Patients and their families
were like small children who had to be told the same thing
again and again. And here he was, a busy man, forced to
answer his own phone at day's end.

"That's wonderful." Relief filled Ray with giddiness. He
soared with a new lightness, and the gladness he felt was so
overwhelming and brilliant that his eyes teared and his hands
trembled. He did not bother to argue with the doctor that he
had not, in fact, told him anything of the sort.

"And there's the other matter of the abortion. I assume
that now you'll want to go right ahead with it."

Why should he make that assumption? Ray wondered.
Why should the knowledge that there was no malignancy
cause them to decide to abort? Surely, from a medical point
of view, if there had been any danger, it would have made
sense for Ina to abort the pregnancy. But perhaps Isaacs was
intent on balance. A life for a death. Hope to offset despair.
Without the danger of death there was no need to hesitate
over a decision for new life. Dr. Isaacs was an orderly man.
Ray imagined him now looking at Ina's chart, wanting it off
his desk, back in its file. Busy men had to keep paper moving,
file folders flowing. Isaacs was impatient with indecision. All
things were clear to him. Surely his checkbook always
balanced. Debit and credit. Life and death.

"There's still some indecision. We'll have to let you know
on that," Ray said.

"By tomorrow afternoon at the latest. I have to schedule it,
and it's pointless for your wife to stay on if you're not going
to proceed." The doctor was firm. Sometimes decisions had to
be forced. Ambivalence was a luxury for which there was no
time in a situation like this. The Feldman woman was six,
almost seven, weeks pregnant. The embryo was maturing, developing a skeletal structure. If she planned to abort, she had
better do it at once.

"We'll call you, Doctor," Ray said. "And thank you."

The doctor hung up without replying, and Ray replaced
the phone gently. His gratitude was superfluous, beside the
point, he knew. Isaacs was not responsible for their luck, was
perhaps not even much interested in it, but Ray's relief overflowed boundaries of reason. Quickly, he left the office, for-
getting the umbrella that leaned sadly against the chair, its
folded black wings still damp from the morning downpour.

The rain had stopped, and he stepped from his office building into the sweet coolness of a twilight spring evening. Long
mauve shadows moved across the pearl-gray sky, and rain-
bowed prisms trapped in small oily pools littered the wet black
streets. A chestnut tree shivered against a breeze and a soft
spray grazed his face. He smiled at the cold fresh wetness and

descended into the subway. He found a seat on the crowded train but offered it at the next stop to a pregnant woman who held a small boy by the hand and thanked him in a language he did not understand.

The ride to midtown was brief, and he emerged from the subway with the perplexed air of a traveler who finds that very little has changed while he switched locations. The shadows were longer and deeper now and had turned deep purple in color. Feathery clouds with fiery gold borders drifted through a gray-green sky. He hoped that Rachel and Jeddy had gone to the window and were witness to this hour of sun death. He remembered that the previous summer, after a rainswept day, he had walked along the shore with the children and watched the great pale sun that had only become visible late in the afternoon sink into the sea. Rachel and Jeddy had gasped then as two gulls soared in tandem across the fading orb. He had clutched their hands tightly, and the three of them had stood with their feet bare against the sodden sand and watched the darkening of the light.

Now, after the long day of rain and worry, he wanted to see that darkening. He would walk uptown, he decided, and the idea seemed to him daring and adventurous, vaguely luxurious. Briskly, he turned north where he could see the chain of lights already lit on the great bridge that linked three boroughs. They glittered gaily in the half darkness, and he walked toward them, whistling softly.

He knew this part of the city well. During the first years of their marriage, he and Ina had lived in a small apartment in the shadow of Grand Central, and each morning and evening they had watched as waves of commuters broke forth upon the city. They sat on their window seat and smiled at each other, feeling a contented superiority to the hurrying men and women on the street below who scurried endlessly between terminal and office. Ina and Ray were city dwellers. They lived where the action was. These broad avenues and crowded side streets were their neighborhood. They knew a fishmonger who sold them pallid slices of sole and flesh-colored strips of

salmon from his shop sandwiched between a mighty bank and
the side entrance of a great department store. They invited
their friends to fondue suppers cooked with cheese they
bought at a small Forty-fifth Street dairy where the proprietor
called Ina "Babe" and saved rectangular wooden boxes for
them so that they might grow their own spices.

No one had worried then about baby-sitters and train
schedules. They were in control of their lives, on their way.
Ina had begun her computer agency with one small account
and desk space in someone's office. Ray had his first job in
Legal Aid. Sometimes, during an evening with friends, after
they had eaten and listened to a couple of records, sitting on
the floor on the oversized pillows Dot had found for them, a
spurt of energy would seize them. They would commandeer
taxis for a ride downtown, where the evening would be
finished at Gerde's Folk City, in a village coffee shop, or in a
Chelsea wine cellar run by guitar-playing Israelis who sang
mournful dirges in Ladino.

Now all that had changed, although they occasionally saw
the friends of those days—at least those few who had not
vanished into the shadows of murky divorces, quiet nervous
breakdowns, or transfers to distant cities. But now they ate
seated around the polished rosewood table and talked in low
voices so that the children would not be disturbed. They
ended their evenings together drinking liqueurs served in tiny
fingers of crystal, while quartet music played on the stereo.
Often, these days, someone fell asleep and wakened with a
start when the record changed.

Ray walked more slowly now because he was on Forty-
third Street where they had lived then. Their house had been
built of narrow red brick and owned by the Bastanis, a shy
Italian couple who had knocked on their door on the evening
of the first day of each month. They were people of rare
dignity who dressed carefully to collect their rent. Mr. Bastani
wore a black suit and a shining white shirt, and his wife wore
a print dress of softest silk. During the monthly ritual they all
drank a small glass of brandy and Ray ceremoniously passed

them the envelope. The Bastanis were long since dead, Ray knew, but he wanted suddenly to see the house.

He turned onto Third Avenue and walked the familiar path, the one he had taken home each night for the first three years of his marriage, and wondered why it was that after they had moved uptown he had never had occasion to walk down this street. He noticed now that the flower shop where he had sometimes stopped to buy Ina a small bouquet (full-blown hothouse flowers in the winter, small buds in spring and summer) was gone and a fast-food shop stood in its place. He was saddened but not surprised. It had been a dying venture then. A new high-rise apartment house stood across the street where once two young men had operated a leather workshop, sharing their frontage with a spice importer. The fragrance of marjoram and coriander had mingled wonderfully with the deep, rich odors of newly tanned skins. He had bought Ina a purse there which she had carried for years, discarding it only when Jeddy went off to school. Ray wondered what had happened to the two young men and to the spice dealer, who had, on the day the Feldmans moved, crossed the street to hand Ina a cushion of cloves sewn of unbleached muslin. "For luck," the man had said, and they had his gift still, hidden among their linens.

He moved up the street and stood finally where the Bastani house of narrow red bricks had risen. It too had vanished. An office building of steel and glass had replaced it, and as Ray stood there, its revolving doors turned, and laughing young women holding leather portfolios and woven bags came through, waved to each other, and hurried off, fanning out in all directions, anxious to reach places of brightness before the long purple shadows faded into darkness. He felt oddly cheated and walked more quickly now, anxious to leave this street where he had been, somehow, betrayed.

The dairy on Forty-fifth Street had also vanished, and a supermarket stood in its place. He continued uptown. Their friends, Stuart and Phyllis, had lived on Fifty-first Street. Stuart had died years before of Hodgkin's disease. Phyllis had remarried and lived now in Toronto. Last year they had not received a New Year's card from her. This year they had removed her from their own list. Some friendships burst asunder. Others fade—immutably, inexplicably.

Each street he passed now was a landmark, a demarcation point of vanished years and distant evenings when loud laughter had echoed against the early darkness. Ina's college roommate, Andrea, had lived on Fifty-eighth Street, almost at the river. They had loved to walk slowly from their own apartment to her huge, low-ceilinged basement flat. Often, they had carried with them cartons of Chinese food which Andrea had not bothered to put on plates. They would have an urban picnic, passing the soggy containers around, mixing up their utensils, giggling when a carton split and a mass of beef and snow peas fell across the floor, which Andrea had painted black. Andrea, who was always laughing then, Andrea, whom Ina loved and whom Shirley Cherne distrusted (both, because of her laughter), had said that the food should be left there and she would find a way to preserve the mess and exhibit it. Andrea had married an engineer who had borrowed five hundred dollars from Ray and another five hundred dollars from Dot and Larry. The money had not been repaid even after Andrea and her husband had bought a house in Larchmont with a pool that faced Long Island Sound. Ray had not minded the loss of the money. It was the death of the friendship, the indifferent, shoddy unraveling of something that had once been woven of such fun and affection, that wounded him.

Good friends went to live in California and returned for a visit transformed into strangers. The men wore their hair long, and gold chains gleamed at their necks. The women wore skintight pantsuits and painted their eyelids the colors of wild flowers. They talked nervously of new dimensions, new horizons, and their voices shrilled with the discontent of unhappy children. Buildings were torn down. Favorite restaurants were closed.

There was no permanence, no guarantees. The couple with whom they had dinner one week had separated by the next.

A colleague with whom he exchanged words in a crowded courtroom was dead of a heart attack two days later. Ray's heart pounded when the phone rang. He awaited news of accidents and death. He anticipated sorrow and loss. His parents had died suddenly, violently, and he was prepared for similar suddenness, similar violence. Prepared and unprepared. With each loss he felt a new weight and feared that he might sink beneath accumulated griefs. The attrition of the passing years frightened him. Losses were compounded.

He awakened in the night and looked down at Ina, wandered into the rooms where his son and daughter slept, their faces pudgy cushions of sweetness and peace in the fearful darkness. They gave him new certainty, relieved his terror. They would not turn into strangers. They were his lien on posterity. He would call Rachel and Jeddy from the hospital, he decided. Ina would want to talk to them, and he wanted to hear their voices. They were growing so quickly. Rachel answered the phone now with a breathy tone, testing her voice for hidden secrets.

He passed a restaurant where he and Ina had eaten many times, years ago. It had a large plate-glass window that had been hung with plants then, and they had speculated cleverly, whimsically, as to how the greenery was watered. The plants were gone, and through the window he saw the smiling faces of jazz musicians emblazoned on huge colored posters. A pianist sat at a piano bar surrounded by a singing, laughing group of young men and women. The music drifted into the street.

A blonde girl in a bright green dress clapped her hands above her head and danced through the room into the arms of a tall, lean youth who lifted her easily from the floor and held her up. In his arms she was a captive fairy, briefly restrained from flitting through never-never land. She kicked her legs prettily and whispered into her captor's ear. She was perhaps six or seven years older than Rachel. Ray thought of Rachel grown up, dancing through such a room in a swirling bright skirt, laughing, singing. Last night, as she modeled her dancing costume, he had noticed the new fullness of her body.

He stood now, staring into the window, like an adult spying on a children's party, admiration and envy in his gaze. The dancers inside were youngsters, but that did not mean that he was old. He was young enough to father a new baby, to want the child, to imagine himself again lightly tossing a laughing toddler up into the air. If there was a new beginning, the ending was distant and not to be feared.

The clarity of the thought startled him. Was that why he had such a yearning for the child they had not planned to conceive? He felt ashamed, apologetic. He had contempt for men who colored their hair and wore brightly colored shirts and large-buckled belts, searching after a youth that had deserted them. Yet he had thought that he would father a new baby to prove that all youth had not yet deserted him, to stanch the flow of days and years, to sponge up the endless recurring losses, to reinforce his holdings. Ina had been angry, and reluctantly, sadly, he understood that anger. What he had told her was true: he wanted the child because it was part of them and because there was no reason not to want it. But what he had not told her (what he had, in fact, not told himself) was that he wanted it also as an expression of spontaneity, of life unexpected and unplanned as it had been in the distant days when they had dashed through these streets laughing and singing, en route to visit friends who, unhappily and mysteriously, had vanished from their lives.

He turned from the window and walked more quickly now, stopping at a corner florist where he bought a plant on which white waxen flowers glowed softly like tiny stars. He held it as carefully as he would an infant and turned toward the hospital. Small yellow flags of light shone in neat symmetrical lines and columns, beaming forth from the large-windowed rooms. He hurried now, eager to be at Ina's side, to tell her that their worry had been in vain and unneccessary. It was as they had thought, as they had hoped. The tiny lump had been

proven benign. Their lives could continue on course. He
would make no demands, exert no pressures. He had recognized his own unfairness, and like a child eager to make
amends for careless mischief, he pondered what he might do to
make things right again. A long weekend at the Cape—the
purchase of a painting she had long admired.

As he passed the outpatient entrance, an Indian woman
wearing a black coat over her red-and-gold sari came out. She
held an infant swaddled in a blue bunting, whose eyes were
glittering coals of darkness in his tiny walnut-colored face.
She spoke softly to the child in her arms as she walked, and
Ray's heart turned. He envied her the tenderness of her words,
the light-as-air sweetness of her burden. Quickly, he averted
his head. His desires, his needs, were his alone. He would not
impose them upon Ina. Too much had been imposed upon her
already. He could not bear to think of the war and her lost
childhood. His heart turned with pity and love for his wife,
with awe at her strength and courage, hard won and pitted
always against the fear and vulnerability that clung to her,
teased her, and haunted her through dream-dark nights.

He pushed through the revolving doors into the crowded
hospital lobby. An elderly, pink-faced lady asked him worriedly if it were still raining and did he think it safe for her to
walk the four blocks to the subway.

"No," he said. "It's best to take a cab."

Nothing was certain. There were no guarantees. Caution,
he knew, had to be exercised at all times.

Ina had eaten her dinner quickly, startled at her own
hunger. She had carried her coffee over to Miriam's side of the
room, where she drank it while chatting with Miriam's
visitors—her parents and her in-laws. Ben Gottlieb, an atten-
tive host, fiddled with the thermostat. The room was too
warm. When Ray entered, Ina waved and motioned him over
as though he had arrived late at a party where she had already
met several people and was enjoying herself. He set the plant

down on her table and remembered that he had not eaten. He
was hungry. He plucked a roll from her dinner tray, dabbed
it with butter, added the small slice of cheese she had left, and
walked across the room.

"You didn't eat." She was accusing and he felt virtuous.

"I wanted to get here quickly." He did not tell her that he
had chosen to walk. He did not tell her that the narrow
bricked building that had been their first home had disappeared.

"Ray, I want you to meet Miriam's parents, Mr. and Mrs.
Rosen, and Ben's parents, Mr. and Mrs. Gottlieb."

The men shook hands with him, and the small, plump
women nodded pleasantly. The two couples looked startlingly
alike. Both men were portly and wore rimless glasses that fell
too low against their fleshy cheeks. Their shirts gleamed white
against their well-cut dark suits, and they wore small knit
skullcaps similar to Ben's. Mr. Gottlieb's was knit of white
and blue wool, and Miriam's father wore one of maroon and
gold. Ray wondered who knit the small skullcaps and thought
that he too would like to own one. Usually he took a plain
black one from the box at the entry of the synagogue, and
he never wore one at home, but it occurred to him now that
it was something he should own, like his prayer shawl and
prayer book. He would buy one for himself and for Jeddy,
too. They were, after all, essential Jewish survival equipment—
items of identity that would define and reinforce.

The women wore neat shantung suits. Ben's mother's was of
black and Miriam's mother wore navy blue, and with them
they wore white blouses whose collars curled softly at their
necks. Ray wondered if they shopped together and spoke
softly in the fitting room of their shared worry. Would the
child live? Would Miriam be all right? Why was their luck
so bad? Mrs. Gottlieb's hair was blue-gray and sprayed into
place, but Mrs. Rosen's, though threaded with silver, was the
same pale brown as Miriam's.

"You didn't eat, Mr. Feldman?" Mrs. Gottlieb held out a
large red-and-white Macy's box lined with aluminum foil.

Golden crusted pieces of chicken, orange wands of carrots, ivory strips of celery nestled within it. "Take, please. There's so much, and Miriam wasn't hungry."

"Ma, please. I was hungry, but I ate dinner. All of it." Miriam pointed to her tray, but her mother-in-law shrugged.

"Well, if you're sure," Ray said, and bit into a piece of chicken. "It's delicious."

The two women beamed. Miriam smiled. Ben sighed with relief.

"You've saved the day," he said. "Nothing hurts my mother more than seeing her food go uneaten."

"The trouble with you young people is that you don't know what it is not to have food to eat," Mrs. Gottlieb said, but there was no accusation in her voice, only calm relief that at least they would be spared. They would never know hunger, and they perhaps would not worry incessantly, obsessively, about food. She cooked too much, she knew, and knew also that there was no need to carry cardboard boxes of food on every journey, when restaurants lined the highways and a coffee shop was tucked into every lobby. But she had lived in Berlin in the thirties when the bread they were lucky enough to find had to be soaked in hot water and eaten as mush, when rotting fungus had to be peeled off vegetables before they could be cooked. The grocery store on their street, where they had shopped for years, was among the first in the city to post the notice "*Juden Verboten*" and later added a smaller sign that read "Jews and dogs not permitted in this shop." They had walked ten blocks to a small Jewish market and later, when that store had mysteriously closed, a mile to another grocery. No. She could not take food for granted. After forty years in America she still gasped when she entered a supermarket and saw the acres of food, all edible, all available. Marketing filled her with joy, cooking was a contentment, an avowal of luck and good fortune.

"Ray loves chicken," Ina confided.

The small gathering had assumed the happy intimacy of a family party. Mrs. Gottlieb pressed more food on Ray. Mr.

Rosen poured him hot coffee from a thermos, offered him a piece of strudel. His wife's. His wife was a wonderful baker. Ray tasted the sweetness of apples and nuts embedded in sweet crusts of dough and smiled his approval. Ina asked for the recipe. Miriam showed her mother the bed slippers knit of yellow wool.

"Ina's sister-in-law brought them for her," she said.

"I could make them." The woman's eye was sharp. She turned them over expertly, studying seam and stitch. Secrets could be gleaned everywhere. She smiled at Ina, who had such a clever sister-in-law. They talked of their friends, of relations, and a novel that all the women had read. They did not talk about the baby. They did not talk about the bandage on Ina's breast. There had, in fact, been good news from the nursery. The neonatologist, a short bespectacled Filipino, had come in to see them and told them that a new formula was being tried on the baby. He was optimistic. But this they could not talk about. They would not tempt fate. They would not expose their fear and hope. It was better to speak of a new movie, to compare reactions to a television show. They knew the rules.

Marnie and her husband, walking the wide corridor with the gait of passengers on the deck of a cruise ship, passed the open door and waved. They waved back, smiled. Miriam found a picture of Marnie in a fashion magazine and showed it to her mother.

Mrs. Gottlieb passed around the basket of fruit, and the two older couples discussed the bus trip they had taken together the year before into Pennsylvania Dutch country. The apple and pear trees had been in full blossom, and the fruit had hung red and gold, blazing like fiery globes amid the thick-leafed branches.

"I don't remember such orchards in Germany. Do you, Lottie?" Mr. Gottlieb asked his wife.

"In Poland we had wonderful orchards." Shirley Cherne had sailed into the room and plucked up the thread of the conversation. She smiled at them with the beneficent ease of a new arrival who is confident that she will be liked and accepted. Norman Cherne stood behind her, the color high in his face. His hands flashed forward in eager greeting to the other men; his smile turned brightly on the women, who thought him handsome and well preserved and did not read the death and fear in his eyes.

Introductions were made. The weather was discussed and discarded. There had been worse springs and better ones, too. Common ground was sought. Norman Cherne's cousin belonged to the Gottliebs' temple. Mr. Rosen had a friend who sold buttons to Cherne Knitwear. Shirley Cherne observed that Miriam looked like her mother, that Ben had his father's eyes. Her observation was assessed, argued over, and accepted. Norman Cherne produced a bottle of Sabra, and they found small paper cups which they filled with the chocolate-colored liqueur that tasted of oranges grown in the Galilee. When Susan Li, the Chinese nurse, looked in on them, they urged a paper cup on her. She giggled and declined and lit the overhead light as she left. Lamps burned at each bedside table and above the sink. The room blazed with brightness and buzzed with talk. They had vanquished the ominous ambience of the hospital.

"A toast," Mrs. Rosen called. The bow of her white blouse had come undone, and her cheeks were very red. Mischief glinted in her eyes. She had always been high-spirited. She still loved a party, any party. Even one held in a hospital room high above a wooded park.

Ray, the lawyer, gifted at oratory, rose at once. He was the family toastmaster. He would do the honors for room 502.

"I give you the ancient toast of our people. *L'Chaim*. Let us drink to life."

Silence reverberated. Their breath was audible in the quiet room. The cups grew soggy in their hands, and when they lifted them to their lips, the liqueur was too warm and there was a strange bitterness to the taste of the citrus. The Gottliebs and Rosens drank and looked at each other gravely. A toast was neither prayer nor pledge. They might be drinking to death. Yet slowly they drained their cups.

Shirley Cherne's tongue darted out to lick at the drink. She did not finish it, but her husband gulped his down and poured himself another. He was not a fearful man. A toast was a challenge, a declaration of faith. He believed in the hand of God moving deliberately through the chaos of history.

Ina sipped slowly, delicately. Her cup split at the bottom, and the remaining drops dripped out. The reddish brown liquid streaked her nightgown, bloodying the fold of fabric that draped her abdomen. She drew her robe over the stain and rested her hands over the soft layers of apricot-colored silk. Beneath that softness, within her body, life nestled, an embryo, a tiny fetal creature clinging to a spongy placenta. She had drunk to life, and the drink had stained her gown.

"*L'Chaim*," she repeated softly, doubtfully, and they looked toward her.

"*L'Chaim*," they all responded at once, impatient at their own silence, and Mrs. Gottlieb found a box of strudel, and Mrs. Rosen passed a package of mints, rattling the paper noisily, banishing unwelcome echoes.

"You're from Poland?" Mrs. Rosen asked Shirley Cherne. "Our families also came from Poland. What city do you come from?"

"My family lived in a small town not far from Warsaw. We ourselves lived in Warsaw when we were married. Before."

There was no need to amend the "before." All Jews of their generation neatly divided their lives into "before" and "after." Before the war and after the war. Cryptically, they flashed each other signals and knew which questions were safe and which were fraught with danger. Dexterously they drew their own boundaries, talked their way through danger zones.

"And your family?" Shirley Cherne asked.

"From Lodz."

"Ah." Her breath exited in a hiss. She and Norman Cherne

looked at each other and then out the window. The leaves of
the trees in the park below were velvet-black against a sky
that was strangely dim.

They knew about Lodz. One of the first ghettoes had been
set up there. They had had family there. A cousin had survived, and they had met him in the displaced persons camp
in Italy. He had held Ina on his knee and told them that in the
great synagogue of Lodz, leaders of the Jewish community
had been locked up without food or water and told that they
would not be allowed out until they had hacked the ancient
carved ark of the Torah to pieces and mutilated the scrolls
within. A frightened crowd had stood in the street outside
and listened to the hacking of metal against wood and to the
anguished cries of the men.

"They had to murder a Torah," the cousin had said, stroking Ina's hair. "That was like to kill a child. Could a man kill
his own child?"

Norman Czernowitz had thought of the soft-spoken, poetry-
loving dentist whose large, gentle hand had stifled the breath
of his infant son.

"A man can do anything," he had replied.

On that they were authorities. They had, after all, seen men
doing anything and everything. Their cousin from Lodz had
gone to Israel and opened an apothecary shop in Tel Aviv.
In 1956 he had been killed on the Suez, but his son had graduated from the Hadassah-Hebrew University Medical School,
and the Chernes had sent him a fully outfitted medical bag,
shopping carefully to find implements that were not manu-
factured in Germany.

"We know about Lodz," Norman Cherne said. What Nachum Czernowitz had known, Norman Cherne would never
forget.

"My family came to the States when I was a baby. Long
before. But some close relatives came after," Mrs. Rosen said.

"Where had they been?" Shirley asked.

"My cousin was in Belsen. My aunt and uncle in Tereisenstadt."

"Tereisenstadt. For some that was not so bad," Norman said.

"My family were all in Mauthausen. My wife's in Buchenwald," Mr. Gottlieb contributed.

"Ah. Mauthausen. Buchenwald." Norman Cherne sighed deeply.

They might have been fellow alumni speaking knowledgeably of distant schools, or countrymen meeting by chance abroad, trading memories of shared experience, shared impression. The Cotswolds in the summer. Bennington in the fall. Buchenwald in the dead of winter. They revealed their knowledge with a muted sigh, an intake of breath, a sudden brightness of eye. Where memory had not been filtered, the harshness of what they could not, would not, speak about masked their faces with pain. "Before" and "after" could be dealt with, but only those who had been there could speak of "during."

"We lost everything, everyone, our whole family," little Mrs. Gottlieb said. "Brothers, sisters, parents, aunts, uncles, cousins. Like dust, like that which had not been. We were alone here. Dry leaves tossed about in a strange land. My husband and I. Our Ben. This baby, the son of Miriam and Benjamin—this baby of ours—he makes us again a family. One generation linked to another. A going on. We begin again to be a family. To build."

"Everyone builds by themselves," Shirley Cherne said softly. "We can't find in our children or in our children's children that which we ourselves have lost. The grandchild does not replace the grandfather." She looked at Ina, who sat very still in her chair, her hands still covering the stain. The new baby would not replace Yedidiah. It would not replace the embryo aborted on the barrack floor. A new life does not cancel the loss of the unforgotten dead. There was compensation but no reduction. Ina turned to her mother, but Shirley had moved to the sink, where she turned the water on so forcefully they had to raise their voices in order to be heard.

Miriam put her arm about her mother-in-law's shoulders. "You know, Mama, you must not be pessimistic. Dr. Ra-

mires said that they are going to switch the baby to a new
IV formula tonight. If he tolerates it, they're sure we have a
better than even chance. The respiratory problem is almost
clear, and his color is better. It's just the digestion now, and
the doctor says they've had terrific success with this formula
in other cases," Miriam said. Her own despair of the long
afternoon was forgotten. She was no longer the desperately
worried mother. Once again she was the good daughter to her
husband's mother, offering hope and comfort to the tired old
woman who had lost so much she could not bear to lose again.

"Let's hope."

Mrs. Gottlieb and Mrs. Rosen wiped the table clear of
crumbs, covered the food, tossed away the soiled napkins.
Diligently they applied their womanly skills. They would restore order to disordered surfaces, reason to unreasonable
lives. Shirley Cherne scrubbed the table with a wet paper
towel. She was an expert on institutional dirt.

"Ma," Ina said, "there's a girl I want you to talk to. If you'll
excuse us for a little while?"

She smiled and they smiled back. The polite social atmosphere had been restored. Mr. Gottlieb produced a chessboard
and Norman Cherne set the pieces up. Ray picked up the *New
York Post* his father-in-law had discarded. He read a headline
and his eyes drifted closed. He was very tired. He had not yet
told Ina about his conversation with Dr. Isaacs. He would talk
to her when she returned, when the Chernes had left and they
were alone.

Ben found a New Jersey station that played chamber music.
Between quartets an announcer told them that a truck driver
had suffered a massive hemorrhage in a turnpike accident. He
was being taken by helicopter to a special unit at Mount
Lebanon. They sighed and looked out the window but saw
nothing. Mrs. Gottlieb produced her needlepoint, and Miriam
and her mother bent over a box and busied themselves with
infant clothing. A small jacket floated over the bedclothes like
a small blue butterfly, the tiny sleeves outstretched like tender

wings. They marveled at it, bewitched by the miracle of its smallness.

Ina and Shirley Cherne walked slowly to the waiting room. They were not in the habit of walking together and awkwardly adjusted their gait each to the other. They passed two women, mother and daughter, their features locked into twinship. The daughter was the visitor, and she walked hand in hand with her mother, who wore a stiff quilted robe on which small rosebuds danced. The robe was too large for her, and her thin fingers worried the belt, which she had pulled too tight. As they walked, the younger woman spoke softly to her in the soothing tone of one telling a comforting story to a frightened child. Her voice was patient. She knew that she had reached that time in life when daughters mothered the women who had borne them and held their hands in wide corridors as once their own small hands had been held on sun-dappled streets. Shirley shivered and smiled as they passed. The sick woman's slippers were loose and fluttered with cushioned throb against the waxed floor.

"Mama," her daughter said, "everything will be all right. The doctor says there is nothing to worry about. You'll see. Everything will be all right."

Endlessly the generations comforted each other—on park benches and in overheated living rooms, across cluttered kitchen tables and in hospital corridors. "Everything will be all right. . . . We will all live happily ever after." Compassion denied truth, and they yearned to believe the fairy tales they knew to be untrue.

The waiting room was crowded, and Ina smiled at faces so newly familiar, introduced her mother to Marnie, was introduced in turn to Marnie's husband, Bob.

"You girls are having a vacation of sorts," he said. His voice was rich and soft, and when he took Ina's hand he did not release his wife's.

"Of sorts," Ina agreed.

What was a vacation, after all, but a change of pace, a

switch of scene? For these few days Marnie had left the bright lights of the photographic studios, the rush from cab to appointment, the long hours of posing in an evening gown while a spring sun blazed or in a bathing suit as a light snow fell. She had instead lived the even-paced, quiet life of the hospital, her day divided up into doctor's visits, technicians' tests, and meals served at precise hours on plastic trays. Ina herself had been far away from the clacking of calculators, the hum of a terminal, the urgent demands of Jeddy and Rachel, Carmen's brisk, automated movement. It had been a time apart, stretches of hours spent thinking backward, looking inward—yes, she supposed it could be called a vacation.

It was on vacations that decisions were made, that lives were often altered. Ruthie had returned from a vacation at a women's commune and left her husband. Dot had returned from a vacation with the decision to adopt another baby, and Simon, silent and wondrous, had come into their lives. Ricky, Ina's secretary, had returned from vacation engaged to be married. Ina smiled at the tall black man whose heavy-browed eyes glinted with arrows of gold.

"But we were cheated," she said. "We didn't get to send any picture postcards."

"Or buy souvenirs." Marnie laughed.

Shirley Cherne stared at them impatiently, uncomprehendingly. Where was the joke? In America they laughed at everything. A hospital stay became a vacation. *Nu?* She shook her head, rubbed her fingers over her rings, flecked a loose thread from her pale green skirt. The black girl was beautiful. She would carry proudly and well. How far pregnant was she? Two months? Three months? Ina would know.

"Have you seen Tina?" Ina asked. "I want my mother to talk to her."

"She's over there," Marnie said, and pointed to the bright blue couch in the corner where Tina sat with her mother and father. They were playing Sorry, desultorily lifting the cards and marching the colorful plastic pieces around the patterned board.

Briefly, Ina explained Tina's situation to her mother. It was not the cancer, the threat of death, that worried the girl. It was the loss of her hair, the fear of ugliness, the specter of her bald scalp shining pinkly, turning her young face into an old woman's death's head.

"She's a kid, a baby," Ina said. "She doesn't understand."

"I wasn't a baby," Shirley answered. "But did I understand? The air stank of death. Bodies burned. My sister went out the door one morning, and I never saw her again. My son died, and I did not know if my husband was alive or dead. But day and night I worried about my hair. Would it grow again? Would the new hair have color, or would it grow in looking like snow? That happened to Bluma Greenwald. She was twenty-four years old. The typhus took her hair, too—it was dark like yours. But when it came in again, it was the color of winter, and she knew that her husband was dead."

"And was he?" Ina asked.

"I told you. Her hair had turned white." Shirley Cherne's voice was firm. There was kitchen wisdom and camp wisdom, unproven but indomitable. If a left-handed person visits a pregnant woman, the child will be born left-handed. If a deserted woman's fallen hair grows in white, she is a widow and must mourn her husband.

All this Shirley Cherne, who knew how to turn a profit on excess yardage of corduroy and how to negotiate a mortgage with a hard-eyed bank officer, believed. And Ina, who fed data into the keyboards of sophisticated terminals, who designed systems in mysterious computer languages—deep within herself, in spite of herself, she believed it too. Years ago her mother had told her never to step over a child or growth would be inhibited. When Rachel and Jeddy stretched across the study floor watching television, she, the mathematician, the woman who spoke up in consciousness-raising groups and at rallies, walked carefully around their prone bodies. Mysteries would not be denied and must not be tempted. The hair of a widow turned white before she knew of her husband's death. In the darkness of the night, in the shadowed hours of late afternoon, women offered cryptic prayers, made ominous bargains. If your child dies, mine will live. Grant me this, and I will not pray for more.

They crossed the room. Ina introduced her mother to Tina and was introduced in turn to Tina's parents.

"Tina told me how nice you and that beautiful model have been to her." The mother was grateful for the kindness to her child. She smiled at Ina as she had, through the years, smiled at sympathetic camp counselors, involved teachers. Now she would train her appreciation on doctors and nurses, therapists and fellow patients.

"Well, Tina's been nice to us too," Ina said, and touched the girl's hand.

Blue bone gleamed through Tina's flesh-bare knuckles. A loss of appetite was a side effect of radiation, chemotherapy. Weight loss often came with remission. Weight loss also came without remission. Arrows pointed in all directions, but they could only play by rules they barely understood and proceed one move at a time. Tina's father drew the Sorry card and bumped his wife's blue playing piece. He moved his own red one to her position. Every game had its moments of luck.

Shirley Cherne drew up two chairs, and Ina chose the nearest and sat leaning forward. The modular seats had been designed to deny comfort. The adhesive on Ina's bandage loosened, and she pressed it back into place. The pain had been replaced by a raw soreness. The incision was knitting. The self-dissolving thread of the suture was being absorbed into her body. Had Ray spoken to Isaacs? What had he said? She touched the bandage tentatively, and the sheer breast skin was hot beneath her fingers. The mounds of glandular tissue were separated from the rest of her body by their tenderness, their manipulable vulnerability. Her breasts were like small animals—the nipples were their flesh-closed eyes that wept milk and hardened with sudden desire, unshed vapor. She drew her arms protectively around them for a brief moment, then sat back, fearful and exhausted.

"Tina was talking to us this afternoon about the radiation treatments," Ina said. "She's afraid that they will affect her hair."

"Her hair?" her father asked.

Disbelief rimmed his voice, overflowed. He worried about his daughter's life, feared her death, brought her gowns of bridal white. He would clothe her in gossamer garments and banish the coarse muslin of hospital gowns from which shrouds are also fashioned. He took jet planes to specialists in distant cities, read obscure medical journals, wrote checks rapidly, eagerly. Money was his only weapon in the terrible war he was fighting. He would win and save his daughter. He did not worry about her hair. It was her life that obsessed him.

"Yes, Daddy, my hair." Tina's voice was piteous. Her hand fluttered to her head, tugged gently. Fine black tendrils formed a net about her fingers, webbed her hand. She held them out to him, trembling, and he brushed them from her fingers. The loosened hairs fell to the floor in a dark silken veil. "I don't want to be bald." Her voice crumbled and broke. His eyes grew moist. She was his baby, his love, his little girl. He had kissed the blood from her scraped knee, licked tears from her cheeks. He had promised her always to make everything better.

"It's nothing. A side effect."

His voice was harsh. He was a large man. He wore no jacket, and his arm muscles rippled as he tensed his fists. He was a strong man, but his daughter's tears melted his strength, and her foolishness twisted his heart. But she would not deter him from saving her.

"So it falls out," he added, softening his tone.

"And it grows back," Shirley Cherne said.

He looked at the woman whose thick chestnut-colored hair, streaked with silver, was pulled into an intricate chignon which she undid, as he watched, working clumsily but determinedly. Her fingers were twisted with arthritis, burdened by rings set with dead-eyed stones. He could not tell her age.

Something in her history had obscured, confused, her years. The hair was freed at last and fell in rich sheaves about her face. She shook it loose, proudly, haughtily.

"I know because once I too lost my hair, all of it. It was in Europe, during the war. I had typhus, and I became bald after the fever. Ina was a small girl then. The baldness frightened her. She cried when she saw me."

Ina was startled. She did not remember her mother being bald. She did not recall her own tears, but she knew that it had all happened. She did remember that during the weeks of Shaindel's illness her Aunt Peshi had cared for her and Bette. It was then that they had played "Moses goes up the mountain, Moses goes down the mountain . . . ," the game that Bette did not remember, even as she herself did not remember Bette's terror. But then, perhaps Bette would remember that Ina had wept to see her mother pale-scalped and skeletally thin.

She and Bette had each plucked out those incidents they could bear to remember from the terrible potpourri of their past. Selective recall, the analysts would call it. Eleanor Berenson would know. The analyst worked at their lives diligently, as though she were involved in the construction of an intricate jigsaw puzzle. Here belongs this jagged piece, and there we will fit the rounded one. The picture will emerge. The riddle will be solved. Fear will be banished and night sweats and sudden tremors of weakness and desolation, woven of the fear that it could happen again, of the certainty that it would happen again—in dream if not in reality.

"It took time," Shirley continued. "My scalp was pink as a new baby's. I wore kerchiefs to cover it. I was ashamed. The war was over. The months went by. My hair grew back. Thicker than before. They say its color is brighter. Only now does silver show in it." She plucked up one silver thread, then another. At her age hair turned the color of ashes, but hers burned like still fire.

They nodded their recognition, their acknowledgment. Unhurriedly, carefully, she twisted her hair again into a coil, pinned it into place. It became a smooth knot held together with pins and clips, a chestnut-colored nest in which strands of silver glinted.

"You see," she said to Tina, "you don't have to worry about your hair. It will grow in again. Thicker. Darker. You will get well. You'll dance at all the parties—the prettiest girl in the room."

Tina smiled. Her mother blushed. Her father grew pale. His large hands trembled.

"Thank you," the mother said. "We appreciate your telling us. Sharing with us. That's the sort of thing you have to hear from someone who has been through it. See, Tina? Don't you feel better now?"

"Yes," the girl replied. "Oh, yes." Tears streaked down her cheeks. The radiation hurt. She would dream of Ina's mother, this lady with twisted beringed fingers, and see her shorn of hair, her scalp glowing pink as a baby's. But she believed her. Her hair had grown back, and so would Tina's own. She would live, and, more important, she would not be ugly.

"Thank you," Tina said, and ran from the waiting room, knocking over the game. Embarrassed, the adults knelt to pick up the cards, the plastic pieces that rolled across the floor.

"She's upset, tired," the mother said.

"Poor kid." The father wept. He was so strong, so prosperous, so powerless. He could not believe his own impotency.

"Yes, of course," Shirley answered. The girl's tears did not surprise her. "She will be fine," she said, and there was strange authority in her voice. Comforted, grateful, they looked up at her, and she and Ina smiled their sympathy and left the room.

In the corridor Ina took her mother's hand, for the first time in many years. They walked through the hall together, talking softly to each other of small things—a new spring coat for Rachel, drapes for the study, a length of fabric Shirley had found to cover the daybed in the Amagansett house. They did not mention sickness and death. The small decisions engrossed and soothed them, and when they passed the elderly woman in her flowered robe, walking hand in hand with her daughter, the other women were murmuring the names of the colors. "Blue," they said, and "Aqua," "Wine red and lemon yellow."

"I will have a lilac suit this spring," the older woman said.

"Yes, Mama, with a dark purple blouse to match."

A nurse came up to them.

"Time for your medication, Mrs. Ingers."

"Yes. Thank you." The older woman nodded. "And a pale green dress," she said to her daughter. "The color of new grass."

"Oh, yes," the younger woman agreed. "Pale green. That will be lovely."

They disappeared into a room and closed the door softly behind them. Ina and her mother continued on their way, walking very slowly, as good friends do after a long evening.

The Gottliebs and the Rosens were preparing to leave. They carried with them boxes and shopping bags, and they checked the bedside table for forgotten items, the scattered litter of their love. Mrs. Rosen gathered up magazines and books.

"You're sure you're through with them?" she asked Miriam worriedly.

She did not want her daughter bored. She belonged to the army of mothers valiantly fighting the ennui of their children, buying them games and toys, magazines and theater tickets, entreating them, imploring them, to be happy. Did we birth you so that you would cry and flounder through empty hours? Laugh and repay us because all we have ever done has only been in the hopes of your health and your happiness.

"Should I take this home?" Mrs. Gottlieb held Ruthie's drawing of the panda.

"No. I like looking at it."

The older couples looked sympathetically at each other. See, she was a child still, this young girl so newly become a mother, so newly initiated into that coven of worriers whose life would never again belong to her alone. She had a baby. She was attached. They laughed because she was a mother, and yet she was their child. There was new hope in the room.

They had, all four grandparents, been to see the baby, to spy on the tiny creature lying within the sterile confines of the isolette. The baby had moved. Its face had curled up and unfolded like a wind-bruised flower. They had counted its fingers and toes. The nurse had told them that the new formula seemed to be working. They had taken heart and opted for hope.

Miriam's mother stroked her hair, tied the bow on her nightgown.

"You shouldn't worry," she said.

"No, Mama."

Her mother-in-law looked out the window where street lamps cast golden columns of light through which the traffic moved slowly, steadily, as though the automobiles themselves were exhausted after the long day of hurrying through the rain, up and down the broad avenues of the city.

"No more rain," she said.

The new sweet dryness of the evening was an omen. When they walked outside the air would smell moist and fragrant, and in the morning young buds would have emerged in blossoms and the leaves of the trees would be a tender green. Mrs. Gottlieb believed in signs. When she was pregnant with Ben, a sparrow had flown into her kitchen window, perched briefly on the table, and winged its way outside again. A neighbor woman had told her that it meant that she carried a boy and that the birth would be easy. Ben had been delivered after a very short labor, and when she first held him, a fledgling sparrow had perched on the window and stared at her with bright hard eyes. The cessation of rain after the long day of near-weeping portended an end to tears. It was only fair that the signs be favorable to them. They had suffered their fill.

The men clutched their folded umbrellas and bent clumsily to kiss the young woman. Her father put his hand under her chin, smiled at her. His skullcap lay askew on his thick hair. He was a secret clown, and one day the tiny baby in the plastic cage would be a small boy who would laugh wildly at his jokes, at his antics. He would pretend to be an elephant for his grandson, and he would slip small gold coins from his ears. He imagined the child's laughter and was assuaged.

"You shouldn't worry," he repeated.

They smiled at Ina, shook hands with the Chernes and Ray, argued with each other about where they had parked the car. In the doorway at last, they looked lingeringly back.

"We'll call in the morning," Mrs. Gottlieb said.

"Fine." Miriam waved to them and leaned back against the pillow as they disappeared down the hallway. Her efforts to appease their anxiety had exhausted her. Her skin was faded to a wintry pallor, and when she closed her eyes, blue veins threaded the fragile lids. Ben pulled the screen about her bed, and Ina and Ray watched their shadows move across the whiteness, watched the wings of his arms move shelteringly about her, heard the murmur of his comforting words.

"Baby. It will be all right. Not to worry. Not to cry. Sweet baby. Good Miriam."

The Chernes too left, her mother's kiss dry against Ina's cheek.

Then there was silence, and Ray turned to Ina, who sat on the side of the bed, her fingers toying with the liqueur stain that had spread like a small petaled flower across the apricot-colored silk.

"It will come out," he said.

"Oh, yes, I know." But still she rubbed at it.

"Ina, I spoke to Isaacs. It was definitely benign. We're home free."

"Oh, Ray!" Her hands fell limp, helpless on the rumpled sheets. A layer of worry floated from her bent shoulders like a gossamer shawl. She was all right. Pain surged through the breast, triumphant, billowing pain. She caressed the wound, laughed at the pain. She would ignore it, vanquish it. She was healthy, and there were a thousand things she would do. Impatience and energy coursed through her in twin currents. Instinctively she touched her abdomen. She was capable of all things. Life grew within her, not death. All decisions were hers. Control of her body, of her own future, had been restored to her. Her cheeks glowed with new color.

"I walked here from midtown," he said.

"A long walk."

"I needed to think. Did you know that they tore down our old house on Forty-third?"

"Yes. I passed it once a year ago."

"You didn't tell me."

"I guess I thought it would upset you. It was strange. It upset me. We had lived there, and now it was gone. There's an office building in its place, all steel and glass. It didn't seem fair somehow. I remember how Mr. Bastani used to wash the windows himself and how they worked together in the small garden in back. They grew herbs there, remember? Marjoram and basil and the large-leafed Italian parsley. Poor garden."

"Yes. But they went back to Italy. We moved. Things happen. Things change."

"Let's plant a herb garden at the Amagansett house," she said. "Our own basil. I'll make a pesto sauce. Gallons of it. We'll freeze it."

"And have a party," he added, and then was quiet, remembering other parties. "I passed Andrea's old street. And the Steins' building where there was no bathtub or shower." He laughed harshly, bitterly. They would have a new guest list for this party. Friends were ephemeral, friendships as vulnerable and expendable as narrow brick buildings that they did not own.

"Ina," he said, "I think I've been unfair. You were right. I should have been more open about my doubts. I guess I didn't talk to you about it even when I had my first feelings about wanting the baby because I knew I was wrong. Wrong to lay what I wanted on you."

"There's no right and wrong when it comes to feelings." That much, at least, she had learned in the darkened room that smelled of Eleanor Berenson's English cigarettes and lavender scent. Feelings soared free of morality. One could not apologize for them or program them into a system.

"The point is," he said, insistent now that she listen and absolve him, "you have to decide on the basis of what's good for you."

"What's good for us," she said, and leaned back against the pillows. "My father was here alone this afternoon. He said that my mother's abortion was like a shadow between them all these years. He's afraid it will happen to us."

The parallel appalled him. They were nothing like the Chernes.

"That's crazy," he said. "We're different."

They had not risen from death to be reunited in a land foreign to them both, to be healed by doctors who did not speak their language, and to be pitied by nurses who fed them semolina in tiny spoonfuls and were startled to see the milky ivory of their bones exposed by sheer and fleshless skin. He and Ina had moved together through shared years, supportive of each other, always talking, discussing. He had encouraged her to start the agency. She had urged him to remain in public service. They were life-smart and fate-free. They had season tickets to the symphony. Yellow school buses carried their children off each morning. No shadows stood between them. They would not tolerate them.

They had, both of them, emerged from pasts so darkened with loss and grief that they could not allow space in which penumbric melancholy might grow. They cluttered their days with activities, their years with achievements. They clung to each other in the darkness of the night, each knowing that the other must be protected from the memory of ineffable, irreplaceable losses. They sought to banish doubt with discussion, confusion with clarity. They shared but they did not trespass. They were completely unlike Shirley and Norman Cherne, who had been catapulted from death to life, from one culture to another, always separated from each other by bitterness and secret. He was hurt, angered, that she could confuse their marriage with that of her parents.

"Of course we're different," she said. "But still."

"But still what?"

She shrugged. The day's uncertainties overwhelmed her. She thought of the system she was working on, imagined moviegoers at a cinema in a Kansas prairie town seeing a film selected by her calculations made in a New York hospital room. She wished herself back at her own desk, wearing her tan linen suit, bent over data sheets, flipping through punch cards. When the phone rang, she would issue terse directives into it, certain of her answers, clear in her choices. "Yes. No. Bill them now. Book computer time for Monday."

"I don't know what to do," she whispered. "I knew, but now I don't. I don't know what I want." Her hands became fists, and she pressed them against her eyes, but she did not cry. He touched her arm, smoothed her hair, filled her water glass.

"Do you want the baby?" he asked.

"I don't know. Does anyone ever know what they want?" Her voice sounded like Rachel's. It quivered in bewilderment.

"We have to decide. Isaacs must know by tomorrow."

"By tomorrow I'll know," she said. The certainty in her voice startled him, but he believed her. He offered no argument, no protest.

"All right."

She reached for the phone. They had forgotten to call the children. Jeddy's voice, shrill and triumphant, streaked out of the phone. He had been selected for the track team. He would need new sneakers. Only three boys had made it.

"Big deal," Rachel said on the extension, but they recognized the pride in her requisite derision and smiled. She had done the assignment she had considered unfair. It had been sort of interesting.

"See?" Ina said. "You never can tell."

Rachel agreed. She had been invited to a party Saturday night. A boy-girl party. A disco theme. Could she go? Yes, of course. Ray and Ina looked at each other. They saw their children streaking away from them, moving faster and faster down the track of their own lives, disappearing into strange rooms, moving their wonderful young bodies to a new and vibrant music. It was all right. It was fine. They had no choice. They were frightened but brave, uncertain but accepting.

"Daddy will be home soon. He's leaving now," Ina said.

"When are you coming home, Mom?" Rachel asked.

"We'll know tomorrow." She made a kissing noise into the phone. They laughed, pleased but embarrassed. They were not babies anymore.

She hung up, and Ray smiled at her contentedly, amused. "Those kids," he said.

"Yes."

"Visiting hours are over. All visitors are requested to leave. Thank you." The woman's voice drifted in over the loud-speaker. There was a stirring along the corridor. Visitors in unbuttoned raincoats, holding furled umbrellas, passed the room. Several phones rang in a sudden desperate symphony. There was an almost palpable murmuring of good-byes. The sound of weeping came from a nearby room.

"Time to go," Ray said. He kissed her cheek, her hand.

Ben Gottlieb appeared from behind the screen.

"Miriam's asleep," he said. "Well, we should have a clear picture tomorrow."

"Yes. By tomorrow." Ina echoed his words.

They all looked out the window to where a red-eyed helicopter was slowly whirring to a landing in the park. Its motor hummed softly, and a cadre of white-coated men and women advanced toward it, a ghostly corps of healers moving swiftly through the moist, sweet darkness. A rush of wind from the propeller ripped the sheet off the waiting stretcher, and it sailed over the trees like a great winged white bird.

"Good night," Ray said.

"Good night." Ben looked from the window back to his wife's bed.

Two police cars circled the helicopter, brilliant golden lights revolving on their roofs.

The two men walked together toward the bank of elevators and glanced automatically up at the clock. They smiled at Marnie and Bob Coleman and at the young girl in the white peignoir who stood quiescently between her parents, like a bride on her way to the marriage canopy.

Ina lay quietly with her eyes closed after they had gone. She did not move when Susan Li came into the room and flicked off both the overhead and sink lights. The nurse tiptoed over to Miriam Gottlieb's bed, and Ina watched her shadowy figure move behind the screen. Like a concerned mother, she bent over the young woman and drew the thin hospital blanket up about her slender form. She draped the pale blue robe over the chair where it would be accessible yet would not crease. She clicked off the bedside lamp, and Miriam was tented in darkness. Then, as softly as she had entered, she left.

Ina was pierced with jealousy. The nurse had ignored her, had left her light burning, had not checked to see if she were awake or asleep. Many years ago Bette had spent several weeks at the Forest Hills apartment, and Shirley Cherne, who took it for granted that Ina could manage the household, worried constantly over her dead sister's child. Had Bette had an egg for breakfast? Did she take vitamins? Why didn't Ina take her cousin swimming, shopping, to a museum in the city? Ina had been resentful, wounded, and she had shouted her hurt out at her mother when Bette (whom she loved and had phoned twice within hours of her leaving) had finally left. "You care more about her than about me! You worried more over her than you ever did over me!" Shirley Cherne had been startled, bewildered. "But she needs it more. She has no mother." Susan Li would, of course, feel the same way about Miriam Gottlieb. She needed more care, more tenderness. She might be bereft of her child. Ina was comforted.

Lazily she got out of bed. The resident had said that she might shower. The hot water would not affect the incision, would in fact be good for it. She gathered towels and a fresh nightgown, preparing for the shower with odd excitement, as though she were undertaking an adventure, crossing a border. She was preparing herself for normalcy, for ordered days and nights.

She stood beneath the spigot, clutched the steel guard, and allowed the water to course down her body in steaming rivulets. The water purified, clarified, bleached the day's doubts and secrets.

The bathroom was lit with bleak wattage, and her skin was pale beneath its cloak of moving water. Where the Amagansett sun had colored them, her arms glowed rose-gold. She soaped herself gently, building frothy columns of foam about her hips, beneath her arms, layering her abdomen with a film of soap. She bent to wash her legs. The bandage at her breast was wet and soggy but remained in place. With light fingers she washed her breasts. They were healthy, tender to her touch. When she rinsed the soap away with a rough cloth, rosy blotches blossomed across them, and their veins snaked bluely in intricate pattern. If the pregnancy proceeded, they would grow large and pearlike, and just before she delivered, golden drops of colostrum would weep through the hardened nipples.

She was a small-busted woman, and she had loved her breasts grown full and overflowing. Ray slept with his head against them, and once in sleep he turned his head and his mouth reached up to her nipple and rested there. He was, that night, her thirsty, undrinking child. She had imagined herself his mother and pressed his lips closer to her flesh.

She had loved nursing Rachel and Jeddy. Their small budding mouths had sucked strenuously at her rounded nipple, and their eyes had remained trustingly, blindly, closed as they drew nourishment from her, urgently, rhythmically. She could not imagine having a baby and not nursing it. But would she want to spend the long hours at home again, listening for the curious infant pant that preceded the wail of hunger?

She remembered how, on signal, with the baby's first cry, a gush of milk would spurt forth, soaking through the nursing pads and brassiere, staining her shirt. Her body's rhythms then had belonged to the babies, but she had reclaimed them years ago. There came a time when a woman's body reverted to her own possession, when her life too became her own. It did not do to reread Camus on a park bench, to fuss with diapers and shirts, and, finally, to swallow an entire bottle of aspirin.

The water grew hotter, and mists of steam clouded the tiny bathroom. She rinsed the veil of soap from her breasts, let the hot water stream over her, then switched it off and shocked her body into sudden wakefulness with a downpour of cool water. She lathered her abdomen. Dark-veined stretch lines streaked her stomach. She drew it in, thrust it out, played at being pregnant. With Jeddy, she had become huge in the last trimester and had moved heavily, a prisoner of her unborn child. She shut off the water and toweled herself dry.

The bandage had peeled off and lay in a sodden heap on the shower floor. She looked for the first time at the incision. It was perhaps three inches long, and beneath the black thread of the suture, the scar line puckered, angry and purple, forming a cruel smile in the featureless face of the breast. She would ask the nurse to bandage it again.

The fresh nightgown was of lime green and high-necked. She had had such a nightgown her first year at the university, and she felt herself a schoolgirl again. She shook her dark hair out of the shower cap. It was damp, and she tied it into a limp ponytail. Peering into the misted mirror, she saw that her color was high. It seemed to her that she was too young to be the mother of a girl verging on adolescence. Yet slivers of gray glinted in her hair. Surely she was too old to mother an infant again.

She folded the towels and used the smallest one to mop the floor where water had leaked from the shower. She was no longer an invalid waiting for a disinterested nurse to cover her, to shut her light and care for her scattered garments. She had taken possession of her life again, and of her body.

She left the bathroom and emerged from its steamy dampness into the dry warmth of the large hospital room. It had filled with the fragrance of spring flowers, of the daffodils and roses her father and Ray had bought and of the great spray of lilac Ben Gottlieb had carried as an offering to his wife. It occurred to her again that the dogwood tree just opposite her bedroom window must be in bloom.

Quickly, she slipped on her yellow robe and left the room, climbing the stairwell to the floor above. She did not want to be seen boarding the elevator. She did not want to be asked questions for which she had no answers.

The Gottlieb baby lay in its bubble beyond the glass window. A tiny plastic tube was threaded to the small arm, and a milky liquid moved through it in slow and silvery descent. The baby wore only a diaper, and as Ina watched, its tiny body shivered and defecated. The yellow-green stain spread across the white cloth, and the tiny face screwed itself into a knot and then relaxed. The small hand opened and closed. The infant arched itself, but its eyes did not open. The dark hair was moist, and a vein at the forehead pulsated like a small spider throbbing through a thin web of its own weaving.

"He looks much better tonight." The elderly nurse she had seen two nights before stood beside her again, as though they had met at this windowed wall by prearrangement.

"Yes. I think so too. Will he live?"

"His chances are much better now." The woman was careful. She had been a nurse for a long time. She had carried many small corpses, as light as air, from the scientifically monitored isolettes that had become their coffins. Sometimes she passed fat and healthy children in the street and wondered who they were, if once they had lain in her steel-barred cribs, connected to life by plastic tubes. She was a nurse who would never recognize the small patients who recovered but would feel always the weightlessness of small and bitter deaths, of tiny creatures rigid in her arms. She hedged her bets, although the dark-haired male infant had good color and his diaper was sullied.

"I hope so," Ina said. Miriam Gottlieb's son opened and closed his fist.

She took the stairs again. They were slippery beneath her feet, and she grasped the handrail for support. Two interns passed and glanced at her curiously, their eyes flitting to her hospital bracelet, but she smiled at them reassuringly and they moved on.

The baby looked much better. Surely it would live. And she would reclaim her life, reorder her days, give up the child she did not want to bear, allow her breasts to remain small and dry and firm. They would plant an herb garden behind the Amagansett house and grow basil and marjoram and large-leafed Italian parsley. They would not think back to narrow brick houses that no longer stood, to faded friendships, to vanished children who had lived long ago in a land cloaked with sad mists of pale blue smoke and talked in a language she no longer understood.

"Yedidiah," she whispered, and waited for an answer, but none came.

The Gottlieb baby would live. Her bargain would be kept. Swiftly she moved down the hall to her room and climbed into the bed that had been mysteriously smoothed and straightened in her absence. She was startled to realize that her cheeks were wet with tears. When she closed her eyes, she saw the trio of faceless soldiers walking very slowly toward the baby who slept within the moist glass walls of the life-sustaining cage.

# FOURTH DAY

THUNDER, ARRIVING STEALTHILY, gathering sonorous momentum, tore mightily, finally, through the night's thick silence. Silver lightning slashed the velvet darkness. On every street and avenue, in parks and vacant lots, branches, brittle from the siege of winter, snapped and fell against turf and pavement. New young leaves and soft emergent buds trembled against the wind and were quiet, weighted down by their wetness, surrendering their brief verdancy. Those who wakened from their sleep and saw the angry sky felt oddly betrayed. They had closed their eyes to a gentle darkness, content that the day of rain had passed. It was unfair that a new storm had broken while they slept. They lay awake and listened to the thunder, stirred to uneasy sadness by the countless inequities over which they had no control—nature's vagaries, life's small and relentless sadnesses.

In the apartment high above the park, Jeddy, always fearful of storms, screamed into the night. Ray rushed barefoot through the shadowed rooms to comfort him. Familiar pieces of furniture loomed menacingly in the darkness. Still half-asleep, the child flailed and twisted in a tangle of ghostly bedclothes.

"Mommy!" he called in a high, sleep-thickened voice. "They're coming for me. Help me. Mommy!"

"Shhhh."

Ray straightened the sheets and blankets, pressed the child's trembling body against his own, smoothed the terror-dampened hair.

"It's a dream. It's a storm. No one's coming. You're home. You're safe. Mommy loves you. Daddy loves you."

The litany of reassurances dropped softly, effortlessly, from his lips. Serial thunderbolts crashed against the brief stillness as though to give lie to his words, but in Ray's arms Jeddy relaxed. The boy's lips curved into a smile. He reached for the blanket's satin binding and pressed it to his chin. He slept as Ina did, with the smoothness of the covering a soft shield against the night.

"Daddy," the child whispered, gladly, contentedly, and Ray bent down and kissed the soft rise of flesh that was his son's cheek. The salt taste on his lips startled him, and then he remembered that Jeddy had been crying.

He paused in Rachel's room before going back to bed. She wore a pale green nightgown, the exact shade and style of one that Ina owned. Once she had slept with a one-eared rabbit, but now paperback books and teen magazines littered her bed. As he watched, she smiled and stirred. She lifted her arm languidly and dropped it carelessly across the newly tender roundness of her breasts.

"I'm coming," she called softly, sweetly, and arched her body; she stretched, half rose, and then slid back into quiet sleep. He saw that fine-tendriled tufts of hair had formed beneath her arms.

He covered her and pondered the penumbral invaders who moved so carelessly through his children's sleep. Jeddy feared the nocturnal specters and Rachel welcomed them, but he thought both his children equally vulnerable and knew himself to be powerless against the amorphous vagrants of the dream-filled night. Certainly he could not battle his wife's nightmares, and he thought sadly of how her slender body trembled, of how terror streaked her eyes with feline brightness when she awakened in the night. Her own fear frightened

him. Who pursued her and would not let her sleep? He felt an
irrational rage, a tense wakefulness.

He went into the kitchen, put the overhead light on, and
welcomed its glare against the gleaming white appliances,
the polished copper bottoms of the hanging pots and pans. He
poured himself a large glass of milk and drank it in long
swallows. He did not want to go back to bed and think of
children who cried out into the night for parents who could
not come to them. He did not want to think of mothers and
fathers who were unable to rush softly through the darkness
to reassure a trembling child.

Ina, whose arms reached out for him in the night, who
murmured fearfully and inaudibly in her sleep, had awakened
just after Rachel's birth, shrieking and shaking. She had told
him that night how her mother had frightened Bette and herself into silence when they awoke with terror-widened mouths
in the barracks night where even darkness was a luxury. Always a single small naked bulb burned in the high-beamed
ceiling.

"Sha! Do you want to be next?" Shaindel would ask
sternly, her fingers clamped against their mouths so that the
guard who patrolled the room (because sleeping emaciated
Jewesses were dangerous and in need of constant surveillance)
would not hear them.

Perhaps small Bette had screamed (as Jeddy did), "They're
coming to get me!" Her terror had not been irrational. *They*
had come to get her mother. *They* might come to get her. If
she survived, *they* might come and get her children.

"I was always afraid to have children," Bette had said once
as the four of them had dinner together. "What if it happened
again? What if I couldn't help the children, save them? Is it
right to bring children into such a world?"

She had been pregnant then with the second of her children,
and although Richard, her husband, had reached for her hand,
she did not look at him. Instead, she stared down at her own
swollen abdomen which moved wondrously beneath the
golden folds of her loose maternity smock. The child she

carried stirred, kicked, as though in protest. Right or wrong, it would be born, it would enter the world.

Bette had fought her fears, had borne the children, but Halina Lansdorf (now Helene Kramer), who had endured the war with them, had remained determinedly childless.

"I would not wish life on anyone," she had said once, dryly, bitterly.

She was a tall, thin woman whom Bette and Ina saw perhaps once a year, meeting in awkward reunion at restaurants that were dimly lit at high noon. Helene headed the beautification committee of her Connecticut town, worked diligently on the board of a museum, appeared beside her fleshy beaming husband at benefits for the Sierra Club and Botanic Gardens. Her husband was not Jewish.

"I don't like 'people causes,' " Helene had told them once, twirling an empty martini glass between thin fingers, so pale they seemed drained of life, just as her athletically spare body seemed dried and drained of sex. "In fact, I don't much like people. For that, of course, you cannot blame me."

Ina and Bette did not blame her. They had, after all, shared her girlhood, and they had trembled with her on the bare planks of the barracks beds and had listened to her weep (weeping themselves, softly and quietly as Shaindel had taught them to) the night that her mother did not return to that long narrow room.

"Mama," small Halina had called into the night. The single electric bulb glared down at her, turned her tears the color of urine.

They had trembled the night Halina returned to the barracks, trembling uncontrollably, the mark of a man's fingers on her face, her dress streaked with damp stains that smelled of darkness. Years later she told them the story, but they had known it then—known it but not acknowledged it. Bette, the child, had known that something terrible had happened to Shaindel. She did not know about the abortion itself, but she knew that her aunt had suffered loss, had been immersed in terror and pain. The children of the camp absorbed horror as though by osmosis but did not speak of it. Silence was a shield, a weapon.

"Mama," Halina had chirped, but no mother had come, only Shaindel who rocked her in skeletal arms and kept a finger pressed against the child's birdlike mouth.

Helene Kramer would not take a chance and bear a child who might, in turn, call out plaintively into the fearful, un-answering darkness. She spared the unborn, ignored the unburied dead, and drank too many martinis through long and empty afternoons. Fear adhered to her like a shadow. She drove swift, low-slung sports cars and always kept her gas tank filled. Infrequently, when they had dinner at her house, the shades were drawn, and it was her smiling, pleasant hus-band who answered the door, vigilant small dogs barking at his heels.

Bette and Ina had been braver. They had become mothers. Ray watched a narrow strip of silver lightning thread its way through the darkness. He lifted his milk glass, toasted his wife's courage, and padded slowly back to bed.

A loosened limb of the giant oak directly across from the hospital crashed to the street. A taxicab skidded crazily to avoid the wild outstretched branches that clawed the air like grasping arms. The driver sounded his horn angrily, harshly. A bolt of thunder roared warningly. Ina awakened suddenly, her sleep pierced by restless sound. A woman's voice, thick and sorrowful, traveled the hospital corridors, bleating sadly into the darkness. Ina strained to listen, but she could not discern the words. Abruptly, the moans turned into a scream and then became a plea.

"Help me. It hurts. I'm scared. Help!"

"I'm coming, I'm coming," Ina called softly. The words sprang automatically to her lips—a mother's verbal reflex. But she did not move, remembering with grateful clarity that she was in Mount Lebanon and that her children were in their beds across town. It was not Jeddy, always fearful of storms, who had moaned into the darkness and riddled its stillness with his strident terror. It was a woman's voice that had given sound to pain—a voice Ina knew but could not place.

Thunder sounded like a muffled drumroll. Silver sparks of fragmented lightning crossed the darkness like small swiftly moving stars. Again the woman cried out, and Ina's heart turned at the sound of her voice. She glanced across at Miriam, but the younger woman slept soundly, heavily, too wearied by the strains of the day to be wakened by the uneasiness of the night.

Ina found her slippers, shrugged into her robe. The woman was weeping now. Small evenly spaced sobs threaded the darkness, and Ina followed them down the corridor like a dutiful child completing a follow-the-dot diagram. Bulbs at half wattage glowed softly in the wide hallway, but the glass-enclosed nurses' station was a booth of brilliant light, an illumined cabin strangely adrift on oceanic darkness. The nurses sat bent over their charts and dropped tiny colored pills into plastic cups. An aide leaned against the doorway and drank coffee from a Styrofoam container. Three residents moved down the hall, their fingers toying with the stethoscopes that dangled from their necks like mysterious amulets. A phone rang and was answered. The weeping continued unabated.

Was she the only one who heard the woman crying? Ina wondered as she moved quickly past the waiting room, where the same small rumpled man slept again on the Naugahyde couch, a flannel blanket tucked about his feet, a pillow bunched beneath his head. His unlaced, unpolished shoes faced each other at an uneasy angle, like cross, uncared-for toddlers who will not play together. Soon, perhaps on this night or the next, a nurse would waken him to tell him that his wife had died and his vigil was over. He would go home then and sleep beneath smooth sheets and polish his shoes for the funeral. Why didn't he stir at the sound of the crying, Ina wondered, or was he attuned only to the throbbing monody of his own grief?

She thought of the old college philosophy problem. If a tree falls in a forest and no one hears it—did it fall? If someone cries out in pain and the cry goes unheard and unheeded, was the pain real? Was the cry sounded at all? If the bodies of hundreds and thousands and millions of people were riddled with bullets and infused with gas, yet no voice was raised in protest, no scream emitted in horror, had the murders occurred at all? The Holocaust became an abstraction, a riddle, a philosophic conundrum. Easier this than to give credence to the incredible or to conceive of the inconceivable. Easier to ignore a woman's weeping than to become involved in the tangle of her grief.

A nurse wheeling a medication cart came down the hall. She looked at Ina and pointed to a door marked "Women."

"Use that one," she said, "but next time please try to wait until your roommate is through."

She sighed deeply and walked on, an exasperated matron who knew that on rainswept nights the orphans in her care rose too frequently to relieve their bladders. Ina nodded and waited until the nurse pushed her cart into a darkened room. Childhood tricks rolled back to her. She was expert at avoiding uniformed authorities, negotiating forbidden hallways. Stealthily, she walked on, following the trail of sobs. Words no longer intruded on the sounds of misery. There was no call for help—only the unremitting moans, the small wordless protests, like the cries of infants who have not yet learned a language that will describe, and perhaps relieve, their distress.

She stopped at last at the room she had visited earlier that day, the small private room where Marnie Coleman's portfolio leaned against the wall and her perfumes and cosmetics filled the air with the varied fragrance of many flowers. Lilac wafted from the doorway, but its sweetness had turned tumid and sour. The light aroma was weighted down by the odor of vomit. Susan Li stood over the bed, a hypodermic needle in her hand.

"This will make you feel better, Mrs. Coleman," she said softly, patiently. The words sprang automatically to her lips— a woman's reassuring promise. The aspirin will make you feel better. There—doesn't the Band-Aid make you feel better?

Small girls comforted and cuddled their dolls, mothers their children, wives their husbands, grown daughters their aged parents. Ina thought of the mother and daughter who had paced the corridor earlier in the evening. "You'll have a purple blouse, a lilac suit—you'll feel better."

"No. It hurts. I don't want it. I don't want to hurt." Marnie's voice, throaty, trained, was coated with pain, resistant to comfort.

Ina moved from the hall into the doorway. Marnie lay rigid on the bed, and when she moved, her body jerked up and down in swift staccato motion, as though to shrug loose the pain that clung to it. Neither limb nor torso moved separately or relaxed: the model's physical frame remained an intact unit, each moving part held in check by the central, sensate agony that controlled it.

On the floor beside the bed, a clump of hospital towels formed a white hillock stained by scarlet blotches of blood. Like a child's painting, the brilliant redness was splashed across the nubby surface of the toweling, and where the blood had gushed out in spongy clumps, it rose from the cloth in distorted small sculptures, plasmic mini-castles of pale pink and deep rose. Carmine ribbons streaked the sheet, ran down the sides of the mattress, formed tiny pools of redness on the floor.

Marnie jerked the blanket upward, and before the nurse could move to cover her, Ina saw that the pads pressed against her vagina were thick with the rust of her body's waste. They rested on the soft, hirsute vaginal rise like bandages pressed against the body of a wounded, furry animal. The blood turned color as the pad absorbed it.

Marnie screamed. Gray lips parted. Her gleaming white teeth shone in a face the color of ash. Translucent tears stood like silvery bullets on the fine high cheekbones. Her hands darted wildly out of the blanket and clutched fearfully at her breasts.

"No!" she cried. "No!"

The nurse moved swiftly. Strongly, decisively, she pushed her over on her side and thrust the needle into the briefly exposed buttock. Then, gently, she drew the cover up and stroked the long black hair that fanned out across the pillow. She passed a damp washcloth across the sweat-streaked face and patted it dry.

Marnie's eyes were closed. The sobs and moans were silenced. Her body was motionless in defeat. She had fought, but there had been no real battle. Nurse Li lifted the chart, made a notation on it with the pen that hung in readiness on a black ribbon about her neck. Hemorrhaging, it would read, caused by a spontaneous abortion. She glanced at her watch and noted the time.

She stooped beside the bloodied linen, then stood abruptly, dropping the stained towel in her hand. An aide would come by with a laundry cart. She glanced again at Marnie, whose lips parted in narcotized sleep. The model emitted a soft sound—"Oh, you're right, Bob," she said. "You're always right."

The nurse sighed, shook her head, and plucked up a peignoir, the color of a summer sky, that had slipped from the chair to the floor. She draped it over the chair, her fingers lingering in its soft folds. Her own uniform was stiff and unyielding, her cap a taut black-rimmed box. She turned to leave and was startled when she saw Ina standing in the doorway, leaning heavily against the jamb as though seeking support against a sudden and inexplicable weakness.

"Mrs. Feldman," she said, sternness rimming the astonishment in her tone, "what are you doing here?"

"I woke up. The thunder. I couldn't sleep."

Apology mingled with explanation. Lie tumbled over truth. She had not realized it was Marnie. She had known there was nothing she could do. But she could not sleep, and the sounds of pain had drawn her to this room.

Was there perhaps a magnetism to sorrow? Did pain gravitate toward like pain? On park benches in late afternoon, lonely widows found each other as they watched long shadows fall. At a crowded cocktail party, she had seen two mothers who had watched young children die come together although they had not known each other before. Once, on a suburban train, Ina had sat opposite a beautifully dressed, wonderfully coiffured woman. But Ina had not been deceived. When the woman raised her sleeve to glance at her watch, the faded violet numbers dotted her skin. And tonight, lost in her own confusion, she had trailed the sounds of Marnie's pain, of Marnie's sorrow.

"Yes. I understand."

The nurse leaned wearily against the opposite jamb. She was tired. She was working double shift. She would spend sixteen hours on this floor where women tended their plants, plucking tiny withered leaves from sturdy stalks of green; where they sat up in bed and pulled long rainbow-colored strands of wool through thick bulks of burlap; where they read brightly jacketed books and talked softly to each other of the wounds concealed beneath their gently colored nightgowns, the scars carved across their yielding flesh. She would mop up tears and blood, offer relief with a needle or a pill, replace a pus-stained dressing with a spotless cushion of gauze, smile her lies, and gravely offer opinions that she did not opine.

"You are looking so much better," she would tell the woman who had just undergone a radical mastectomy and who wandered the halls with bandages packed across her chest and beneath her arms. "A miscarriage is very common. It's nature's way of righting a wrong," she would tell Marnie Coleman tomorrow, repeating the words she had uttered so many times before to weeping young women whose faces she no longer remembered.

"Mrs. Coleman had a miscarriage—a spontaneous abortion. The resident will be here to check her soon, and I guess her own doctor will be in in the morning."

"How?" Ina asked. "I mean, why did it happen?" Marnie had been feeling fine, had thought of that brief bleeding as negligible. Her doctor had assured her that it was nothing. And she had been so determined to have the child. What had she said to Ina that afternoon—something about all that she and her husband had achieved being worthless if there was no child? But when it came to problems of health, determination counted for very little. Doubt did not induce a hemorrhage. Uncertainty could not create a sudden weakening of the placental wall, a swift lurching death of fetal life, nor did certainty ensure uterine strength. Women did not exercise emotional strength over their bodies, did not determine their physical destiny. Dot, yearning for children, was childless. Ina herself, unwillingly, unwittingly, was pregnant. But over this pregnancy she did have some control. She pressed her hands to her stomach, rocked back on her heels, and retched briefly and imperceptibly.

"I don't know why," Nurse Li said. "Of course, she had had some slight bleeding before. That was why she was admitted. It could have been any number of things. But she's a young woman. She'll have another child. Other children. This sort of thing is not uncommon."

"No. Of course not," Ina agreed. That was what they had said years before when she too had suffered a miscarriage, a "spontaneous abortion"! The expression must have been formulated by men who thought in terms of mismanagement and failure, of affairs of business suspended before completion—suddenly if not spontaneously aborted.

"I miscarried the first time I was pregnant," Ina said. "But there was no bleeding, nothing like this." She pointed to the mass of linen, stained maroon now by the seeping blood. "Just a clot in the toilet."

"Yes. Well, you didn't hemorrhage, and you probably were not as far along as Mrs. Coleman was."

"I suppose not," Ina said.

"Mrs. Feldman, you had better go back to your room." The nurse had resumed her professional tone.

Two residents walked down the hall, their stethoscopes swinging from side to side, their heads nodding. One wore glasses and the other smiled widely, showing wonderfully straight teeth. They were very young. The newness and power of their knowledge glinted proudly in their eyes. They moved quickly, determinedly. The nurse went to meet them, and Ina, forgotten, turned back toward her room.

"I'll go back to sleep now," she said, but the nurse was deep in conversation with the doctors and did not hear, or, hearing, did not answer.

"I heard her buzzer, and then I heard her scream," Susan Li reported to the earnest young men and then added, "It must have been after two."

They nodded. It was important to fix the time of suffering, the hour of loss.

Ina continued on down the corridor and climbed gratefully back into bed. She remembered the long-ago day, that first pregnancy, that first loss. Rachel had been conceived six months later, and it occurred to her now that if that first pregnancy had endured, another, a different, child would have been born to them. Rachel would not be Rachel, and Jeddy would not be Jeddy. He too would have been conceived at a different time, within a different gametic pattern. Chance, not choice, had given them their children. Small miracles, tiny accidents, sudden swift sadnesses and gladnesses of soaring, startling joy had formed their family. Their lives had been shaped by unexpected laughter on sunswept mornings, by chance meetings on a summer evening, by mysterious passages on nights when thunder ripped the sky. Her very survival was an accident—the benevolent oversight of a careless guard. She remembered how Ray's shoulder had gleamed like ivory in the darkness the night she had conceived this child whom she would select now for life or death (as she had been selected—by accident, by chance). She had not dreamed that night, she knew. The thunder had been a sonorous companion; she had followed the lightning into dreamless sleep.

A shaft of silver lightning slid across the dark sky now, and she thought of how Ray's hair was streaked with gray. He feared age. A new baby promised men youth, Dot had said. An infant's cry into the night's darkness renewed strength and promise.

Ina touched the thin hospital blanket, longed for the satin trim of her bedroom comforter, and wondered if Ray had remembered to draw the shades in Jeddy's room. Storms frightened her small son.

"Poor Jeddy," she thought, "poor Ray. And Marnie. Poor Marnie."

She did not form words of pity for herself but fell into a sleep, strangely light and dreamless.

Bette Abramson disliked talking on the phone. The small, colored instruments, scattered in convenient places throughout her large suburban home, remained oddly exotic objects to her. Always their ring startled her, and always she lifted the receiver apprehensively, surprised that anyone should be calling her, fearful that the voice at the other end would bring her news of sadness and danger. Breathlessly she whispered her "Hello" into the receiver. Her hand trembled as she accepted a dinner invitation, canceled a dental appointment, volunteered a contribution to the United Fund. Her father had slept in his clothing so that he would be ready when the dreaded knock at the door was sounded. She, his emotional heiress, waited fearfully (and foolishly, she knew, but could not help herself) for the call that would threaten her children, destroy her life.

"But why," Eleanor Berenson had asked her once, deceitful wonderment heavy in her voice, "why should the ringing of a telephone have such an effect on you?"

The analyst's phone had rung just then, and Bette had shivered although the room was warm. The answering service picked up, and the room was quiet.

"I never used a phone until we came to the States," Bette said.

"But surely you had seen them, knew about them."

"Yes."

There had, in fact, been a wall phone in the barracks—an ugly black phone screwed into the rotting wooden walls. It had no dial face, but on its surface were two brass bells which

Bette and Ina had polished diligently. It was a small task
benevolently allotted to the small girls by the guard whose
pale hair was twisted into whips and who tiptoed over to
Shaindel in the darkness of the night to whisper dank secrets,
ugly fears.

"I am a good woman," Bette had heard the guard say
urgently. She had gripped Shaindel's arm, imprinting the
seal of her fingers across the trail of pale blue numbers that
made Shaindel her property, her slave.

"Of course you are," Shaindel had assured her. Slaves did
not argue with their mistresses. They complied. They offered
reassurances. They smiled to please and danced and sang to
amuse and polished ornaments on ugly telephones to an oxi-
dized metallic brightness. Above all, they remained alive and
saved their children.

In order to make calls outside the barracks, a small crank
had to be turned. The guard carried the crank in the jacket
pocket of her uniform where she kept her keys. The keys
were strung along a thick chain, and sometimes, in the night,
the heavy woman toyed with them, as women sometimes toy
with a lovely necklace. Occasionally, she allowed the little
girls, Ina and Bette, Manya and Halina, to touch them and
make them jingle. She was, she thought with satisfaction, kind
to these little girls whom she allowed to live. The lump in her
breast had grown smaller. God loved her.

The guard liked to touch the keys for which she had little
use. The barracks building was unlocked then, as were the
bathhouses and latrine areas. No one would run away. There
was no strength for flight; no refuge offered sanctuary. One
key fit the storeroom of the clothing warehouse where the
shelves were barren. All the clothing taken from the Jews
was sent to Germany now. Another key fit a storage closet
where the metal teeth pried from the jaws of corpses and the
wedding bands removed from yielding, despairing fingers cast
a topaz glow across the shadowed dimness. The guard had
seen that room only once, and the lock had since been
changed, but still she kept the key. It was a small metallic

symbol of power, of privilege, like the telephone which only she was allowed to use.

"When did it ring?" Eleanor Berenson had persisted.

"Not often. Almost never."

Yet Bette could remember still how its sound riddled the air, how the women trembled and sobbed at its ring, how the guard's boots had stamped against the wooden floor as she hurried to answer it and shouted her name into the mouthpiece. She clutched the receiver to her ear so that its long black wire was taut as a whip stretched into readiness.

"Did it ring sometimes, and then afterward prisoners would disappear?" Like an expert hunter, the analyst followed a trail, would not lose her scent.

"No," Bette answered firmly. "That didn't happen. No phone call took my mother. She had already surrendered herself. She went away one morning and never came back. That's all. "

That was all and that was enough. The analyst's small Dresden clock delicately chimed the end of the hour, and Bette rose from the couch, left the room, and spent the next two hours at Saks Fifth Avenue. She bought two striped dresses which she returned the next week. She never wore stripes. She had never again, during an analytic hour, spoken of the way her heart stopped and her hand trembled at the ringing of the telephone.

"It's Ina calling," she thought involuntarily, irrationally, when the phone rang that morning. Something had happened to Ina in the hospital. Mattie, the baby, toddled into the room pushing his wooden walker. It was a bright yellow wooden horse, and its ears and eyes were fashioned of red felt which Mattie had chewed and licked to a faded pink.

"Tell-the-phone," he said gleefully and pointed to the yellow kitchen phone which rang for the third time while Bette stared at it.

"I'll tell the phone," she agreed, smiling.

The child's pudgy cheeks, his mass of chestnut-colored curls (the same shade as her Aunt Shaindel's—the same thick-

ness and color of her mother Peshi's hair, which had blazed in
a fiery, tangled mass above her skeletal face even after the
features had sunk into the *mussillman*'s mindless surrender),
his solid little body, dispelled fear. She reached for the receiver, but before she could lift it, he had grasped it.

"Hello," he said happily. "Hello tell-the-phone." Then he
laughed merrily and tossed the receiver down.

"Mattie." Annoyance replaced amusement. "That was
naughty. Go away."

Bewildered, the child looked at her. He opened his eyes
wide, disbelieving her anger. If she sustained it, his dimpled
chin would quiver, and his pert features would collapse in
misery as tears rolled down his cheeks. She softened. It was
not worth it. Whoever had called would call back again. It
had not been Ina. Ina was fine.

"Play in the other room," she said, and as he waddled out
the door, pushing his horse, the phone rang again. He giggled
and waved good-bye as she lifted the receiver.

"Hello. Is this Bette Abramson?"

The caller's voice was sharp and clipped. It belonged to a
woman who wasted little time, betrayed no hesitancies.

"Yes."

"This is Ruthie Bradley. Ina's friend."

"Oh, yes. She has told me about you. I even have one of
your drawings in my daughter's room. But is Ina all right?"
The uneasiness returned. Why should a friend of Ina's, whom
she had never met, be calling her?

It occurred to her suddenly that it was a neighbor of her
father's (whom she had never met) who had phoned to tell
her of his collapse. ("Mrs. Abramson, this is Mr. Tulchin—I
live next door to your papa. This morning I heard a crash.
The door was locked, but I got the super. An ambulance
came. A nice intern. By Lenox Hill your papa is . . .")

Tragedy brought strangers together with swift spontaneity
—it linked them in an odd network of involvement, compassion, sorrow. (I do not know who you are, but I know you
hurt.) Even in the camp, inmates had sidled over to women

they did not know who had suffered an illness, a loss. A scrap of onion, a tattered box, a crust of bread, was passed to grieving strangers. When Peshi died, women had found small bits of ribbon, a broken clothespin, a bunch of sorrel grass, to give to the orphaned Batya. Someone in another barrack had fashioned a doll for her out of an odd sock, sewing on bits of charcoal for eyes, beads of the blood-colored bittersweet that grew above the quarry for a mouth. When the doll ripped on the ship going to America, Bette and Ina had discovered that it was stuffed with hair, stolen, they speculated, from the great storeroom where the shorn tresses of the dead formed feathery mountains until they were compacted and used for pillow stuffing, jacket linings. None of the hair within that doll was chestnut-colored, but strands of black and gray clung to their fingers. Bette had dropped the limp doll overboard and watched it bob briefly on the black-tipped waves before it disappeared from sight.

Sometimes in the beauty parlor she watched the attendants sweep up the clippings of hair and thought to tell them that it was wasteful to discard the freshly washed curls of suburban ladies. They could serve a useful purpose, fulfill a useful function. Work equals freedom, the camp guard had told the little girls. Waste not, want not. Bitter laughter, like droplets of gall, choked her with such thoughts, such memories, and she subdued them and turned the pages of her fashion magazine like the normal ladies who sat beside her under the whirring dryers, who had never, when they were small girls, played with dolls stuffed with human hair.

"Oh, Ina's fine," Ruthie Bradley assured her hastily. "I spoke to Ray. I'm sure he must have told you that the final report on the biopsy was that it was benign."

"Yes. He phoned me last night."

"I'm only calling because I know you're very concerned about Ina. She's told me that you're like sisters."

"Yes." They were in fact closer than most sisters who had shared only life. She and Ina had shared death and fear of death.

"I'm sort of concerned about Ina's indecision over this abortion. You know, she's worked so hard building her business, and her life is really set—just where she wants it to be. I'm really frightened that if she goes ahead with this pregnancy, she'll be very sorry."

"Surely that's her choice." Ice edged Bette's tone. Revulsion stirred within her. How could this woman whom she did not know, had never met, call her to discuss Ina's intimate decision?

"I'm sorry. I didn't mean to intrude." Ruthie was embarrassed. The sharpness of her voice was muted. She had overstepped boundaries that she no longer recognized but that others still lived by. Bette heard her confusion, her indecision, and softened.

"I know you care about Ina. I do too. But some things people decide for themselves. We have a friend—Helene. She was in the camp with us. She decided not to have children at all. Her choice."

"But Ina's decision is part of the guilt trip that's always being laid on women."

"Not so simple," Bette said. She wondered if Eleanor Berenson would have simply hung up on this woman she did not know who treated an uninvited phone conversation as a forum for a consciousness-raising session. Bette's goal in analysis, she decided, would be to achieve the ability to hang up on people she did not want to talk to, to decline invitations she did not want to accept. A modest aim, but her own.

Ruthie was talking rapidly now, quoting statistics, case histories, medical probabilities. Bette paced the kitchen, cradling the phone, attached to its long yellow cord as though to a leash. She washed a dish and put it away.

Ruthie talked on. Ina was such a super person. Her kids were terrific. Wouldn't this new baby traumatize Rachel and Jeddy?

"You know I have three children of my own. My two oldest are almost the same ages as Rachel and Jeddy. My youngest is only eighteen months old. The older children were not traumatized by his birth," Bette said drily. Where was Mattie? she wondered as Ruthie talked on. His training cup, still half full of the morning orange juice, sat on the table.

"Look, I must hang up now," Bette said. The conversation was wearying her. Her palms were damp, and the fresh cotton blouse she had put on that morning clung to her body although the morning was cool. Where had Mattie gone?

"I thought you would help." Ruthie's voice was plaintive, half disappointed, half accusatory. Bette realized with instant clarity that Ruthie was not calling on Ina's behalf but on her own. Ina must validate Ruthie's own decisions, must opt for a course that would not conflict with Ruthie's philosophy, with Ruthie's life-style.

"Of course," Ruthie said coolly, "we only want what's best for Ina. It was good to talk to you, Beatie." She managed disinterest, disowning the conversation over which she had lost control.

"Bette," Bette corrected, but Ruthie had already hung up.

"Mattie!" Bette called.

There was no answer.

"Mattie!"

She raised her voice, struggling with her own irritation and against the nacre of anxiety she could feel fermenting. She hurried into the family room. It was strewn with the debris of the previous evening—her daughter's recorder, her son's open chemistry set, Mattie's Tinker Toy construct. The television set played soundlessly. A bright green Kermit the Frog waltzed with pink Miss Piggy. She turned on the volume, then switched the set off and ran into the dining room.

She looked beneath the table where the child sometimes hid. Leafy shadows trailed across the thick rug and snaked their way beneath the carved legs of the chairs. The dining room set had belonged to her in-laws, and Bette marveled still at the wonder of a family retaining possessions that might be passed from one generation to the next. Dimly, from her own childhood, she remembered an oaken chair upholstered in red velvet that she had thought of as a throne. It had, she sup-

posed, been burned for firewood, or perhaps it had been
appropriated for the Berlin apartment of a Gestapo officer.
It did not matter. It was lost. Her children would never know
the soft touch of its seat, the intricacy of its carved legs.

"Mattie—" she kept her voice gentle, controlled, "I'm counting to three. Come out, come out, wherever you are. One—
two—three!"

There was no rush of small feet, no answering giggle. The
silence in the house frightened her, and she ran now into the
empty living room and out to the glassed-in sun porch that
overlooked the street.

It was a quiet block, closed to truck traffic, a good distance
from any main thoroughfare—the type of street selected by
the overcautious parents of small children. Often hours passed
without a car cruising down it. But now a car horn bleated
long and powerfully, like a large and frightened animal that
has lost control. Brakes screeched wildly. Someone shouted.
Frozen, Bette remained in the middle of the room, staring at
a hanging philodendron, her eyes riveted to a long leaf that
had inexplicably wilted. She moved toward the plant, slowly,
painfully. It hung near the window, and when she had moved
so close that she could no longer avoid looking out, she
turned to the street.

A car, a long tan station wagon, stood in front of her house.
Its tire marks had blackly seared the street. The woman who
lived next door, wearing her bright red jogging suit, talked
to the driver. He was a tall young man. He gesticulated
wildly, pointing straight ahead, pointing toward the sidewalk.
Bette watched them as she had watched Kermit dance across
the soundless screen. Then the neighbor moved aside, stooped,
and Bette saw the splintered mass of yellow wood, the red
wheel lying in the street, the faded felt of the horse's tongue
licking the black tarmac. Only last night at dinner Mattie had
amused them by standing on his horse and turning the
doorknob.

"Mattie big," he had said, and they had clapped and
laughed.

"No!" she screamed. "No! Mattie!" She ran to the front door which stood wide open and hurled herself into the street.

"Mattie!"

Her neighbor and the driver turned, started toward her, but before they could reach her, Mattie flew into her arms, clutched her, wept against her breast, mingling his tears with the sweat that ran down her body and drenched her skirt.

"No more horse," he cried, and she held him tighter. She would not fall while she held him. The weakness and dizziness that had threatened her vanished. The child's fingers pinched her neck flesh. The pain revived her, reassured her. He was safe. He was all right.

"Silly boy. We'll buy you a new horse. It was just a horse."

He grew calmer, pressed his head against her shoulder, hugged her with arms and knees.

"I'm awfully sorry, lady," the driver said. "I saw the kid push the horse into the street, and I tried to stop, but I just couldn't make it in time."

"Of course you couldn't help it," Bette said. "Thank you for trying."

She marveled that she lived in a country where strong young men apologized for mangling a toy. She had come from a country where strong young men boasted gleefully of the children they had mangled. Once she had stood between Ina and Halina, at the edge of a sports field, and watched two guards play a game of catch, tossing a screaming infant through the air. The baby had been a little gypsy girl, and the sun had sparkled on her tiny gold earrings.

Her neighbor carried up the horse's splintered body, the battered red wheel.

"Maybe with a little glue it could be fixed," she said. Bette was unconcerned. Things could always be replaced. Wooden horses and oaken chairs and even fallen hair and vanished wedding bands. The small boy was heavy in her arms.

"A giraffe," he said sleepily. "Let's get a giraffe."

"All right," she agreed and smiled conspiratorially at her

neighbor and at the driver, who put the broken toy on the lawn, waved apologetically, and drove away.

Bette carried Mattie into the house. She put him to bed and returned to the sun porch. Gently, carefully, she plucked the wilted leaf from the philodendron and saw that a new finger of green was unfolding. She touched the new leaf and noticed that her finger trembled and that her knees had grown oddly weak and rubbery. She stumbled into a chintz-covered wicker chair and sat quietly, sorting her fear, gathering her strength and her thoughts.

She had, in her mind's dark eye, seen Mattie dead, crushed beneath the wheels of the large tan car. If it had happened, people would have comforted her, would have flocked to the house to offer sympathy. "You are not alone. You have other children. Think of how fortunate you are," they would say to her.

She remembered a woman in the camp saying that to her Aunt Shaindel when Yedidiah died. "You are lucky. You still have your Ina." The woman's own three children had gone up the chimneys. The odds had been with her, and still she had lost. All three had died. Their own family had been luckier. Only Peshi and Yedidiah had died, and Yedidiah had not been gassed. He had died in his sleep of illness, of weakness.

Bette remembered the night of Jeddy's terrible and inexplicable fever. She had sat beside Ina in the hospital and searched for words of comfort to offer her cousin. "It's all right. You still have Rachel." She had formed the thought but had not uttered the words, had not had to utter them. Jeddy had recovered. The fever had vanished as swiftly and mysteriously as it had gathered.

She and Ina had clutched each other in joyous relief. They were women who were vigilant always to sustain themselves against loss. Their history necessitated insurance, a stockpiling of securities. Always they hedged their bets against fate.

Had Ina had such thoughts during this time? Bette wondered. She pressed the dead leaf, and it flaked into brittle green teardrops across her palm. Ina should have this baby, she thought. A new infant would be security, indemnification. The luxury of choice belonged to women who had been exempt from loss, who did not tremble at the ringing of a telephone or an unexpected knock at the door, who did not anticipate death because a car horn honked. She had to talk to Ina, advise her. Her cousin was her sister in grief, her twin in survival.

Together, she and Ina had learned their lessons, had mastered the small secrets of survival. They had been tiny, skeletal girls weighted down by fear and misery, but they had learned to dance and sing, to simulate an innocence that had never been theirs. Ina had led and Bette had followed. They had held hands and danced together. Their reedlike voices had filled the smoke-darkened air of the pseudo-café in the camp where the guards and soldiers went to drink and play cards. They sang sweet *lieder* which they did not understand, taught to them by a woman who wept as she mouthed the strangely tender words. The Germans smiled and sang along and tossed them rusks of bread or small bones to which scraps of meat clung with a bloody redness. They ate the raw meat, gnawing it like the grateful cubs they were.

Bette remembered the night when her mother did not return. Ina had come to her in the darkness, had hugged her cousin, had refused to allow her to invite death to take her too.

"We will grow up," Ina had promised her. "We will go to America. Soon, soon, the war will be over."

Ina spoke with such certainty that Bette had believed her. She had believed her even after she knew that Ina too sometimes cried alone in the darkness. She could not afford not to believe her.

"We will be happy," Ina had promised fiercely. "We will be warm. We will not be hungry." They shivered with cold and trembled with weariness. Ina snatched a thin blanket from the bed of a dead woman and wrapped it about her cousin. Bette plucked a moldy heel of bread from a pile of garbage. They sucked at it together.

Bette knew with absolute certainty that without Ina she

could not have survived the war. Without her cousin who wept only when the curtain of night had fallen, who whispered secrets of hope into the empty darkness, she, Bette, would have trailed after her mother into that netherworld where neither life nor death counted for anything.

"We will be all right," Ina had promised, and she had been right. They, who had searched for crumbs between splintered planks, sat now at laden tables, in carpeted rooms, felt the gentle hands of their husbands, the sweet merriment of their children.

Laughter came slowly to Ina and Bette. The happiness they sought was elusive, mysterious. Bette felt it now at rare and wondrous moments—when Richard sang as he walked up the path, when her children played peacefully on a winter evening. Now, at last, she surrendered to brief contentment, letting her guard down, allowing herself to believe that this, finally, was hers and that it would not be taken from her, neither by a knock at the door nor by the ringing of a phone.

But her cousin, she knew, had never known such sweet submission. Poor Ina, who was so good, so strong, who could not allow herself the luxury of weakness, of spontaneity. She had so long simulated strength when she shivered with weakness and feigned certainty when she trembled with doubt that she could no longer discern between them. Like the systems she designed on specially lined paper, her life was programmed, organized. She could not afford deviation. Pity for her cousin chafed at Bette.

She reached for the telephone and dialed Mount Lebanon but replaced the receiver before the connection was established. She could not call Ina. She was not Batya, the shivering child. She was Bette, the capable, rational woman who thought things through and lived in a large, many-windowed house. The argument she had offered Ruthie applied to herself, as well. She could not impose her own feelings and fears on Ina. Reason overtook her galloping fantasy. Her hand was steady now, and her heart beat in even rhythm. Mattie was fine. He had never been in danger. Certain scales could not be balanced. In given situations all arguments were equally valid and equally invalid.

She went upstairs and looked into the sun-streaked room where her son slept on a low bed. A bright blue plush panda pressed against his cheek. He smiled in his sleep and lifted a pudgy hand to brush away a chestnut curl. Bette went into her own room and changed into a fresh cotton dress. When the phone rang, she answered it on the first ring. It was Richard, and when he asked how she was, she told him that she was fine, just fine.

Over breakfast that morning, Ina told Miriam about Marnie's miscarriage.

"Poor girl," Miriam said. "I know what that's like."

"Yes." Ina too knew what that was like. "I wonder how her husband will feel."

"How can he feel?" Miriam asked. "Awful, of course."

"Marnie told me that he really didn't want a baby. Not just yet. Their business is just getting started, and he needs her. He felt that they should wait another year. He was pretty ambivalent about the pregnancy."

"I don't know." Miriam buttered her toast, finished her egg. She grimaced but downed a glass of milk. She was watching her diet carefully, calculating her intake of protein and calcium. She wanted to nurse her baby, to keep her milk rich and flowing even while the infant was nourished by intravenous feeding.

She had the nursing mother's absorption in vitamins and nutrients. Ina knew women who had, all their lives, skipped breakfasts and lunched on a Chock Full o' Nuts doughnut; during their pregnancies they became absorbed in calorie charts and had argued the merits of bananas and granola. It was the first step in motherhood, the first acknowledgment that others had claim on one's body, that life could no longer be lived foolishly, carelessly. After Rachel's birth, Ina, the veteran New Yorker who had always dashed across broad avenues in defiance of traffic lights and traffic, had begun waiting patiently at corners for red controls to turn green. Mothers had more at stake, had to be more careful.

"Without you and Bette," her mother had told her once, "I would not have been as careful of myself during the war. I would not have tried so hard to remain alive."

Through symbiotic stress they had, all three, survived. It was common knowledge in the camps that if a child perished, the mother did not long survive. Miraculously, the generations worked to sustain each other. Life clutched at life. Death led to death.

"I think," Miriam said, "that ambivalence is a luxury you can indulge in while you think you're on safe ground. It's an intellectual game. What do I want? Why do I want it? But once something happens, once a child is lost, the game is over. Marnie's husband will feel it as a loss." Her voice trembled. Her own child had not been drowned in her blood. He had been born alive, swaddled and touched. How much more profound then would be her own loss and her husband's? And what of their parents, the two older couples who stood nightly vigil in front of the glass window to watch their grandson stir and sleep? She would not think about it.

Carefully, she sliced the orange which would give her vitamin C. The megagrams that fought colds would travel into her milk ducts. Her baby would imbibe them and be protected. He would live. She would not let him die. She ate the fruit and with forefinger and thumb manipulated her nipple. Pale colostrum leaked a narrow ribbon of dampness down her nightgown, and she smiled in satisfaction at the stain.

"Every situation is different," Ina offered mildly.

She put on her robe and walked down the corridor. Bob Coleman sat in the waiting room. He wore dark slacks and a camel-colored jacket. His pigskin attaché case was at his side. His head rested in his hands, and his shoulders quivered, yet it took Ina a moment to realize that he was crying. She hesitated and moved on. A library cart stood in the hall, and she took a book from it and flipped the pages. The jacket came loose in her hand and fluttered to the floor. The volunteer, a tall young woman whose fair hair fell in silken folds about the pink shoulders of her hospital smock, hurried to retrieve it as Ina herself bent.

"No. Please let me," the volunteer said. "You mustn't."

"But I'm fine," Ina protested.

The other woman would not be cheated out of her concern, her benevolence. A large diamond ring sparkled on her finger, a long gold chain encircled her throat. She spoke to Ina in the slow, reassuring tone that the fortunate use to address those who do not share their luck.

"This is a good book. I read it and liked it. It has a tricky ending."

"Thank you."

Ina could not refuse her courtesy. She took the book and recognized it as a gothic tale that Rachel had read with heart-chilling delight that winter. Its graphic cover showed a beautiful blonde young woman rushing down a staircase pursued by tongues of flame. Always, in such books, women fled danger, dashed from one precarious situation to another. Perhaps those who marketed them knew something of the floors that hospitals set aside for "women's problems."

Holding the book, she retraced her steps. In the waiting room, Bob Coleman stood at the coffee machine. It had been repaired and yielded him a Styrofoam cup of pale steaming liquid. Turning, he saw Ina and nodded. His eyes were blood-shot, and trails of damp grief grooved their way down his dark cheeks.

"Want some coffee?" he asked.

She shook her head but sat down, and he sat next to her on the bright red couch.

"You know about Marnie?" he asked.

"I woke up last night," she said. "I know. Is she all right?"

"They're doing a curettage now. A scraping. Routine, they say. Just to make sure everything is all right."

"Yes, that's important," Ina said. "Was she very upset this morning?"

He laughed harshly, bitterly.

"You could say. But she'll be all right. She's a fighter. My girl's a fighter. "

"Yes. And how are you?"

Her own intrepidity startled her. She was a private person who respected the privacy of others. She did not know Bob Coleman and would perhaps never see him again. Yet the question came naturally, easily. On this corridor, all barriers were bridged. Sorrow became common property. Grief was shared and exchanged. Briefly, destinies were intertwined. The life of one child became entangled with the death of another. Foolish promises were whispered into reverberant darkness. Old women shared their secrets with young girls. Men revealed their grief, sought solace, removed their unpolished shoes in rooms where yesterday's newspapers were scattered across Formica tables scarred by cigarette burns in the shape of black-rimmed teardrops.

"Lousy. Awful. I feel terrible for Marnie. Nothing ever came easy for her. Nothing. And I didn't make this easy for her either. I kept telling her I needed a year—another year. But now I'm cut up, bleeding inside. It was my baby. Jesus— I'm crying for a baby I didn't want to have."

Tears clouded his great dark eyes, matted his thick lashes. He did not cover his face now. He was not ashamed. Fathers mourned their lost children. It was fitting. It was manly. He mourned his baby, his lost baby.

"You'll have other children," Ina said. "You're young. Marnie's young and healthy."

"Oh, I know." He covered her hand with his own. "I know. But other children won't be this one. What's lost you don't find again. And I gave her such a damn hard time. Why the hell didn't I know what I wanted?"

"It wouldn't have made any difference," she said, and added, very softly, "I think it's so hard to know what we want."

"You're going home today?" he asked.

"I don't know. No, not today. Maybe tomorrow. Maybe not. I don't know."

She felt a sudden dizziness, a new bewilderment. The book she did not want to read fell to the floor again, and he picked it up and looked at her. His dark eyes were soft with concern. A new gentleness had been born in him. Always now, he would be kind to women who spoke with a tremor in their voices and who wept suddenly, inexplicably.

"You all right?" he asked.

"Yes. Fine," she assured him, but still he took her arm and guided her slowly down the hall. He watched from the doorway until she had safely hoisted herself up into bed and was propped up against the pillows. The dizziness had subsided and was replaced by a nausea so swift and sharp that she leaned forward and gasped for air. A virus, she thought, I must have a virus. Laughter at her own foolishness welled within her. She did not have a virus. She was pregnant and experiencing morning sickness. Retching (remembering that she had retched the night before), she got off the bed and lurched to the bathroom. Dry heaves did not yield vomit, but she washed her face with cold water and felt better.

Miriam was not in the room. Gratefully, Ina sank back against her pillows and closed her eyes. Always during her pregnancies she had napped briefly in the morning, a sweet luxury earned and taken. It occurred to her that now she had no right to that morning respite, yet mysteriously, wondrously, she fell asleep.

Dot called Ray at eleven that morning, forcing him to leave a hearing through which he had sat like a spectator at an uninteresting sports match. The witnesses seemed dull, the attorneys obtuse. His own rulings bored him. He was tired. Office matters seemed peripheral, unimportant. He wanted the day to pass and Ina's decision to be taken. His mother-in-law, Shirley Cherne, too had called him that morning.

"*Nu*?" she had asked. "What will be?"

He peeled the harshness from her tone and heard the trembling concern, the unarticulated plea.

"Whatever Ina decides," he had replied.

"And you? What do you want?"

"I want what you want." A new alliance had been forged between him and his wife's mother. They both had the survivor's understanding of cruel unnatural death. He had buried his parents. She had buried her son. Both of them loved Ina.

His answer to her was clear, his decision fair, but still he moved through the morning hours in a haze of uncertainty, unable to concentrate. His mail bewildered him. His secretary spoke to him of matters of urgency, and he offered vague answers, indifferent shrugs. Twice during the hearing he had confused the names of witnesses and asked for testimony to be repeated. Still, Dot's call annoyed him.

"I was in a hearing," he told his sister petulantly.

She apologized. It was important. Classes at the school Rachel and Jeddy attended had been suspended for the day. A water pipe had burst, and they had called Dot. She herself was committed to accompanying Claire's school on a class trip to the aquarium. Rachel and Jeddy could come with her, of course, although she thought they would not be enthusiastic about the idea.

"Why can't they just go home?" Ray asked, signing letters he could not remember dictating.

"It's Carmen's day off."

"They're not babies. They've stayed alone in the apartment before."

Dot did not reply. Her disapproval hung heavy on the silent wire. It was not right to ask children to stay alone in the apartment while their mother was ill and worry rimmed the family.

He glanced at his calendar. There were no appointments scheduled for the afternoon.

"I'll tell you what," he said. "Do me a favor and call the school. I'll wrap up this hearing and zip up there and take the kids out for lunch. Tell them I'll be there in about an hour."

"That's a good idea," Dot said.

Her tone was the one she used when Ethan or Claire had picked up a suggestion she had cloaked in subtlety and innuendo. "Don't you think it would be a good idea . . . ?"

The subliminal approach to motherhood, Ina called it. She preferred to be direct with Rachel and Jeddy. She was her mother's daughter.

Ray smiled. He did not mind having fallen into his sister's trap. He looked out the window and saw that sunlight splayed the street. The day was suddenly a holiday. With his son and daughter at his side he would walk the wide bright avenues. They would look in shop windows, browse in the large Japanese market on Eighty-sixth Street. Perhaps they would find a kite that Jeddy could launch that weekend. He would take them to Rumpelmayer's for lunch, and they would all have enormous sundaes. He hurried back into the hearing room, startled the witnesses with the acuteness of his questions, the clarity of his decision, and adjourned. His secretary was pleased that he was taking the afternoon off.

"You work too hard," she told him, and watched with a maternal smile as he left the office. He was five years her senior, yet she thought of him as her son. Poor boy, poor man. An afternoon off would do him good.

Rachel and Jeddy stood in front of the school and watched the workmen who scurried in and out of the building. They wore the stoic, patient expressions of children who are conditioned to waiting for mini-buses and station wagons and who know themselves to be units of human cargo who must be shuttled endlessly from school to dance lessons, soccer practice, music studios, and the carpeted offices of orthodontists and ophthalmologists. Rachel studied a magazine, and she glanced indifferently from a color photo of Robin Williams to the overalled workman who hefted a length of pipe on his shoulders.

"What's that for?" Jeddy asked. "Is that to replace the one that busted?"

The man did not answer. Beads of sweat rimmed his upper lip. He walked past the boy into the building. Jeddy shrugged and turned toward the street. He saw Ray coming toward them and waved wildly.

"Rachel—it's Daddy."

She did not lift her eyes from the magazine but waved lazily, languidly, like a girl who has been waiting indifferently for an unimportant date. Ray felt oddly hurt. Rachel, the toddler, had hurtled through the apartment into his arms screaming, "Daddy, my daddy!" Her fat little arms had curled around his neck. She knew how to hoist herself up across his chest and ride his shoulders. "Daddy, my daddy."

Around and around the apartment they went, and he would laugh with the full force of his love, with all the pride of his strength while Ina looked at them with a curious, wistful smile on her face. Ray understood and avoided that wistfulness, that shadowed reminder of the small Ina he had not known.

No happy shouts, no playful games dotted the bleak and death-colored landscape of her childhood. She and Bette had lived beneath the shadows of plank board beds, obedient children following Shaindel's fierce dictum—out of sight meant out of danger. Once, when Ina was angry at Rachel and had banished her to her room for some small infraction, a punishment with which Ray disagreed, he had argued with her.

"You're hard on the child."

"Children are resilient. They survive most things," she had replied.

"Must she suffer because you did?" Could it be that his wife was jealous of her own child?

The thought, the words, had startled and shamed him. He did not believe them. It was just that he loved his small daughter, his evening princess, so much that he could not bear to hear her whimper in misery.

"I'm sorry," he had told Ina, but she did not reply, and later he realized that she had not denied his words.

When she was a small girl Rachel had waited for him in front of rented beach houses, had thrown herself into the path of his shadow as he approached, her shrill voice trembling with excitement at all that had happened in the brief hours since she had seen him last. A flock of egrets had soared through the pale blue sky. The Italian potato farmer had given her a ride in his wagon. She had fallen. Jeddy had pushed her. She stood on one foot and lifted her scraped flesh-cushioned knee for his healing kiss.

But now his Rachel waved to him absently and turned to the glossy pages of her magazine to scan bits of essential adolescent wisdom. Dorothy Hamill washed her hair every day. John Travolta was not interested in acting on Broadway. Hot water and lemon juice was an effective solution against acne. Her father's shadow did not divert her.

"Hey, Dad," Jeddy said, "they've got this neat soldering iron. The guy let me watch, but old Hornstein kicked me out."

"Just as well." Ray tousled his son's hair, tucked the boy's cambric shirt into his dungarees. Jeddy squirmed away from him.

"Aw, Dad, cut it out."

Another boy, still waiting to be picked up, grimaced at them, and Ray straightened, blushing slightly. He had not meant to embarrass his son with his affection, his love.

"What do you want to do?" he asked them.

"Have lunch. I'm starved," Rachel said. She slipped the magazine carefully into her bookbag and pulled her red shetland sweater down over her plaid skirt.

"I thought we'd walk all the way down to Rumpelmayer's. Maybe stop at the Japanese shop and find a kite. There should be a good wind on the beach this weekend."

"A kite?" she asked.

"Yeah. A kite," Jeddy replied. "You know, with a tail and a string. Maybe we'll find one for you shaped like John Travolta."

"Shut up."

"Come on. Cut it out."

Ray struggled to maintain a paternal situation-comedy voice. The amused, understanding father, the wise solver of all sibling squabbles. He and Dot, with ten years separating them in age, had never quarreled. Later, they had been too dependent on each other for disagreement. Their parents' death had caused them to cleave together; they were drifting orphans clinging to frayed familial ropes. One cross word and the rope would give. He wanted his own son and daughter to love each other mightily, to be kind to each other, to insure each other against solitude and sorrow. Had Ina and Bette ever bickered? he sometimes wondered.

"I don't want to go to Rumpelmayer's," Rachel said. "I don't want ice cream. I have a lot of homework to do."

"Let's go somewhere different. Rumpelmayer's is boring." Jeddy added his protest to his sister's. It seemed to Ray that his children had made peace between themselves and formed a league against him, betraying him, exposing his naiveté.

But they followed him into the large Japanese shop and walked with him down the aisles lined with tiny china bells and diminutive figurines. Rachel lifted a small coffee-colored bell and listened to its lovely jingle, the gentle melodic kiss of the fragile clapper against the pale thin body. Once she had collected china ornaments, pleaded with him for possession, acquisition.

"Do you want it?" he asked, willing her to claim it. He would buy her a toy and restore her to childhood.

She lingered over it, made it ring again, but set it down at last.

"I have no room," she said. "I have to get rid of some of my junk."

Incense hung heavy in the air. Clerks in wondrously colored silk blouses hurried from counter to counter. They moved swiftly but took small steps. Rachel did not glance at the papier-mâché toys, the bamboo mobiles, the haughty dolls in their elegant kimonos. Instead she paused in the cookware section where a white-aproned chef clutched a cleaver that danced in metal frenzy above a cutting board, slicing green scallions and zucchini, huge earth-colored mushrooms and curling strands of ivory bean sprouts. A smiling woman assistant, wearing a kimono of peacock blue, transferred the vegetables to a flat pan of thin black iron in which oil sizzled in golden pools.

"What are they trying to sell?" Rachel asked.

"The cooking implements, I think," he replied.

"We ought to buy Mom a cleaver. There's nothing sharp at the Amagansett house."

"Not today," he said harshly.

The cleaver, he supposed, was as sharp as a surgeon's knife. The Japanese cook lifted the cutting board and scraped off the bits of clinging vegetables. The metal ripped across the wood. Ina had told him that morning about Marnie's miscarriage.

"How is she now?" he had asked.

"She's having a curettage—a sort of scraping to make sure there's nothing left." Ina's voice had been small, almost frightened.

The cook smiled widely, triumphantly. Small white teeth flashed against his pale pink gums. A strip of mushroom had resisted, but he had dislodged it. He had scraped the cutting board with his cleaver.

Just so, with such graceful expertise, would the steel of Isaacs's surgical instrument move across the nacreous surface of Ina's womb. The scrap of clinging life would shrink before its thrust and surrender finally. It would be tossed, like a quivering vegetal scrap, into the debris of operating room waste.

"Dad, your fingers are cold." Jeddy withdrew his hand, wandered off to look at the display of kites. Ray followed him, his heart beating too rapidly, his toes and his fingertips strangely numb.

They selected a kite shaped like a dragon, fashioned of brilliant reds and golds, the color of a full-blooded sun. Emerald eyes sparkled in the painted face. Even Rachel admired it and urged Ray to buy an extra spool of string, a new reel.

"Jeddy needs it," she said, and he was pleased and knew that she would run with her brother across the dunes and watch the wind carry the fierce dragon skyward. She was a small girl still, his baby, his evening princess. He hugged her, and she giggled shyly.

They did not exit on the avenue but took a street door and so did not pass the cook again, although, glancing back, Ray saw him score the air with a stainless steel spatula. Flecks of sunlight bounced off the silvery surface, and a bit of tomato clung like a brilliant scarlet blood clot to the gleaming metal.

It was Jeddy who spotted the restaurant and insisted on eating there. A classmate had told him about it. It was supposed to be terrific. A real fun place. Cool gimmicks. As though to support the child's claims, a waiter dressed in kelly-green knickers, a green-and-white-striped shirt, and a tweed cap set at a jaunty angle, handed out sample menus. Tiny antique cars bordered the printed sheet, and Ray, who had thought the waiter was dressed as a jockey, now realized he was supposed to be a racing car driver.

"Please, Dad," Jeddy urged, and Ray looked at Rachel, who nodded.

She was, for that moment, a compliant, resigned adult, recognizing her younger brother's harmless whim and submitting to it. They started in, and the sidewalk waiter flashed them a brilliant smile of gratitude.

The restaurant was designed to resemble an auto race track. Patrons sat in booths shaped like cars and used ancient horns to summon the waiters. Their seats came from vintage vehicles; springs creaked although they were newly covered in handsome wine-colored velour. A dashboard enabled the children to switch on the headlights in the front of each booth, to signal a left turn or a right. The room was bathed in swaths of colored lights as the children played with the switches. A small steering wheel projected from beneath the table, and Jeddy crouched over it, swerving widely to the left and to the right, flashing his signals and sounding his horn. A giant screen flashed Technicolor replays of famous auto races. As they read their menus, a car on the screen swooped down the Indianapolis course and burst into flames. Ray shivered, looked away. Cars had blazed in the collision that his parents had died in. Their own car, a bright red Ford, had exploded in a burst of flame that could be seen for miles. He had returned once to

the country road where it had happened, expecting perhaps
to see the outline of a car seared into the tarmac, but of course
the road was clear and lined with aged apple trees that were in
full bloom that day. Soft white petals littered the road where
he had become an orphan. Larry had identified the bodies.
Ray had been too young. The coffins had been closed, and it
was his imagination that the funeral parlor stank of flesh and
singed hair. He had been an imaginative boy, and sex and
death flew through his dreams and fantasies.

He read the menu through twice, and when he looked up to
give the waiter their orders, a parade of model-T Fords moved
across the screen, all driven by young men in bowler hats,
accompanied by ladies who covered their bouffant hair with
driving veils.

Ray ordered a "Studeburger," and the children ordered the
"Auto-Burger" special. Service was swift because only three
booths were occupied. This was, after all, a school day.

"We get a big crowd on weekends," the waiter said, as
though apologizing. "On Sunday in the winter you have to
wait a half-hour, sometimes an hour."

Ray believed him. Winter Sundays stretched in endless
hours before urban parents with small children. Spacious
apartments became isolated islands wandered by whining unhappy children. He and Ina had passed that stage. They were
mobile now. They could pack the children off to visit friends
or go with them to a matinee, a museum, a movie. But he remembered the days when they had exhausted all amusement in
the apartment, and the sounds of small squabbles, irritable
crying, and persistent demands had sent them to the telephone
in search of respite. They would visit Dot or drive to Connecticut to share tasteless pizza with Bette's family. Sometimes
they searched out restaurants like this one where cartoons
mesmerized the children and guitar-playing clowns obviated
the need for talk. Would a new baby mean the beginning of
all that again? he wondered, and shook the thought away.
There would be no new baby. He anticipated Ina's decision
and mentally reiterated its validity.

His "Studeburger" (a hamburger into which fried onions had been ground) tasted like sawdust in his mouth, and the coffee was bitter and tepid. He left the table abruptly and dialed the hospital. There was no answer in Ina's room, and when he returned, neither Jeddy nor Rachel asked where he had been. They ate with relish, watched the screen, and smiled absently as a waiter, cruising the room on a moped, delivered their Cokes. In such a restaurant whole meals could pass, and families would not have to exchange a word. The American Dream, he thought wryly. No interaction and therefore no conflict. Zero population growth resulting in zero familial contact, all made possible by money, gimmicks, and technology.

But over dessert, Jeddy, his mouth crammed full of apple pie, small bits of crust snowing down on the table, asked, "Daddy, is Mom coming home today?"

"Probably tomorrow," he said. "Or perhaps the next day."

He would not commit himself. The abortion might be slated for that very afternoon or for the next morning. It was, Isaacs had assured him, a simple, routine procedure. Some women rested for a couple of hours afterward and went home. Ruthie had told them about a friend who had returned to work the same day. Ray, however, could not be that casual about the human body, about Ina's body. Mysterious metal implements would pierce her flesh. Blood would flow. Sedatives would assuage taut and jangled nerves. A tiny life, like a minute, unknown, and uninvited dybbuk, would be exorcised, routed by drug and steel. It was necessary perhaps, and it was wise perhaps, but it was not so routine, not so simple.

Jeddy went to the bathroom, and Rachel looked at Ray across the table. There was a shrewdness in her dark eyes, and her expression reminded him of her grandmother, Shirley Cherne. His daughter would not be fooled. She had, her teachers always reported, an extraordinary gift for abstraction. Like her grandmother, like Ina herself, Rachel would know how to turn an extra yardage of corduroy into a profit, how to economize on computer time, how to survive against incalculable odds. Her question now was direct.

"How come Mom is in the hospital for so long? If it's nothing serious, why is she still at Mount Lebanon?"

"Dr. Isaacs thought she needed a little more time to rest. No two operations are alike. Different people recover differently. Rosa recuperated quickly. Your mother needed a few extra days."

"I called her from school while we were waiting for you. Twice. Mrs. Gottlieb, the lady in her room, said she had gone out for a walk. I mean, how sick can she be if she goes for walks? She could rest at home, too." Rachel took a long sip of her Coke. "Don't worry," she said, "I didn't tell Jeddy what I think."

"What do you think?" he asked.

His voice was hoarse. Fear clutched his throat. His small daughter, his evening princess, knew too much. Questions of life and death glinted in her dark eyes. She was too old to be diverted by china bells and dolls in silken dresses. She was the daughter and granddaughter of survivors. Their skills and instincts were her heritage. She sought out white when black confronted her, searched for exits to sealed rooms.

"I think maybe she has a bad disease. Cancer. I think maybe she's going to die." Tears filled her eyes, trailed down cheeks pale with fear. Her mouth twisted into a knot of misery, and flecks of spittle whitened her trembling lips. Her words were awesome. She had not known how they would sound when spoken aloud.

"No," Ray replied quietly. "She doesn't have cancer. She has no disease at all. She is not going to die. She is going to come home in a day or two, and this summer we are going to plant a herb garden at the Amagansett house."

He handed her his handkerchief and watched her blot at tears that fell swiftly, freely.

"But why is she in the hospital so long?" Rachel asked.

"There are reasons, but they have nothing to do with cancer or any other illness." He could not tell her the truth, but he would not tell her a lie.

Acknowledging defeat, she did not persist, and they sat

opposite each other in silence. How soon would it be, he wondered, before she guessed what it was? Lying awake on a summer's night, she would piece together small scraps of knowledge and devise a patchwork cloth of near-truth. Perhaps one day, Ina herself would tell her about it, echoing Shirley Cherne's belated confidence. ("It is something you must know because you are my daughter . . .") But now in this foolish room with its Stop signs and hooting horns, the unspoken words separated him and Rachel, and the unanswered question stretched between them like a dividing line they were powerless to cross.

Jeddy returned and Ray paid the bill, toted up on a green betting form, proffered to him on a hubcap tray.

"What are you going to do now, kids?" he asked as they stood on the sidewalk.

"I'm going home to change for soccer practice," Jeddy said.

"I've got a paper to do." Rachel's tone was subdued, and she did not look at him. "A book report."

"You going to the hospital, Dad?" Jeddy asked.

"Yes," he said and hailed a cruising cab and hurried them into it. "I'll call you later."

"Hey, Daddy, thanks for lunch," Jeddy called through the open window, and Ray smiled and waved.

But when he turned, he did not walk toward the hospital but in the direction of Dot's apartment. His sister was not home, but the baby, Simon, would be there, and quite suddenly Ray wanted to hold his adoptive nephew, the small Oriental princeling, born and alive and happy against all odds.

Ina's office called twice that morning. An important client needed a system urgently. Could they take the job?

"Why not?" Ina asked.

She calculated costs, computer rental time, the extra freelance people that would have to be hired. She herself would design the system. The problem was an interesting one. As she scribbled notes, she thought of the new language she could use in the program, a new technique to store the data.

She phoned the client herself, accepting the job, outlining the plan. The client's questions were brusque and to the point. There were no subtleties of decision, no nuances involved. She answered him briefly, directly, pleased to be confronted with questions to which she knew the answers. Doubt and indecision did not trail her into the fastness of her professional world where whirring machines offered solutions and certain knowledge was economically stored on narrow reels of tape.

The second call reported receipt of a Telex from the movie firm. Could a messenger pick up the programs Ina had taken to the hospital with her?

"They'll be ready," she promised Ricky, her assistant.

She was pleased that Ricky was taking a strong initiative, seizing the administrative reins. Ricky could really be relied on to keep the office running if Ina chose to work at home. The thought surprised and irritated her. She felt suddenly claustrophobic in the empty hospital room. The aide who had made up the bed had raised the steel sides, and both her own bed and Miriam's looked like steel cages. The tables and chairs had been pushed too close together, and the rhythmic dripping of the faucet grated on her. She had been too long in this room. Almost four days. Two of her full-blown yellow roses had wilted, and the velvet petals were rimmed with rusty decay. Her water glass left a small circlet of moisture on the Formica tabletop. The room was completely quiet. Miriam had gone to see her baby.

"We'll know today," she had said, and she had put on a crisp new nightgown of pink batiste and tied her hair up with a matching ribbon. Hope and fear struggled against each other, and when she applied toilet water, her hands trembled as she held the bottle, and the amber liquid spilled and filled the room with a cloying sweetness.

Ina did not want to be in the room when Miriam returned. She did not want to be in the room at all. Outside her window a window washer hoisted himself up on a swaying platform. He wore a red-and-black shirt and smiled and waved a dirty rag at her as he drifted past. Her lack of privacy shamed and astonished her. Hastily, she gathered together her papers, her sharpened pencils and manuals, and went to the waiting room, where she appropriated two of the small Formica tables and spread out the huge coded printout sheets.

She worked steadily, completely absorbed in the words and numbers, triumphantly fielding a problem, formulating a solution. The small man who spent the nights sleeping on the couch came in carrying an overnight case. He looked carefully around the waiting room, like a hotel guest who is about to check out. He found a paperback novel that had fallen behind the couch. A white handkerchief was draped like a small banner of surrender over a blue chair. He plucked it up, furtively, opened and shut the valise, and left the room. He smiled apologetically to Ina from the hallway, and she smiled back. He was a nice man. He had not meant to intrude upon her with his own small, mysterious misery. Tears had stood in his eyes, luminous liquid bullets that he could not wipe away because he had packed his handkerchief. Probably he was a neat man. His belt buckle was polished to a gleaming brightness, but now his shirttail trailed out of his trousers, which were bunched and creased.

Ina turned back to her sheets. She could not share his grief. She had nothing to offer him. In the camp, strangers had sent frayed scraps of ribbon to comfort the newly motherless Bette, a half a potato to silence Halina's sobbing, but in this New York hospital, she had nothing to offer the small man who walked slowly to the elevator, his shoulders stooped beneath the weight of his sadness.

She concentrated on her work. She saw how a step could be eliminated from one program and how two processes could be incorporated into one. Four computer hours would be saved. She smiled with satisfaction and wrote a concise memo of explanation.

Tina wandered in, looked at her curiously, and smiled shyly. "I'd like to learn about computers," she said.

"There are all sorts of courses," Ina replied.

"The thing is, I really want to concentrate on my music.

I'm into classical guitar. I'd like to perform. Maybe compose. Maybe work with a group. Or I could teach."

She was fourteen and touching all bases. Life stretched before her in an intriguing maze of endless possibilities and combinations. She would one day sit on a stage, a small bright figure shining in a pool of golden light. Music would spring from her fingers, and young men would look at her and think of love. She had put death behind her and hung her white peignoir away. Her hair would grow in thick and luxuriant. She wore plaid pajamas and a loose robe to match, and above her hospital bed she had taped her poster of Julian Bream in concert.

"They'll be serving lunch soon," she said.

"Yes. I know." Ina glanced at her watch, corrected a minor error.

"They brought Marnie back. I passed her room. She's just lying there, so quiet. I was afraid to go in."

"She needs some time probably. You'll see her later," Ina said. She too would see Marnie later, offer her the conventional words of comfort and reassurance that would neither comfort nor reassure. "We'll visit her together, Tina."

"Okay. Swell."

Tina walked down the hall, smiling at the nurses she passed. She bent to pick up a slip of paper. She was the helpful child again, with the lovely smile she practiced nightly before her mirror.

Ina finished the work, organized the printout sheets into a neat package which she left at the nurses' station for the messenger service. She felt the special pleasant fatigue that came for her with a job done, an end achieved.

"What I hate about this baby business," a sandbox mother had said to her once, "is that you're never finished."

An aide and a volunteer greeted Ina by name. She nodded and smiled, briefly confused. She welcomed their recognition and resented their familiarity. But no matter. She was pleasant, compliant. They wore uniforms and thus had power over her.

She had learned that lesson well, years ago, in a half-forgotten land.

"Oh, I'm fine," she assured them brightly. (Always say you're fine, Shaindel had fiercely cautioned Bette and Ina. The sick were in danger of death that would not come from germs. And they had been sick. Rickets bowed their legs; their stomachs were distended. Still, they learned to do little dances and to sing German love songs in high sweet voices. Once Ina had known all the words to "Lilli Marlene." Once she had known a song called "My Beloved Fraulein." How had they learned all those songs—she and Bette?) She continued down the corridor, softly humming "Lilli Marlene."

The door to her own room was closed, and from within came the murmur of many voices. They rose and fell like measured, rationed sobs. Ina paused and wondered if she should knock, but then the door opened, and Nurse Li came out. The Chinese nurse's face was drawn, and her beautiful almond-shaped eyes were rimmed with swollen ridges of flesh. She nodded at Ina and hurried down the hall, leaving the door wide open behind her.

Ina's heart sank. Her hands trembled. She grasped the doorknob, as though for support. A shaft of pain shot through her breast, and the white high cage of her bed seemed very far away.

Miriam's bed was encircled. The two elderly couples, her parents and her in-laws, stood at either side of her. Each man clutched his wife's hand as mourners do at funerals, grasping for ballast against insupportable sorrow. The small stocky women wore new spring suits in pastel shades and pert hats to match. Miriam's mother had chosen a bright pink, shades deeper than her daughter's nightgown. Ben's mother wore a suit of silken fabric, the color of early pale lilacs. A sprig of lilac darted out of the grosgrain band of her hat. She touched a handkerchief, dotted with small purple flowers, to her eyes. They had all dressed in the colors of gaiety, seeking perhaps to deceive fate. Ben's hand rested on Miriam's hair, moved down her head in soothing strokes, took up the brave pink ribbon and played with it.

Certain knowledge weighed Ina down, paralyzed her. The baby was dead. She was entering a room of mourning, and she was a poor consoler. She had nothing to say to these four old people, stooped and grayed by multiple bereavements, compounded by betrayals. She had no words to offer the young couple who had waited and hoped and believed that a new formula, a young doctor's indifferent wisdom, a nurse's optimism, would save their child.

Ina cursed her own optimism. She too, only hours before, had watched the tiny infant soil his diaper, stretch lazily like a minuscule sunbather beneath the ultraviolet light, open and close his small bud of a fist. She had believed then that he would live and grow to be a sturdy boy, a boy like her own Jeddy, who would one day stand at ocean's edge and marvel at a sunset. She had willed him life and offered her own unborn child as hostage. But the infant had died, and now his parents and grandparents, trapped in a circle of grief, stared at her as she stumbled toward her bed struggling for words.

"Ina. Do you feel all right?"

Miriam's voice was oddly light and clear, although Ina saw that her cheeks were wet with tears. Perhaps, then, the baby's death had been a relief after all, an end to worry and anxiety.

"Yes. But you? How are you?" The questions ripped painfully from her mouth. She did not want the answer.

"Us? We're marvelous. The baby is fine. Terrific. They're not worried anymore about anything. The formula is working, and everything is under control. Now it's just a question of his gaining weight, and he has put on at least an ounce. You should have seen us when they told us. Everyone began crying—even Nurse Li!"

She laughed. Her anxiety was banished now to a whimsical episode, a precious beginning to her child's history. He was so special, her little boy. He was in fact a miracle. She would tell him, when he was old enough to understand, about all the people who had hovered over him, who had smiled to see the jaundiced yellow face pinken and the tiny nails harden over the circlets of pink-and-white flesh.

"Thank God," Ina said.

She fell back against her pillows, and from a secret, mysterious source, sudden tears welled up, and she too began to cry. Her body heaved, and her mouth twitched uncontrollably.

Her tears fell from an obscure, secret source, from a mysterious vein of sorrow long untapped. She wept for her brother who had died and for Miriam's baby who would live. She wept for the child her mother had not borne and for the childhood that had been lost to her. She wept with relief because light had followed darkness and life endured where death had swept over them with a long and terrible shadow. Tears flowed because she was relieved of her promise and was no longer hostage to another woman's fortune.

"I'm so glad," she gasped, feeling that she must explain.

They looked at each other and moved toward her. Mrs. Gottlieb offered her a tissue. Miriam's mother poured her a glass of water and held it to her lips as though she were a small girl who had awakened suddenly in the night. They understood and accepted her tears and did not question them.

"Here's your nice lunch," Mrs. Gottlieb said.

An aide set down the tray. Ina glanced without interest at the pale slab of meat surrounded by colorless viscous vegetables. Idly she ripped open the plastic packet of salad dressing and oozed out a design across the single slice of tomato perched on faded lettuce leaves.

Across the room, the Gottlieb family chatted happily. They talked for the first time of a name for the child. Ben's father suggested the name Maurice. His own father had been known as Moshe. Miriam offered the name Alan, for her grandfather Aaron. Maurice Alan. They savored the name and then played with others. Scott Matthew perhaps, for Shimon Mendell. Robert Jason for Reuven Yaakov.

They had no difficulty with choices and combinations. Their dead were numerous, and their melodic ancient names resonated in troubled memory. Their bodies were turned to ashes, no headstones marked their passing, but their names lingered on.

Ina had read a modern Midrashic tale once that told of how the souls of the departed drifted through the nether regions, moaning and weeping until at last their names came to rest on a newborn child. The story had haunted her, and she had named Jeddy for her brother, Yedidiah. Her mother had objected to the name. Each time her grandson was called, she would see the face of the small boy who had died of weakness while she slept. Even Ray had been hesitant. He did not want his child named for his wife's brother who had vanished in a pale blue wisp of smoke. Children should be named for the strong, for those who had lived long lives. He was not a superstitious man, yet he had fought the name and later felt a swift irrational anger when Jeddy had become ill with that fierce nocturnal fever. In the quiet of the pediatric corridor at Saint Luke's, he had silently blamed Ina for endangering their son with the name she had plucked from her dark and terror-streaked past. He had wanted to call the child Jimmy. But Ina had insisted. "This child shall be known in Israel as Yedidiah," the officiating rabbi had said at Jeddy's circumcision, and Norman Cherne had grown pale and left the room.

"I like the sound of Maurice Alan," Miriam said now.

"All right. Moshe Aaron. Maurice Alan. A fine name. A good name," Mr. Gottlieb asserted, and they all nodded and agreed but continued to offer new combinations.

Ina thought of her cousins in Israel. They had discarded the names of the past. Geulah, her doctor cousin had called her first-born daughter. "It means Redemption," she had written to Ina. Oded, they had called their son. "The name means Encourager," her cousin had written. There were two cousins named Shlomo. Peace. The name came from the word *shalom*, and both boys had been born after the war of '67. Ina closed her eyes, and little Mrs. Gottlieb tiptoed over and drew the curtain about the bed.

With the curtain shielding her from the Gottlieb family, Ina poured herself a cup of coffee but did not drink it. She had not eaten since breakfast. Dr. Isaacs might fit her in that afternoon, and the anesthesiologist would want her stomach empty. She set the cup down.

"Mrs. Feldman?"

A tall blonde woman had come into the room, moving quietly on very high-heeled black patent-leather shoes, their soles cushioned in crepe. She wore a black suit and a white shirtwaist with a narrow black ribbon about her collar. Slender, her cheeks brushed with the glow of an early spring tan, her bright hair tied neatly back, she emanated good health, prosperity, organization. Ina had never seen her before.

"I hope you don't mind my visiting you." She smiled brilliantly; white teeth gleamed. No one had ever objected to a visit from her. "I'm Emily Anders. I've brought some literature that might interest you."

"I have plenty to read," Ina said, but Emily Anders had already opened her black portfolio, removing pamphlets and single sheets of softly colored papers. Numbers and words marched neatly across mimeo bond of pink and blue, yellow and green—baby colors chosen for tiny kimonos and minute bed jackets.

"This is our newest leaflet. We're very proud of it."

Tastefully designed in black and white, its cover featured a laughing, chubby baby. A balloon above the baby's mouth had it saying, "Don't I have a right to live?"

"Get out of here," Ina said through clenched teeth.

She brushed the pamphlets away from her. One flew open to show the standard picture of a dead fetus curled up in a bottle of formaldehyde.

"Why are you afraid to read our literature?" Emily Anders asked. Her lips were full and moist, and her smile moved with rubbery mobility across her face.

"I'm not afraid to read it," Ina said, keeping her voice low. There was no reason for Miriam to hear this conversation. "In fact I have read it or material like it. But it doesn't seem to include any pictures of neglected children or mental defectives and mongoloids. And I've never seen any discussions of fifteen-year-old girls made pregnant by rapists. And what about all the young girls who died on the kitchen tables of back-room abortionists? Shouldn't you deal with that problem? I'm not afraid of your opinions, but I think perhaps you're afraid of mine."

"No. I'll read anything you give me. Truly." Emily Anders was gentle, conciliatory. She had been well-trained. She knew how to keep her cool. "I'd be interested in discussing your philosophy."

"I'm afraid I'm a little tired," Ina said. She turned her head and yawned.

Emily Anders gathered up her material and placed it in a neat pile on Ina's bedside table.

"Don't you think your baby has a right to live?" she asked softly. Her smile radiated beneficence, concern.

"Is that any of your business?" Ina asked and was annoyed with herself for rising to the other woman's carefully placed bait.

"Ah, but we are all responsible for each other in this world." How reasonable was Emily Anders's voice, how appealing her tone.

Anger soared within Ina. She remembered suddenly the voice of a woman crying out in the night—a night when planes flew so low that even from the narrow windows they saw the flash of moving airborne lights, heard the hum of hovering motors. "Why don't they do something for us," the woman cried. "Is no one in this world responsible for us?"

She turned to Emily Anders.

"No one felt responsible for my grandparents. They were killed in 1941. Or for my mother. She had an abortion because she had no choice. Pregnant women were killed at once. How can you say that we are responsible for each other?" Her voice was harsh, and her hands trembled.

"My father was Jewish," Emily Anders said, but the smile had bounced off her lips, and her eyes were too bright.

"I'm very tired," Ina said and realized that it was true.

Fatigue rested on her like a heavy cloak. She leaned back. "Who told you about me?" she asked wearily.

Emily Anders did not answer. She stood. A white thread caught on her black skirt.

"I wish you luck," she said stiffly.

Ina did not answer. She tossed the literature into the wastebasket. The dead fetus stared up at her, and she covered the leaflet with a mass of tissues. When the phone rang, she glanced at it nervously, suspiciously, and did not lift it until the third ring.

"Ina, I'm at Dot's," Ray said. "Larry had some papers for me to sign."

He would not tell her that he had come to hold Simon in his arms, to listen to the toddler's playful chortle, and to stroke his fat little neck that breathed out the smell of baby powder and small-boy sweat.

"Oh."

"I had lunch with the kids. There was dismissal because of a burst pipe, so I picked them up at school."

"Oh, great."

She was briefly, irrationally, envious of his freedom. She prowled corridors thick with the smell of antiseptic and the dank odor of worry; her room was accessible to roaming invaders like Emily Anders, while he hailed taxis and walked with the children from sun-dappled streets into shadowed restaurants.

"We had a good time," he admitted. "Ina, Rachel asked me about what was happening at the hospital. She's a pretty sensitive kid. She suspects something."

Her daughter then was smarter than she had been. She had suspected nothing. She had guessed nothing. Her mother's loss and pain had never touched her. It was Bette who had noticed the difference, who had guessed that "something" had happened. "Something."

"Perhaps when it's all over, we'll tell Rachel about it."

"You're decided then?" Defeat weighed his tone.

"Yes."

"I see." Disappointment withered the words.

"You said you wouldn't be angry."

"I'm not angry."

He would not argue with her. Simon clutched his hair, twisted in his arms, and hurled his small body against his uncle's torso.

"I the king," the child announced and frowned imperiously. "I the count. One, two, three." He laughed jovially at his own joke.

Ray stroked the small boy's wonderfully straight back, felt the miracle of the child's evenly knobbed spine.

"Ray, it's what I have to do," Ina said.

"All right. I'll see you later."

She hung up. The receiver shimmered wetly where she had grasped it. She dialed Dr. Isaacs's office. He was out, but she left a message with the secretary. Mrs. Feldman had decided to go ahead with the procedure. Would the doctor call back when he had scheduled her?

When she hung up, she was suffused by a new calm. The issue now seemed clear, defined. She did not want another child.

It was her decision, and she had a right to it. She had earned control over her own destiny. Once her life had belonged to the pale-haired guard who carried a whip and a phone crank in her pocket. But that time was past. Now her body and her life belonged to her alone. Her decision was clear and had been clear since the night she had stretched out beside Ray in the darkness, when the knowledge of her pregnancy was new to her. Slivers of glass from the broken street light had glided soundlessly to the street below. She had thought that with just such quiet swiftness her luck could be shattered. And she had had the dream again that night. Defenseless in sleep, she had held Bette's hand and watched the trio of faceless soldiers advance toward her, death streaking from their organs of life. She shook herself free of the memory, conditioned herself to calm. The turmoil was over.

She had made a nocturnal bargain while looking at the struggling newborn. It had been a foolish bargain, one that she would not have to keep. Anger and sorrow had released her. The tears she had shed over the Gottlieb baby had washed away cobwebs of doubt, obfuscating dust mice of memory. She was not responsible for her mother's past, her husband's future. She was, finally, responsible only for herself.

Across the room, names continued to flutter through the air.

"If we ever have a little girl, I love the name Caroline Elizabeth," Miriam said dreamily.

"Nina. I always liked the name Nina," her mother offered.

"Elana. That's a Hebrew name. Doesn't it have a pretty sound? I wonder what it means."

"A young tree," someone replied.

Ben, the new father, stood at the window and looked down at the park where a magnolia sapling had blossomed forth that day. The star-shaped white flowers weighed down its fragile branches. Even from a distance, he could see the red veins that bled across the flower's heart.

Nurse Li stopped at their room before going off duty. She had worked a double shift, and she walked very slowly, lifting one white oxforded foot carefully in front of the other, as though fatigue made every step a precarious undertaking. But she smiled brightly at Miriam.

"I just wanted to say good-bye and good luck," she said. "I'll be off for the next four days, and I'm sure you'll be discharged before then."

"Yes," Miriam said, "but we'll be coming back because the baby—I mean, Maurice Alan—" She smiled at her parents and in-laws, and they nodded. A baby that had a name would live. Maury, they would call him, and Moshe. Now they planned his circumcision ceremony. One day they would plan his bar mitzvah. They would celebrate birthdays, graduations. A miracle had been wrought, a generation had been restored.

"In my town," little Mrs. Gottlieb said softly, "they never told a baby's name before the circumcision."

"Superstitious nonsense. From that place. From that time." Her husband brushed away her words. He did not want to think of that time, of that place. Death stalked the streets of their past. He would look toward the future, to days of gladness as a child grew. His child's child. His grandson. Maurice Alan.

"Anyway, Maurice will be in the hospital for a few more weeks," Miriam concluded, "so I'm sure we'll see you."

"I hope so," the nurse said. "And don't worry. My son had the same problems at birth, and he's a third-year medical student now."

"Wonderful."

They all beamed at her, understanding now her involvement, her concern. She was a good woman who worked double shift to pay the tuition of her medical student son who had also struggled for breath in the first days of his life. He wrought strange miracles, this strange and incomprehensible God. He caused children to suffer and turned the sufferers into healers. Perhaps Maurice Alan would also go to medical school. They trembled at the wonder of his life, his future.

Miriam's father reached into a pocket and took out an envelope. He walked over to the nurse and held it out. A blush turned her cheeks a mottled rose gold. She shook her head, smiled.

"No. I couldn't take it. I only did what I could. It's my job."

"Please. If you don't want it, give it to charity," he insisted. He was a man used to paying for services and redeeming his luck.

"All right. I'll put it in the children's Christmas party fund. Good-bye. Good luck."

She shook hands with each of them and on her way out stopped at Ina's bed.

"Good-bye, Mrs. Feldman. I wish you the best."

"Thank you," Ina said.

The nurse's words drifted across her consciousness as though across a filtered screen. The new calm protected her. She would make her own luck. Life did not simply happen to you.

There were controls to be exercised, choices to be made. Her
mother had never trusted to luck. Neither would Ina.

"Such a lovely nurse," Miriam's mother said.

"Wonderful."

Ben's mother prepared to leave. She gathered up the department store boxes, golden-veined with grease lines, in which
she had packed the cakes and chicken. She put Miriam's soiled
nightgowns in a small net bag which she slipped into her large
purse. She was expert at packing and conserving space. When
they left Germany, they had been allowed to take only two
valises, and her husband proudly told of how one had contained their cutlery wrapped in undergarments. His prayer
shawl had been wound around a carving knife that pierced
the heavy linen in transit. He had never repaired it. The
severed fabric was a reminder; often in synagogue, he ran his
fingers across the ragged edges, counting each stray strand as
though he were counting lives lost, vanished faces, fragmented echoes of laughter, and words whispered in the lost
language of his youth.

The elder Gottliebs left the hospital room in a flurry of
good-byes, a spattering of reminders. There were relatives to
call, purchases to make. They had to see about a skirt for the
bassinet, curtains for the baby's room.

"Don't forget to call Sophie," Miriam's mother told her as
she and Miriam's father at last prepared to leave.

"I won't," Miriam assured them, smiling. She did not be-
grudge them their involvement.

A new torpor settled over the room with their departure—a
drowsy silence not unlike the silence of a children's bunk at
camp rest hour, when all activity has been suspended. Miriam
dutifully reached for her phone but let the receiver drop back
into the cradle without dialing.

"I'm tired," she said contentedly, and leaned back, her eyes
closed.

Ina too eyed her phone. She wanted Dr. Isaacs or his nurse
to call back and tell her when she was scheduled, whether the
abortion would take place that afternoon or the next morning.

She was hungry. If there was no surgery scheduled, she could eat. She thought longingly now of the laden lunch tray she had sent back. Even the overcooked meat and the pulverized vegetables seemed appealing now. She longed for the soft round roll covered with the golden film of butter and the rich, hot coffee through which prisms had floated. She reviewed other meals—lavish after-theater dinners in the string of restaurants along Fifty-sixth Street, sumptuous brunches in dining rooms hung with plants and rimmed with aquariums, gay lunches with clients at salad bars and sushi counters. She thought of these meals and remembered how the women had lain awake at night in the camp and discussed food, exchanged recipes.

"I used a whole chicken in my soup," Halina's mother had said. "And leeks. No onions. Only leeks."

"It's fresh parsley that makes the difference," Shaindel contributed. "Always, I grew my own parsley."

They wore rags. Translucent bones glimmered beneath the bloodless parchment of their skins. Their fleshless breasts hung slack. They were starving. Their menstrual blood did not flow. But they talked on, their voices taking up the tone of vigorous, virtuous housewives. Peshi had always put carrots in her pot roast, and the secret of Shaindel's gefilte fish rested in the matzoh meal she blended into the ground carp.

The little girls, Batya, Halina, and Ina, had clutched their bellies, swollen with emptiness, distended with gas and air, and listened to the tales of golden chickens and crisp green vegetables as though they were fairy tales, miracles that belonged to a never-never land to which they had been denied entrance.

It was hunger that excited such memories of food, Ina knew, and she knew too that hunger terrified those who had once felt the stale sour breath of starvation. She could not fast beyond lunch on Yom Kippur. Panic overtook her. Even now, having missed only one meal, she trembled with nervousness.

She called the doctor's office again. The nurse's voice betrayed annoyance. The doctor had not returned. When he did, she would certainly give him Mrs. Feldman's message. No. She did not know exactly when she would hear from him. He was performing surgery that day and was scheduled for a Caesarian section delivery. Her tone was clipped, accusatory, her implication clear. Her doctor's skills just now were involved in saving lives. He would call Ina back when he could schedule the minor, death-related procedure.

"Thank you," Ina said.

Miriam had fallen asleep. The mournful strains of a violin drifted in from a radio across the hall. Somewhere along the corridor a heavy book slipped to the floor with a dull thud. Visitors had left, and the patients were dozing, propped up against their many pillows, as pale, voiceless shadows floated across their television screens. The nurses who patrolled the corridor walked slowly and spoke in soft voices.

Ina slipped out of bed. She was too hungry to sleep. She put on her robe and the knit bed slippers Dot had brought and walked down to the waiting room. The floor had just been washed, and the tables and chairs had been shoved into corners or piled on the couch. She was saddened, disappointed, like a child who has arrived at a playground and finds the gate padlocked.

"Ina—do you want to go visit Marnie?"

Tina stood beside her, a small transistor radio held up to her ear. A breathless voice, accompanied by a rasping guitar, sang of getting on a jet plane, going far away from home. Tina tapped her feet to the music.

"Sure," Ina said. "But Tina, remember, she may not feel like having visitors. She's been through something pretty grim."

"I understand," Tina answered. She too, after all, had been through something pretty grim.

The overpowering fragrance of a spring garden in full bloom leaped out at them as they entered Marnie's room. Vases of pale lilacs, full-blooming pink tulips, sun-gold daffodils were scattered on every surface. Ina glanced involuntarily down at the floor where, only hours before, she had seen a pool of blood the color of the scarlet rosebuds that rested on Marnie's bedside table. Surrounded by her flowers, wearing a white nightgown cut like a schoolgirl's shirt, Marnie sat up in bed. She flashed them her wonderful smile, but her great dark eyes were dull and the lids were swollen. She waved and then dropped her arms listlessly. They rested, like abandoned ebony wands, in the white wings of her sleeves. Her fingers were splayed and her palms turned upward. The pink pads of her pinkie and her thumb rubbed against each other in a child's gesture of nervousness.

"Hi," she said. "I guess you guys heard about it."

"Yes. Gee, I'm sorry, Marnie," Tina said.

"Not to worry. It happens. And usually you're better off when it does. It's nature's way of telling you something is wrong."

Marnie, the dutiful student who had learned how to stand and walk, how to modulate her voice and drape a cowl neck into a sculpture in fabric, had easily absorbed the doctors' explanations, the nurses' glib assurances. The explanation had not been altered or improved through the years. "It's nature's way of telling you something is wrong," Dr. Isaacs had told Ina that long-ago day when she had called to tell him about the pink plasmic mass that had slipped, with a sudden violent cramp, from her body into the toilet.

"It's for the best," Marnie asserted now, surely echoing the words of a nurse who had mouthed them more than once.

"Yes. I suppose so," Tina said.

The girl toyed with her radio, and Ina knew that Tina wanted her music. She wanted to hear her mournful songs played with a raucous intensity. She had the teenager's need for a loudness that would mute the insistent whispering of her own fears, her own uncertainties. She needed the power of violent rhythm to overcome the mysterious sweet stirrings in her own body and to blot out the fears engendered by other people's worries. Rachel too had begun to play her radio too loudly, and she talked constantly of her friends who were buying stereos with too many speakers. At a decibelic pitch

it was possible for unasked, inaudible questions to be smoth-
ered and silenced.

"Tina." A nurse stood in the doorway. "They're waiting
for you in chemotherapy."

"Oh. Right." She grasped her radio. "I'll see you later then,
Marnie. Maybe after dinner. You know, I don't always feel
too great right after a session."

She followed the nurse with stoic, accepting submission,
walking slowly, carefully, as women do when their pregnancies are near term and they are overpowered by their own
bodies.

"How are you feeling, Marnie?" Ina asked. She settled into
the bedside chair, shifting the frothy peignoir that hung
over it.

"Awful," Marnie said. "Rotten. Mad. And maybe just a
little relieved. The doctors and nurses are probably right.
Probably it's for the best. And I guess it really is for the best
as far as timing goes—the agency and all that."

"Bob was really awfully upset when I talked to him this
morning," Ina said.

"Yes. Well, now he can afford to be upset and concerned.
But he didn't give me any support when I needed it. And
these flowers won't make up for what wasn't."

Her voice hardened. She sought a scapegoat for her sorrow,
a sponge to absorb her bitterness. She would remember always
that her husband had not wanted the child who had been lost,
unborn, on a stormy spring night. He could weep now for its
loss and send her flowers for consolation, but she would not
forgive his hesitancy, his uncertainty. It had carved a searing
fissure on the smooth surface of their marriage. Always they
had pulled together, but in the brief months and weeks of her
pregnancy, he had allowed her to pull alone. She could not
forgive him, and forgiving, she would not forget.

Ina remembered a neighbor of Bette's whose husband had
not wanted children. Finally, years into the marriage, the
woman had become pregnant and given birth to a beautiful
blonde baby girl. When Ina congratulated her, she had looked

at the baby and then at her husband and said, "Yes, but she
was born five years too late." The couple was divorced when
the child was two. The woman could not forget or forgive
her years of barrenness.

Such stories frightened Ina. Marriages could only sustain so
much. Repeated scars, compounding wounds, weakened them.
Differences, unforgotten and unforgiven, festered and spread
poisonously beneath a deceptive surface. Silences gathered and
thickened, forming a metastatic carapace, impenetrable and
unyielding. Ina's parents had lived through decades, locked
into such a silence. Last night she had seen them touch hands
for the first time in years, speak of a trip together, perhaps to
Israel, perhaps even back to Poland. They thought they might
once again walk through Warsaw's Saski Gardens. Would
the new life of their marriage be built on the death of her
own? She tasted the bitterness of her own thought. Her saliva
thickened and soured within her mouth. A coating of fear
clung to her teeth.

"You're not angry?" she had asked Ray.

"No," he had replied, but she had felt his disappointment in
the sheer weight of his voice, the softness of his sigh.

Poor Ray. She pitied her husband, who loved small things,
who held his Steuben miniatures up to the light and smiled
like a child to see a rainbow captured in a crystal lion's tiny
paw. She pitied him because he had been orphaned young and
because he would not again father a tiny infant. She pitied
him because he saw age encroaching, because his hair was
threaded with gray and his children grew too quickly, eluding
the protection of his shadow, abandoning him to a solitude for
which he was unready. But her compassion extended to herself. She would not have a child she did not want. Her life
was her own. She thought bitterly, contemptuously, of Emily
Anders, who argued for life dressed in the color of death. The
admissions clerk must pass information to her, or perhaps one
of the volunteers.

"Marnie," Ina said, "you have to stop blaming Bob. You'll
have other children. It's the marriage that's important."

"Yes. Of course I'll have other children. But I wanted this one. For once in my life I wanted to have something when I wanted it."

The model's eyes burned with the memory of all that had been denied her. Her demands had not been great. She had wanted a mother and father and a home. She wanted sisters who did not walk the streets and a brother who was not periodically remanded to reform school. She had wanted her husband's family alive and well, not incinerated in a tenement fire, leaving her with the scent of their scorching flesh forever in her nostrils, their screams ringing through the dark nights of her life. And she had wanted the baby that had thrust itself from her body in a stream of blood, an agony of body-breaking cramps. She wept now with the desperate, impotent fury of those who, deprived as children, struggle as adults to grasp that which is forever lost to them.

"Was it so much to want?" Marnie asked, crying now. The sobs rolled over her in soft waves of grief, and her body rose to meet them as a swimmer yields to gentle breakers.

"No," Ina assured her. "No. It wasn't."

She put her arms around Marnie, felt the young woman's tears damp against her shoulder.

"It wasn't Bob's fault. Of course I know that."

The grief, the flood of tears, drowned her bitterness, clarified her anger. She would not forget that he had not wanted the child, but she would not blame him for its loss.

Ina smoothed her hair, patted her shoulders, eased her back against the pillows. She pulled the covers over Marnie and saw pellets of blood on the sheet, carmine teardrops forming a tiny path on the white patched hospital linen. Tears formed in her own eyes. It was unfair. Marnie's miscarriage should have happened to her, to Ina herself. A miscarriage would have relieved her of decision, of self-recrimination, of her husband's sorrow and her mother's will. She would not have had to answer to Ruthie or to young women who carried pictures of jarred fetuses to her hospital room. The thought repelled and shamed her. She was done with doubt and recrimination.

She knew what she wanted, and she would follow through. Perhaps Dr. Isaacs's office had called back.

Marnie's eyes were closed.

"I'm sorry, but I'm tired, so tired," she murmured.

"Yes, of course you are," Ina said softly.

She kissed Marnie's cheek, and on her way out of the room she shut off the light. The drapes were drawn, and the flowers glowed like varicolored jewels in the new dimness.

But back in the corridor she hesitated. Miriam would be asleep, and Ina did not want to read. Her work was accomplished. She did not want to lie in bed in the silent room and wait for the phone to ring. She paused at the pay phone in the hall and fingered the coins in the pocket of her robe. Dot was on a class trip with her children, and her parents were visiting a customer. She dialed Bette's home and allowed the phone to ring several times, knowing how Bette hated the phone and resisted answering it. There was no answer. She dialed Ruthie, who answered on the first ring.

"Ina, hi. I can't talk. I'm just leaving," Ruthie said breathlessly. "Someone's here right now, and I've got to get some illustrations over to a publisher across town. Do you need anything? Is everything okay?"

"Yes, of course," Ina said. "I won't keep you."

"Swell." A man laughed in the background, and Ruthie clicked off.

Ina hung up, disappointed but not surprised. Ruthie was not a friend who would hold herself available to share and soothe the sudden, piercing loneliness of early afternoon. She had no patience with whispered worries, secret tears. She could manage arguments when facts were on her side and offer advice brusquely and bluntly. Her world was divided into black and white, and she stood carefully clear of gray areas.

"I don't understand myself. I need help," a newcomer to their consciousness-raising group had sighed one night.

She was a slight young woman who had recently left her

husband and slept with all the lights on in her barren apartment.

"What kind of help?" Ruthie had asked briskly, her pad open.

She was prepared to help the woman find a job, to lend her money, to find a room for her in a women's center.

"I don't know."

The woman had shivered in the overheated apartment and choked on the lipstick-smeared joint being passed desultorily from hand to hand.

"Then I don't see what we can do to help," Ruthie said. She was a busy woman herself and had no time to struggle with nameless fears.

They had heard somehow that the sad-eyed newcomer had suffered a nervous breakdown and returned to her home in the South. Ina thought vaguely of writing her but had realized, of course, that she had nothing to say.

If Ruthie had not hung up so quickly, perhaps Ina too would have whispered into the phone, "I need help"—and Ruthie's answer, inevitably, would have been, "What kind of help do you need?"

Ruthie, of course, was being realistic, Ina decided. Beyond a certain point, people could not help each other. She fingered her remaining dime, and finally, with unsteady fingers, she dialed Eleanor Berenson's office. Her own nervousness bewildered her, and she leaned against the wall for support while the phone rang again and again. A recorded voice filled the earphone, speaking with great clarity and sweetness. "The doctor is not available just now. Please wait for the beep and speak slowly. A message will be taken. Thank you."

"No, thank you," Ina said, without waiting for the beep. She hung up. She was annoyed with herself. Why was she calling Eleanor Berenson anyway? Her decision was taken. Mentally she reviewed the messages she might have left on the recording machine. "I am calling because I feel a free-floating sadness—different, I think, from a free-floating anxiety." "I am calling because I have come to a decision, and I want you to congratulate me on the systematic clarity and maturity of my thinking." "I am calling because I need to hear your voice, a voice that makes no demands on me, and because I do not want to return to the room where I have already spent four days and where the velvet petals of my flowers drift to the floor and my thoughts wander across borders I do not recognize."

She left the phone and stood in the hallway like a forlorn child, struggling against the small despair of having nothing to do.

A nurse walked by carrying a sheaf of green phone message slips.

"Nurse, I haven't been in my room for a while. Did anyone take any calls for me?" Ina asked.

The nurse shook her head.

"No. I have no messages for you, Mrs. Feldman."

"I'm waiting for a call from Dr. Isaacs's office."

"Well, he would call the nurses' station if your room didn't answer," the nurse replied. "I guess Mrs. Gottlieb is napping. Isn't the news about the baby marvelous?"

"Yes," Ina agreed, and she felt suddenly lighthearted and decisive.

She knew what she would do with this brief stretch of time, so echoing in its emptiness. She would go to see the Gottlieb baby—Maurice Allan, Moshe Aaron. She had visited the infant at night with worry and concern sour in her mouth, her steps weighted down by the grim nocturnal bargain she had made with herself. She had walked through the darkened corridor as rain streaked down the wide windows of her room, where Miriam Gottlieb lay with her face to the wall, mourning the infant who had not yet died. Now Ina would visit the baby who was getting better and growing stronger with each passing hour. Now, in sunlight and certainty, she would marvel at the tiny fingers, the lovely little limbs, the fine dark hair that grew in shining tendrils across the soft pink scalp on which networks of intricate cranial nerves glowed bluely in the false light of the isolette. Hunger made her light-headed, increased the excitement that propelled her through the doorway and up the iron-grate stairs.

There was a flurry of activity on the neonatal floor. Nurses rushed by, shoving equipment ahead of them—medication carts, small lamps, minuscule respirators, the paraphernalia of healing, in gleaming stainless steel. Somewhere a baby cried, rhythmically, desperately. Two doctors bent their heads over a single chart. They were angry with each other. One waved a pencil through the air. The other twirled his stethoscope. An alarm sounded—an urgent staccato beep that continued in rhythm with an infant's wail. The doctors turned and went swiftly down the hall, their white coats swinging behind them, twin-uniformed partners in a walk race.

But within the violet glow of his plastic bubble, Maurice Alan, named for Moshe and for Aaron, whose lives had drifted skyward in wisps of smoke in strange and distant lands, stirred and waved a tiny leg limb, opened and closed his palm.

Ina watched him, mesmerized with pleasure, with relief. This, at least, was fair. It was wonderfully right that this baby on whom such love and hope rested should live and grow from strength to strength with each passing day. What was it her mother had said last night? Something about everyone building by themselves. Oh, yes. Shirley Cherne, who wore the dark-hearted gems of death on her fingers and could not sleep in the blackness of the night, she had told her that what was lost could not be found again. The grandchild did not replace the grandfather. Maurice Alan Gottlieb, born in Mount Lebanon Hospital in New York City, would not reclaim the men, whose death-days were unknown. And yet he would. In small and precious ways, compensation would have been made. In rooms that had long been silent, a child's laughter would be heard. A name, long unspoken, would be intoned before the ark of the law. Moshe Aaron would ascend to the Torah and kiss the fringes of his prayer shawl. A tradition would be sustained, a life extended, because this infant lived.

"Sweet baby," Ina whispered, and planted a kiss from her fingers onto the window that stood between her and the child she would, in all probability, never see again.

There had, then, been some equity, some justice during these four days. Miriam's baby lived. Ina would soon be done with a pregnancy she had not wanted. Tina walked with new hope. Marnie would have other children, would assimilate this loss until it became a dim memory, a night of unremembered pain and a mysterious surging of blood.

Ina opened the stairwell door and started down the steps, humming softly to herself. "Lilli Marlene" teased her memory. She did not hold the handrail but walked slowly, trying to remember the gestures she and Bette had made when they sang. They had curtsied, held each other's hands, skipped on spindly legs. Their feet were bare. Small crescents of dirt rimmed their ragged toenails as they sang and danced. Sometimes Ina would look down as they danced, and often she was unable to tell which gray-fleshed, skeletal limb belonged to her and which to her cousin.

Once they had danced before three young officers. They had not dared look up at the men who stood before them, but kept their gaze at eye level. They were small girls, and the soldiers were tall. They could see how their thighs strained against their gray trousers and how the penis of the middle soldier swelled into an erection. Ina feared that protuberance of maleness. She did not understand it. Trembling, she danced on. It seemed that the man's organ would plunge through the cloth. He would bludgeon them with the pink muscle of his sex. The women whispered of such things in the night, and the small girls listened, mesmerized with fear and fascination.

She clutched Bette's hand and they waltzed together. Her cousin's bones were fragile and birdlike to her touch. One of the soldiers laughed and reached into his pocket, perhaps to toss them a kopeck or a candy, but the sudden movement frightened Bette.

"They mean to shoot us," she had hissed. "Run! Oh, run!" And they had run, while behind them the officers laughed at their fear, and one of them sang the last lyric of the song in a surprisingly rich baritone.

She had forgotten the incident until now, Ina thought, but not the melody or the improvised dance step. Down the iron-runged hospital stairwell she moved and swayed to the half-remembered dance. Right foot so and left foot so. One step, then another. Turn and whirl and turn again. She glanced down at her own feet, mittened within their yellow cocoons of wool. How terrible it had been to dance barefoot over icy, rough cement. How terrible to live in fear, to play hide and seek with death. Nausea and giddiness broke over her. She lost step. The woolen bed socks were slippery against the metal surface. She could not grasp a foothold and felt herself falling. She pitched forward and clawed at the wall for support. Terror constricted her breathing. The iron steps yawned, opened wide their ugly metal teeth to receive her. Thought and fear tumbled over each other. Fantasy overwhelmed her. She saw herself huddled at the foot of the stairwell. The enemy would prevail. The child she carried would be killed just as her mother's child had been killed.

A sudden fury grasped her, strengthened her legs. With frightening clarity she realized that she could resist her phantom enemies only by enduring. She could vanquish their death-sperm of hate by transforming the seed of love into life. She could not fall. She would not allow herself to. With one arm she protected her abdomen, and with the other she grasped for the bright yellow handrail that seemed to move beyond her reach with sudden, eerie mobility.

"Help!" she screamed.

She heard the sound of her terror and pitied the desperate woman who had uttered such a scream.

Below her a shadow moved.

"Help! I'm falling. Save my baby. Catch me."

She curled her toes within their soft wool shrouds against the rims of the steps. Her back arched and her arms flailed. The walls of the stairwell were green. She lunged toward them and felt her foot slide. In defeat, she closed her eyes

against a sudden whiteness. She thought of snow and dogwood blossoms and an infant's tender skin.

"I only care because of the baby." She wept piteously. A
chlorinated odor filled her nostrils. She gagged, nausea jerking
her into wakeful reality. A man's calm voice sounded then, as
though from a distance.

"You're fine. You're all right. Nothing happened. You
didn't fall. You just got dizzy, lightheaded. I caught you."

The voice belonged to a tall young doctor who held her
steady. He had rushed up to her and caught her. His finger
expertly felt her pulse, and the pocket of his clean white
jacket was smeared with the pale pink of her lipstick where
she had pressed her face.

Gently, as though leading a blind child, he guided her down
the stairs, opened the heavy stairwell door for her.

"Can you make it to your room all right?" he asked.

"Yes. Oh, yes. Thank you."

The door slammed behind her. She leaned against the corridor wall, sucking the air, gasping. Her robe and nightgown
were soaked with sweat. Her back ached with the great effort
she had made. How mightily, how vigorously, she had struggled to save the child she had been so certain she did not want
to bring to birth. Joy surged within her. They had lost—that
vanished, vanquished trio—and she had won. She would laugh
and mock her own foolishness—how she had sought to weigh
and balance, to make bargains, to seek for rights that would
cancel out wrongs. The absurdity of it all bewildered her.
Tears came. They glided down her cheeks in a steady flow.
She was surprised. She felt no sadness, no unhappiness, but
the tears would not stop.

Weeping, she walked back to her room, ignoring the curious and worried glances of nurses and aides. They had no
power over her now. Miriam was not in the room, and as she
lifted the receiver to dial, she saw that petals had dropped
from the full-blown roses. Dr. Isaacs's nurse picked up on the
first ring. The calmness of her own tone surprised Ina.

"Please tell the doctor that I'm canceling—" She fumbled for the word, smiled, and settled. "—the procedure."

The nurse asked no questions, requested no explanations, asked only that Ina repeat the spelling of her name.

She replaced the receiver and sank back, exhausted. Vaguely, she thought to change the nightgown that clung to her body, damp and stained with her fear. But she did not move. Instead, she turned her face toward the window. Its newly washed glass was brushed now with golden fringes of sunlight. She stretched toward its warmth, closed her eyes, and slept.

It was dark when she awakened. Ray sat beside her. He held her hand within his own in tender grasp, as though a frightened, trembling bird had fallen into the safety of his protection.

"It will be all right," he said.

Framed in the window's darkness two early stars glinted.

"I know." Her words were the merest whisper, and she lifted his fingers gently to her lips.